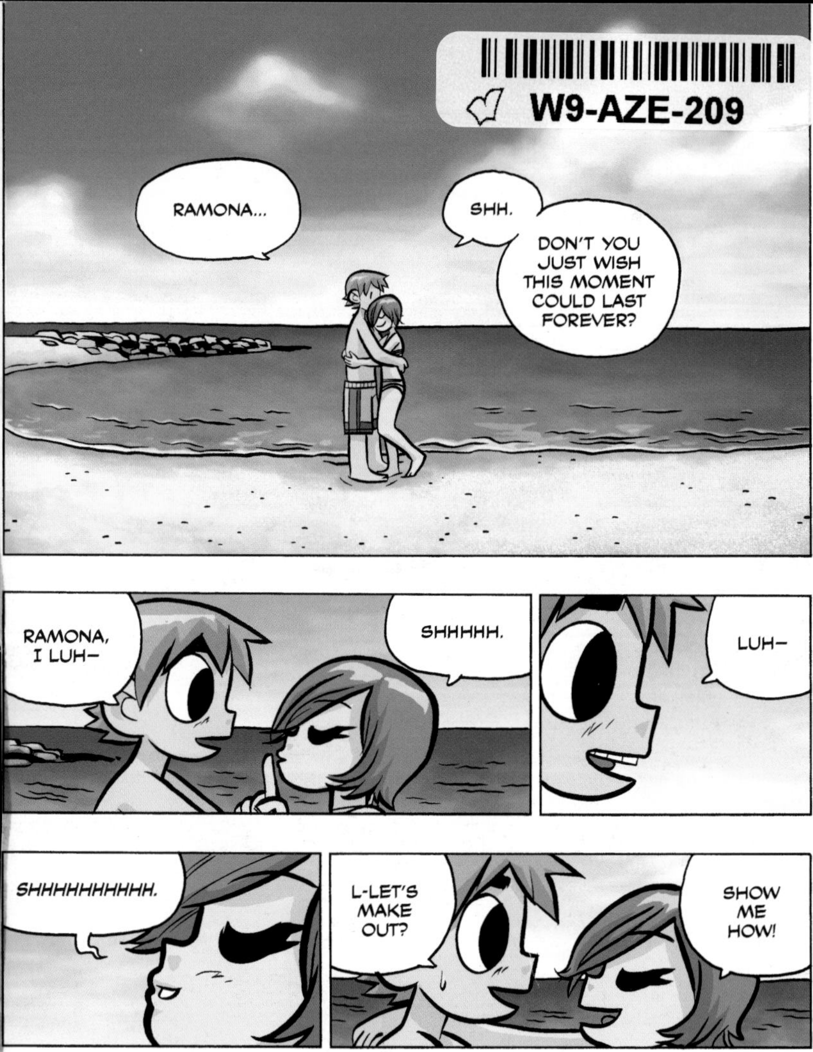
RAMONA...
SHH.
DON'T YOU JUST WISH THIS MOMENT COULD LAST FOREVER?
RAMONA, I LUH–
SHHHHH.
LUH–
SHHHHHHHHHH.
L-LET'S MAKE OUT?
SHOW ME HOW!

ONI PRESS presents **BRYAN LEE O'MALLEY's**

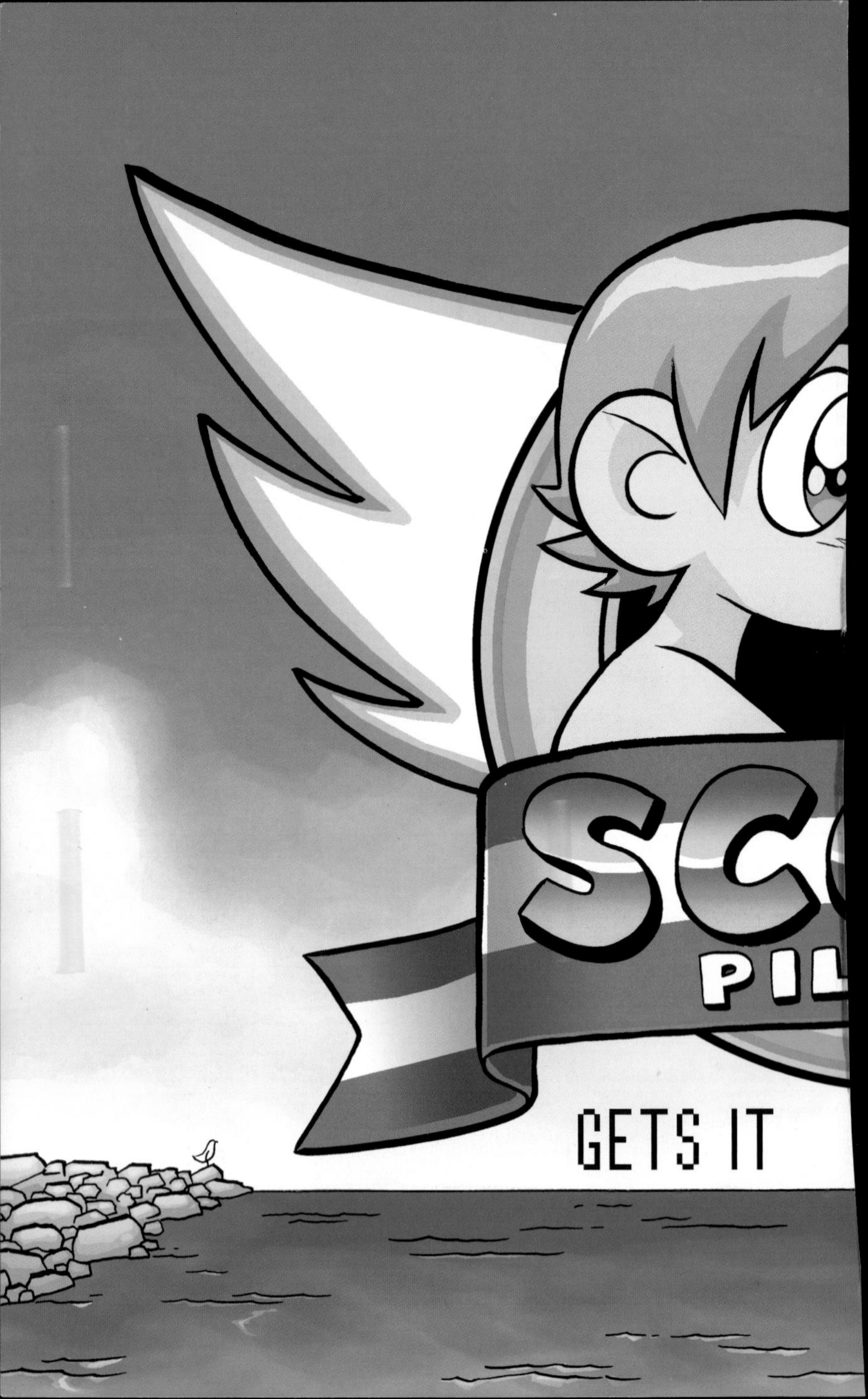
GETS IT

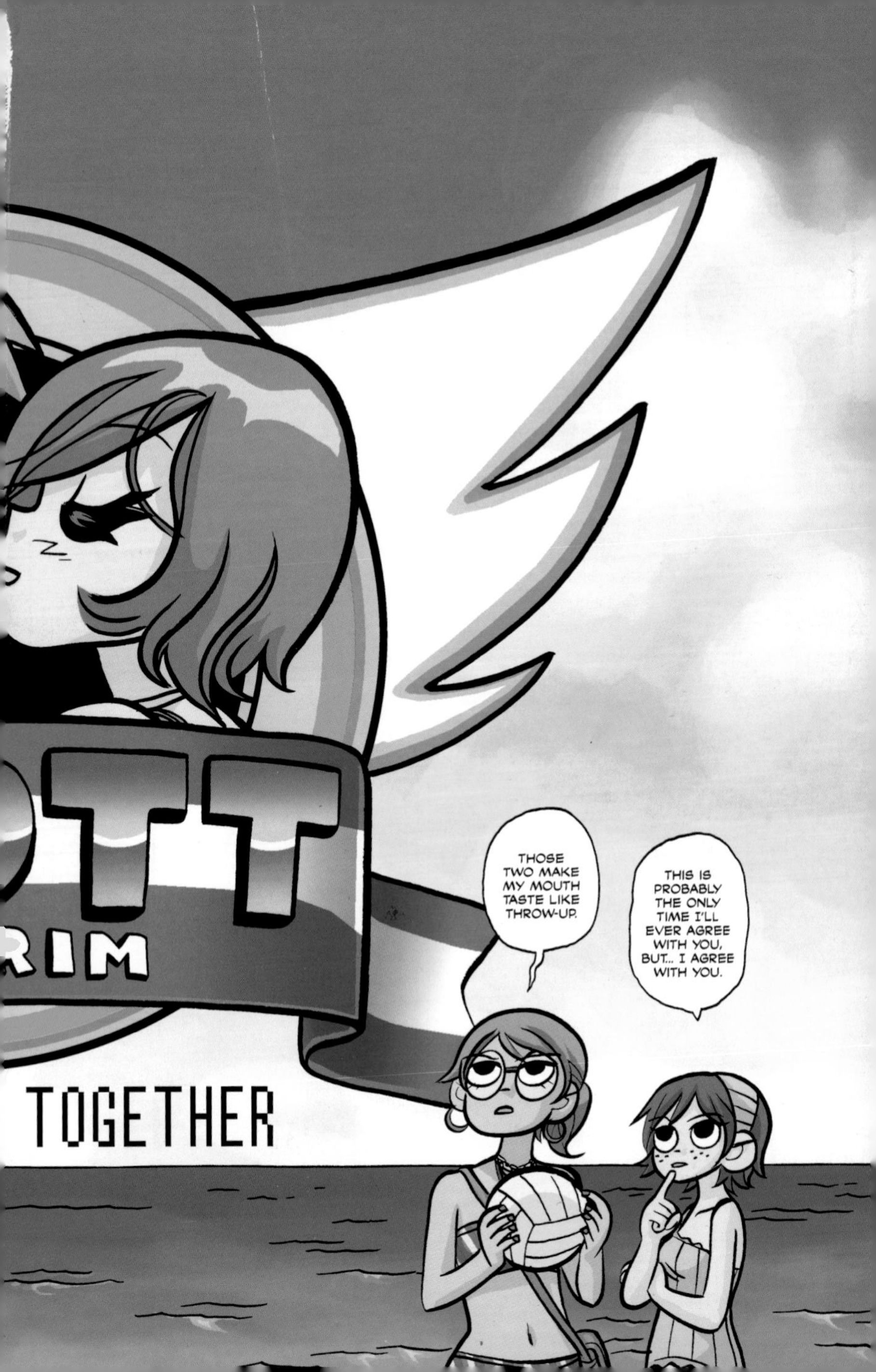
OTT
RIM
TOGETHER
THOSE TWO MAKE MY MOUTH TASTE LIKE THROW-UP.
THIS IS PROBABLY THE ONLY TIME I'LL EVER AGREE WITH YOU, BUT... I AGREE WITH YOU.

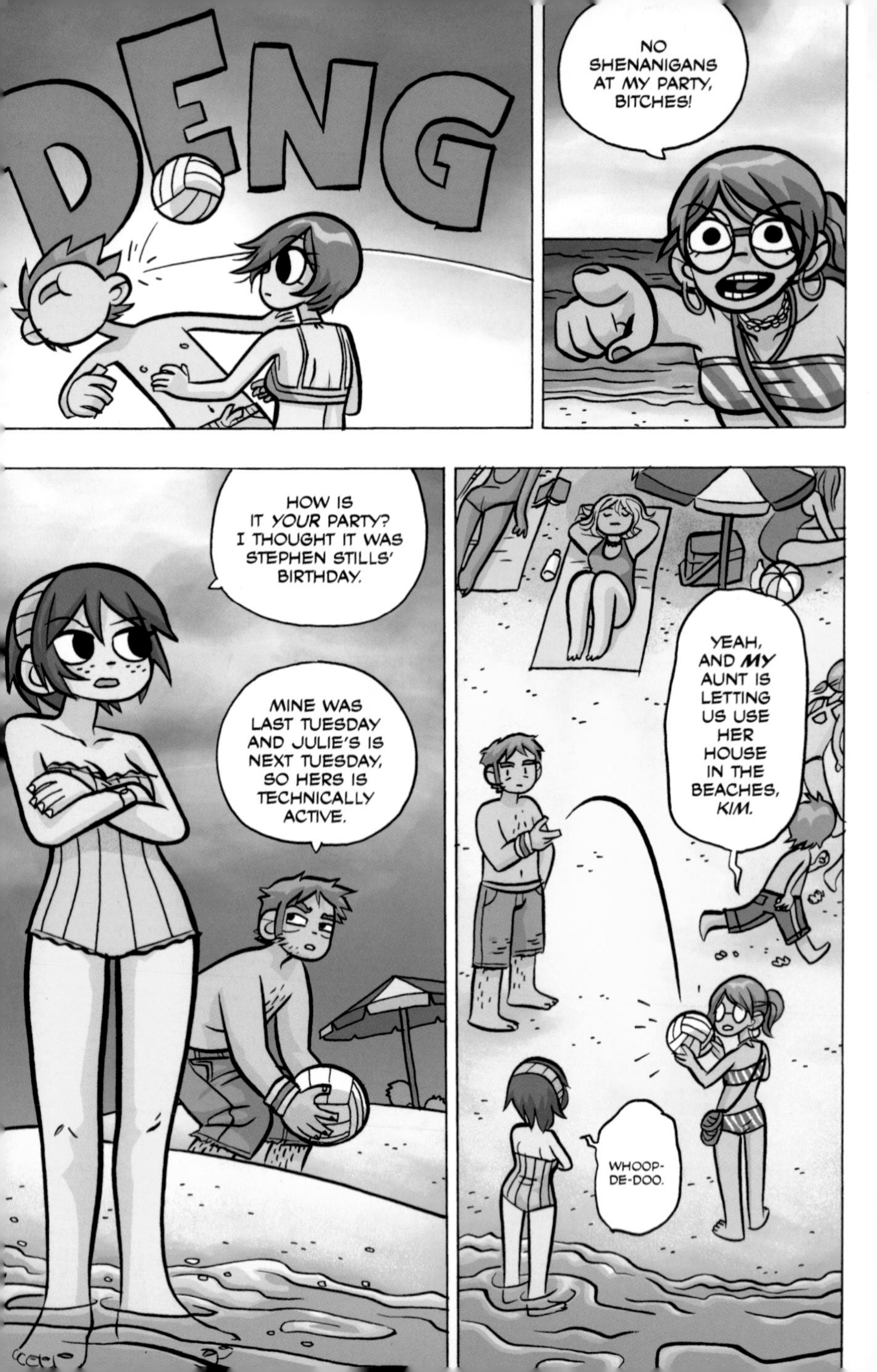
DENG
NO SHENANIGANS AT MY PARTY, BITCHES!
HOW IS IT *YOUR* PARTY? I THOUGHT IT WAS STEPHEN STILLS' BIRTHDAY.
MINE WAS LAST TUESDAY AND JULIE'S IS NEXT TUESDAY, SO HERS IS TECHNICALLY ACTIVE.
YEAH, AND ***MY*** AUNT IS LETTING US USE HER HOUSE IN THE BEACHES, *KIM.*
WHOOP-DE-DOO.

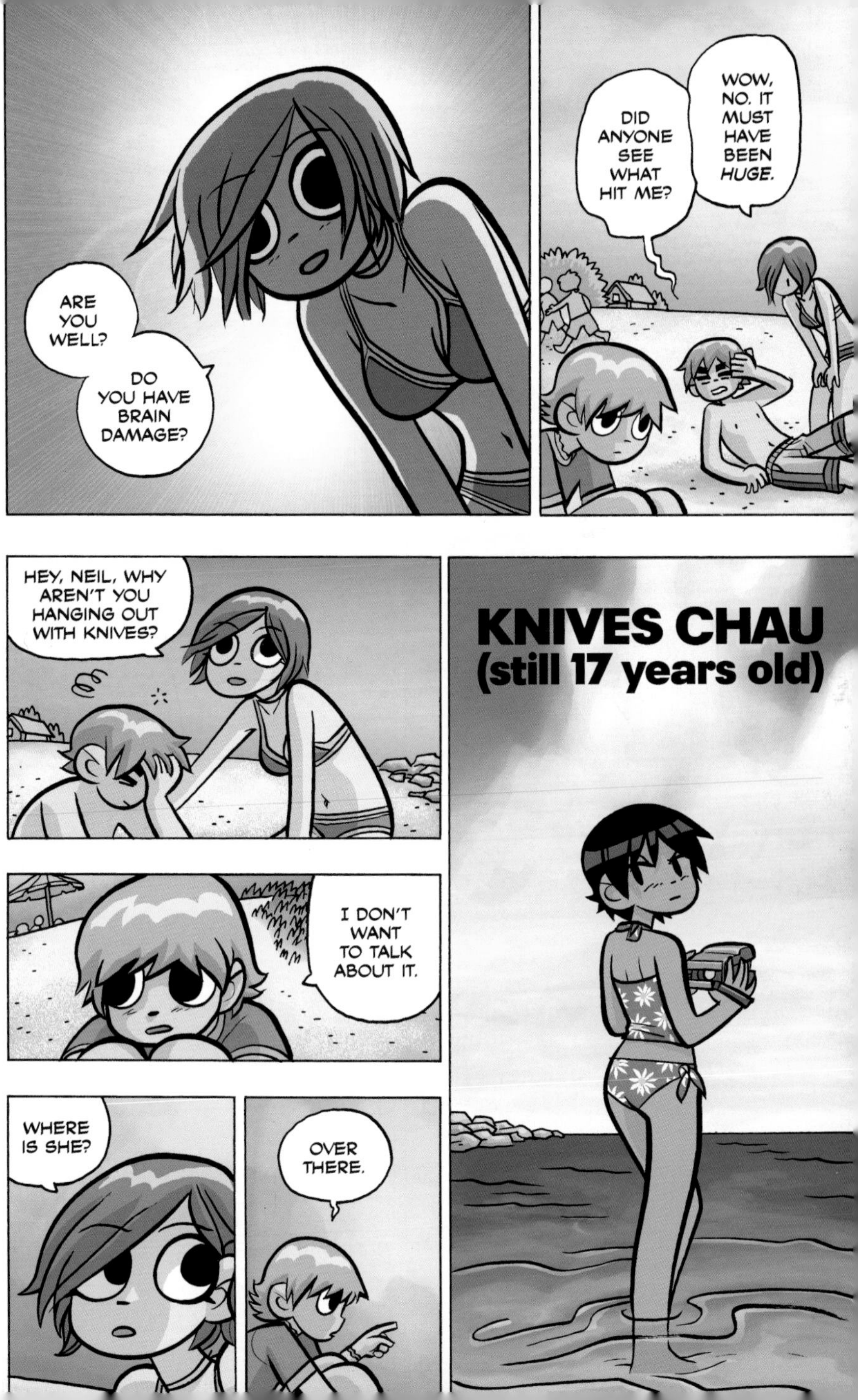
ARE YOU WELL?
DO YOU HAVE BRAIN DAMAGE?
DID ANYONE SEE WHAT HIT ME?
WOW, NO. IT MUST HAVE BEEN *HUGE*.
HEY, NEIL, WHY AREN'T YOU HANGING OUT WITH KNIVES?
I DON'T WANT TO TALK ABOUT IT.
WHERE IS SHE?
OVER THERE.
KNIVES CHAU
(still 17 years old)

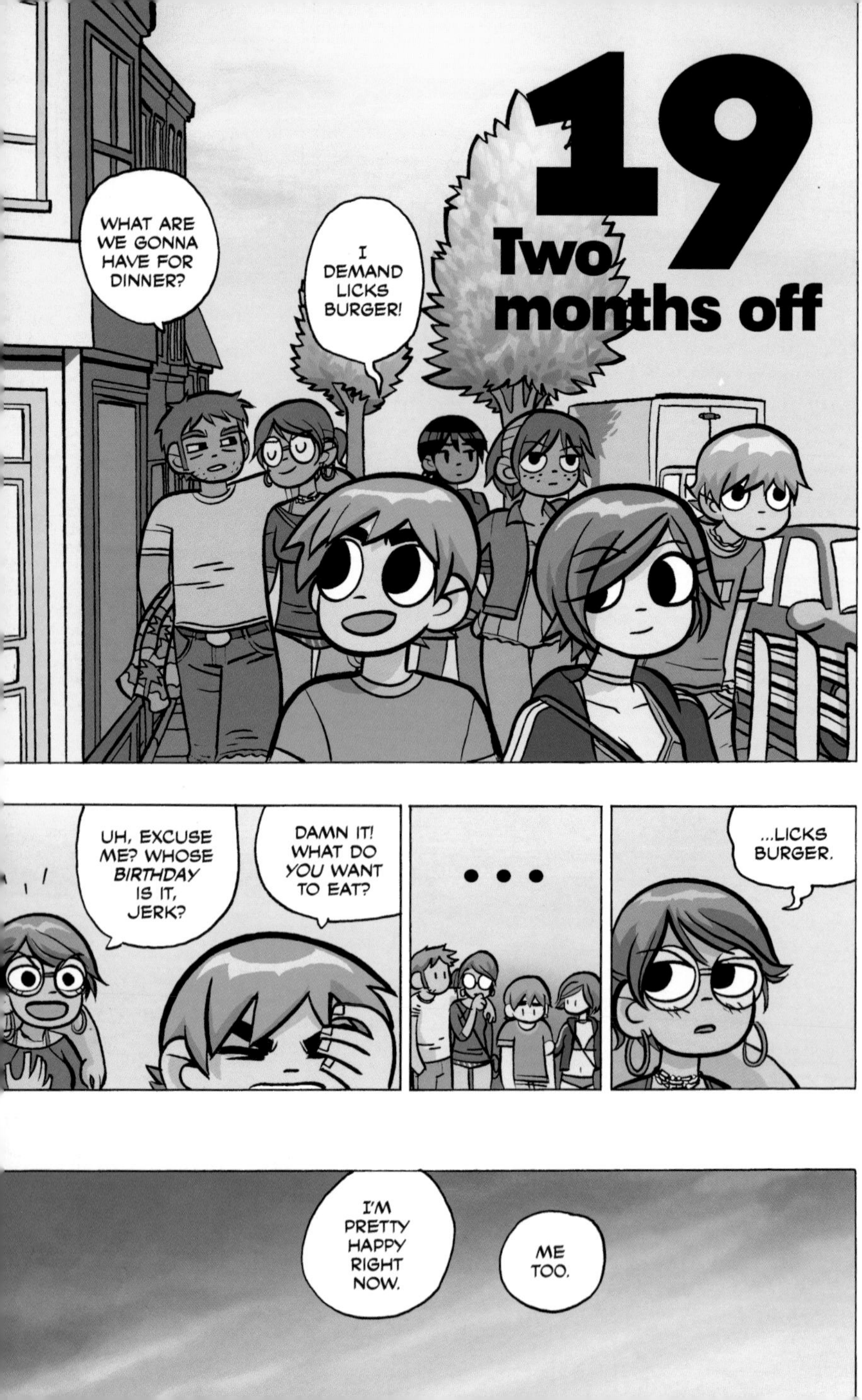
19
Two months off
WHAT ARE WE GONNA HAVE FOR DINNER?
I DEMAND LICKS BURGER!
UH, EXCUSE ME? WHOSE *BIRTHDAY* IS IT, JERK?
DAMN IT! WHAT DO *YOU* WANT TO EAT?
• • •
...LICKS BURGER.
I'M PRETTY HAPPY RIGHT NOW.
ME TOO.

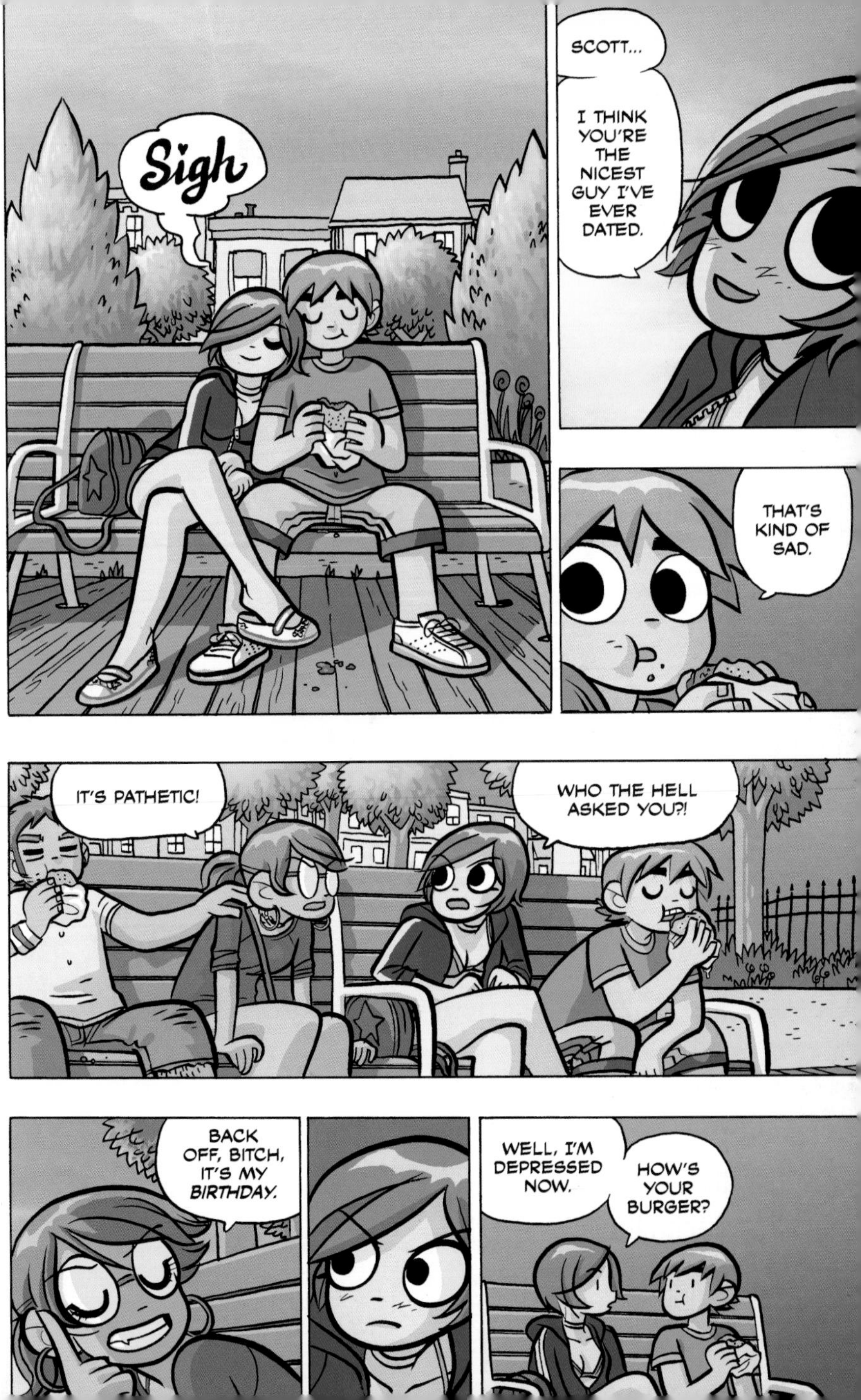
Sigh
SCOTT...
I THINK YOU'RE THE NICEST GUY I'VE EVER DATED.
THAT'S KIND OF SAD.
IT'S PATHETIC!
WHO THE HELL ASKED YOU?!
BACK OFF, BITCH, IT'S MY *BIRTHDAY.*
WELL, I'M DEPRESSED NOW.
HOW'S YOUR BURGER?

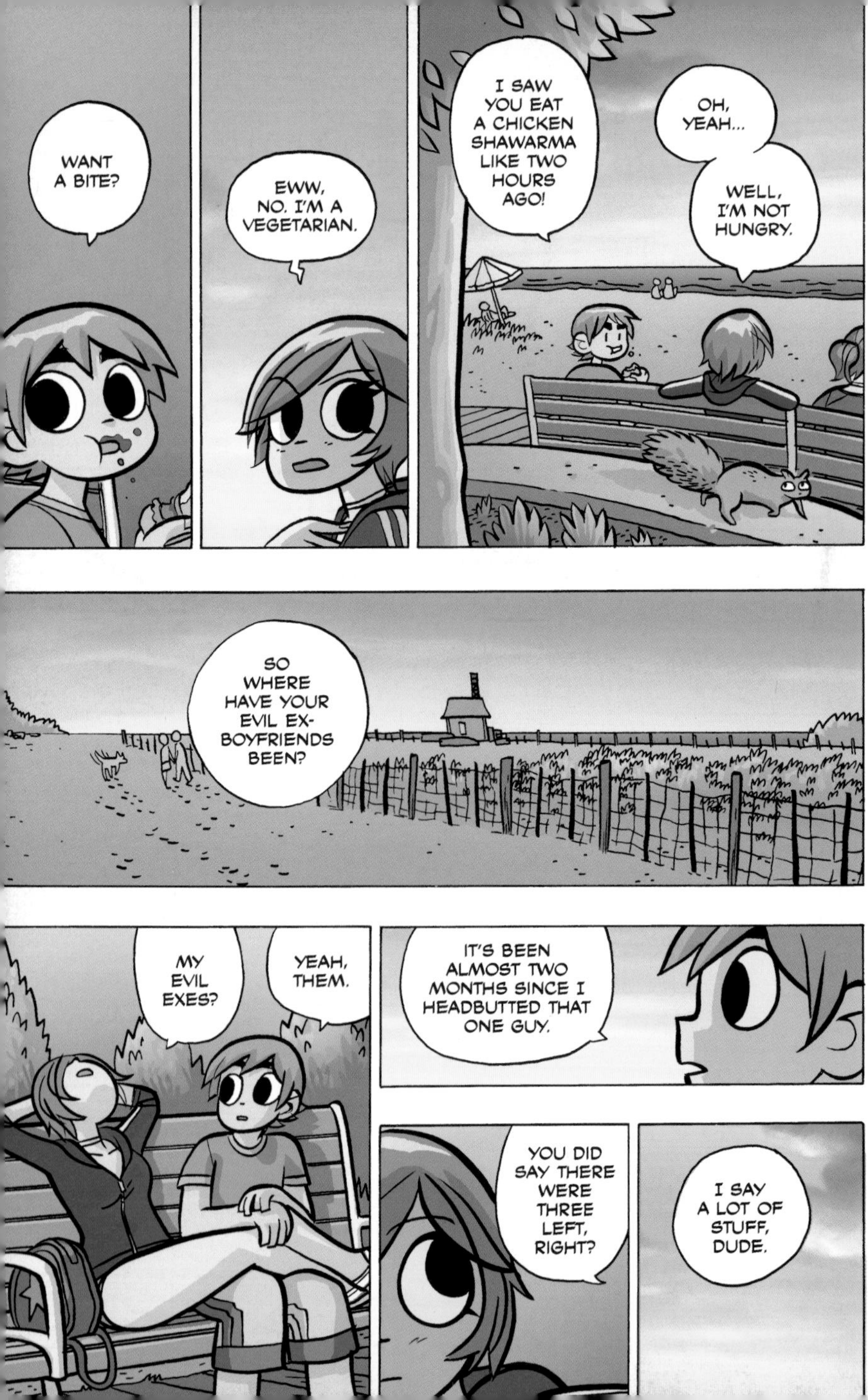
WANT A BITE?
EWW, NO. I'M A VEGETARIAN.
I SAW YOU EAT A CHICKEN SHAWARMA LIKE TWO HOURS AGO!
OH, YEAH...
WELL, I'M NOT HUNGRY.
SO WHERE HAVE YOUR EVIL EX-BOYFRIENDS BEEN?
MY EVIL EXES?
YEAH, THEM.
IT'S BEEN ALMOST TWO MONTHS SINCE I HEADBUTTED THAT ONE GUY.
YOU DID SAY THERE WERE THREE LEFT, RIGHT?
I SAY A LOT OF STUFF, DUDE.

edited by James Lucas Jones
design and layout by Bryan Lee O'Malley
production assistance from Steven Birch @ Servo
pages 1-8 colored by Steve Buccellato
back cover pixel art by Miguel Sternberg

published by Oni Press, Inc.
Joe Nozemack publisher | James Lucas Jones editor in chief | Randal C. Jarrell managing editor
Douglas Sherwood editor in goober | Jill Beaton editorial intern

ONI PRESS, INC.
1305 SE Martin Luther King Jr. Blvd.
Suite A
Portland, OR 97214
USA

Special thanks to: Hope, the Oni boyz (DOUG!!), Gitter, E.W.Jr., Michael B., my peeps in Toronto and London, the Halifax crew and the HGPA, mom & dad, bro & sis, kitties, Kanye West, Clark and Michael... and YOU! Winners don't use drugs, except Claritin this time of year.

WWW.ONIPRESS.COM
WWW.SCOTTPILGRIM.COM

First edition: October 2007
ISBN: 978-1-932664-49-2

10 9 8 7 6 5 4
PRINTED IN CANADA (WOO)

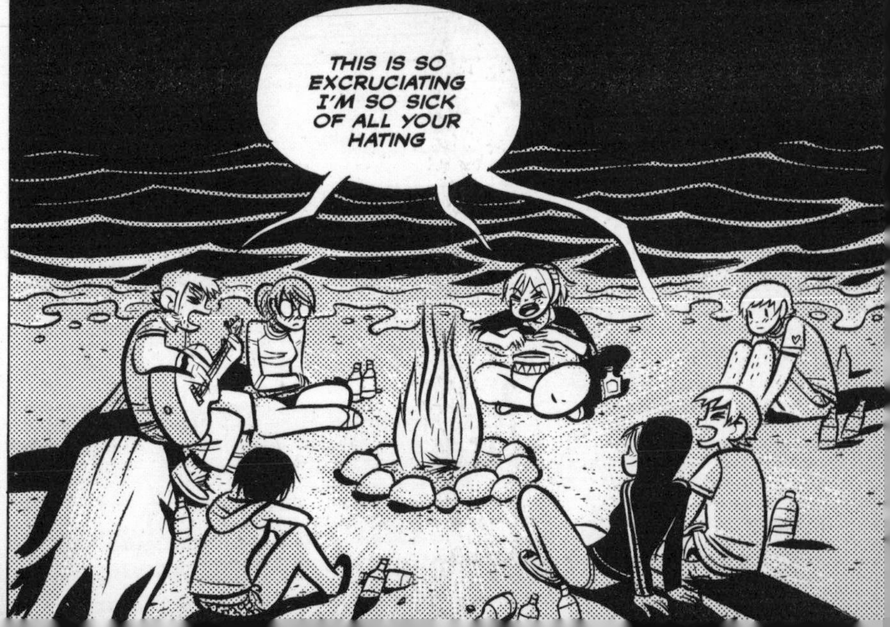
THIS IS SO EXCRUCIATING I'M SO SICK OF ALL YOUR HATING

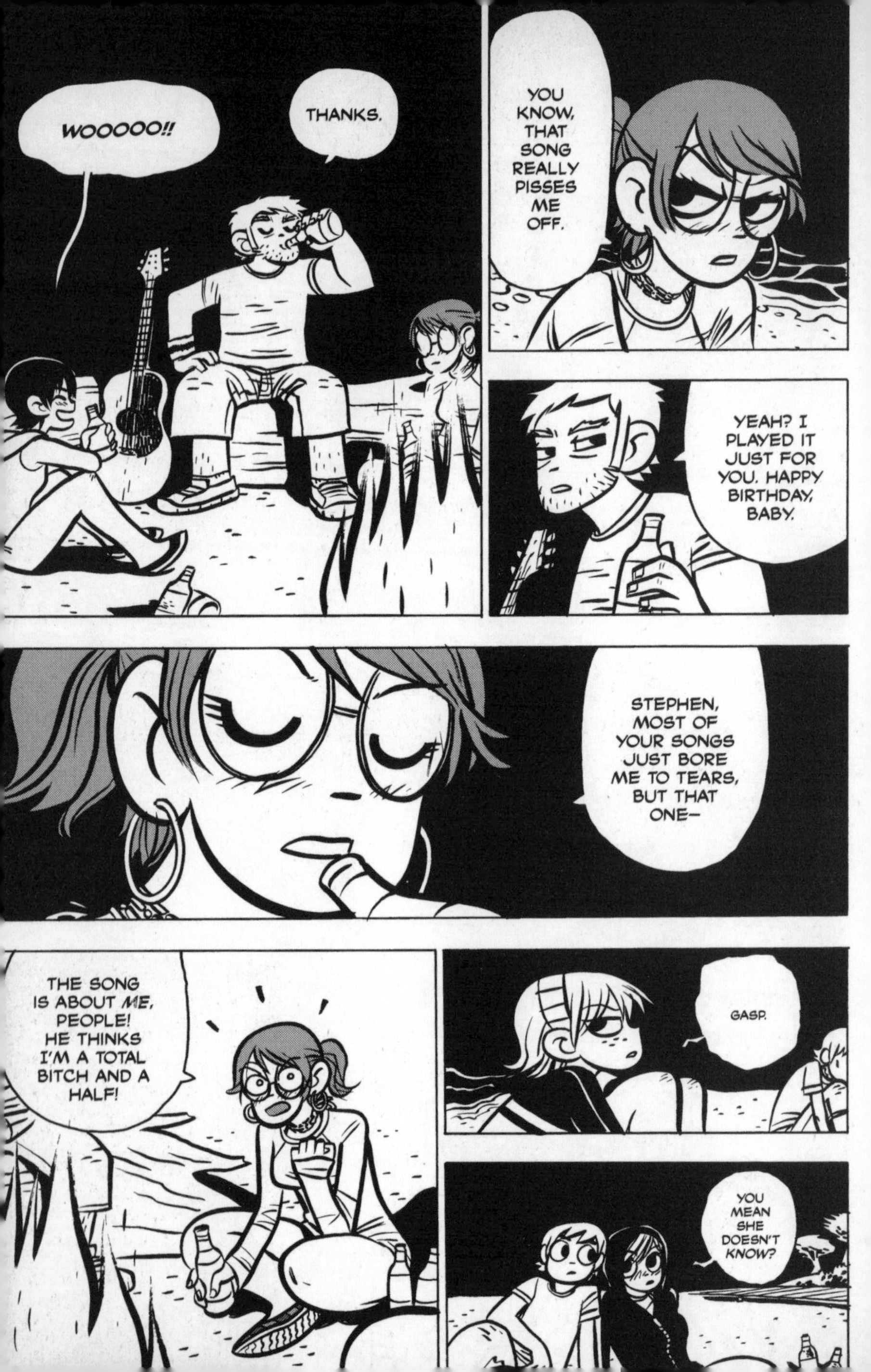
WOOOOO!!
THANKS.
YOU KNOW, THAT SONG REALLY PISSES ME OFF.
YEAH? I PLAYED IT JUST FOR YOU. HAPPY BIRTHDAY, BABY.
STEPHEN, MOST OF YOUR SONGS JUST BORE ME TO TEARS, BUT THAT ONE–
THE SONG IS ABOUT ME, PEOPLE! HE THINKS I'M A TOTAL BITCH AND A HALF!
GASP.
YOU MEAN SHE DOESN'T KNOW?

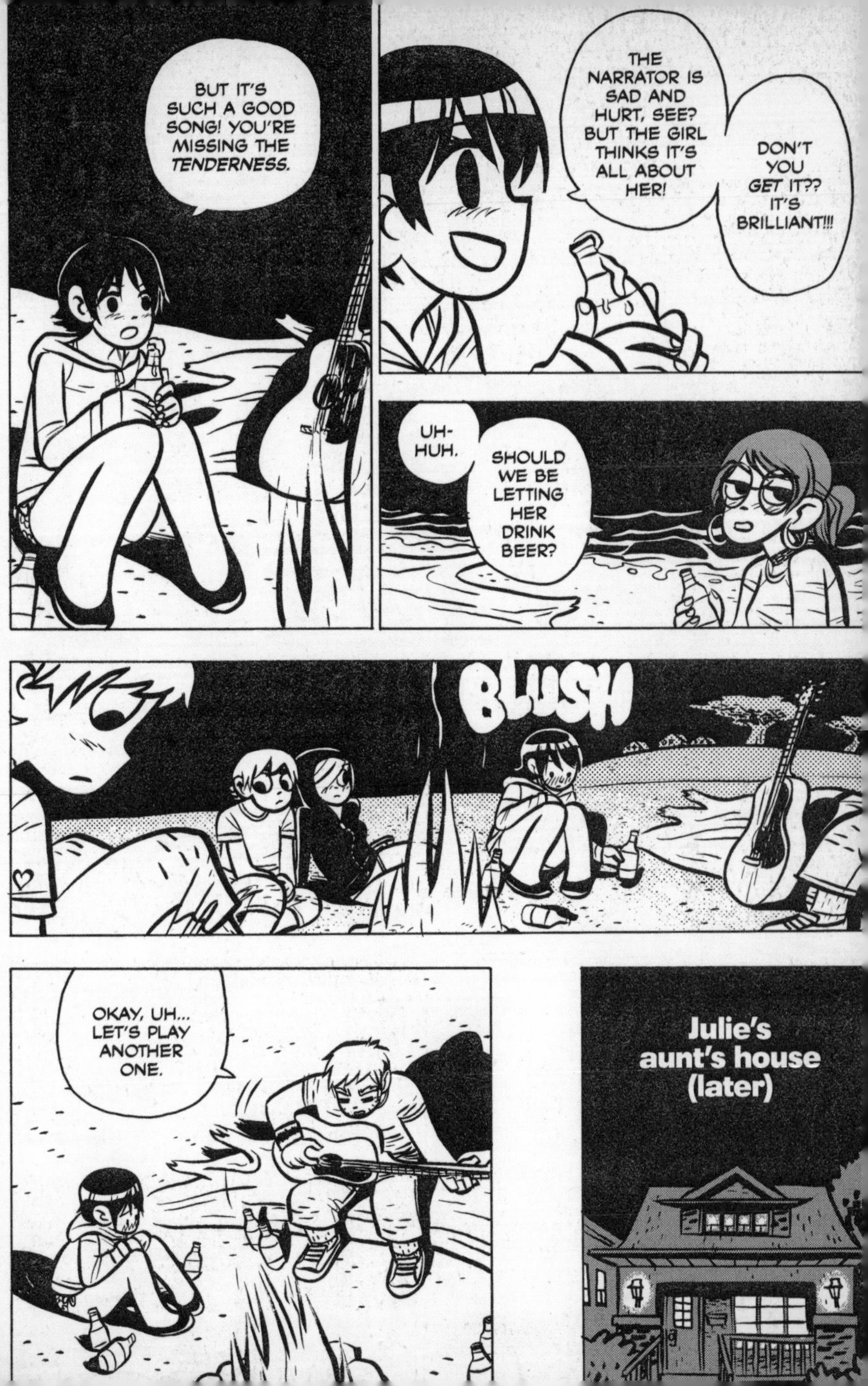

BUT IT'S SUCH A GOOD SONG! YOU'RE MISSING THE *TENDERNESS.*
THE NARRATOR IS SAD AND HURT, SEE? BUT THE GIRL THINKS IT'S ALL ABOUT HER!
DON'T YOU *GET* IT?? IT'S BRILLIANT!!!
UH-HUH.
SHOULD WE BE LETTING HER DRINK BEER?
BLUSH
OKAY, UH... LET'S PLAY ANOTHER ONE.
Julie's aunt's house (later)

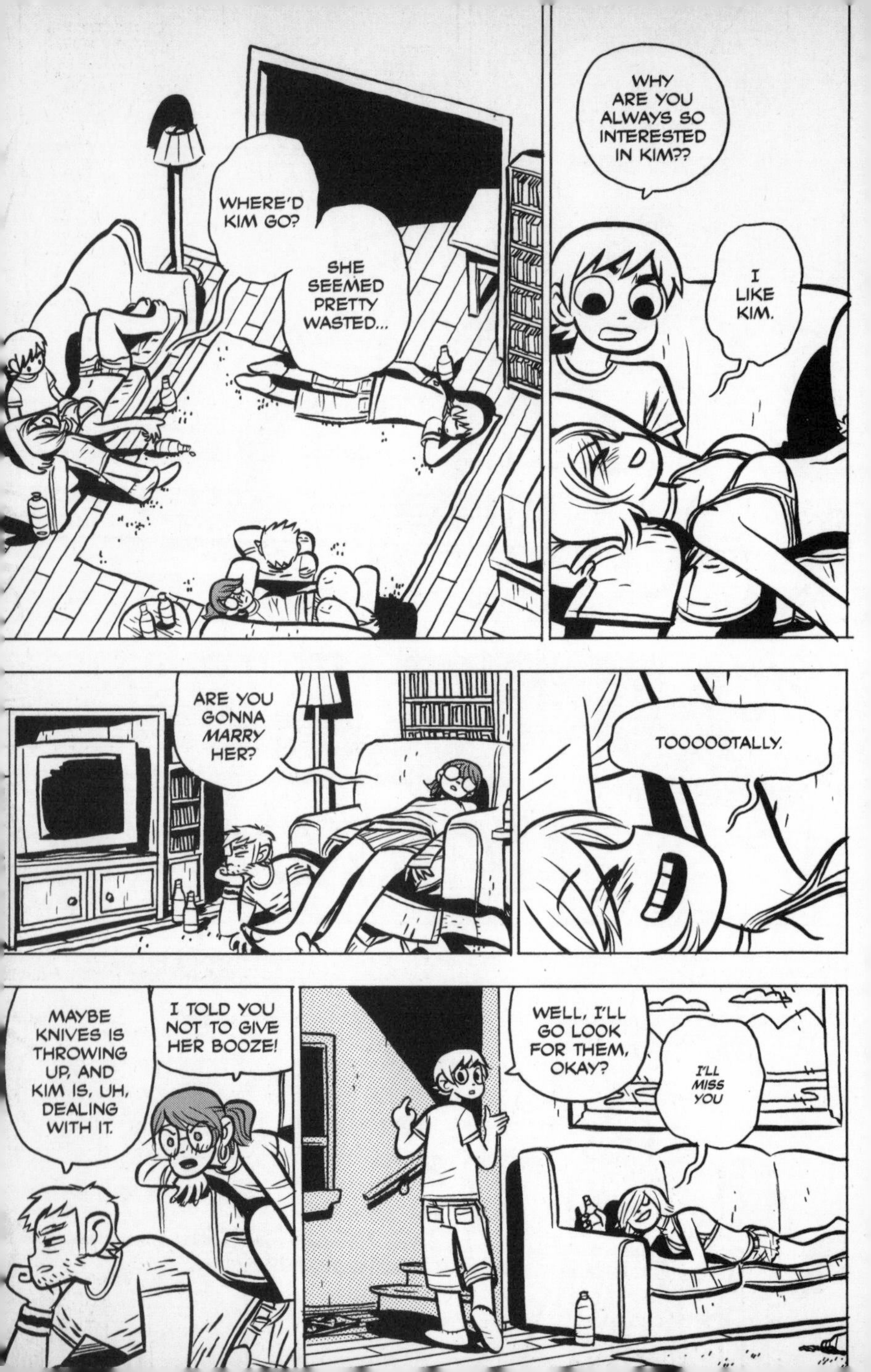
WHERE'D KIM GO?
SHE SEEMED PRETTY WASTED...
WHY ARE YOU ALWAYS SO INTERESTED IN KIM??
I LIKE KIM.
ARE YOU GONNA *MARRY* HER?
TOOOOOTALLY.
MAYBE KNIVES IS THROWING UP, AND KIM IS, UH, DEALING WITH IT.
I TOLD YOU NOT TO GIVE HER BOOZE!
WELL, I'LL GO LOOK FOR THEM, OKAY?
I'LL MISS YOU

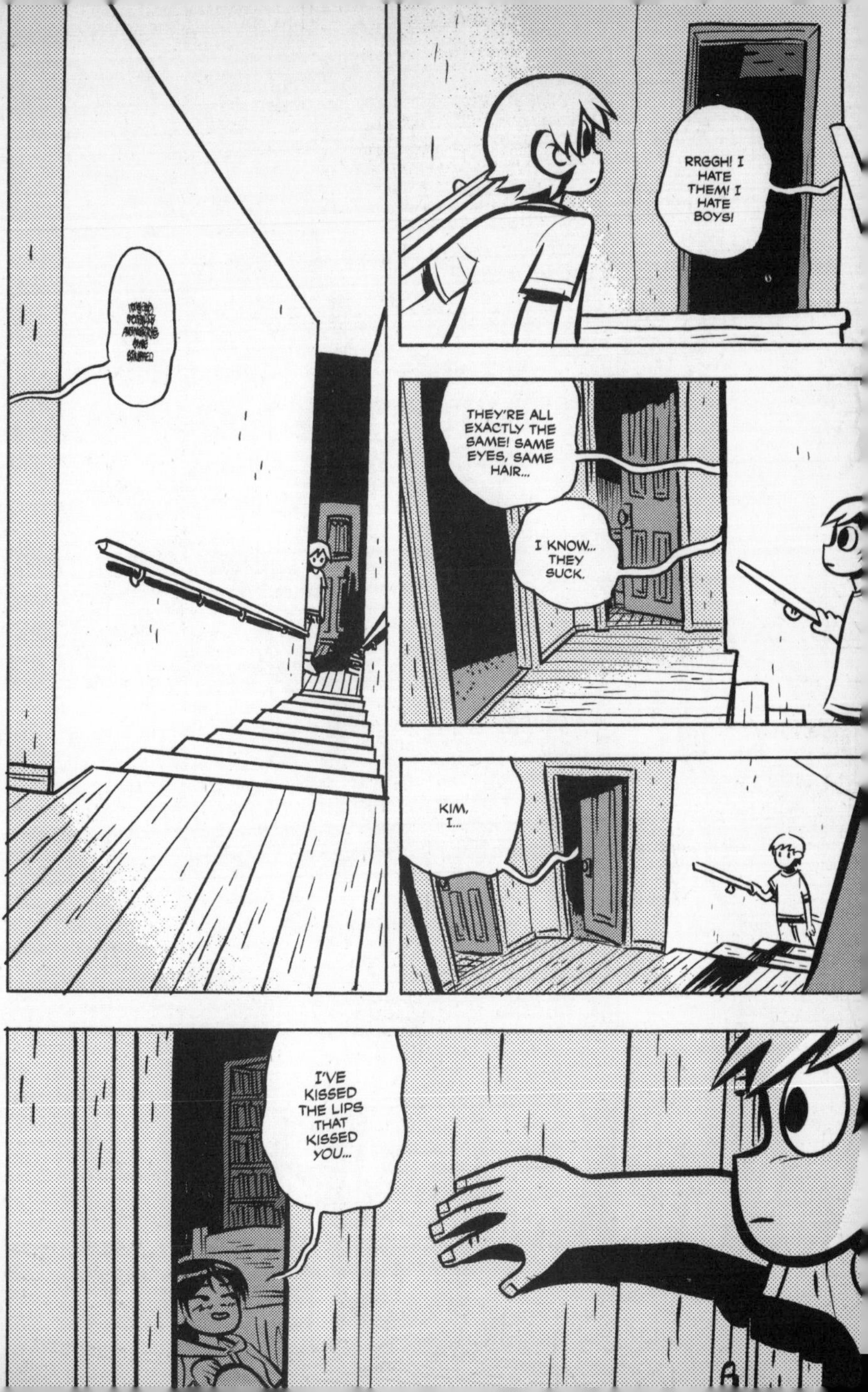
RRGGH! I HATE THEM! I HATE BOYS!
THEY'RE ALL EXACTLY THE SAME! SAME EYES, SAME HAIR...
I KNOW... THEY SUCK.
KIM, I...
I'VE KISSED THE LIPS THAT KISSED YOU...

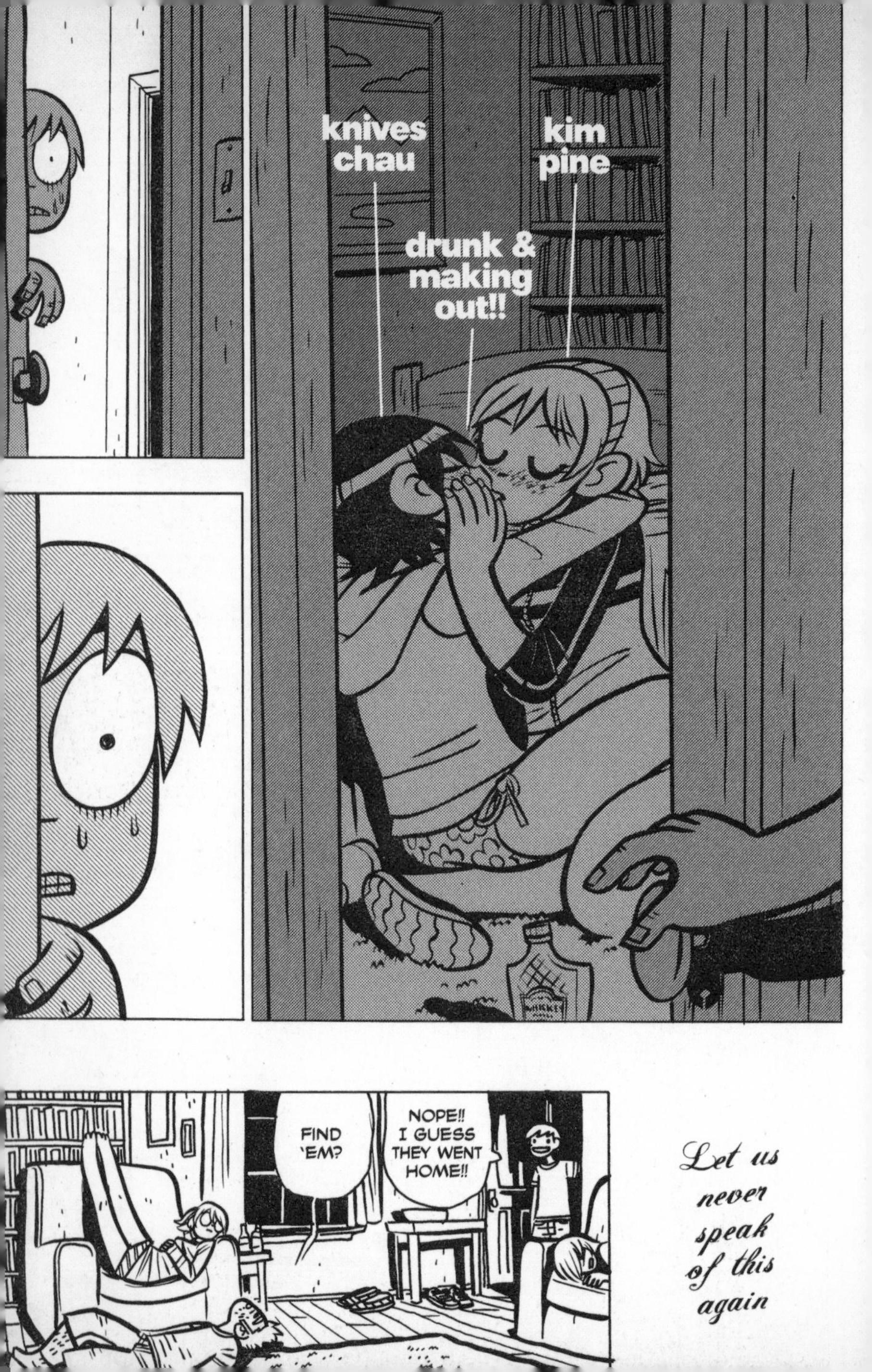

knives chau
kim pine
drunk & making out!!
FIND 'EM?
NOPE!! I GUESS THEY WENT HOME!!
Let us never speak of this again

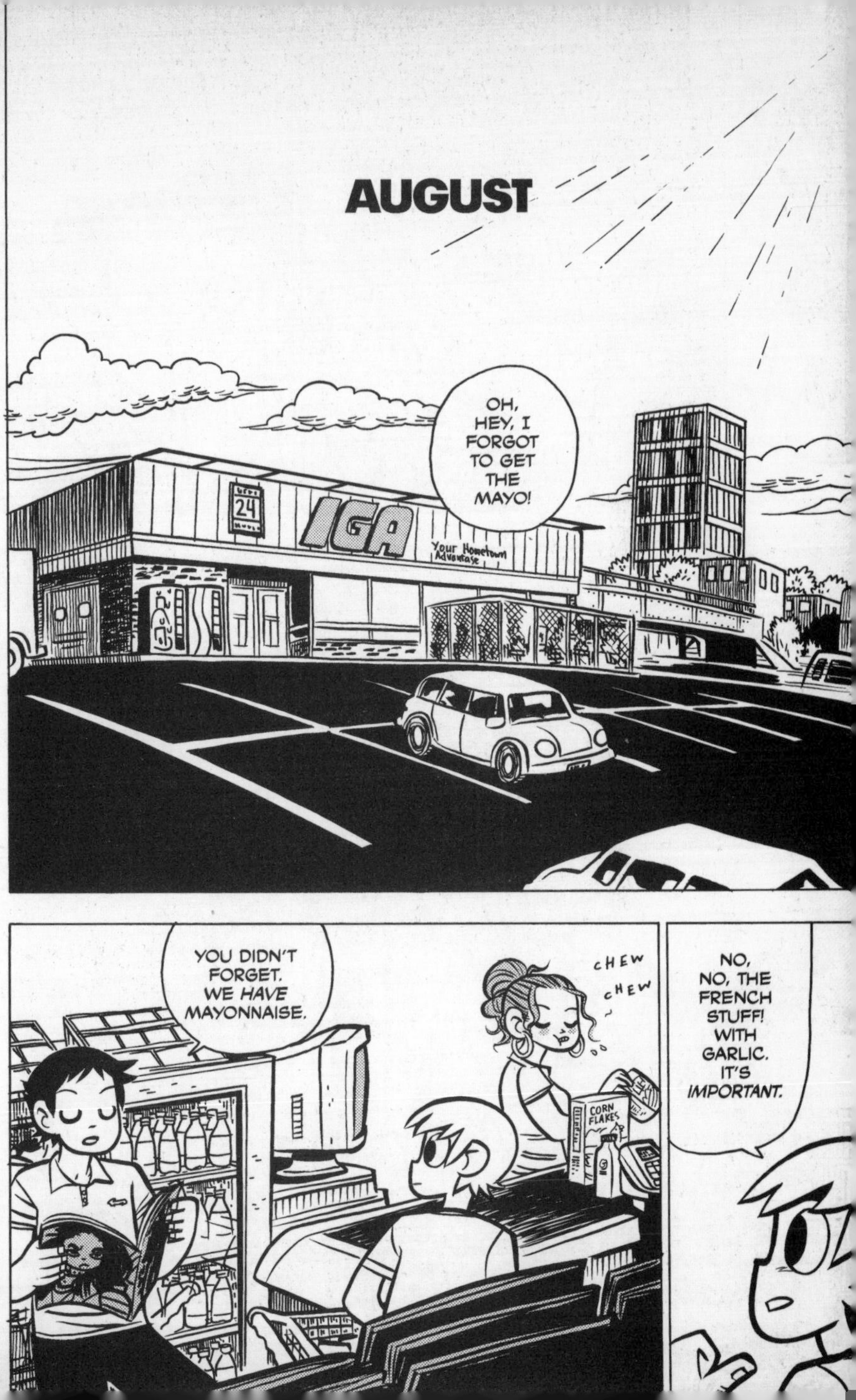
AUGUST
24
IGA
Your Hometown Advantage
OH, HEY, I FORGOT TO GET THE MAYO!
YOU DIDN'T FORGET. WE *HAVE* MAYONNAISE.
CHEW CHEW
CORN FLAKES
NO, NO, THE FRENCH STUFF! WITH GARLIC. IT'S *IMPORTANT.*

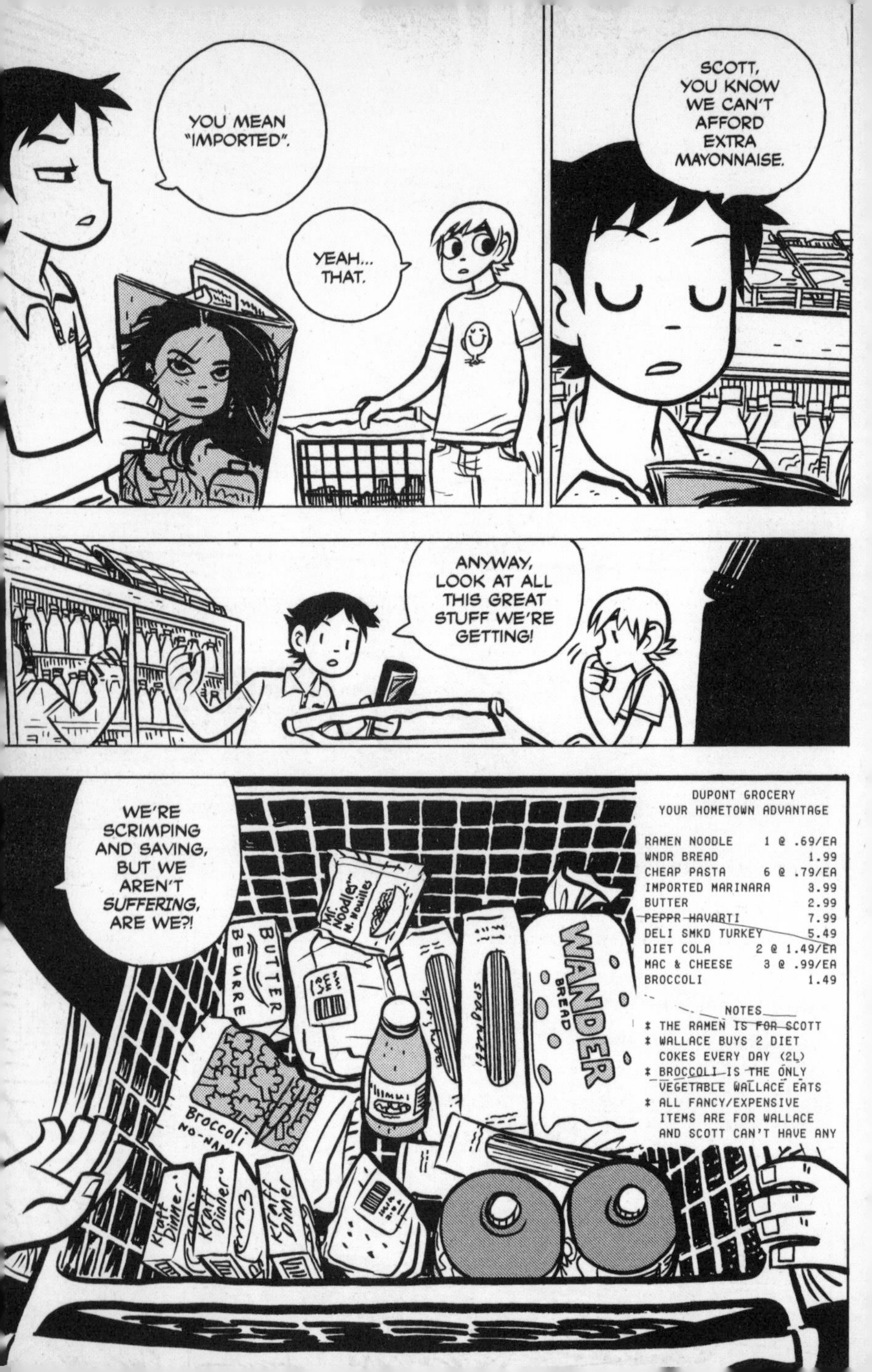
YOU MEAN "IMPORTED".
YEAH... THAT.
SCOTT, YOU KNOW WE CAN'T AFFORD EXTRA MAYONNAISE.
ANYWAY, LOOK AT ALL THIS GREAT STUFF WE'RE GETTING!
WE'RE SCRIMPING AND SAVING, BUT WE AREN'T SUFFERING, ARE WE?!
DUPONT GROCERY
YOUR HOMETOWN ADVANTAGE
RAMEN NOODLE 1 @ .69/EA
WNDR BREAD 1.99
CHEAP PASTA 6 @ .79/EA
IMPORTED MARINARA 3.99
BUTTER 2.99
PEPPR HAVARTI 7.99
DELI SMKD TURKEY 5.49
DIET COLA 2 @ 1.49/EA
MAC & CHEESE 3 @ .99/EA
BROCCOLI 1.49
NOTES
* THE RAMEN IS FOR SCOTT
* WALLACE BUYS 2 DIET COKES EVERY DAY (2L)
* BROCCOLI IS THE ONLY VEGETABLE WALLACE EATS
* ALL FANCY/EXPENSIVE ITEMS ARE FOR WALLACE AND SCOTT CAN'T HAVE ANY
Mr. Noodles M. Nouilles
BUTTER BEURRE
WANDER BREAD
spaghetti
Broccoli NO-NAME
Kraft Dinner
Kraft Dinner
Kraft Dinner

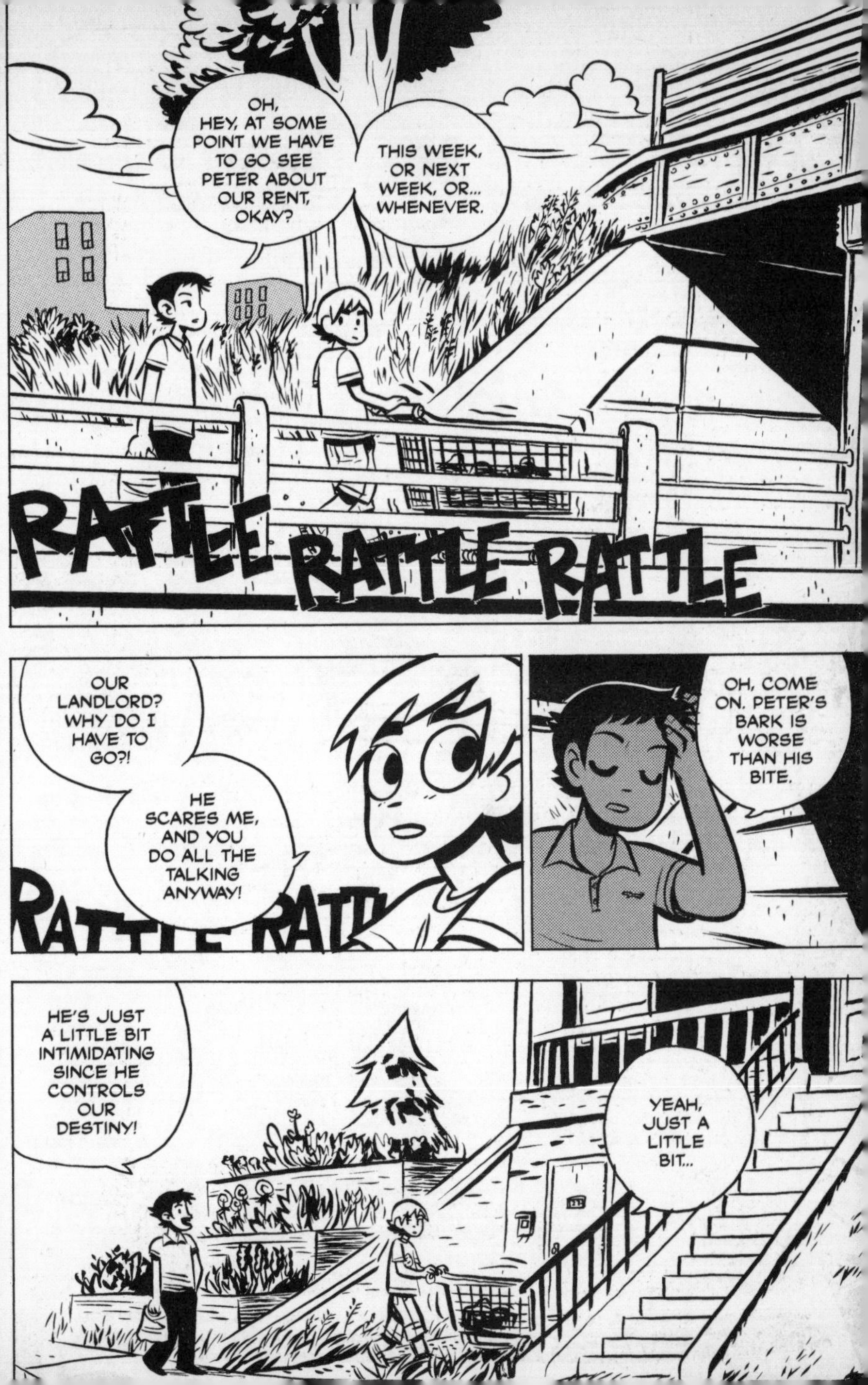
OH, HEY, AT SOME POINT WE HAVE TO GO SEE PETER ABOUT OUR RENT, OKAY?
THIS WEEK, OR NEXT WEEK, OR... WHENEVER.
RATTLE RATTLE RATTLE
OUR LANDLORD? WHY DO I HAVE TO GO?!
HE SCARES ME, AND YOU DO ALL THE TALKING ANYWAY!
OH, COME ON. PETER'S BARK IS WORSE THAN HIS BITE.
HE'S JUST A LITTLE BIT INTIMIDATING SINCE HE CONTROLS OUR DESTINY!
YEAH, JUST A LITTLE BIT...

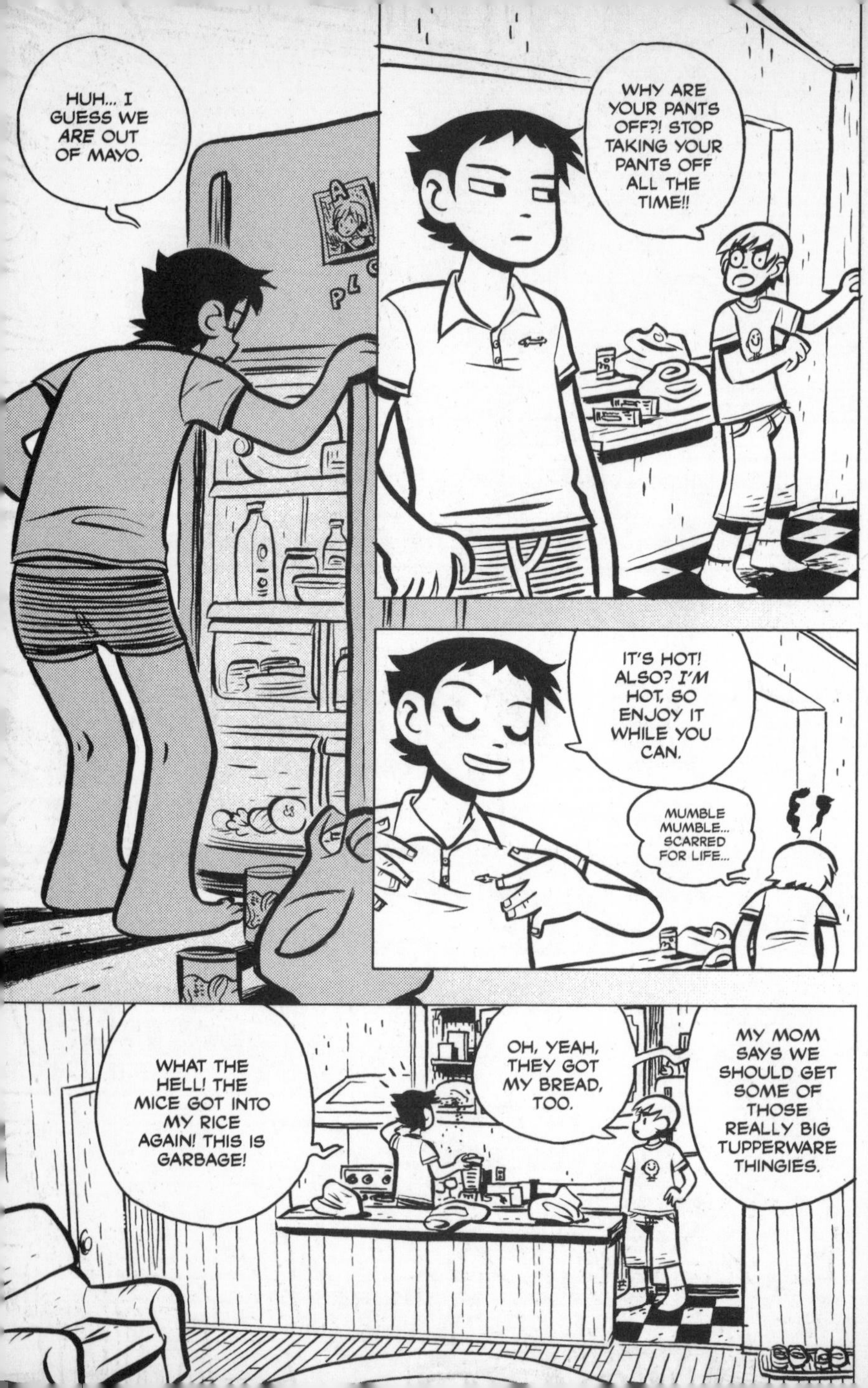

HUH... I GUESS WE ARE OUT OF MAYO.
WHY ARE YOUR PANTS OFF?! STOP TAKING YOUR PANTS OFF ALL THE TIME!!
IT'S HOT! ALSO? I'M HOT, SO ENJOY IT WHILE YOU CAN.
MUMBLE MUMBLE... SCARRED FOR LIFE...
WHAT THE HELL! THE MICE GOT INTO MY RICE AGAIN! THIS IS GARBAGE!
OH, YEAH, THEY GOT MY BREAD, TOO.
MY MOM SAYS WE SHOULD GET SOME OF THOSE REALLY BIG TUPPERWARE THINGIES.

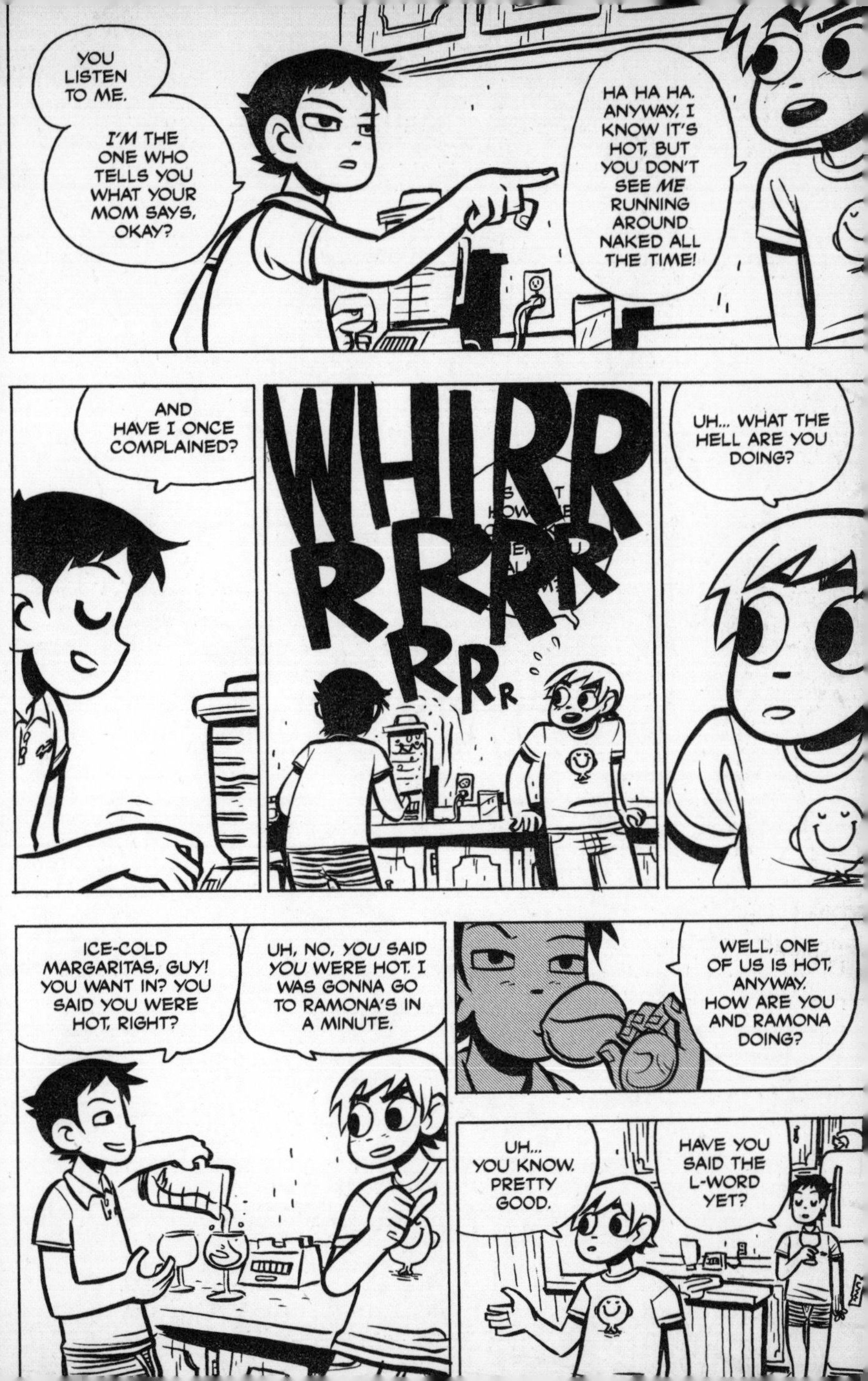
YOU LISTEN TO ME.
I'M THE ONE WHO TELLS YOU WHAT YOUR MOM SAYS, OKAY?
HA HA HA. ANYWAY, I KNOW IT'S HOT, BUT YOU DON'T SEE ME RUNNING AROUND NAKED ALL THE TIME!
AND HAVE I ONCE COMPLAINED?
WHIRR RRRR RRR
UH... WHAT THE HELL ARE YOU DOING?
ICE-COLD MARGARITAS, GUY! YOU WANT IN? YOU SAID YOU WERE HOT, RIGHT?
UH, NO, YOU SAID YOU WERE HOT. I WAS GONNA GO TO RAMONA'S IN A MINUTE.
WELL, ONE OF US IS HOT, ANYWAY. HOW ARE YOU AND RAMONA DOING?
UH... YOU KNOW. PRETTY GOOD.
HAVE YOU SAID THE L-WORD YET?

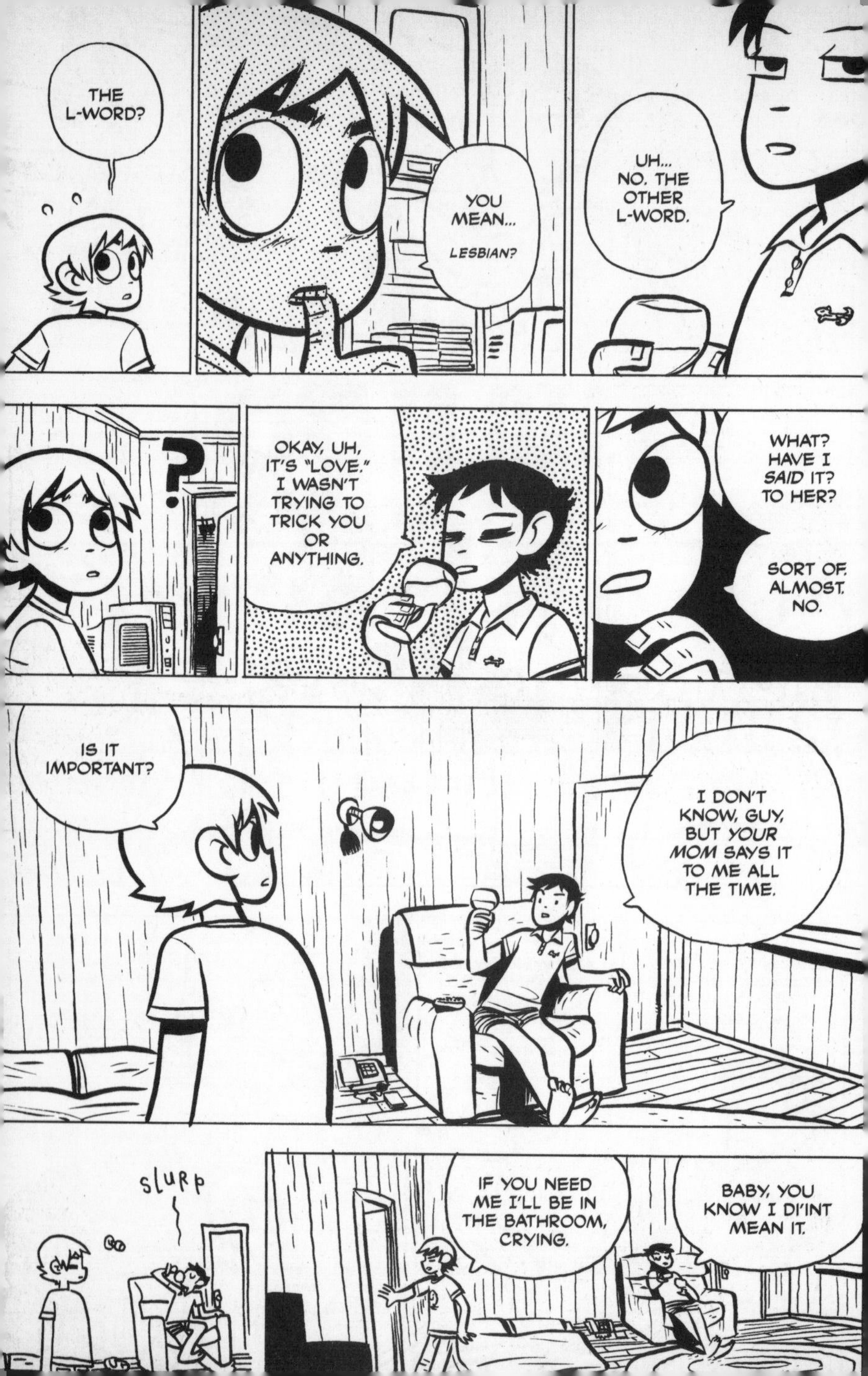
THE L-WORD?
YOU MEAN... LESBIAN?
UH... NO. THE OTHER L-WORD.
OKAY, UH, IT'S "LOVE." I WASN'T TRYING TO TRICK YOU OR ANYTHING.
WHAT? HAVE I SAID IT? TO HER?
SORT OF. ALMOST. NO.
IS IT IMPORTANT?
I DON'T KNOW, GUY, BUT YOUR MOM SAYS IT TO ME ALL THE TIME.
SLURP
IF YOU NEED ME I'LL BE IN THE BATHROOM, CRYING.
BABY, YOU KNOW I DI'INT MEAN IT.

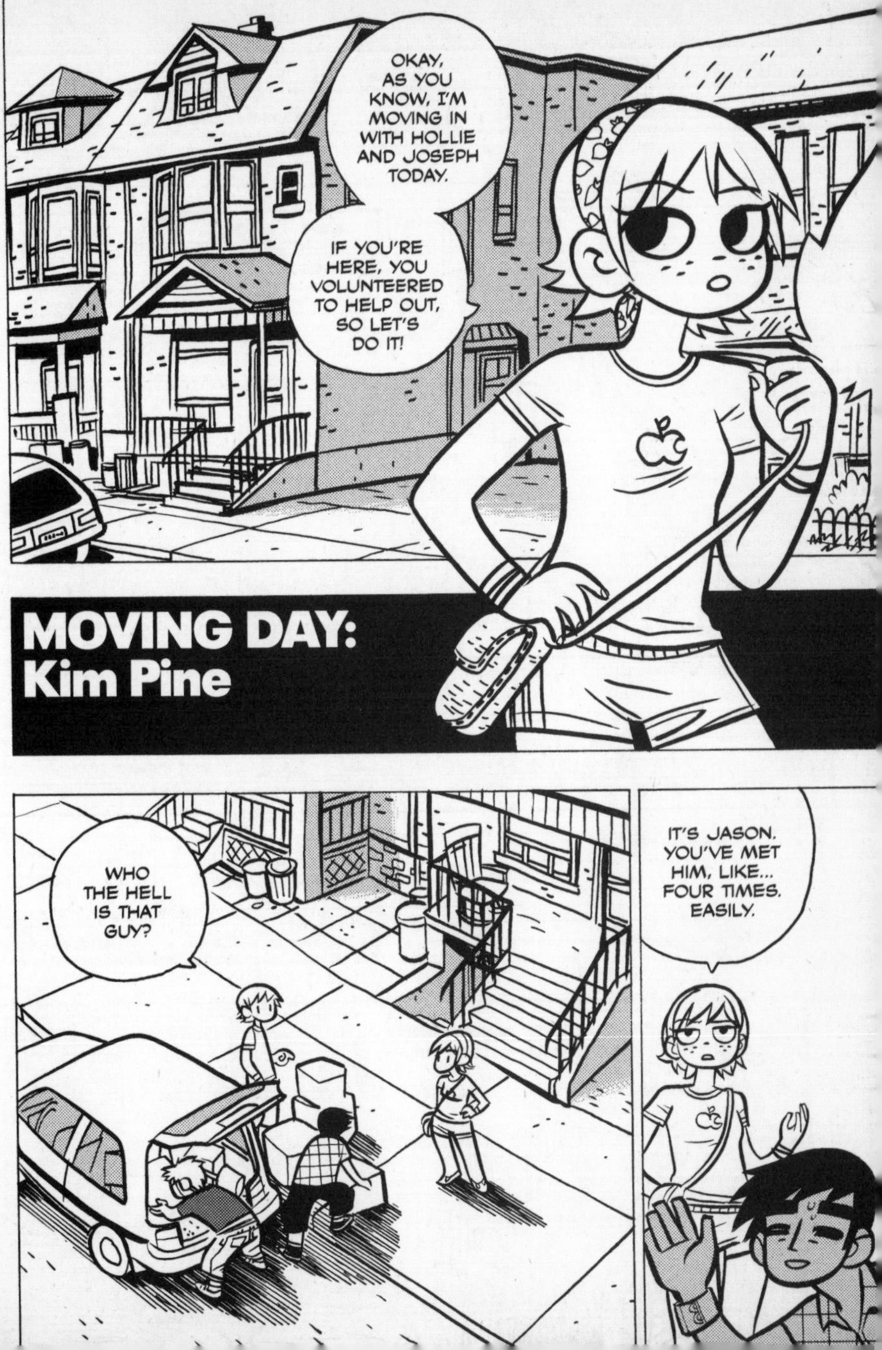
OKAY, AS YOU KNOW, I'M MOVING IN WITH HOLLIE AND JOSEPH TODAY.
IF YOU'RE HERE, YOU VOLUNTEERED TO HELP OUT, SO LET'S DO IT!
MOVING DAY:
Kim Pine
WHO THE HELL IS THAT GUY?
IT'S JASON. YOU'VE MET HIM, LIKE... FOUR TIMES. EASILY.

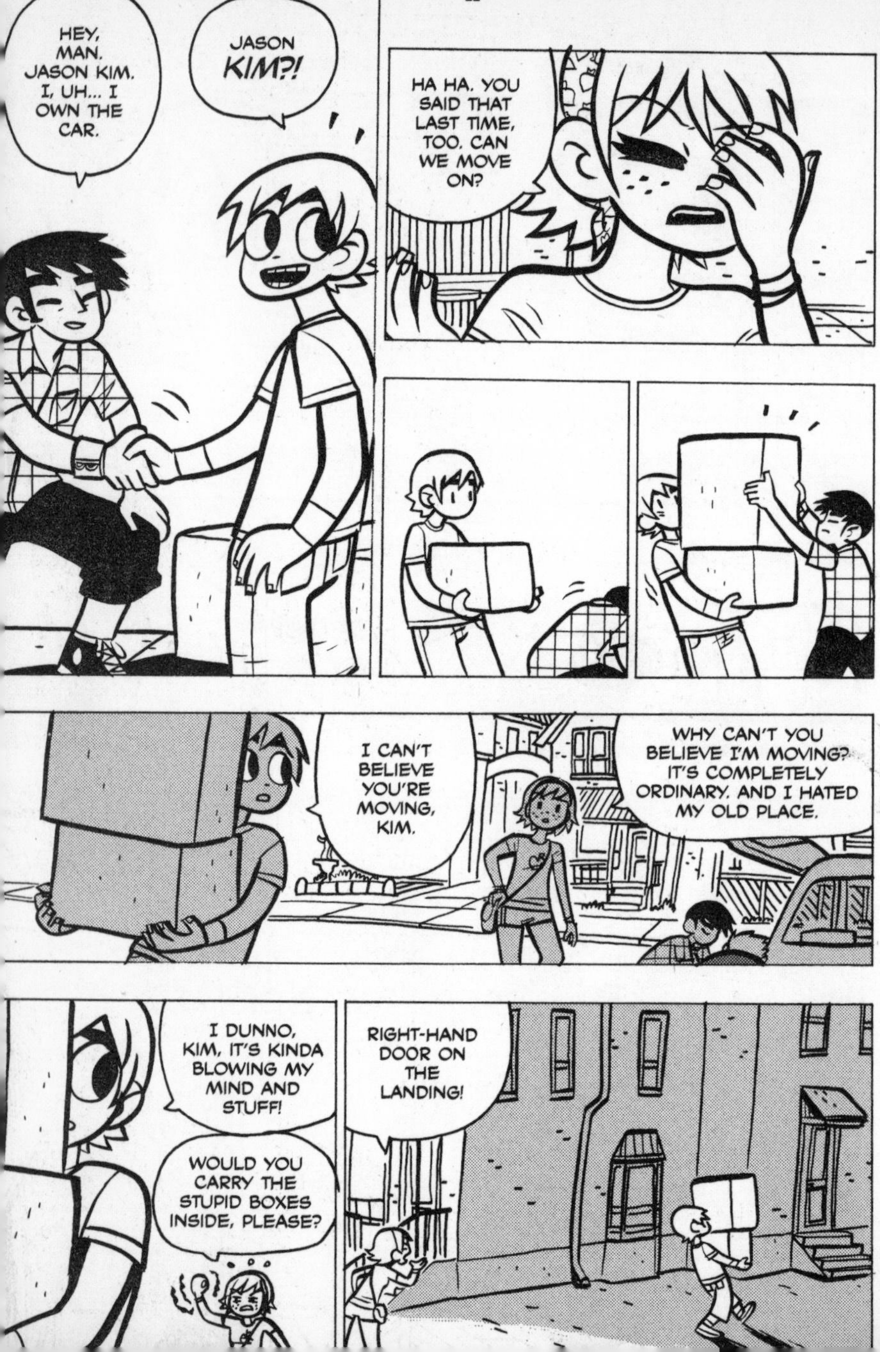
HEY, MAN. JASON KIM. I, UH... I OWN THE CAR.
JASON KIM?!
HA HA. YOU SAID THAT LAST TIME, TOO. CAN WE MOVE ON?
I CAN'T BELIEVE YOU'RE MOVING, KIM.
WHY CAN'T YOU BELIEVE I'M MOVING? IT'S COMPLETELY ORDINARY. AND I HATED MY OLD PLACE.
I DUNNO, KIM, IT'S KINDA BLOWING MY MIND AND STUFF!
WOULD YOU CARRY THE STUPID BOXES INSIDE, PLEASE?
RIGHT-HAND DOOR ON THE LANDING!

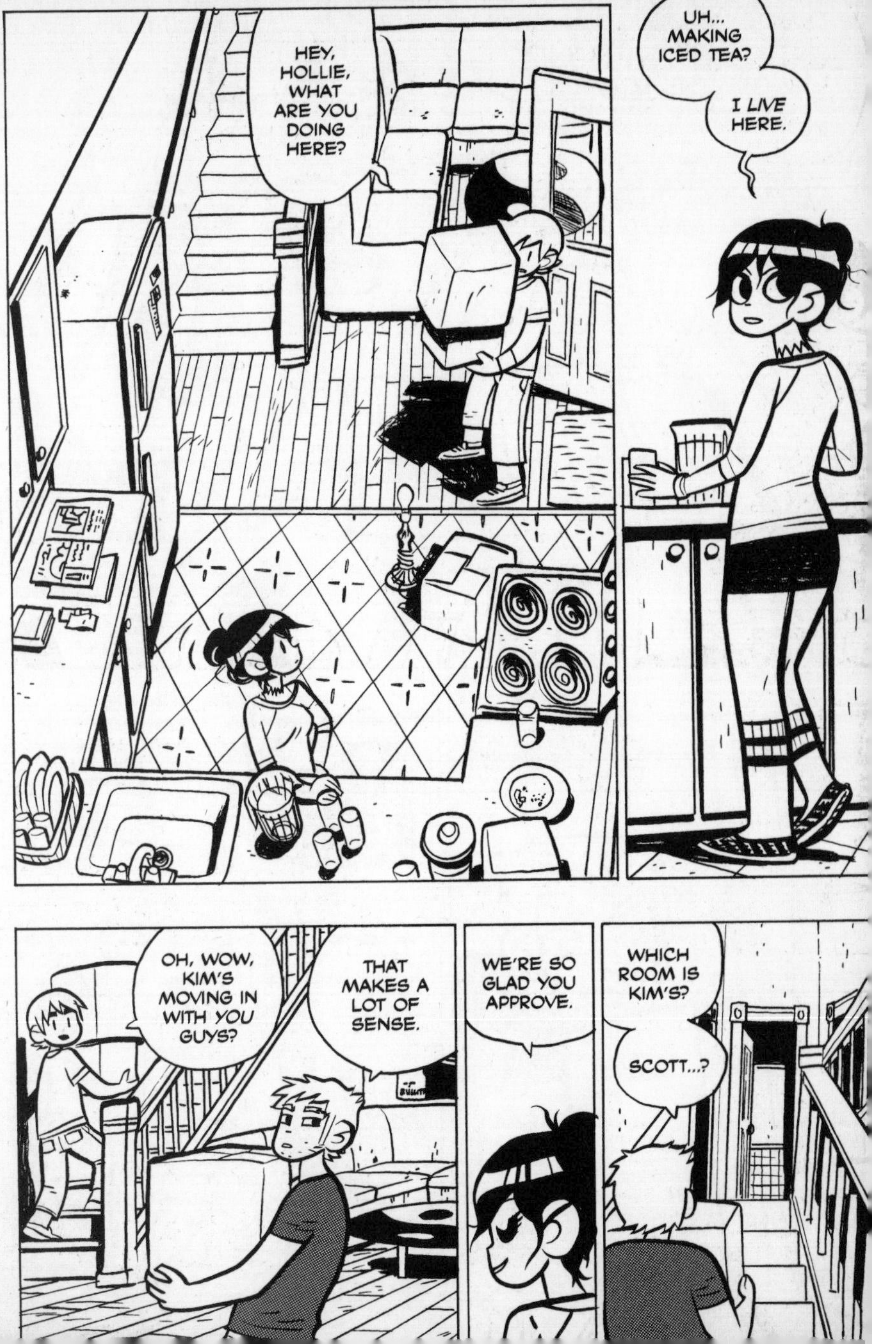
HEY, HOLLIE, WHAT ARE YOU DOING HERE?
UH... MAKING ICED TEA?
I *LIVE* HERE.
OH, WOW, KIM'S MOVING IN WITH *YOU* GUYS?
THAT MAKES A LOT OF SENSE.
WE'RE SO GLAD YOU APPROVE.
WHICH ROOM IS KIM'S?
SCOTT...?

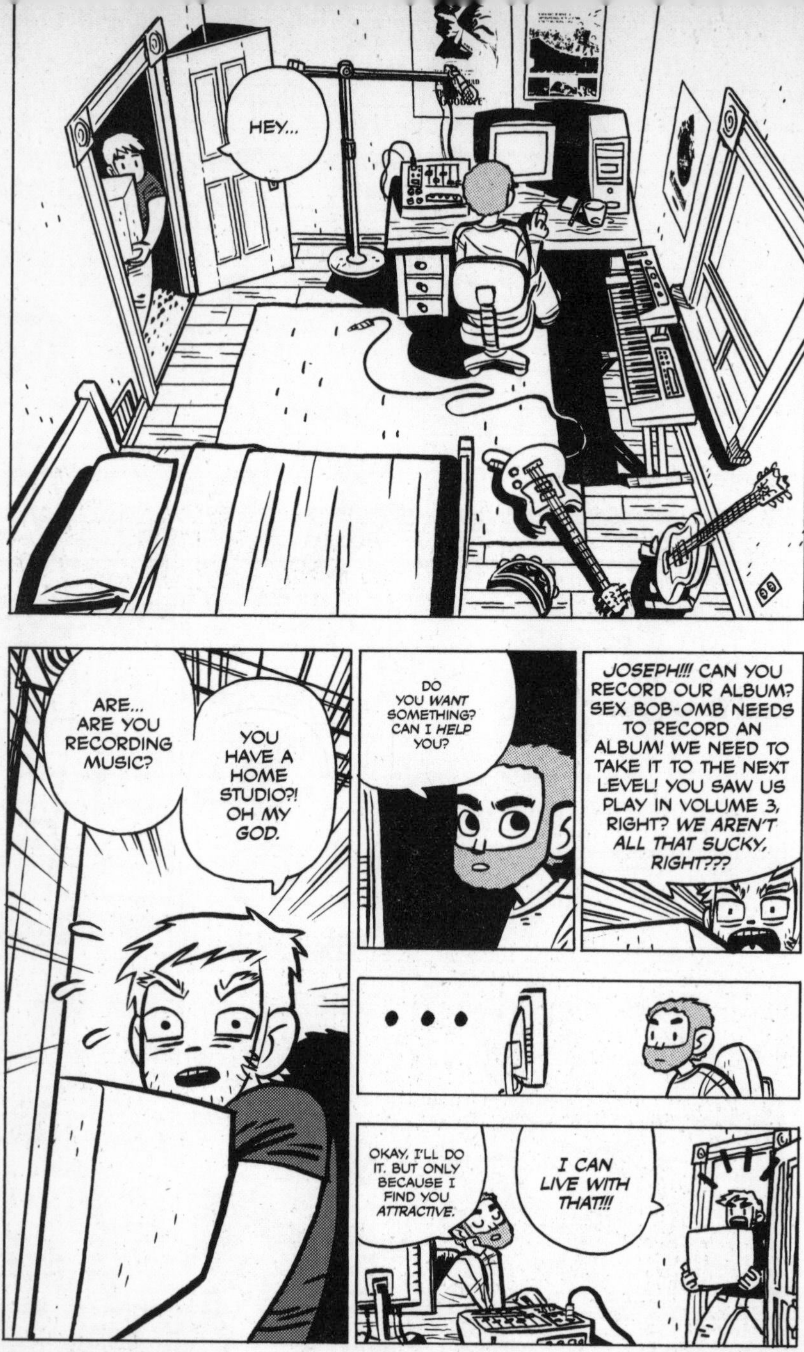

HEY...
ARE... ARE YOU RECORDING MUSIC?
YOU HAVE A HOME STUDIO?! OH MY *GOD.*
DO YOU *WANT* SOMETHING? CAN I *HELP* YOU?
JOSEPH!!! CAN YOU RECORD OUR ALBUM? SEX BOB-OMB NEEDS TO RECORD AN ALBUM! WE NEED TO TAKE IT TO THE NEXT LEVEL! YOU SAW US PLAY IN VOLUME 3, RIGHT? *WE AREN'T ALL THAT SUCKY, RIGHT???*
• • •
OKAY, I'LL DO IT. BUT ONLY BECAUSE I FIND YOU *ATTRACTIVE.*
I CAN LIVE WITH THAT!!!

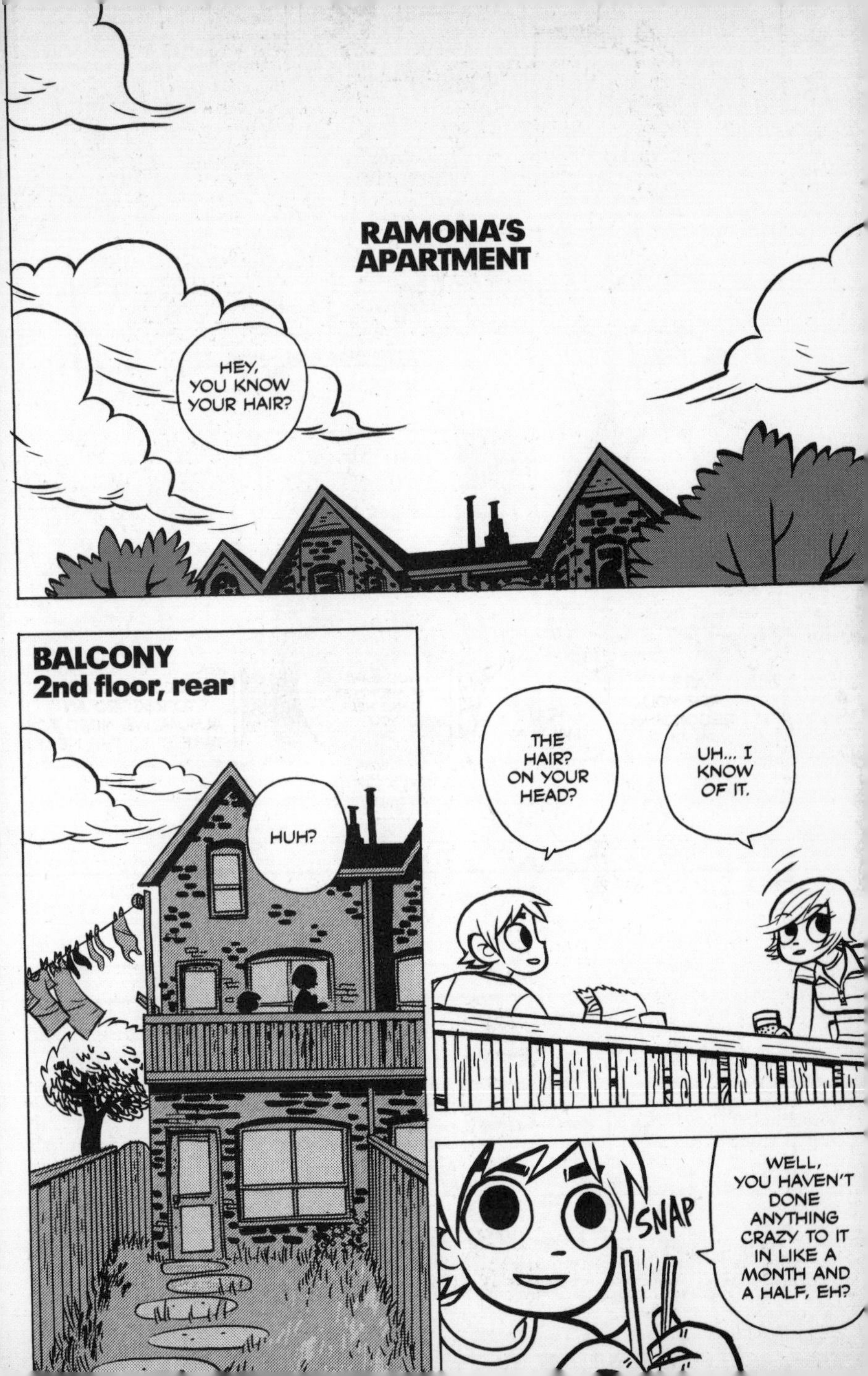
RAMONA'S APARTMENT
HEY, YOU KNOW YOUR HAIR?
BALCONY 2nd floor, rear
HUH?
THE HAIR? ON YOUR HEAD?
UH... I KNOW OF IT.
SNAP
WELL, YOU HAVEN'T DONE ANYTHING CRAZY TO IT IN LIKE A MONTH AND A HALF, EH?

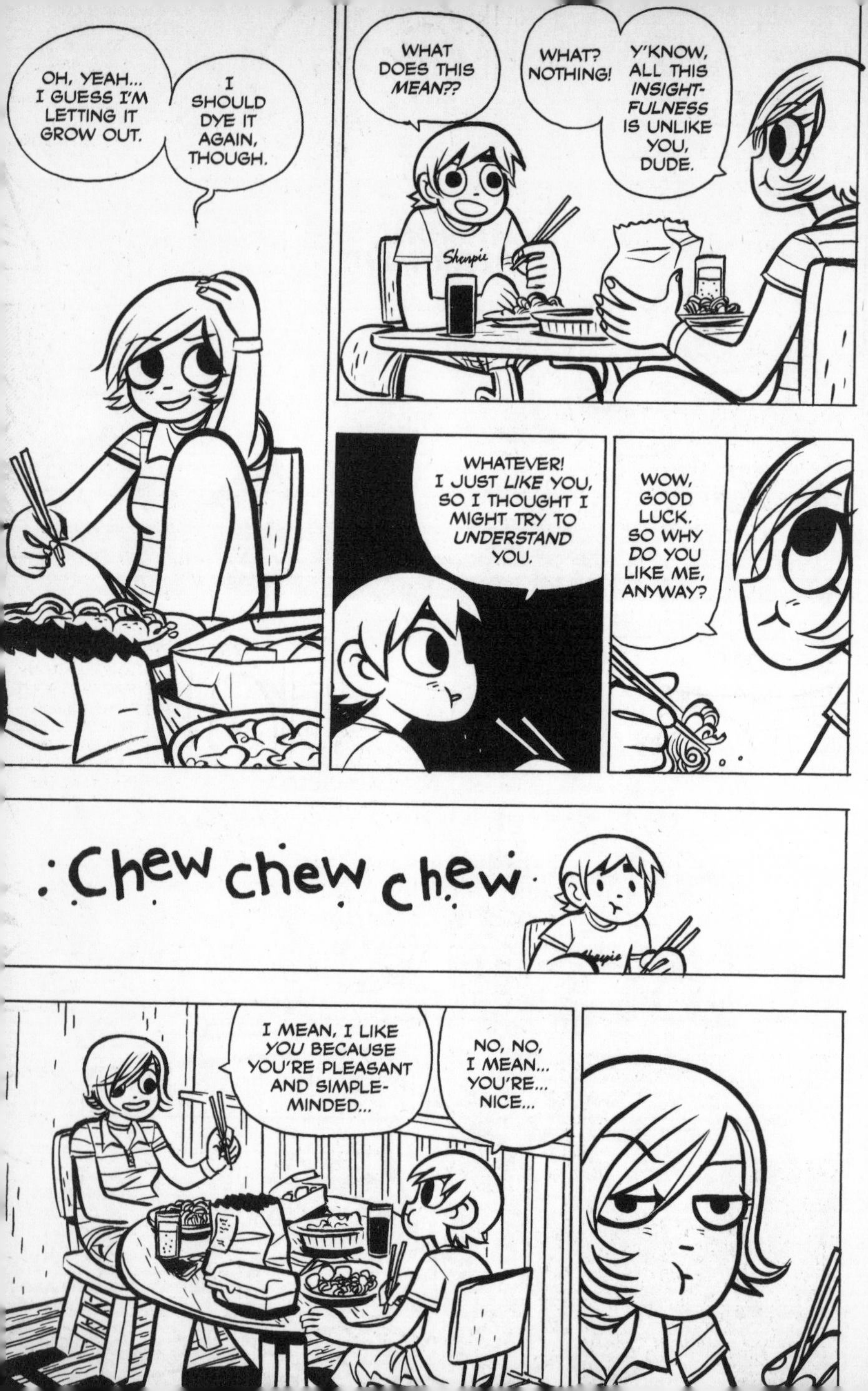
OH, YEAH... I GUESS I'M LETTING IT GROW OUT.
I SHOULD DYE IT AGAIN, THOUGH.
WHAT DOES THIS MEAN??
WHAT? NOTHING!
Y'KNOW, ALL THIS INSIGHT-FULNESS IS UNLIKE YOU, DUDE.
Sharpie
WHATEVER! I JUST LIKE YOU, SO I THOUGHT I MIGHT TRY TO UNDERSTAND YOU.
WOW, GOOD LUCK. SO WHY DO YOU LIKE ME, ANYWAY?
Chew chew chew
I MEAN, I LIKE YOU BECAUSE YOU'RE PLEASANT AND SIMPLE-MINDED...
NO, NO, I MEAN... YOU'RE... NICE...

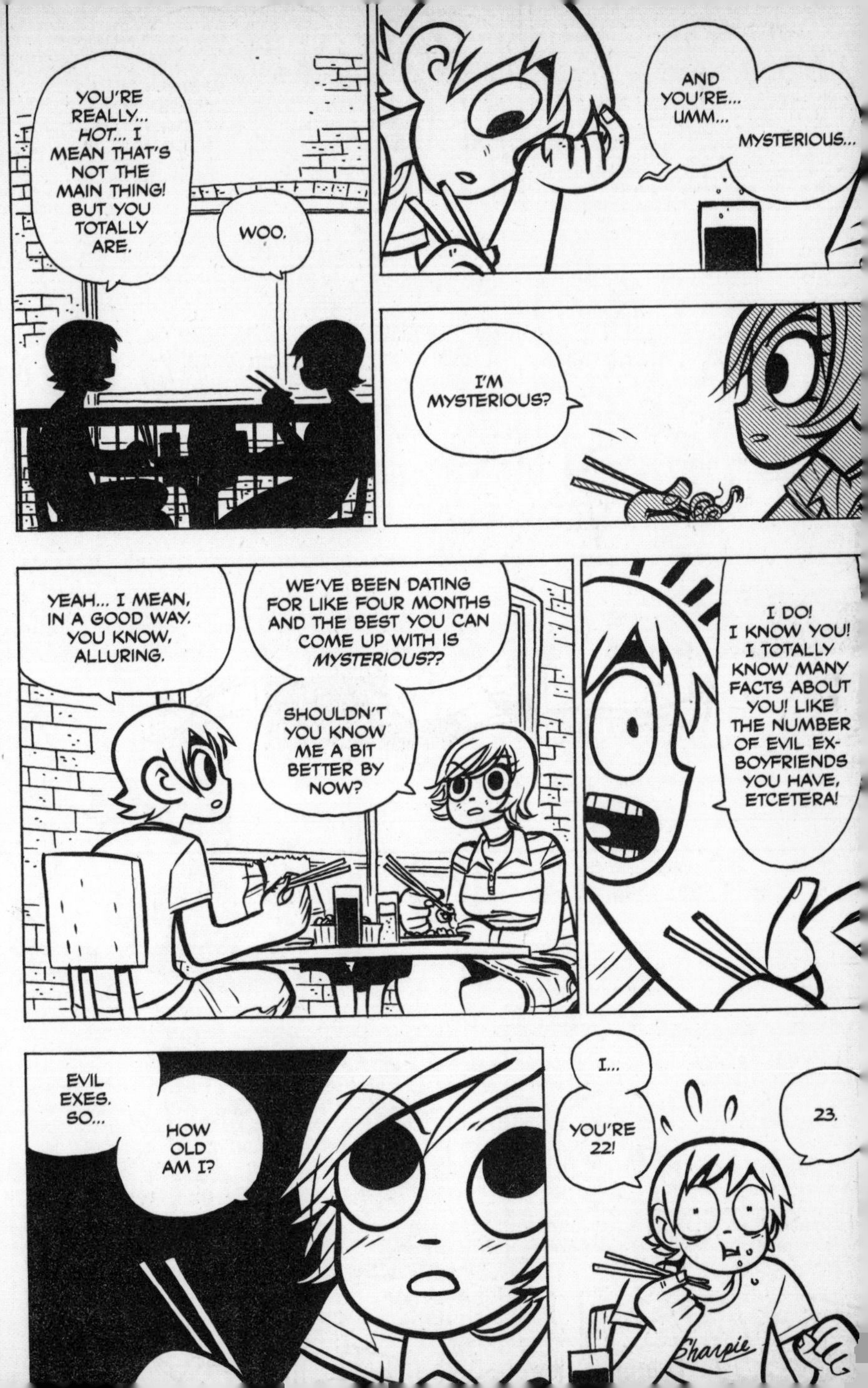
YOU'RE REALLY... HOT... I MEAN THAT'S NOT THE MAIN THING! BUT YOU TOTALLY ARE.
WOO.
AND YOU'RE... UMM...
MYSTERIOUS...
I'M MYSTERIOUS?
YEAH... I MEAN, IN A GOOD WAY. YOU KNOW, ALLURING.
WE'VE BEEN DATING FOR LIKE FOUR MONTHS AND THE BEST YOU CAN COME UP WITH IS MYSTERIOUS??
SHOULDN'T YOU KNOW ME A BIT BETTER BY NOW?
I DO! I KNOW YOU! I TOTALLY KNOW MANY FACTS ABOUT YOU! LIKE THE NUMBER OF EVIL EX-BOYFRIENDS YOU HAVE, ETCETERA!
EVIL EXES. SO...
HOW OLD AM I?
I...
YOU'RE 22!
23.
Sharpie

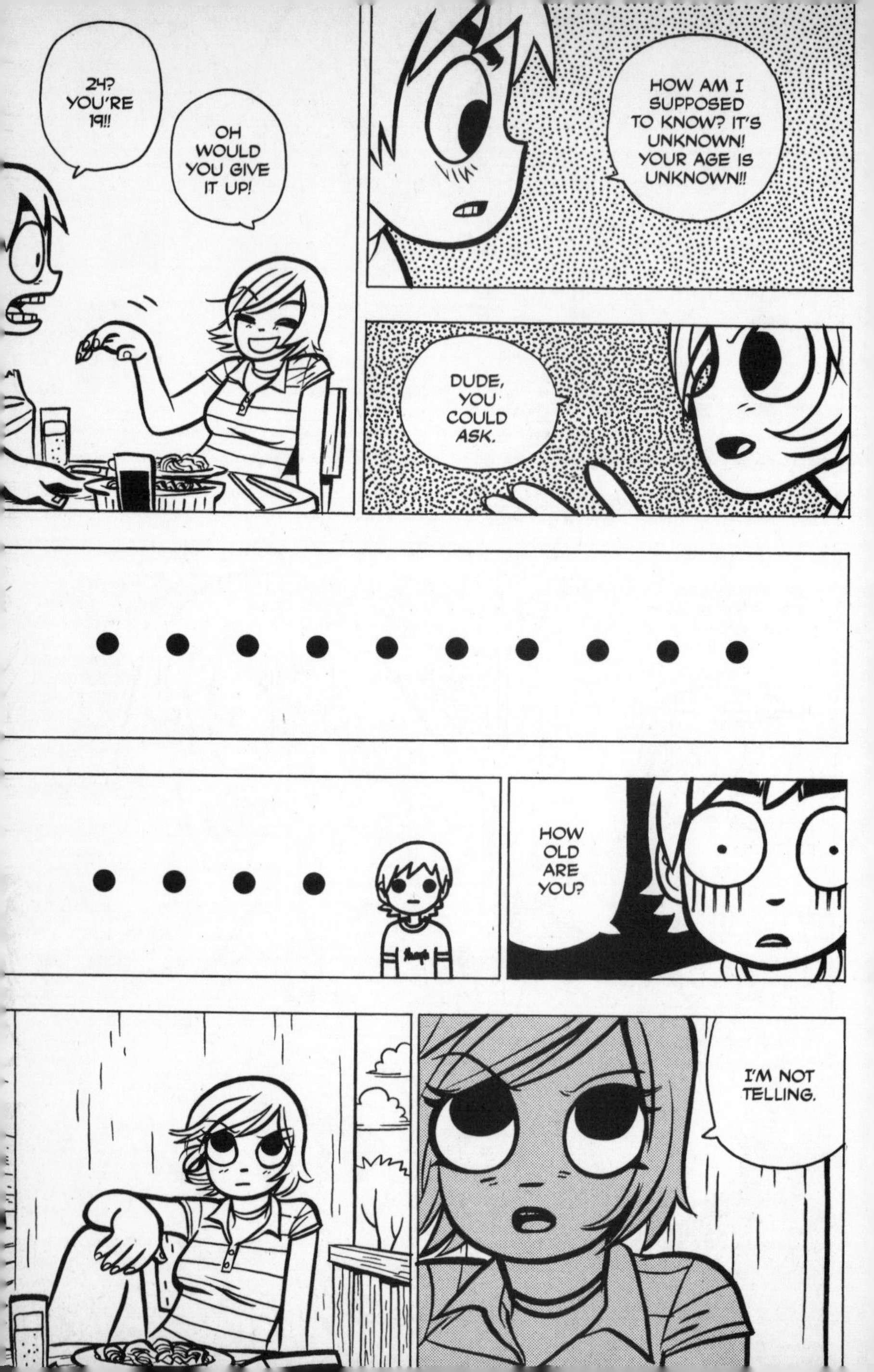
24? YOU'RE 19!!
OH WOULD YOU GIVE IT UP!
HOW AM I SUPPOSED TO KNOW? IT'S UNKNOWN! YOUR AGE IS UNKNOWN!!
DUDE, YOU COULD ASK.
HOW OLD ARE YOU?
I'M NOT TELLING.

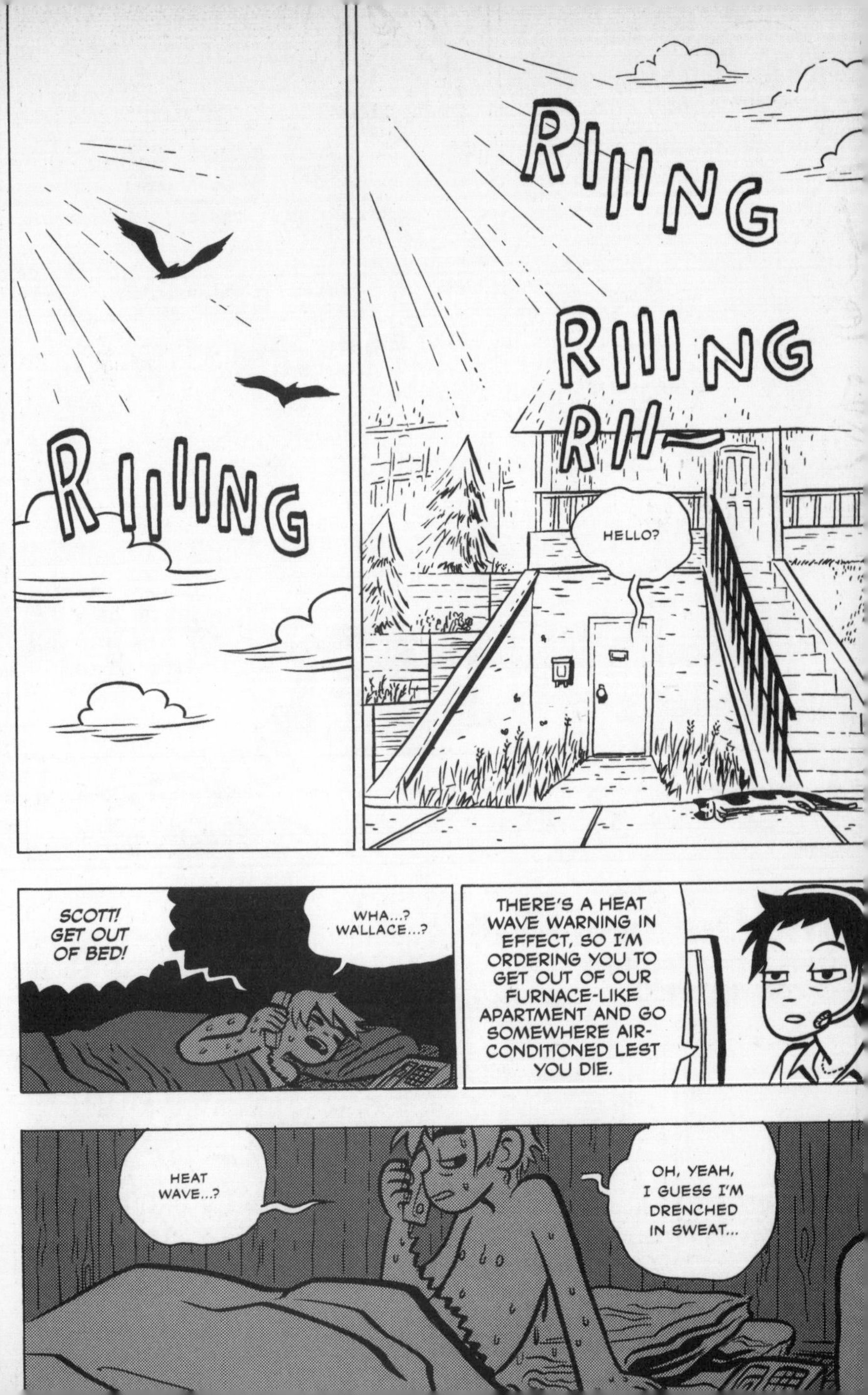
RIIING
RIIING
RIIING
RII—
HELLO?
SCOTT! GET OUT OF BED!
WHA...? WALLACE...?
THERE'S A HEAT WAVE WARNING IN EFFECT, SO I'M ORDERING YOU TO GET OUT OF OUR FURNACE-LIKE APARTMENT AND GO SOMEWHERE AIR-CONDITIONED LEST YOU DIE.
HEAT WAVE...?
OH, YEAH, I GUESS I'M DRENCHED IN SWEAT...

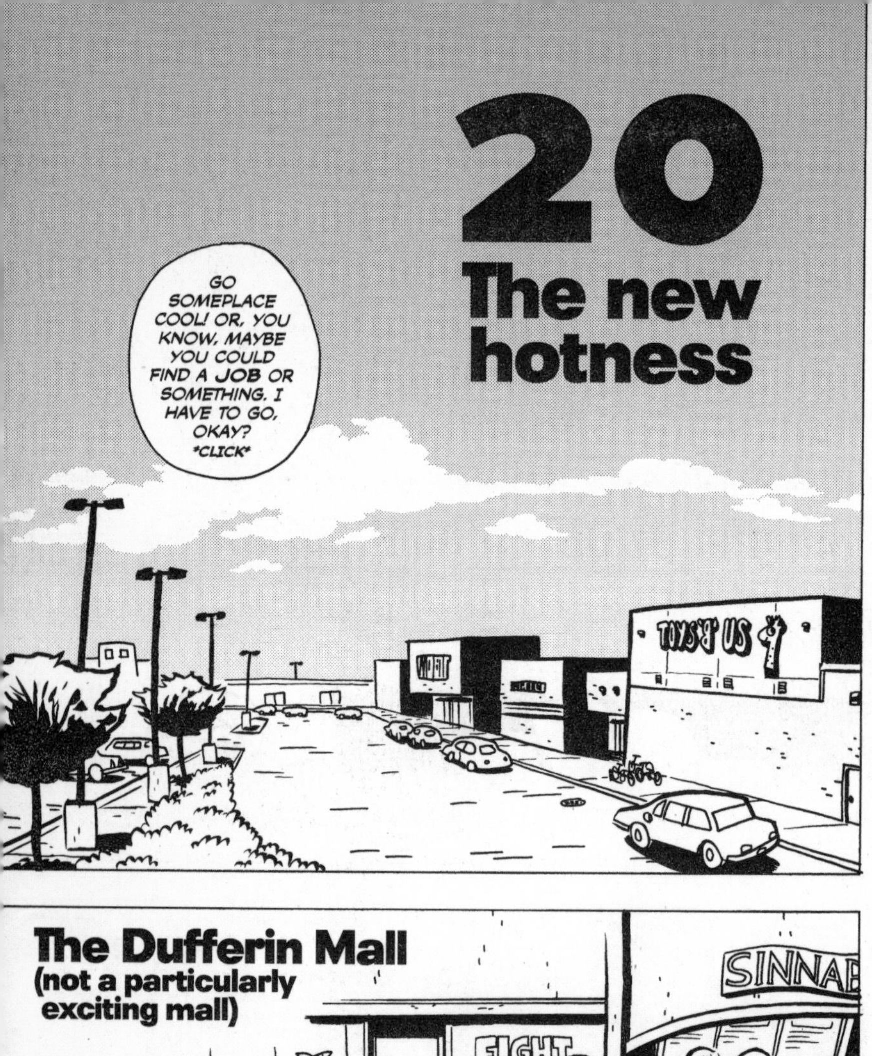
20
The new hotness
GO SOMEPLACE COOL! OR, YOU KNOW, MAYBE YOU COULD FIND A JOB OR SOMETHING. I HAVE TO GO, OKAY? *CLICK*
TOYS'R' US

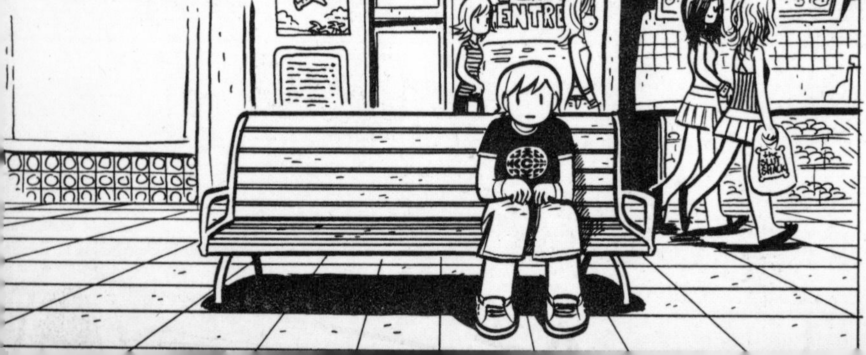
The Dufferin Mall
(not a particularly exciting mall)
SINNAB
FIGHT CENTRE

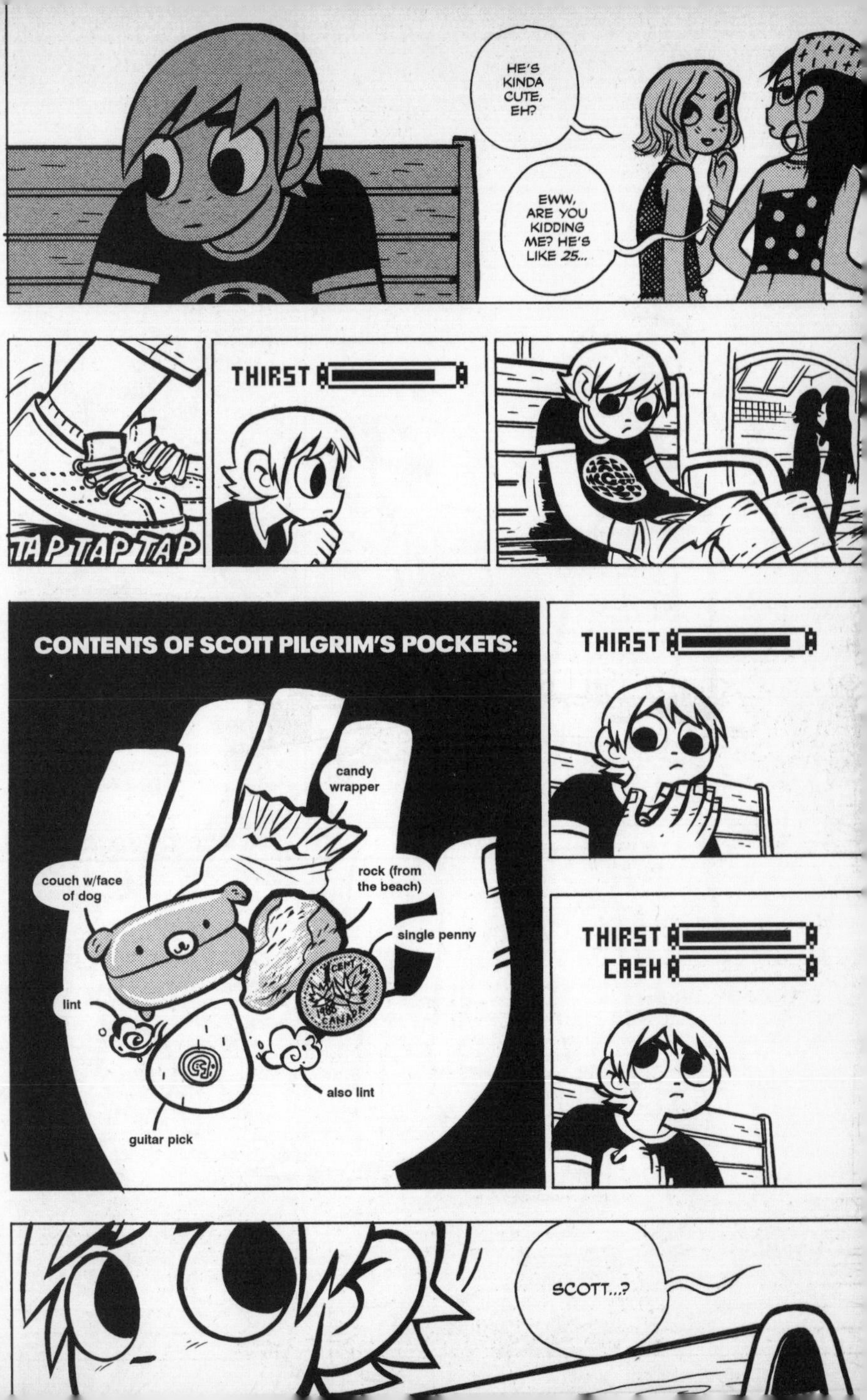
HE'S KINDA CUTE, EH?
EWW, ARE YOU KIDDING ME? HE'S LIKE *25*...
TAP TAP TAP
THIRST
CONTENTS OF SCOTT PILGRIM'S POCKETS:
candy wrapper
couch w/face of dog
rock (from the beach)
single penny
lint
also lint
guitar pick
THIRST
THIRST
CASH
SCOTT...?

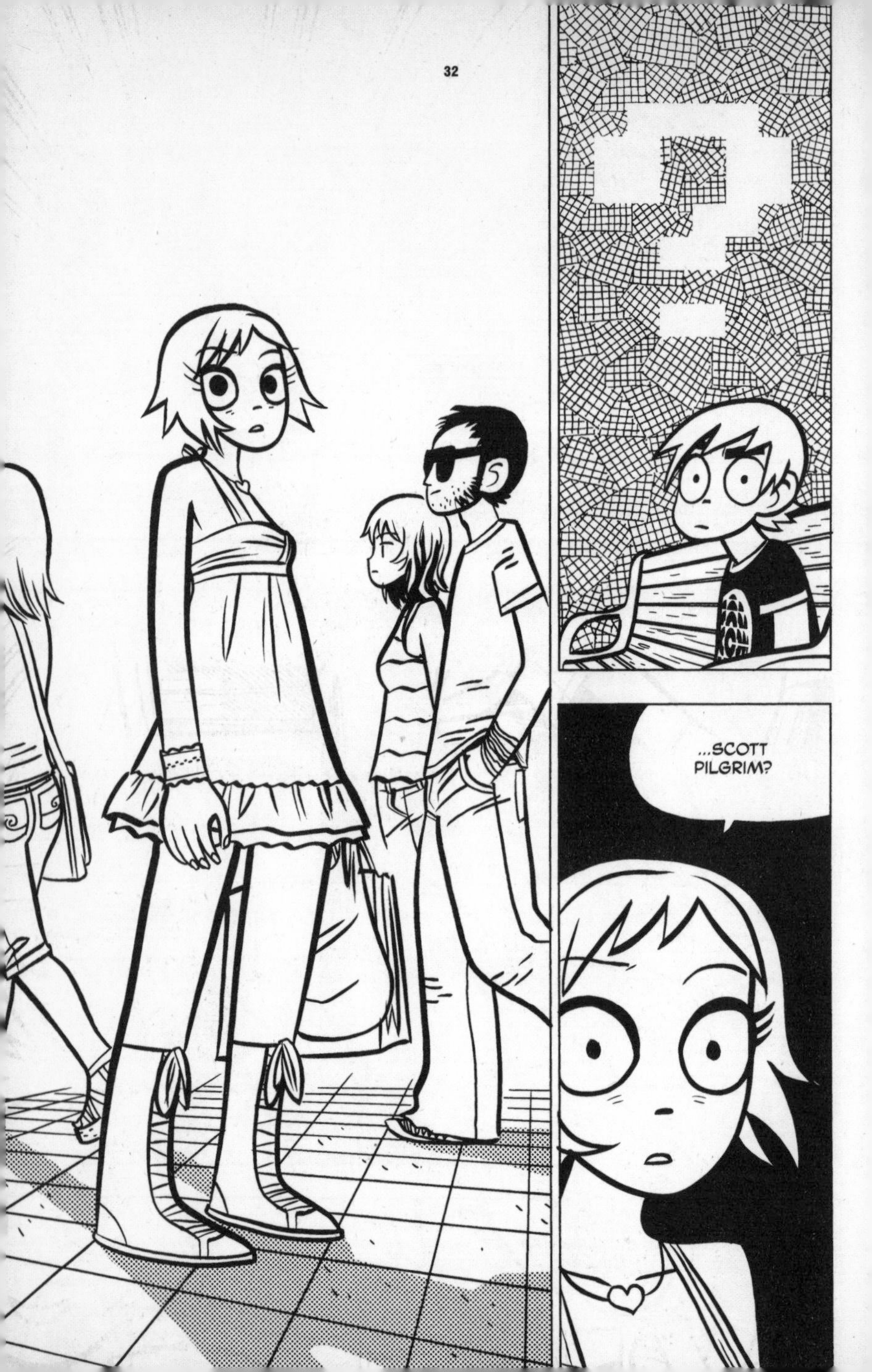
...SCOTT PILGRIM?

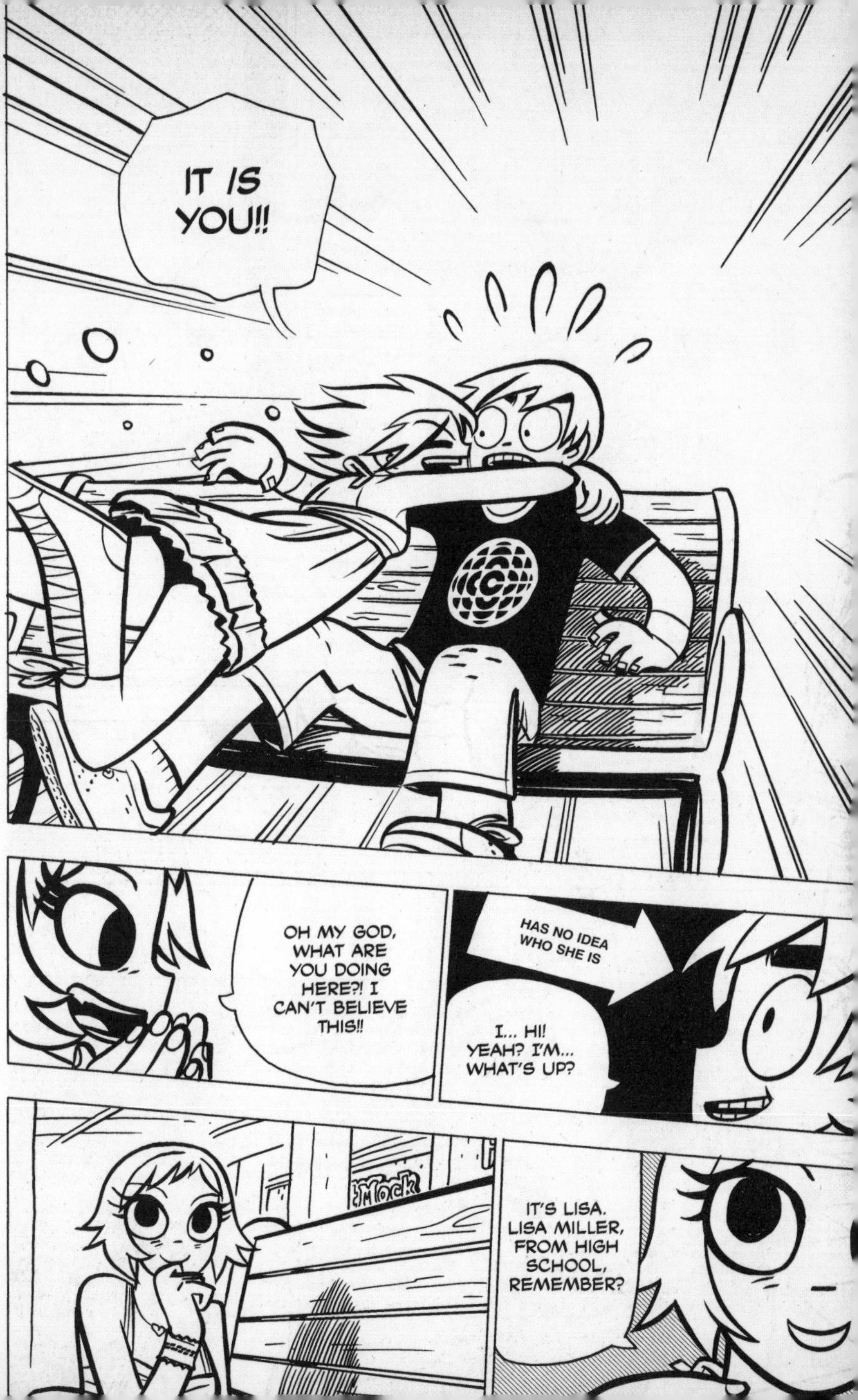
IT IS YOU!!
OH MY GOD, WHAT ARE YOU DOING HERE?! I CAN'T BELIEVE THIS!!
HAS NO IDEA WHO SHE IS
I... HI! YEAH? I'M... WHAT'S UP?
IT'S LISA. LISA MILLER, FROM HIGH SCHOOL, REMEMBER?

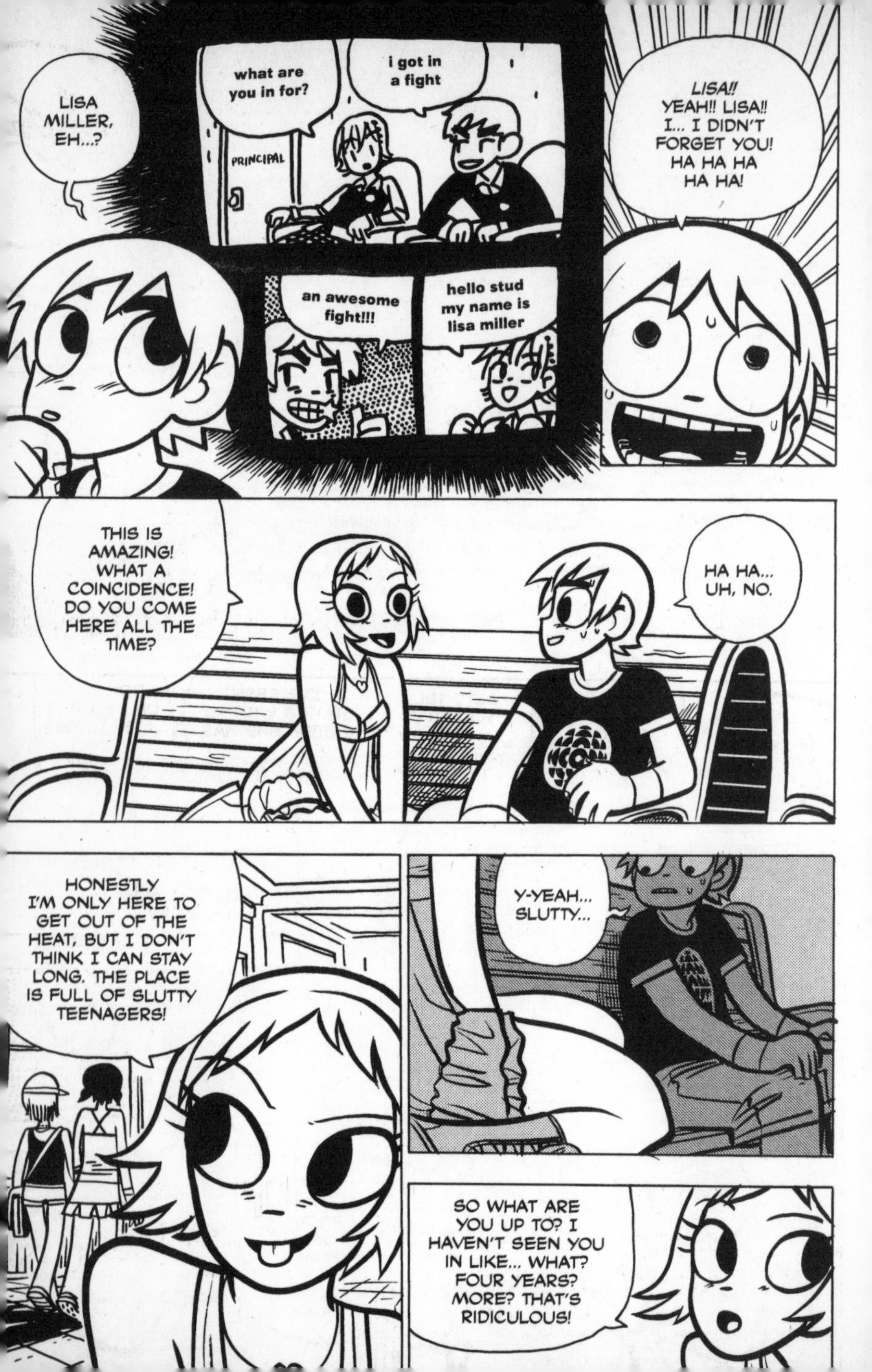
LISA MILLER, EH...?
what are you in for?
i got in a fight
PRINCIPAL
an awesome fight!!!
hello stud my name is lisa miller
LISA!! YEAH!! LISA!! I... I DIDN'T FORGET YOU! HA HA HA HA HA!
THIS IS AMAZING! WHAT A COINCIDENCE! DO YOU COME HERE ALL THE TIME?
HA HA... UH, NO.
HONESTLY I'M ONLY HERE TO GET OUT OF THE HEAT, BUT I DON'T THINK I CAN STAY LONG. THE PLACE IS FULL OF SLUTTY TEENAGERS!
Y-YEAH... SLUTTY...
SO WHAT ARE YOU UP TO? I HAVEN'T SEEN YOU IN LIKE... WHAT? FOUR YEARS? MORE? THAT'S RIDICULOUS!

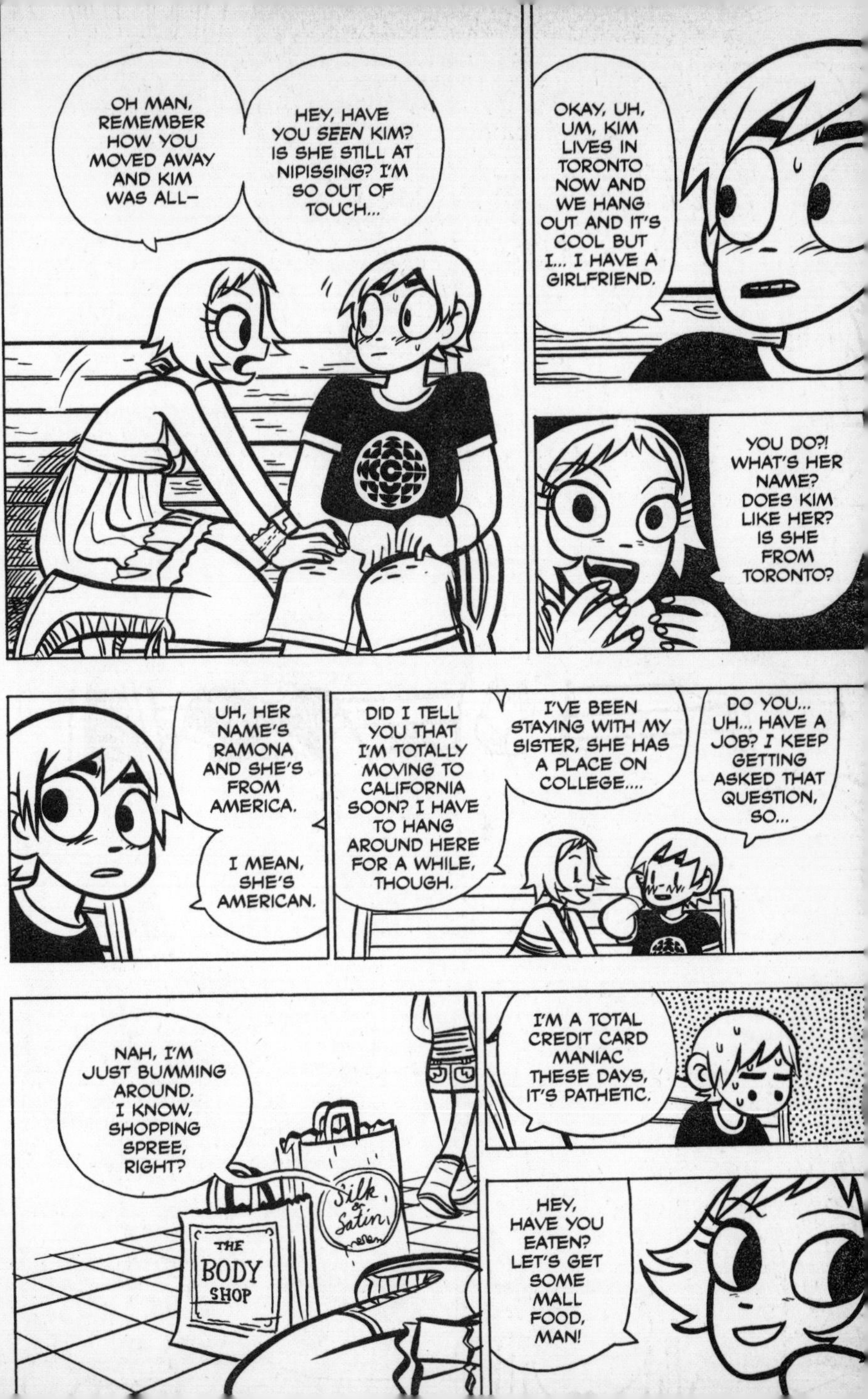
OH MAN, REMEMBER HOW YOU MOVED AWAY AND KIM WAS ALL–
HEY, HAVE YOU *SEEN* KIM? IS SHE STILL AT NIPISSING? I'M SO OUT OF TOUCH...
OKAY, UH, UM, KIM LIVES IN TORONTO NOW AND WE HANG OUT AND IT'S COOL BUT I... I HAVE A GIRLFRIEND.
YOU DO?! WHAT'S HER NAME? DOES KIM LIKE HER? IS SHE FROM TORONTO?
UH, HER NAME'S RAMONA AND SHE'S FROM AMERICA.
I MEAN, SHE'S AMERICAN.
DID I TELL YOU THAT I'M TOTALLY MOVING TO CALIFORNIA SOON? I HAVE TO HANG AROUND HERE FOR A WHILE, THOUGH.
I'VE BEEN STAYING WITH MY SISTER, SHE HAS A PLACE ON COLLEGE....
DO YOU... UH... HAVE A JOB? *I* KEEP GETTING ASKED THAT QUESTION, SO...
NAH, I'M JUST BUMMING AROUND. I KNOW, SHOPPING SPREE, RIGHT?
Silk & Satin
THE BODY SHOP
I'M A TOTAL CREDIT CARD MANIAC THESE DAYS, IT'S PATHETIC.
HEY, HAVE YOU EATEN? LET'S GET SOME MALL FOOD, MAN!

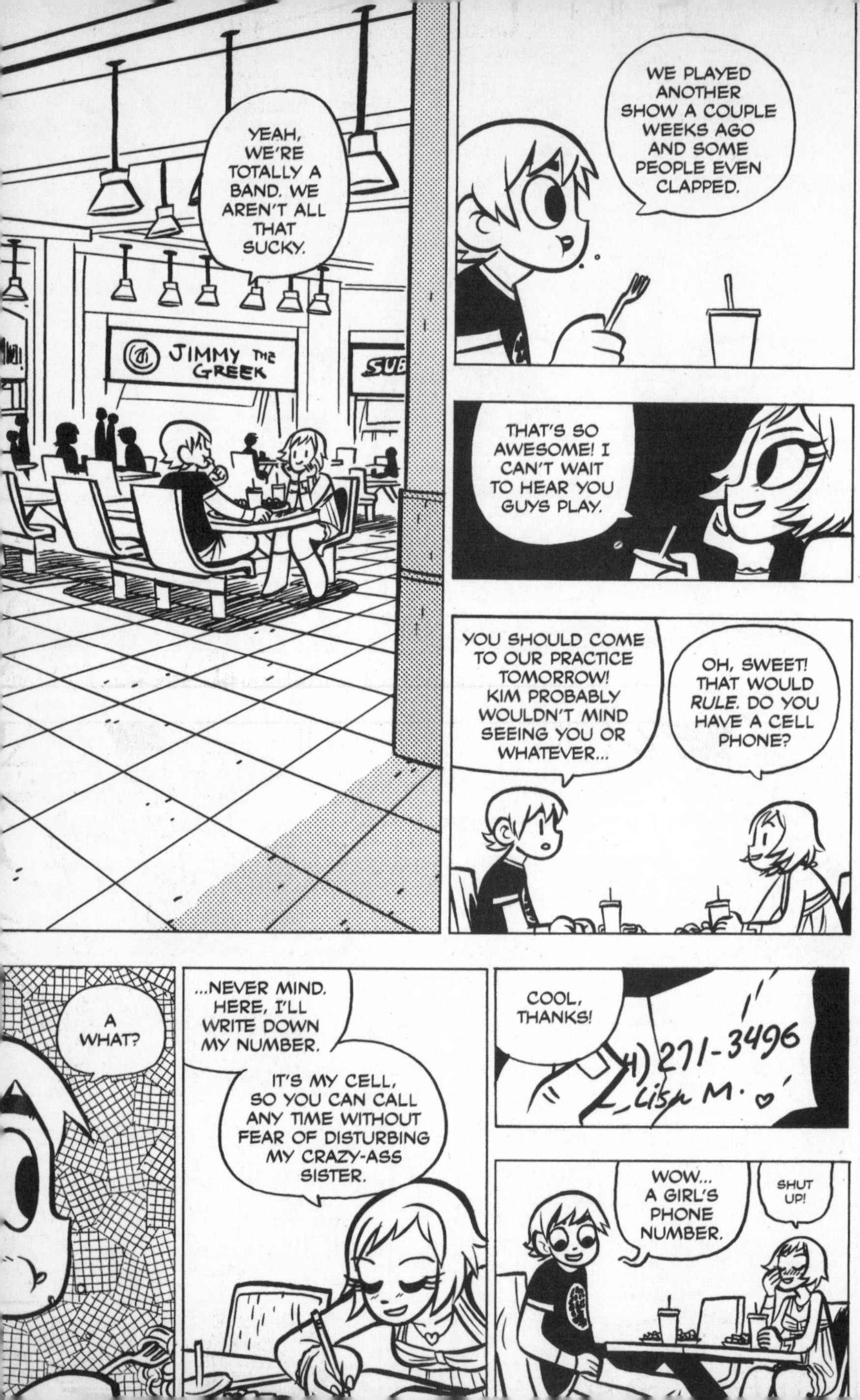
YEAH, WE'RE TOTALLY A BAND. WE AREN'T ALL THAT SUCKY.
JIMMY THE GREEK
WE PLAYED ANOTHER SHOW A COUPLE WEEKS AGO AND SOME PEOPLE EVEN CLAPPED.
THAT'S SO AWESOME! I CAN'T WAIT TO HEAR YOU GUYS PLAY.
YOU SHOULD COME TO OUR PRACTICE TOMORROW! KIM PROBABLY WOULDN'T MIND SEEING YOU OR WHATEVER...
OH, SWEET! THAT WOULD *RULE*. DO YOU HAVE A CELL PHONE?
A WHAT?
...NEVER MIND. HERE, I'LL WRITE DOWN MY NUMBER.
IT'S MY CELL, SO YOU CAN CALL ANY TIME WITHOUT FEAR OF DISTURBING MY CRAZY-ASS SISTER.
COOL, THANKS!
4) 271-3496
Lisa M.
WOW... A GIRL'S PHONE NUMBER.
SHUT UP!

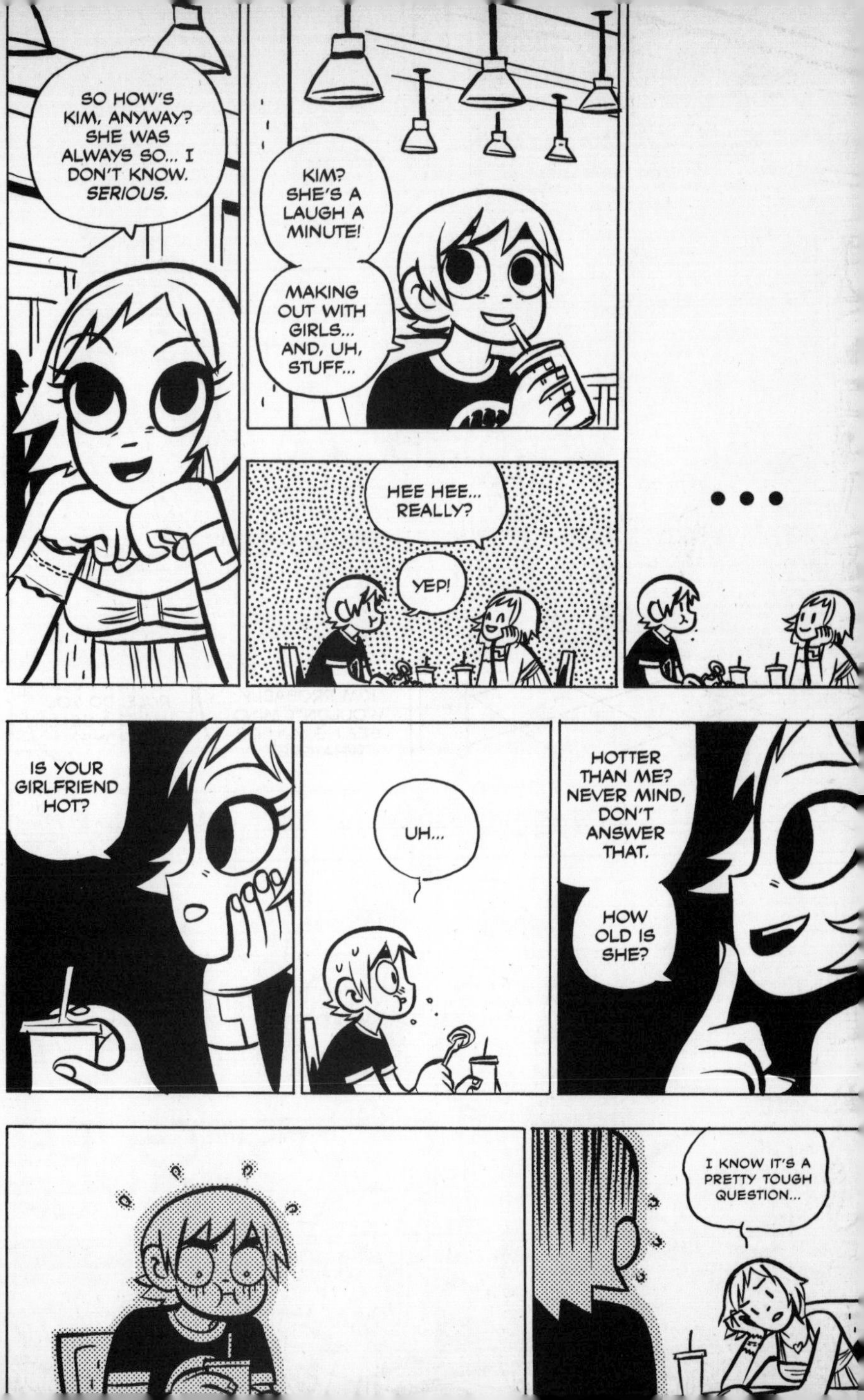
SO HOW'S KIM, ANYWAY? SHE WAS ALWAYS SO... I DON'T KNOW. *SERIOUS.*
KIM? SHE'S A LAUGH A MINUTE!
MAKING OUT WITH GIRLS... AND, UH, STUFF...
HEE HEE... REALLY?
YEP!
• • •
IS YOUR GIRLFRIEND HOT?
UH...
HOTTER THAN ME? NEVER MIND, DON'T ANSWER THAT.
HOW OLD IS SHE?
I KNOW IT'S A PRETTY TOUGH QUESTION...

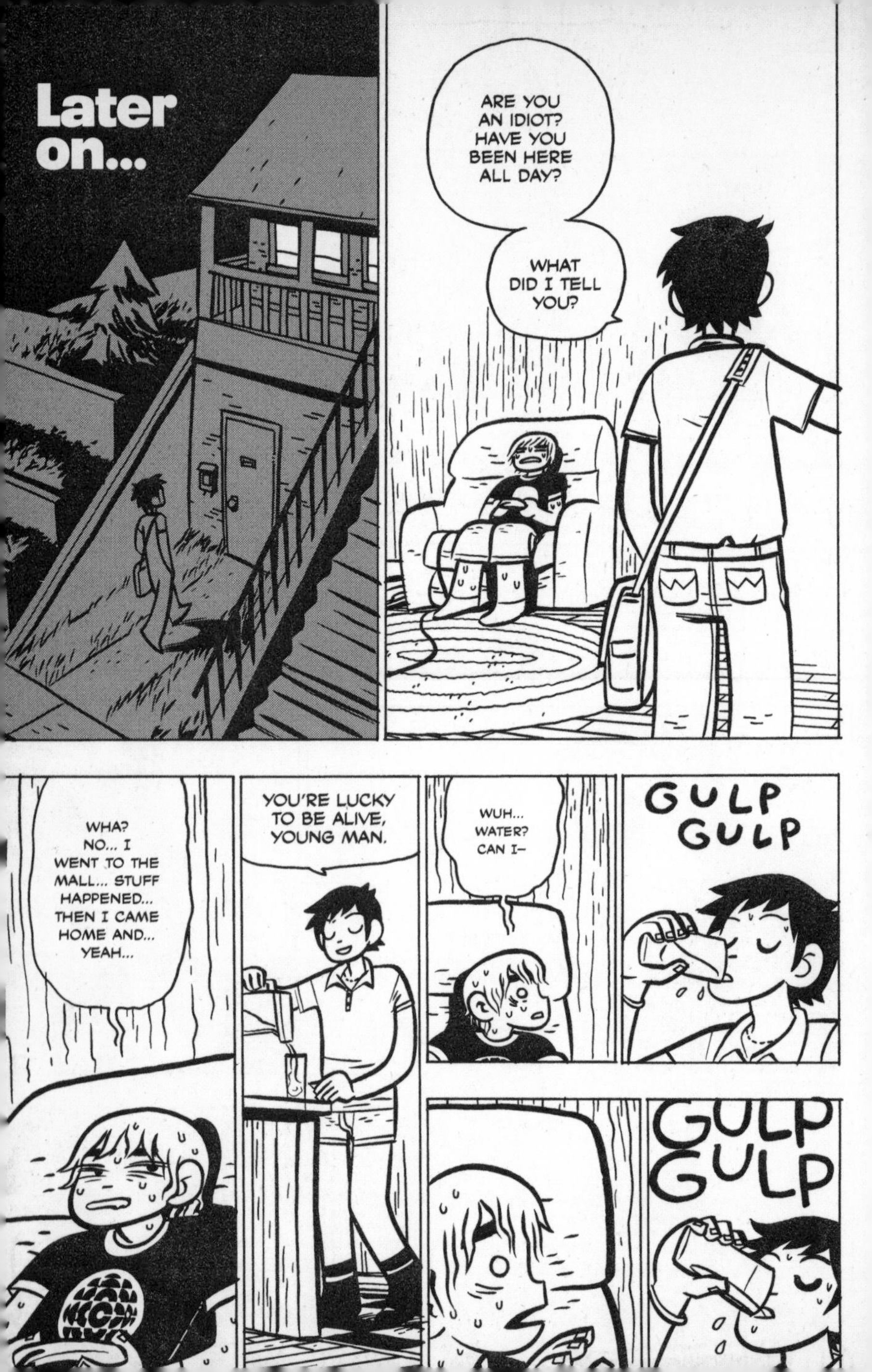
Later on...
ARE YOU AN IDIOT? HAVE YOU BEEN HERE ALL DAY?
WHAT DID I TELL YOU?
WHA? NO... I WENT TO THE MALL... STUFF HAPPENED... THEN I CAME HOME AND... YEAH...
YOU'RE LUCKY TO BE ALIVE, YOUNG MAN.
WUH... WATER? CAN I—
GULP GULP
GULP GULP

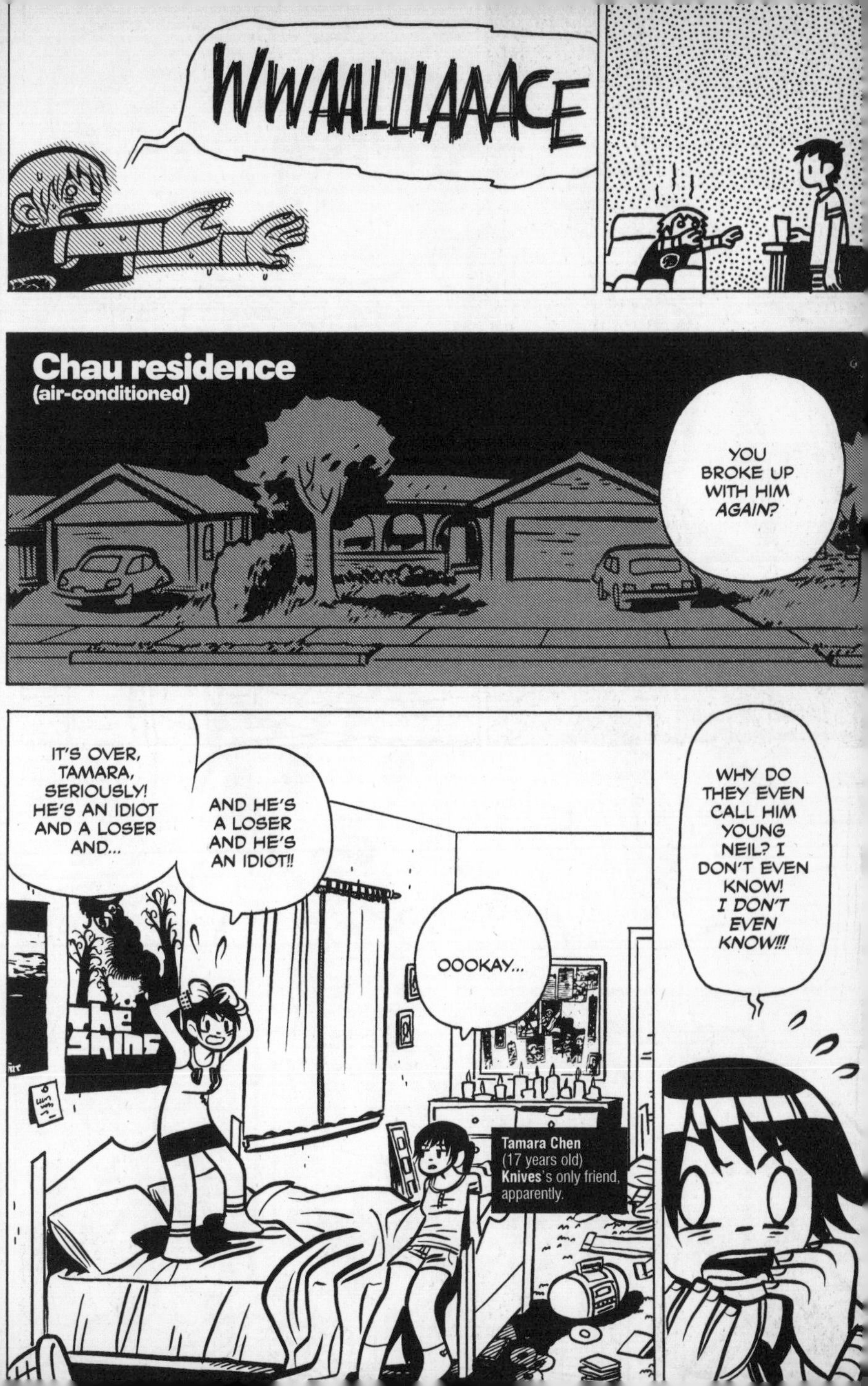
WWAALLLAAACE
Chau residence
(air-conditioned)
YOU BROKE UP WITH HIM *AGAIN?*
IT'S OVER, TAMARA, SERIOUSLY! HE'S AN IDIOT AND A LOSER AND...
AND HE'S A LOSER AND HE'S AN IDIOT!!
OOOKAY...
WHY DO THEY EVEN CALL HIM YOUNG NEIL? I DON'T EVEN KNOW! *I DON'T EVEN KNOW!!!*
The Shins
Tamara Chen (17 years old) **Knives**'s only friend, apparently.

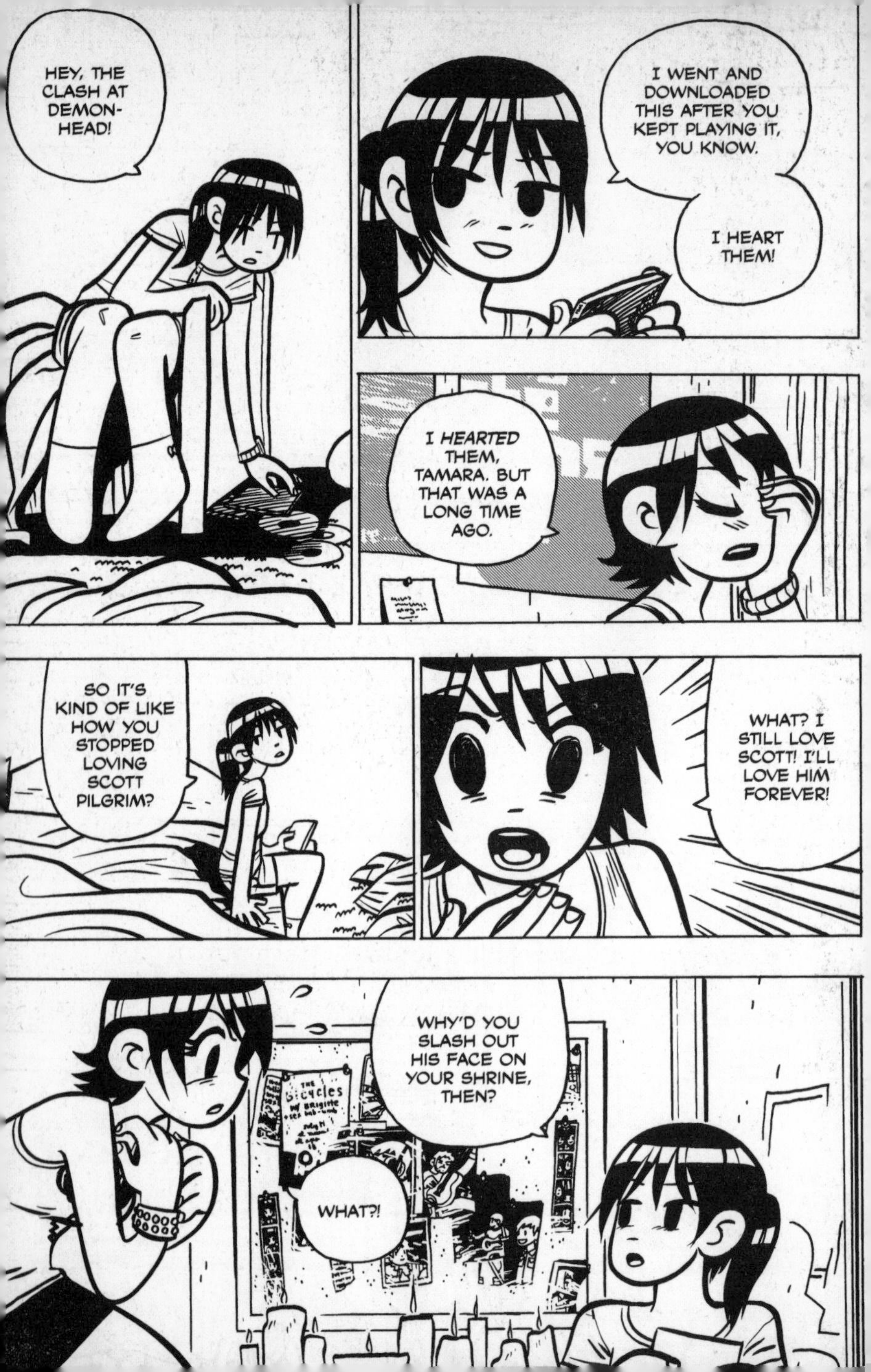
HEY, THE CLASH AT DEMON-HEAD!
I WENT AND DOWNLOADED THIS AFTER YOU KEPT PLAYING IT, YOU KNOW.
I HEART THEM!
I *HEARTED* THEM, TAMARA. BUT THAT WAS A LONG TIME AGO.
SO IT'S KIND OF LIKE HOW YOU STOPPED LOVING SCOTT PILGRIM?
WHAT? I STILL LOVE SCOTT! I'LL LOVE HIM FOREVER!
WHY'D YOU SLASH OUT HIS FACE ON YOUR SHRINE, THEN?
WHAT?!

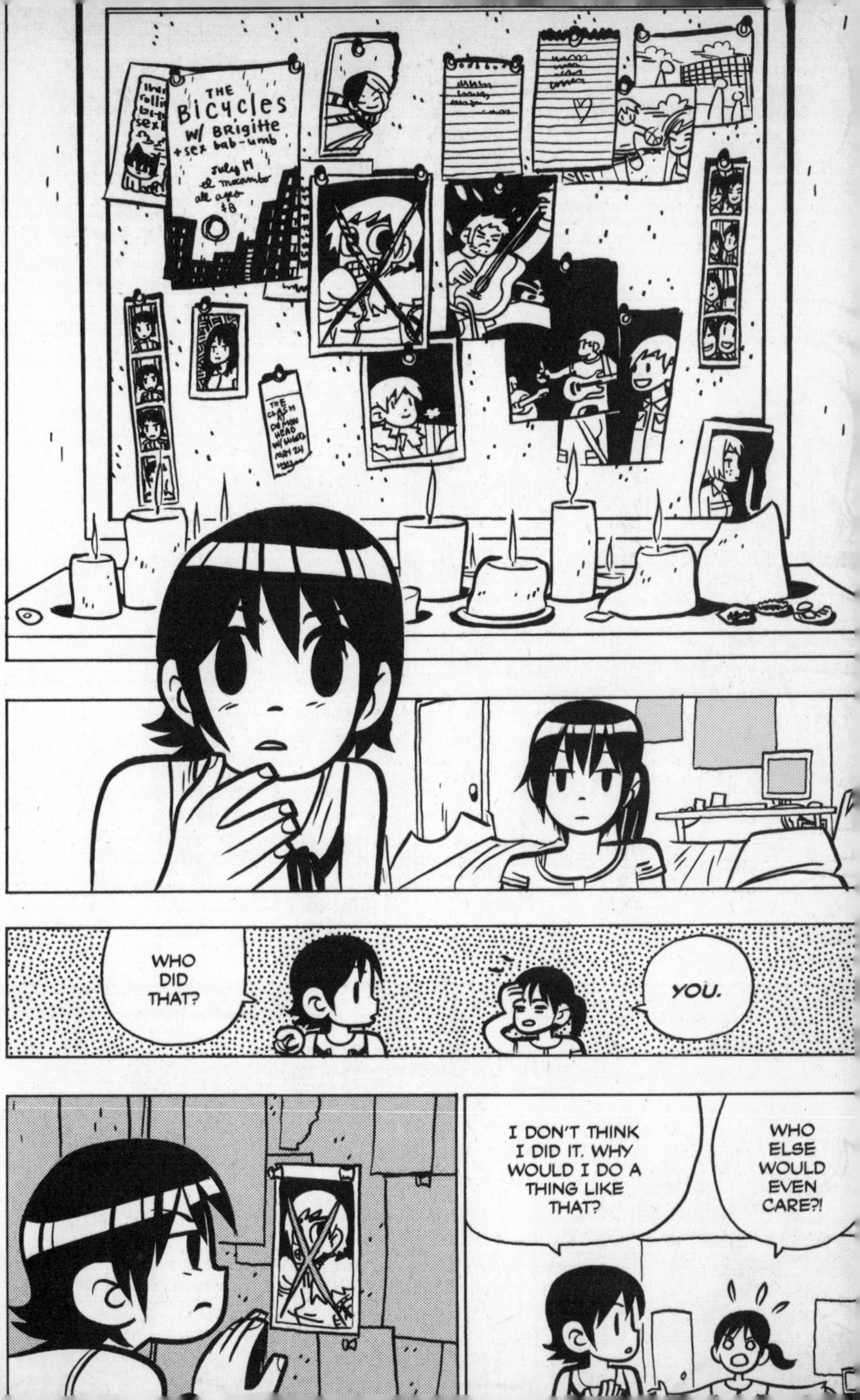
THE
Bicycles
W/ BRIGITTE
+ sex bob-umb
July 14
el mocambo
all ages
$8
WHO DID THAT?
YOU.
I DON'T THINK I DID IT. WHY WOULD I DO A THING LIKE THAT?
WHO ELSE WOULD EVEN CARE?!

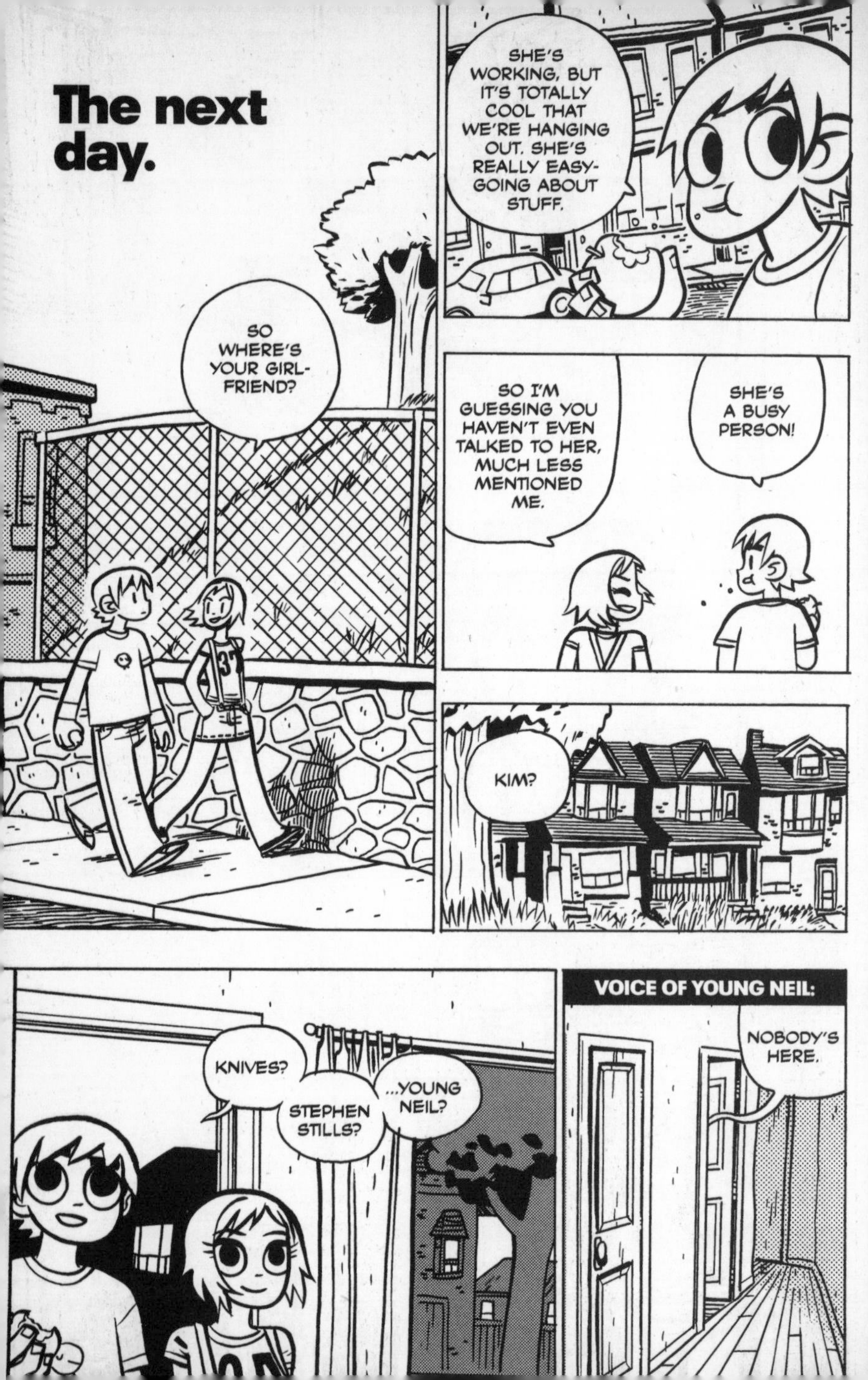
The next day.
SO WHERE'S YOUR GIRL-FRIEND?
SHE'S WORKING, BUT IT'S TOTALLY COOL THAT WE'RE HANGING OUT. SHE'S REALLY EASY-GOING ABOUT STUFF.
SO I'M GUESSING YOU HAVEN'T EVEN TALKED TO HER, MUCH LESS MENTIONED ME.
SHE'S A BUSY PERSON!
KIM?
KNIVES?
STEPHEN STILLS?
...YOUNG NEIL?
VOICE OF YOUNG NEIL:
NOBODY'S HERE.

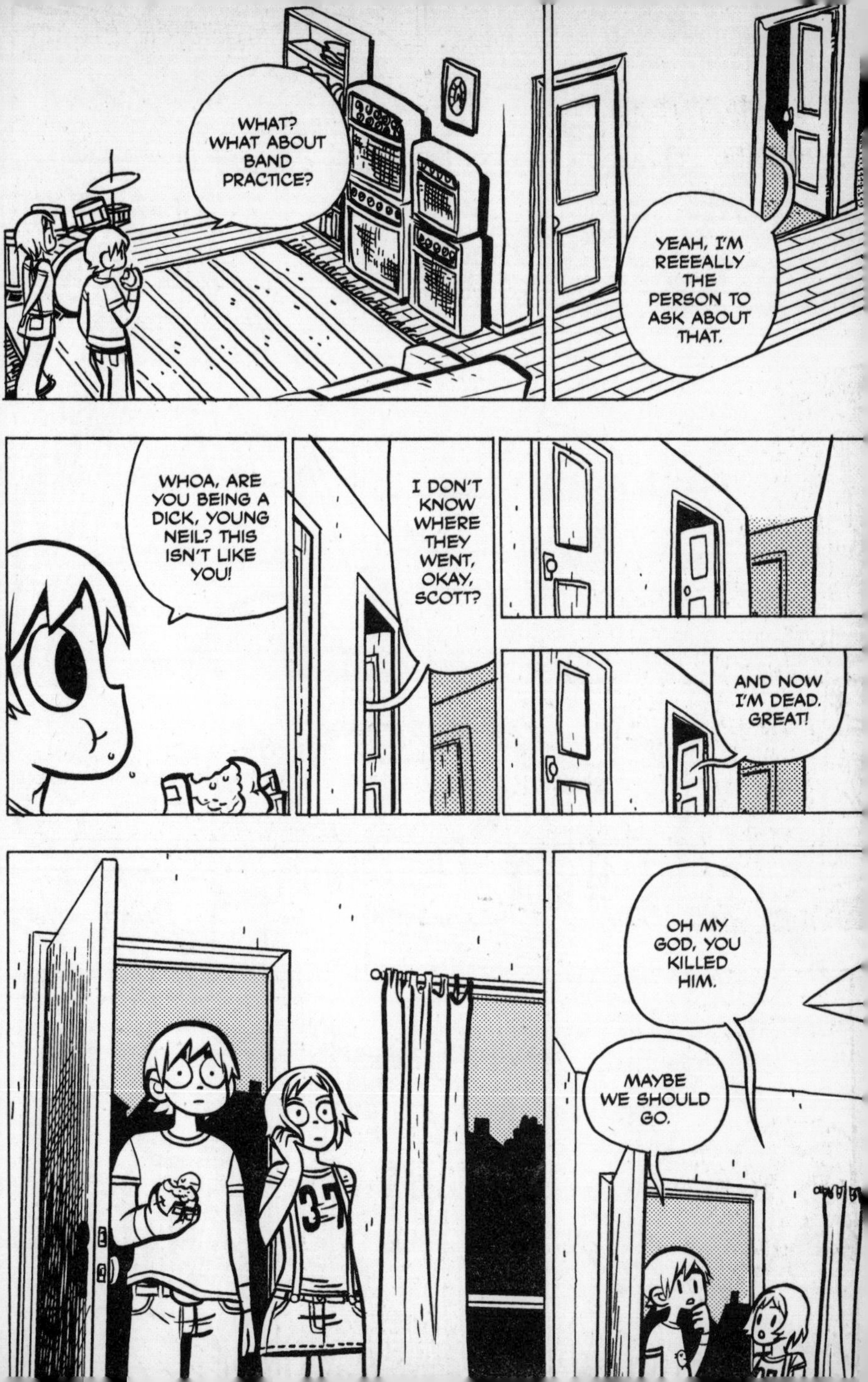
WHAT? WHAT ABOUT BAND PRACTICE?
YEAH, I'M REEEALLY THE PERSON TO ASK ABOUT THAT.
WHOA, ARE YOU BEING A DICK, YOUNG NEIL? THIS ISN'T LIKE YOU!
I DON'T KNOW WHERE THEY WENT, OKAY, SCOTT?
AND NOW I'M DEAD. GREAT!
OH MY GOD, YOU KILLED HIM.
MAYBE WE SHOULD GO.

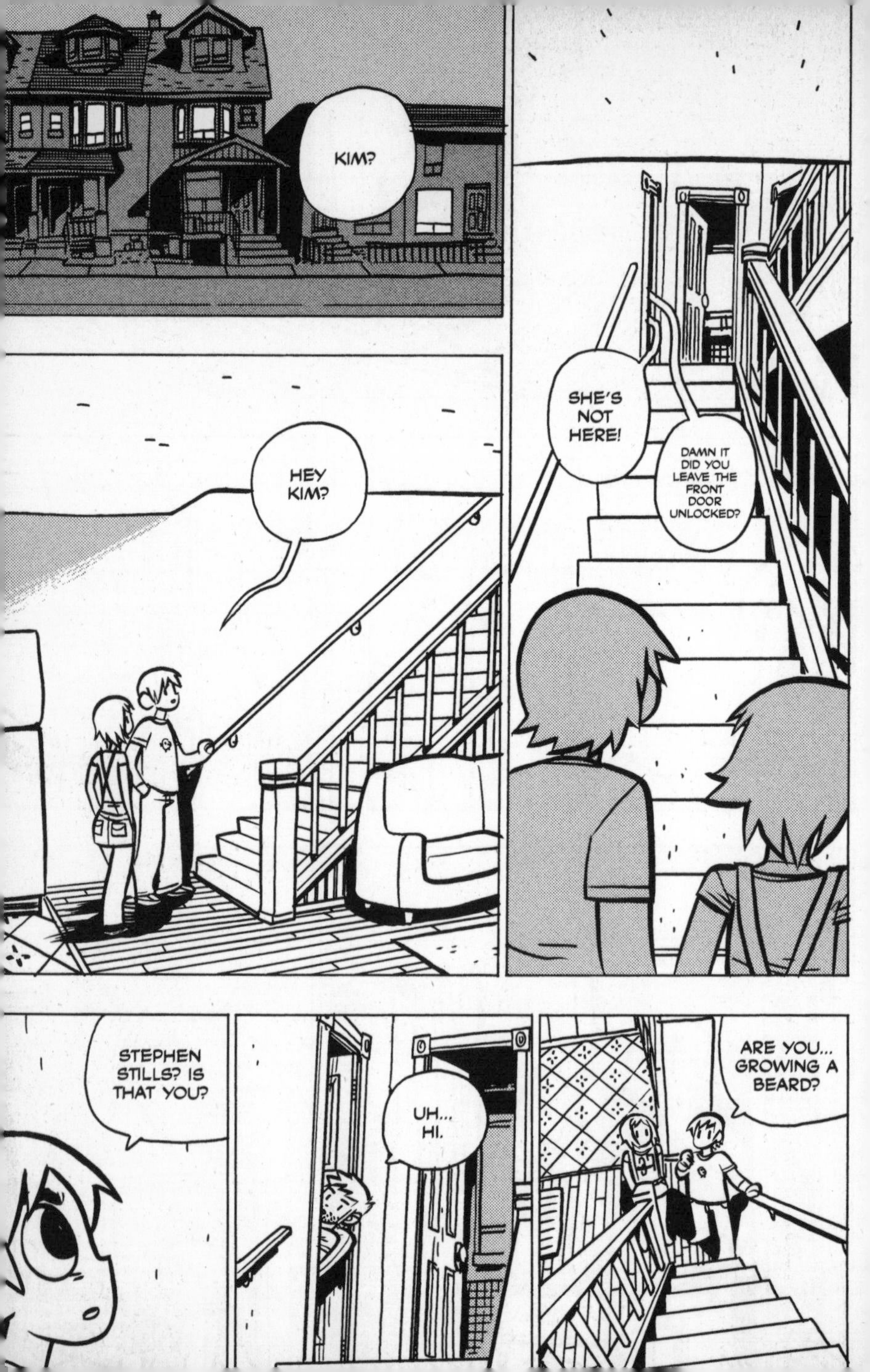
KIM?
HEY KIM?
SHE'S NOT HERE!
DAMN IT DID YOU LEAVE THE FRONT DOOR UNLOCKED?
STEPHEN STILLS? IS THAT YOU?
UH... HI.
ARE YOU... GROWING A BEARD?

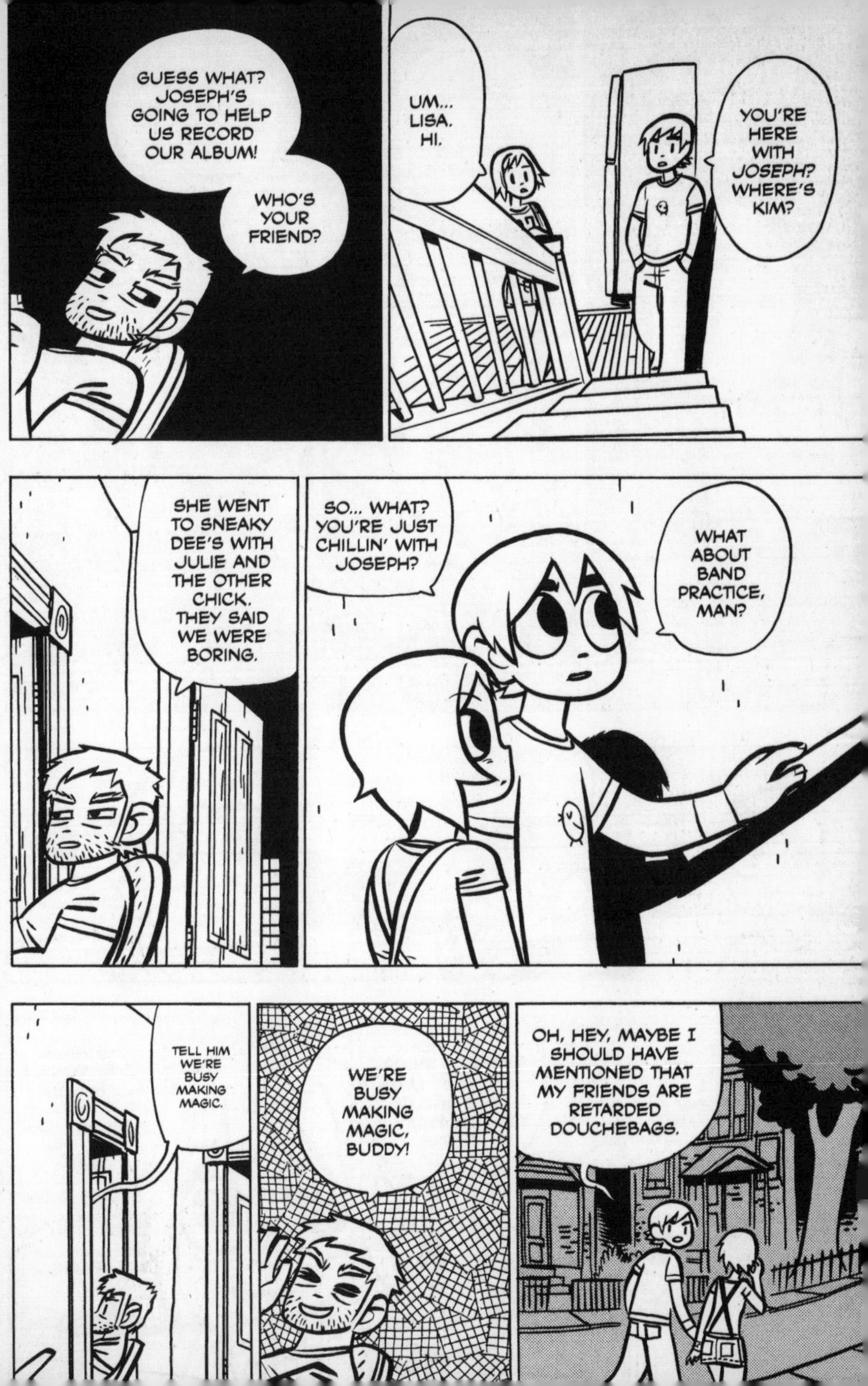
GUESS WHAT? JOSEPH'S GOING TO HELP US RECORD OUR ALBUM!
WHO'S YOUR FRIEND?
UM... LISA. HI.
YOU'RE HERE WITH JOSEPH? WHERE'S KIM?
SHE WENT TO SNEAKY DEE'S WITH JULIE AND THE OTHER CHICK. THEY SAID WE WERE BORING.
SO... WHAT? YOU'RE JUST CHILLIN' WITH JOSEPH?
WHAT ABOUT BAND PRACTICE, MAN?
TELL HIM WE'RE BUSY MAKING MAGIC.
WE'RE BUSY MAKING MAGIC, BUDDY!
OH, HEY, MAYBE I SHOULD HAVE MENTIONED THAT MY FRIENDS ARE RETARDED DOUCHEBAGS.

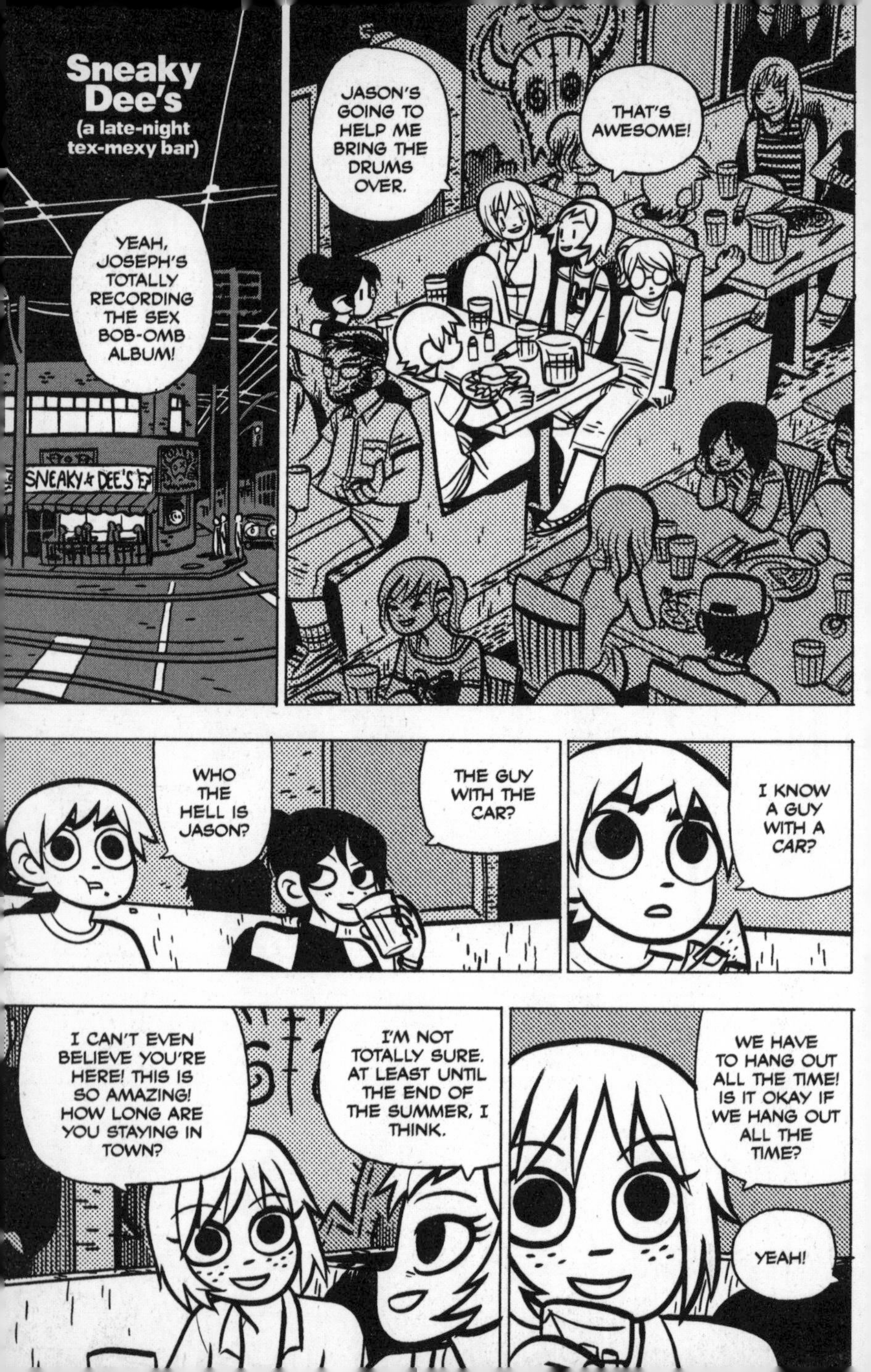
Sneaky Dee's
(a late-night tex-mexy bar)
YEAH, JOSEPH'S TOTALLY RECORDING THE SEX BOB-OMB ALBUM!
SNEAKY DEE'S
JASON'S GOING TO HELP ME BRING THE DRUMS OVER.
THAT'S AWESOME!
WHO THE HELL IS JASON?
THE GUY WITH THE CAR?
I KNOW A GUY WITH A CAR?
I CAN'T EVEN BELIEVE YOU'RE HERE! THIS IS SO AMAZING! HOW LONG ARE YOU STAYING IN TOWN?
I'M NOT TOTALLY SURE. AT LEAST UNTIL THE END OF THE SUMMER, I THINK.
WE HAVE TO HANG OUT ALL THE TIME! IS IT OKAY IF WE HANG OUT ALL THE TIME?
YEAH!

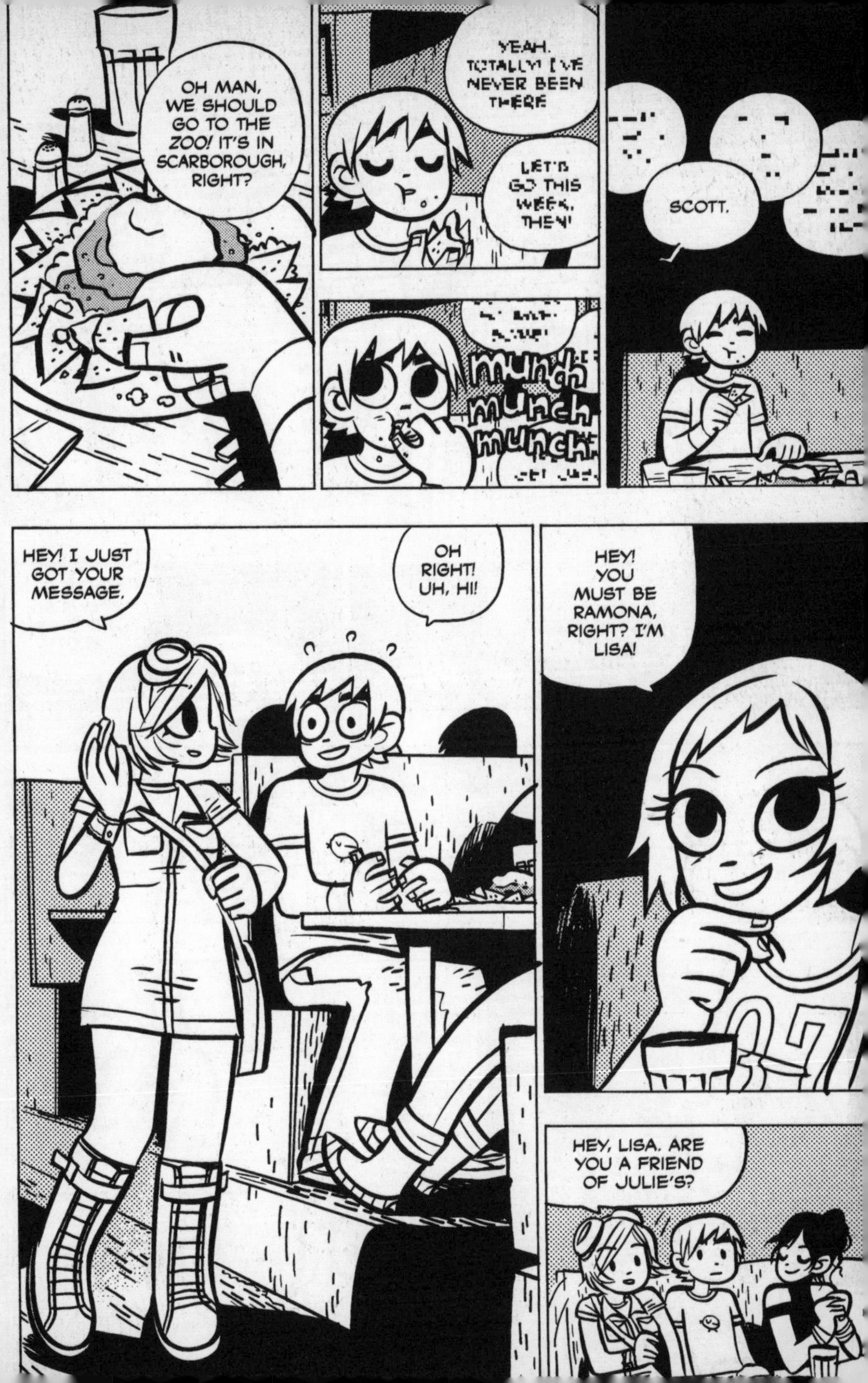
OH MAN, WE SHOULD GO TO THE ZOO! IT'S IN SCARBOROUGH, RIGHT?
YEAH. TOTALLY! I'VE NEVER BEEN THERE
LET'S GO THIS WEEK, THEN!
munch munch munch
SCOTT.
HEY! I JUST GOT YOUR MESSAGE.
OH RIGHT! UH, HI!
HEY! YOU MUST BE RAMONA, RIGHT? I'M LISA!
HEY, LISA. ARE YOU A FRIEND OF JULIE'S?

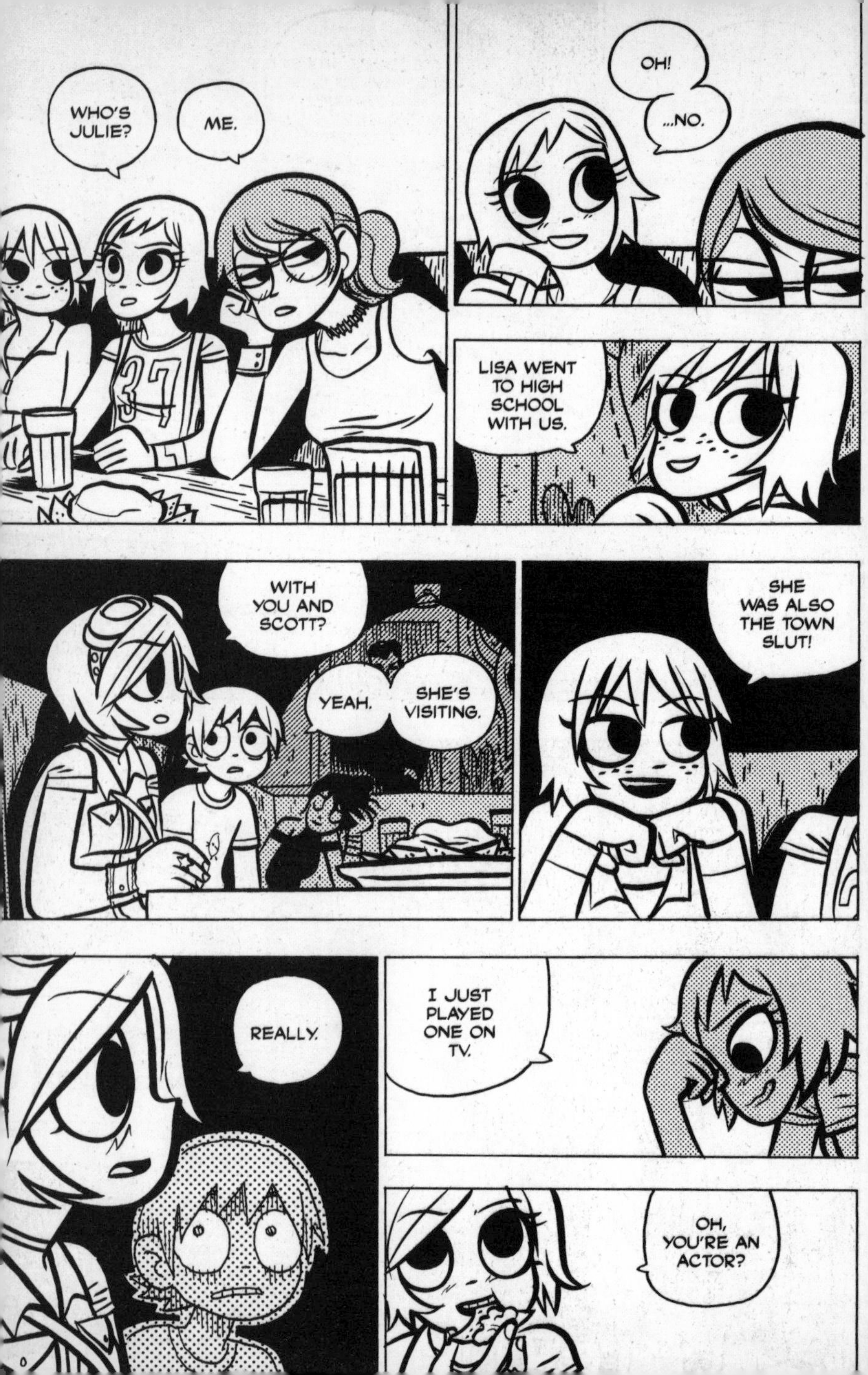
WHO'S JULIE?
ME.
OH!
...NO.
LISA WENT TO HIGH SCHOOL WITH US.
WITH YOU AND SCOTT?
YEAH.
SHE'S VISITING.
SHE WAS ALSO THE TOWN SLUT!
REALLY.
I JUST PLAYED ONE ON TV.
OH, YOU'RE AN ACTOR?

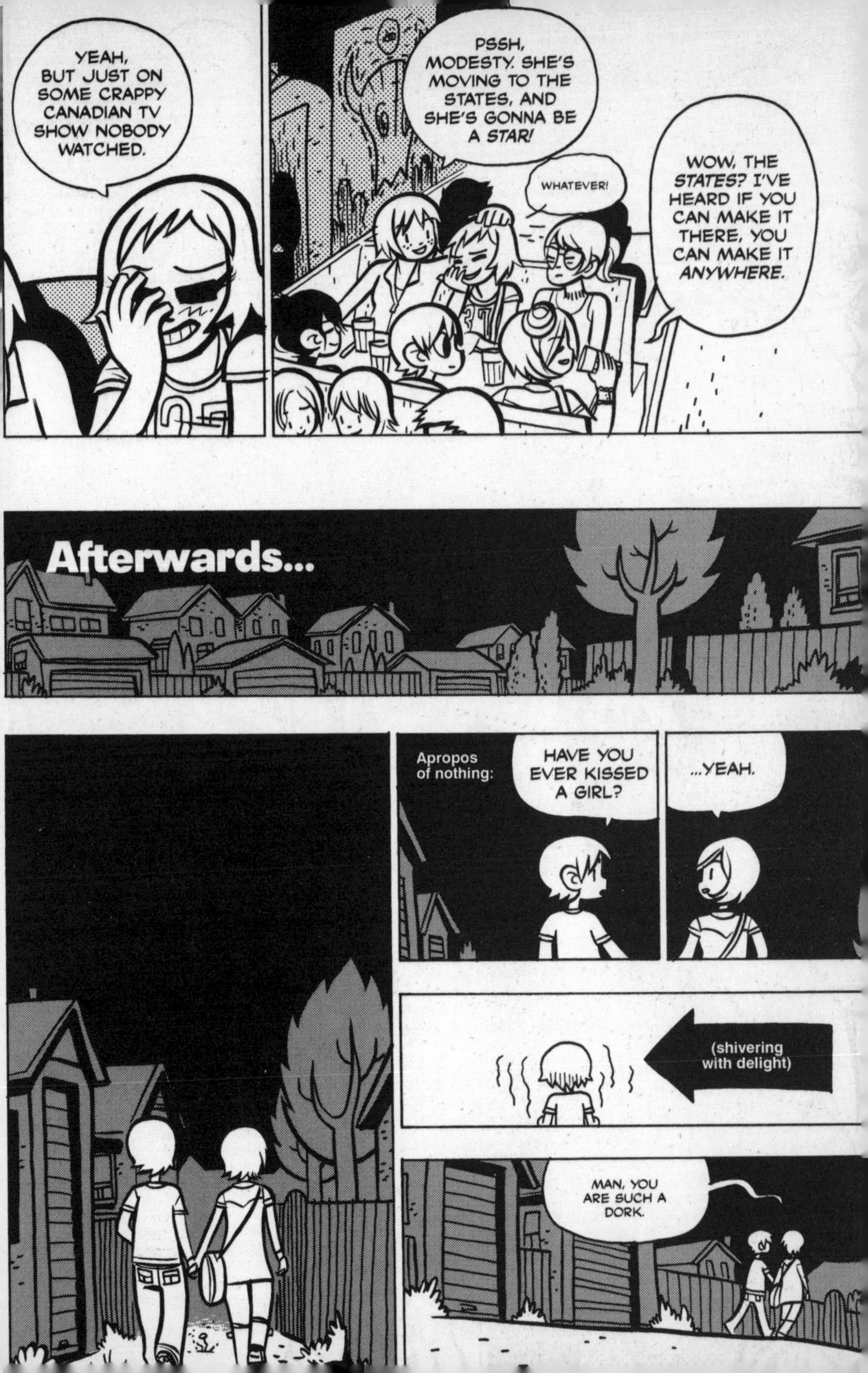
YEAH, BUT JUST ON SOME CRAPPY CANADIAN TV SHOW NOBODY WATCHED.
PSSH, MODESTY. SHE'S MOVING TO THE STATES, AND SHE'S GONNA BE A STAR!
WHATEVER!
WOW, THE STATES? I'VE HEARD IF YOU CAN MAKE IT THERE, YOU CAN MAKE IT ANYWHERE.
Afterwards...
Apropos of nothing:
HAVE YOU EVER KISSED A GIRL?
...YEAH.
(shivering with delight)
MAN, YOU ARE SUCH A DORK.

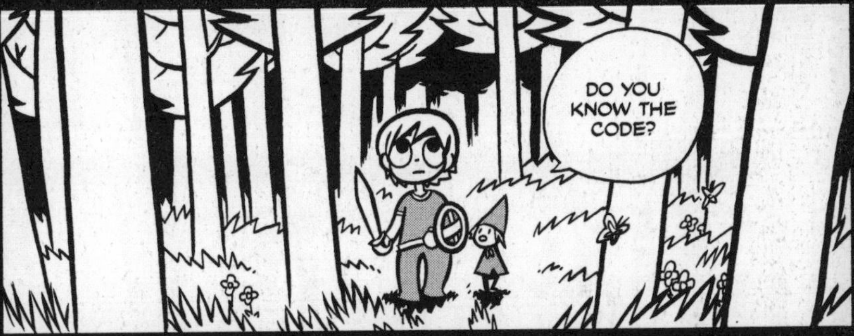
DO YOU KNOW THE CODE?

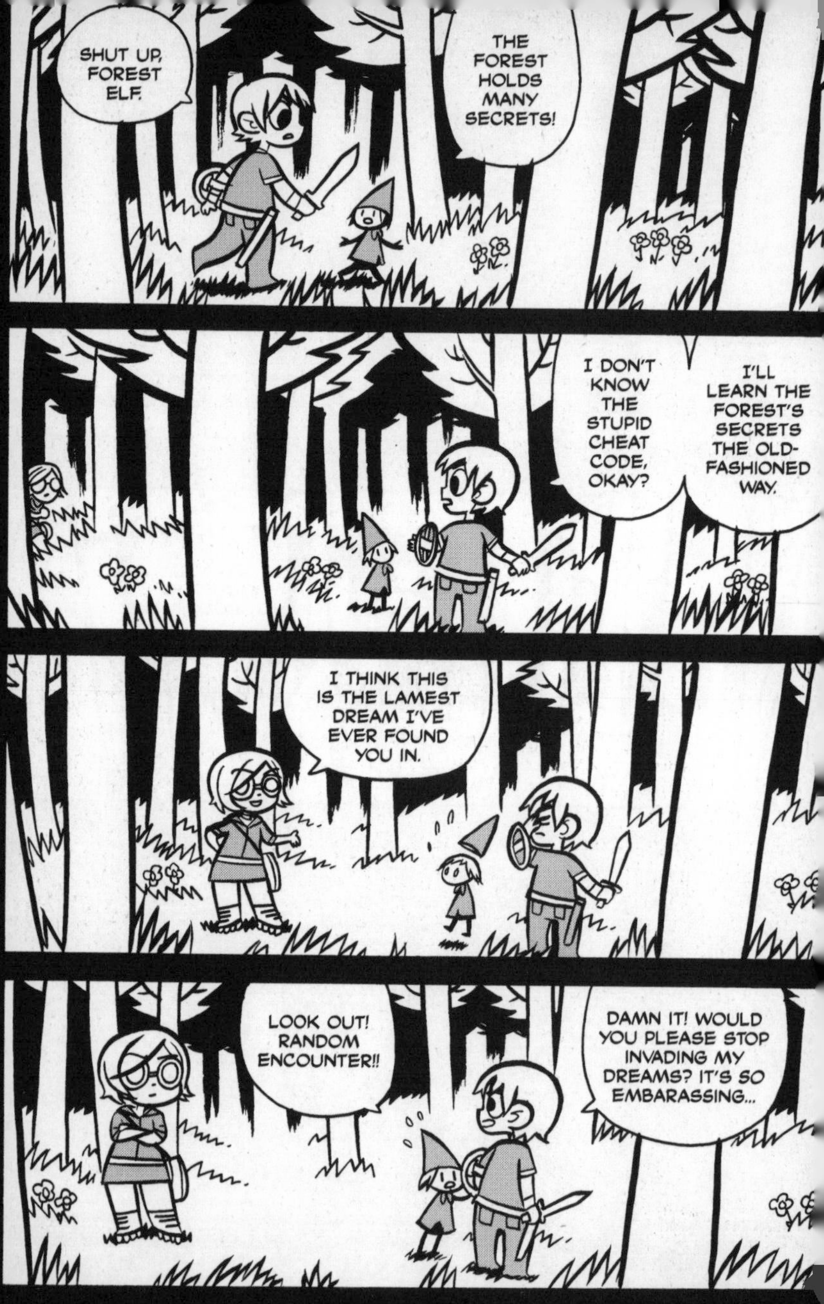
SHUT UP, FOREST ELF.
THE FOREST HOLDS MANY SECRETS!
I DON'T KNOW THE STUPID CHEAT CODE, OKAY?
I'LL LEARN THE FOREST'S SECRETS THE OLD-FASHIONED WAY.
I THINK THIS IS THE LAMEST DREAM I'VE EVER FOUND YOU IN.
LOOK OUT! RANDOM ENCOUNTER!!
DAMN IT! WOULD YOU PLEASE STOP INVADING MY DREAMS? IT'S SO EMBARASSING...

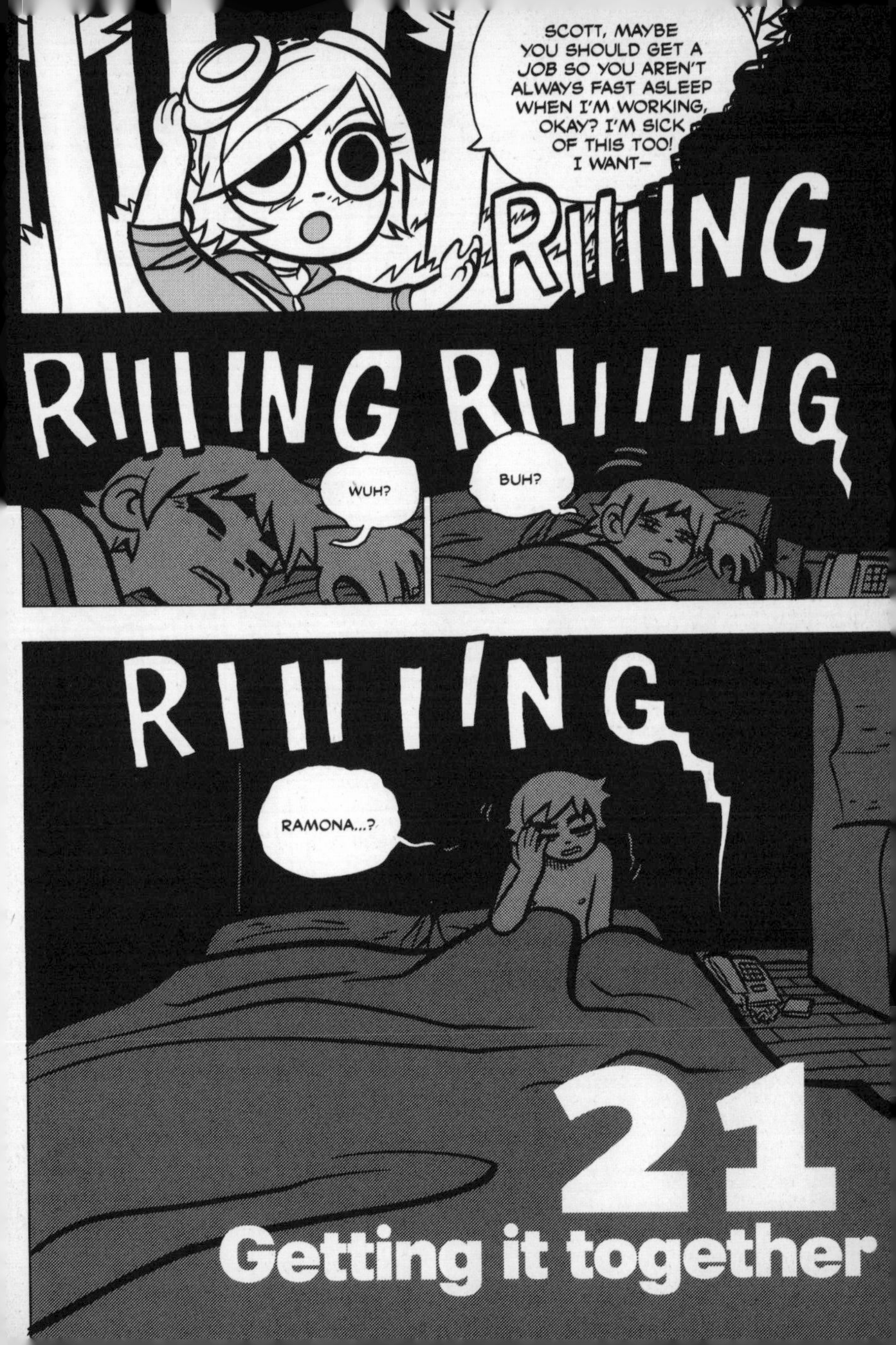
SCOTT, MAYBE YOU SHOULD GET A JOB SO YOU AREN'T ALWAYS FAST ASLEEP WHEN I'M WORKING, OKAY? I'M SICK OF THIS TOO! I WANT—
RIIIING
RIIIING RIIIING
WUH?
BUH?
RIIIING
RAMONA...?
21
Getting it together

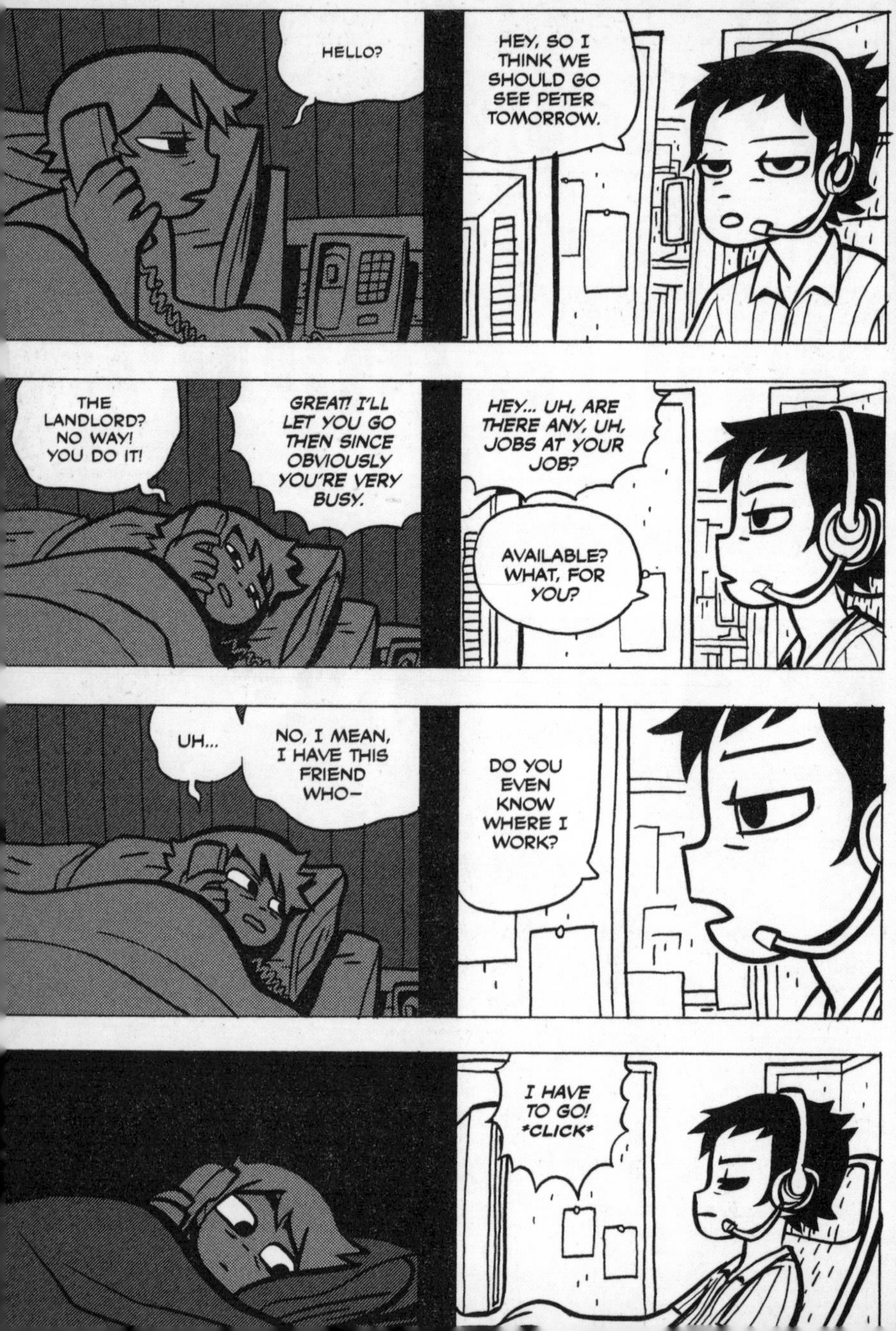
HELLO?
HEY, SO I THINK WE SHOULD GO SEE PETER TOMORROW.
THE LANDLORD? NO WAY! YOU DO IT!
GREAT! I'LL LET YOU GO THEN SINCE OBVIOUSLY YOU'RE VERY BUSY.
HEY... UH, ARE THERE ANY, UH, JOBS AT YOUR JOB?
AVAILABLE? WHAT, FOR YOU?
UH...
NO, I MEAN, I HAVE THIS FRIEND WHO–
DO YOU EVEN KNOW WHERE I WORK?
I HAVE TO GO! *CLICK*

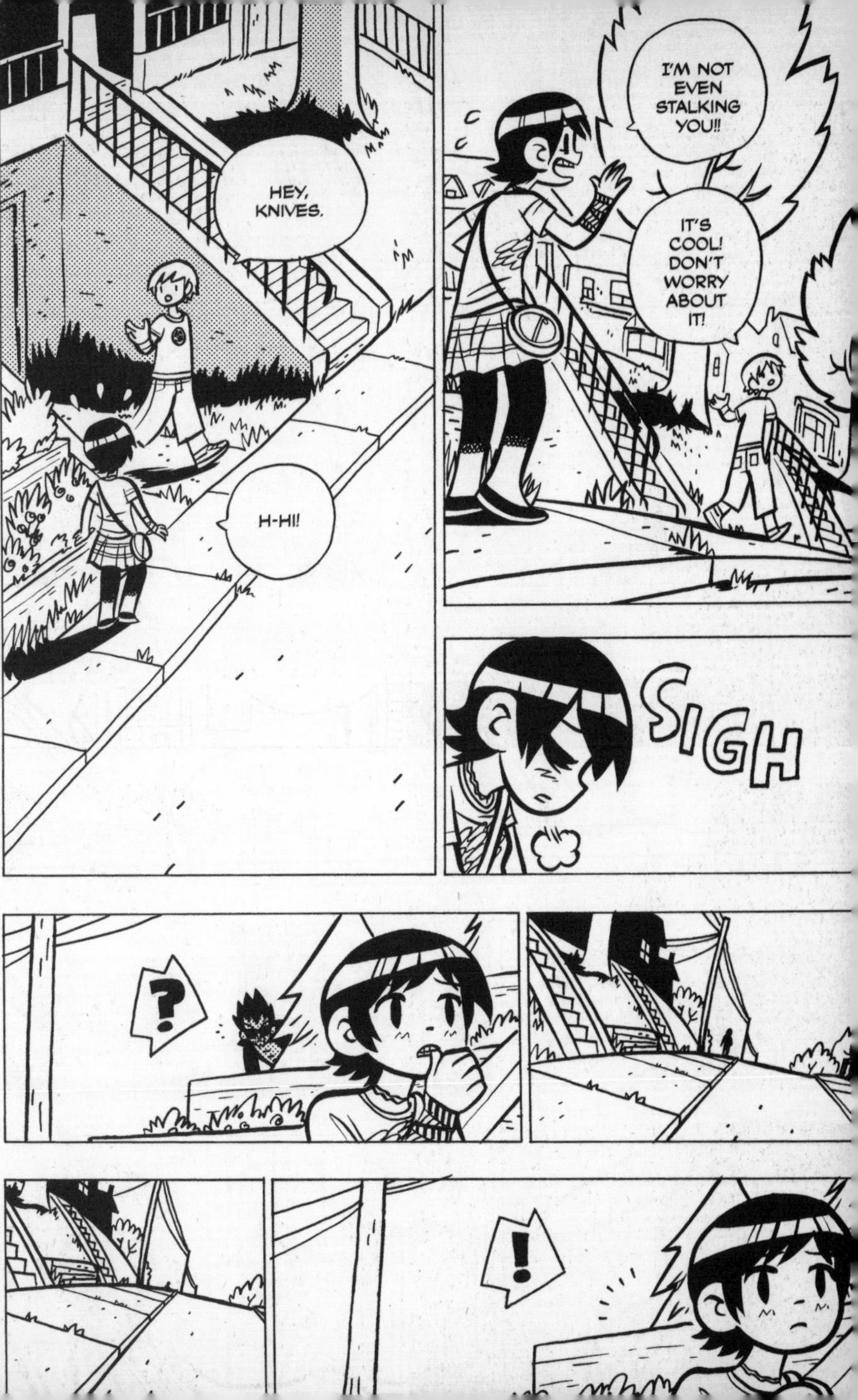
HEY, KNIVES.
H-HI!
I'M NOT EVEN STALKING YOU!!
IT'S COOL! DON'T WORRY ABOUT IT!
SIGH
?
!

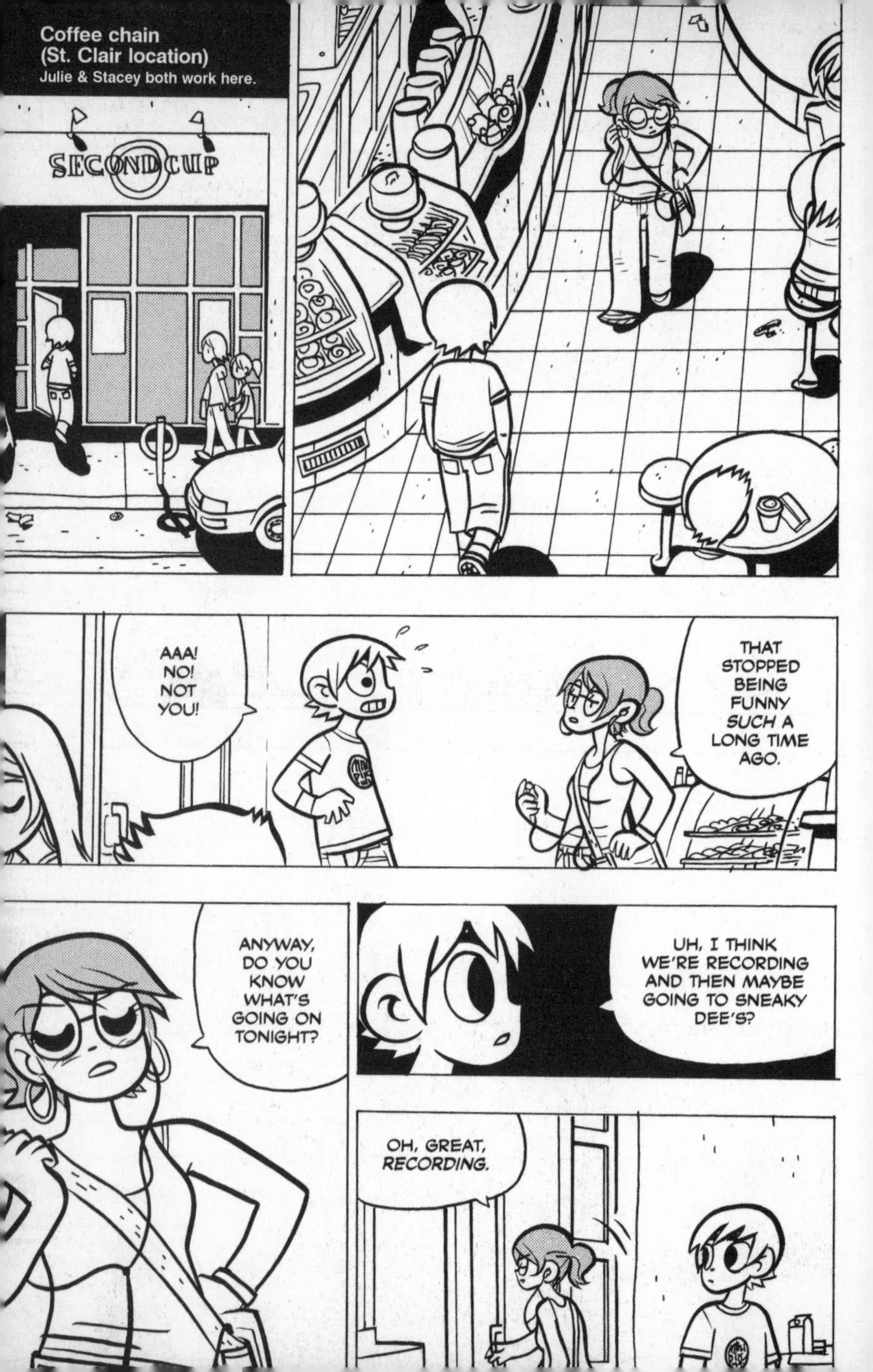
Coffee chain
(St. Clair location)
Julie & Stacey both work here.
SECOND CUP
AAA! NO! NOT YOU!
THAT STOPPED BEING FUNNY *SUCH* A LONG TIME AGO.
ANYWAY, DO YOU KNOW WHAT'S GOING ON TONIGHT?
UH, I THINK WE'RE RECORDING AND THEN MAYBE GOING TO SNEAKY DEE'S?
OH, GREAT, *RECORDING.*

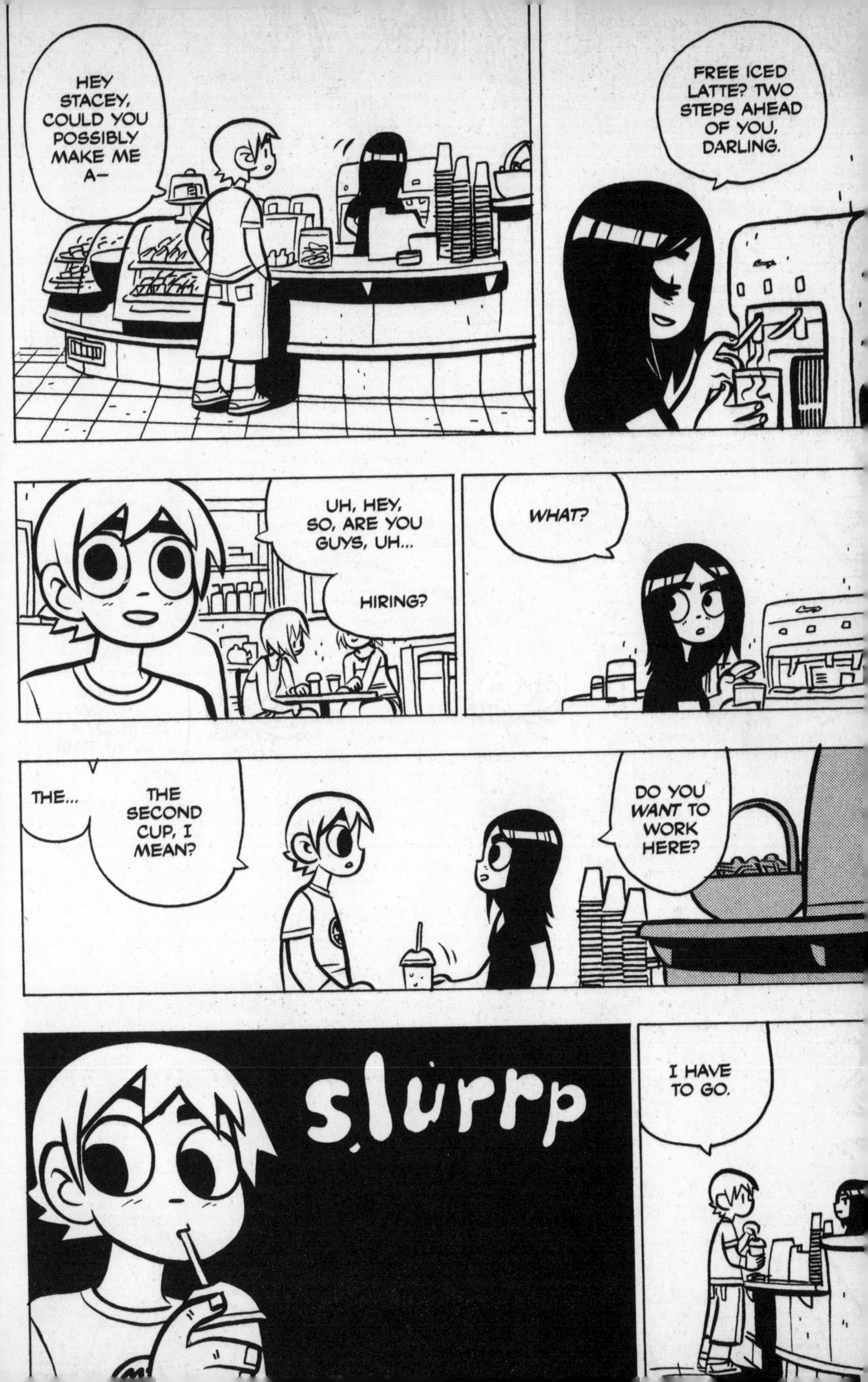
HEY STACEY, COULD YOU POSSIBLY MAKE ME A—
FREE ICED LATTE? TWO STEPS AHEAD OF YOU, DARLING.
UH, HEY, SO, ARE YOU GUYS, UH...
HIRING?
WHAT?
THE...
THE SECOND CUP, I MEAN?
DO YOU WANT TO WORK HERE?
slurrp
I HAVE TO GO.

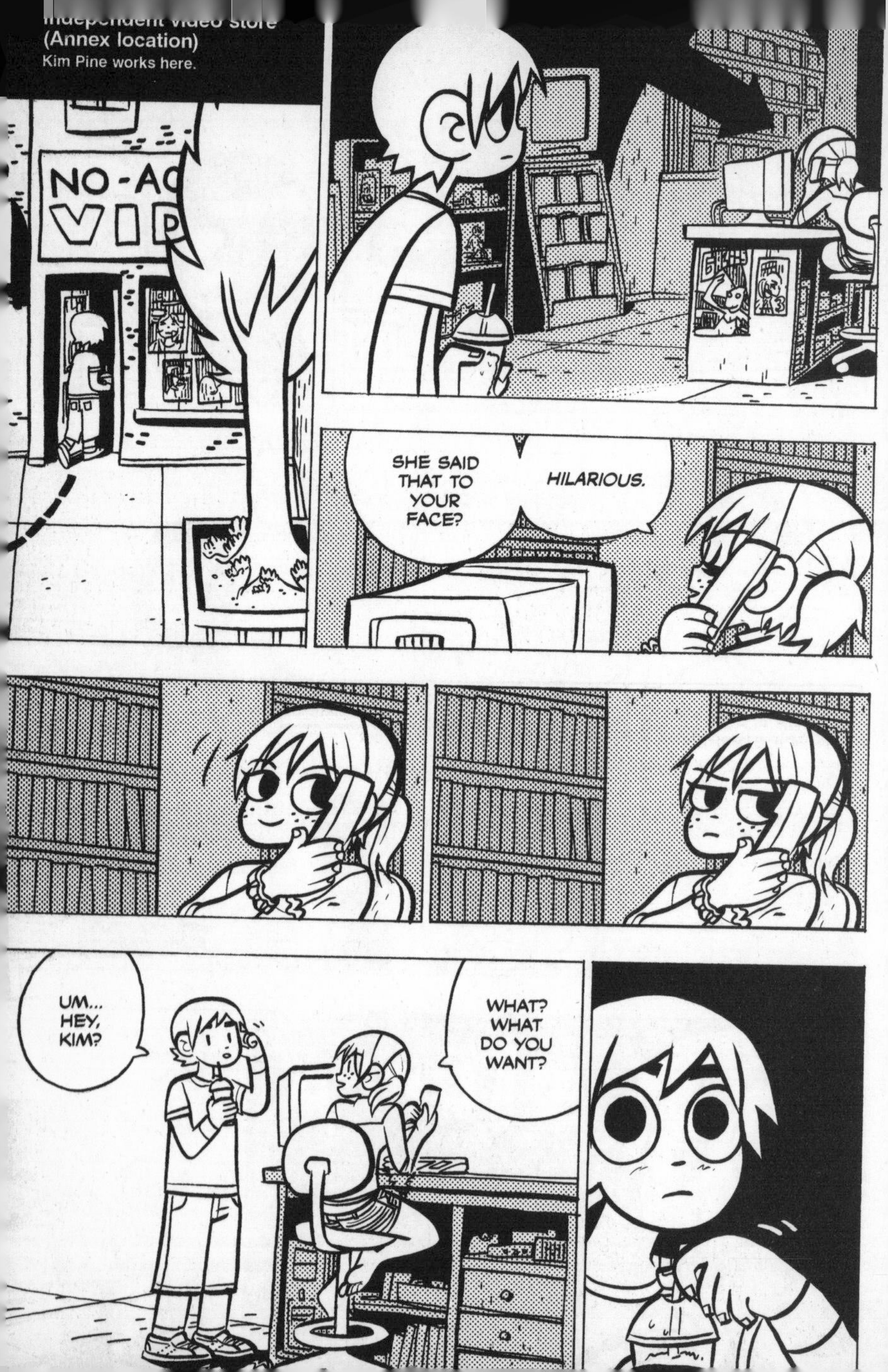

Independent video store
(Annex location)
Kim Pine works here.
SHE SAID THAT TO YOUR FACE?
HILARIOUS.
UM... HEY, KIM?
WHAT? WHAT DO YOU WANT?

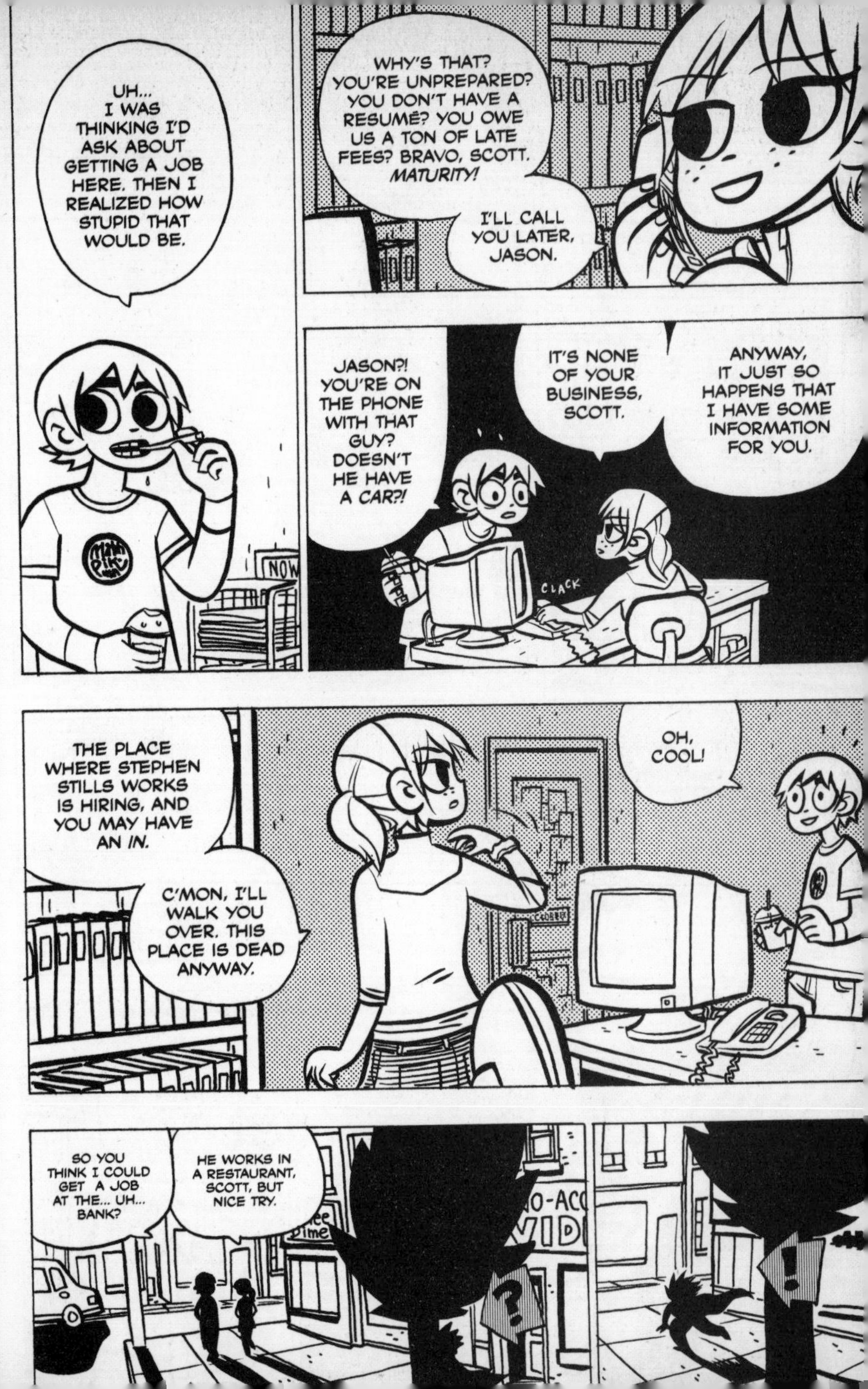
UH... I WAS THINKING I'D ASK ABOUT GETTING A JOB HERE. THEN I REALIZED HOW STUPID THAT WOULD BE.
WHY'S THAT? YOU'RE UNPREPARED? YOU DON'T HAVE A RESUMÉ? YOU OWE US A TON OF LATE FEES? BRAVO, SCOTT. *MATURITY!*
I'LL CALL YOU LATER, JASON.
NOW
JASON?! YOU'RE ON THE PHONE WITH THAT GUY? DOESN'T HE HAVE A *CAR?!*
IT'S NONE OF YOUR BUSINESS, SCOTT.
ANYWAY, IT JUST SO HAPPENS THAT I HAVE SOME INFORMATION FOR YOU.
CLACK
THE PLACE WHERE STEPHEN STILLS WORKS IS HIRING, AND YOU MAY HAVE AN *IN.*
C'MON, I'LL WALK YOU OVER. THIS PLACE IS DEAD ANYWAY.
OH, COOL!
SO YOU THINK I COULD GET A JOB AT THE... UH... BANK?
HE WORKS IN A RESTAURANT, SCOTT, BUT NICE TRY.

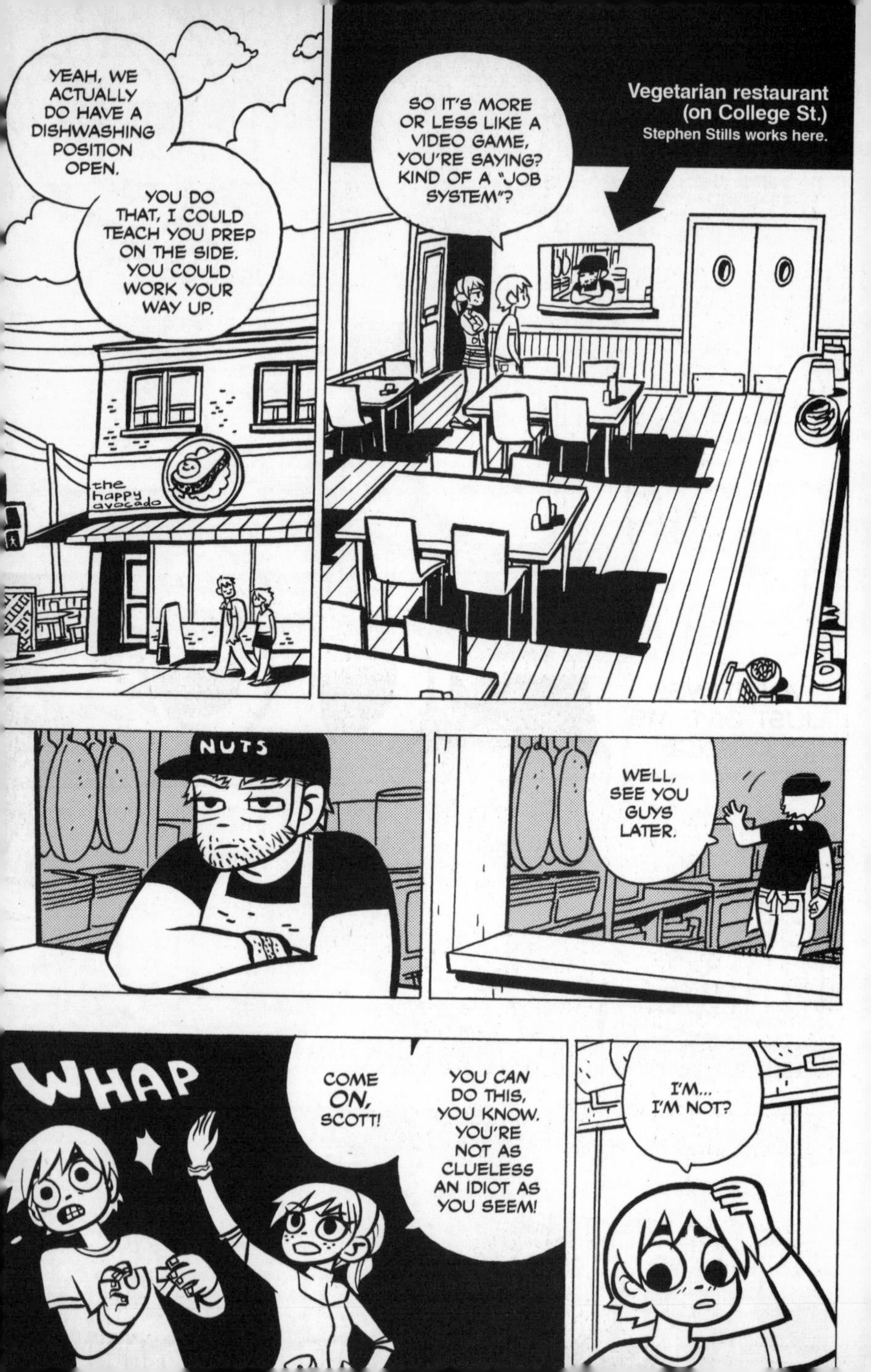
YEAH, WE ACTUALLY DO HAVE A DISHWASHING POSITION OPEN.
YOU DO THAT, I COULD TEACH YOU PREP ON THE SIDE. YOU COULD WORK YOUR WAY UP.
the happy avocado
SO IT'S MORE OR LESS LIKE A VIDEO GAME, YOU'RE SAYING? KIND OF A "JOB SYSTEM"?
Vegetarian restaurant (on College St.)
Stephen Stills works here.
NUTS
WELL, SEE YOU GUYS LATER.
WHAP
COME ON, SCOTT!
YOU CAN DO THIS, YOU KNOW. YOU'RE NOT AS CLUELESS AN IDIOT AS YOU SEEM!
I'M... I'M NOT?

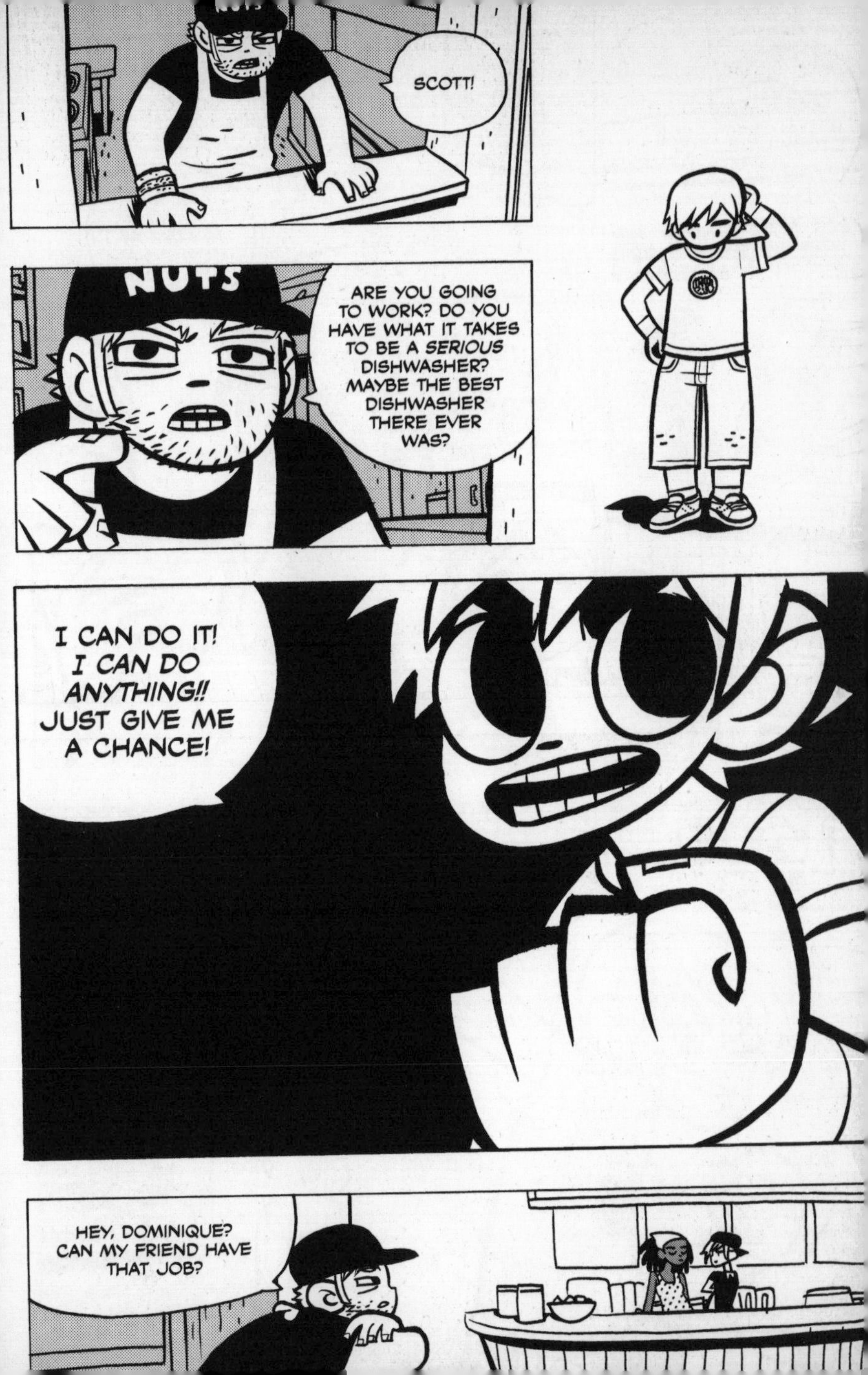
SCOTT!
ARE YOU GOING TO WORK? DO YOU HAVE WHAT IT TAKES TO BE A *SERIOUS* DISHWASHER? MAYBE THE BEST DISHWASHER THERE EVER WAS?
I CAN DO IT! *I CAN DO ANYTHING!!* JUST GIVE ME A CHANCE!
HEY, DOMINIQUE? CAN MY FRIEND HAVE THAT JOB?

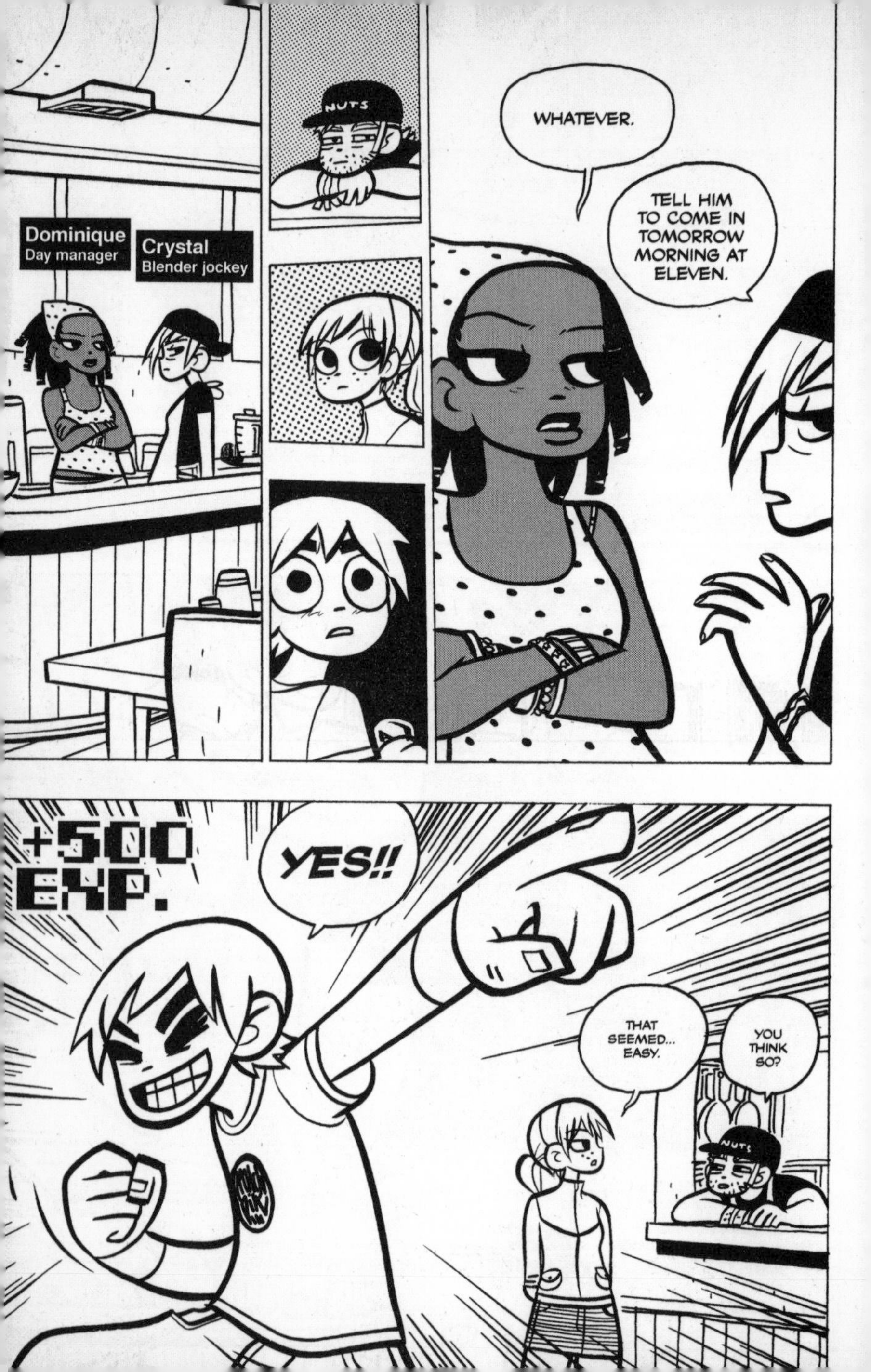

Dominique
Day manager
Crystal
Blender jockey
NUTS
WHATEVER.
TELL HIM TO COME IN TOMORROW MORNING AT ELEVEN.
+500 EXP.
YES!!
THAT SEEMED... EASY.
YOU THINK SO?
NUTS

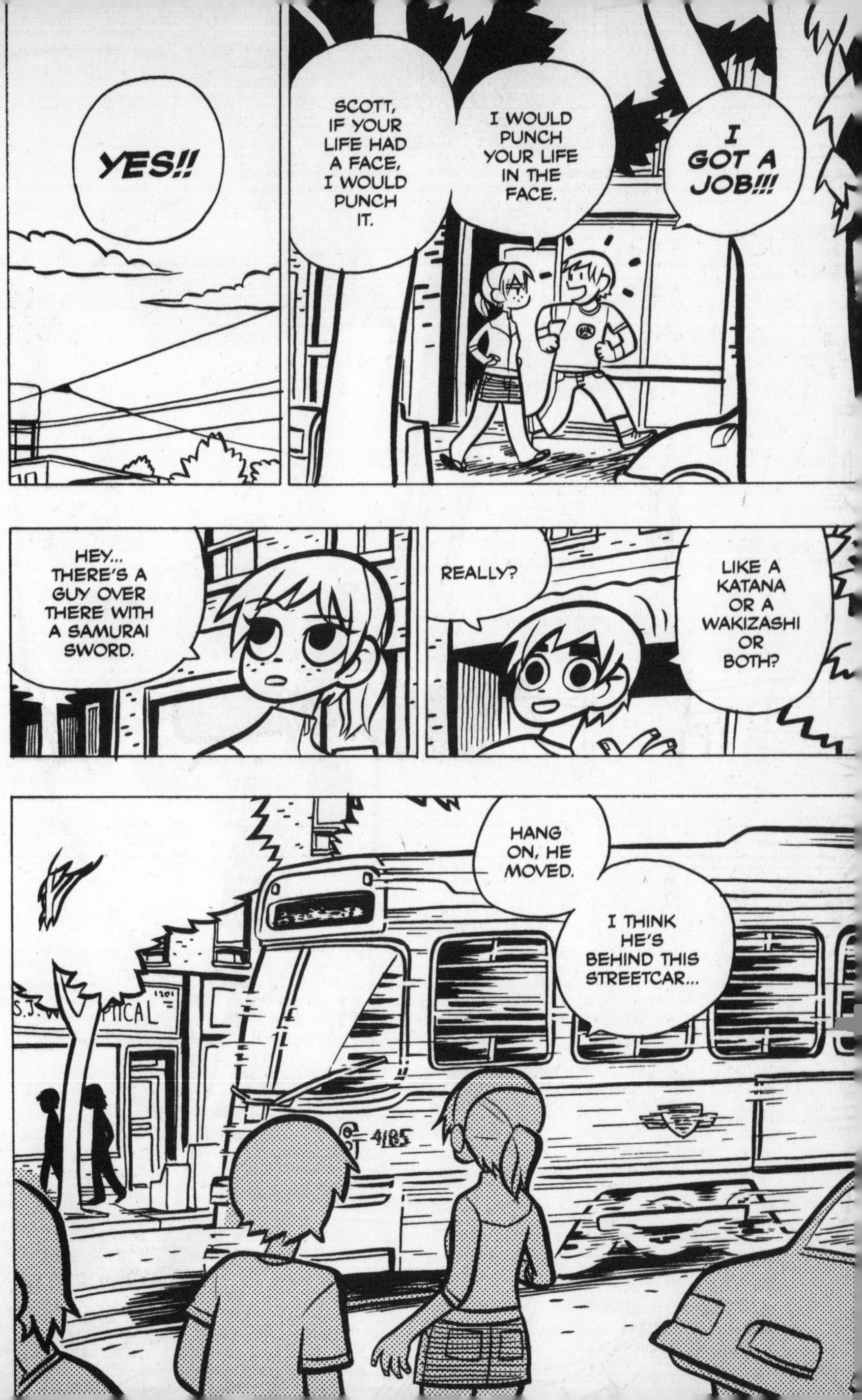
YES!!
SCOTT, IF YOUR LIFE HAD A FACE, I WOULD PUNCH IT.
I WOULD PUNCH YOUR LIFE IN THE FACE.
I GOT A JOB!!!
HEY... THERE'S A GUY OVER THERE WITH A SAMURAI SWORD.
REALLY?
LIKE A KATANA OR A WAKIZASHI OR BOTH?
HANG ON, HE MOVED.
I THINK HE'S BEHIND THIS STREETCAR...
S.J. W OPTICAL
4185

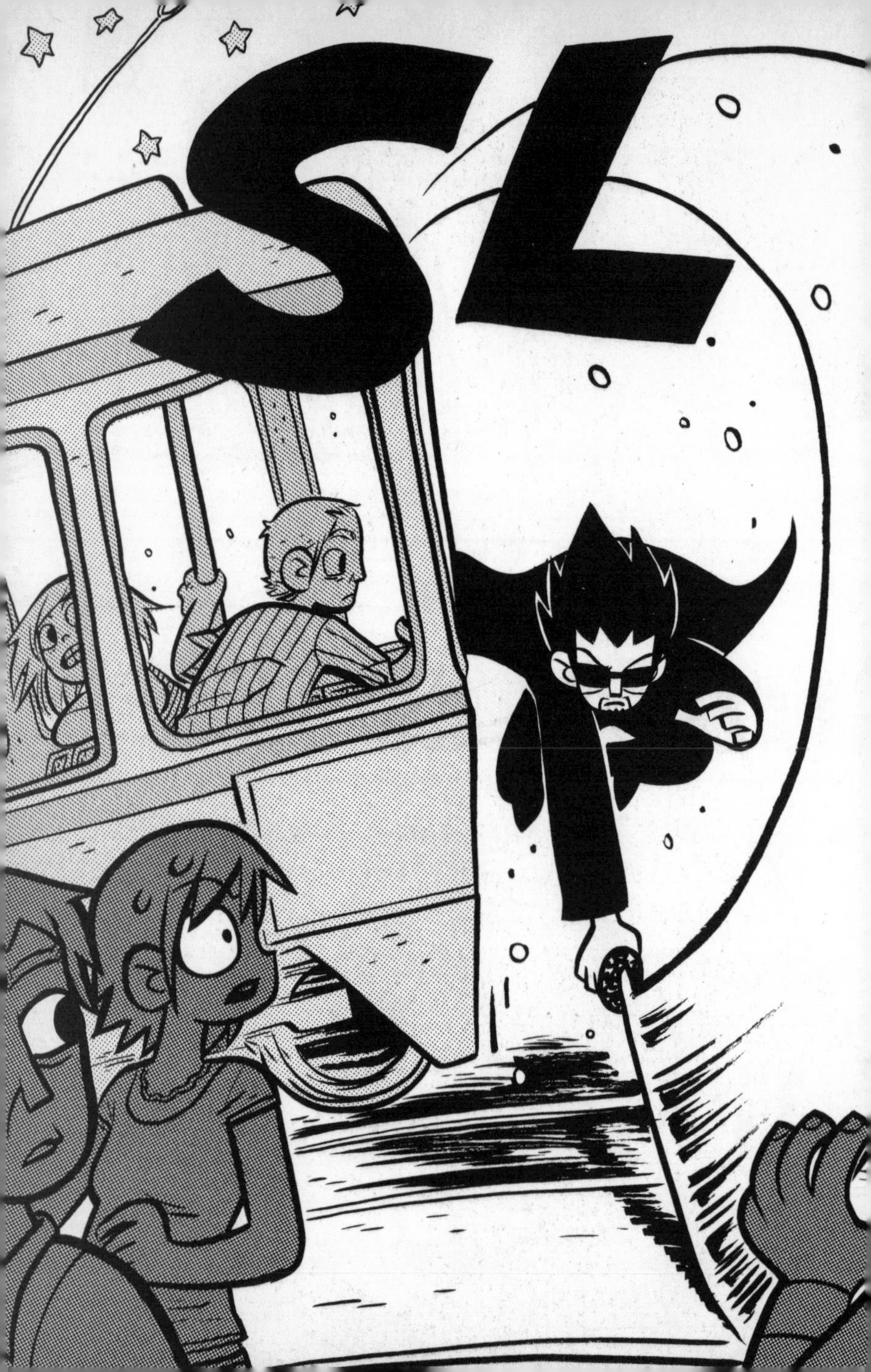
SL

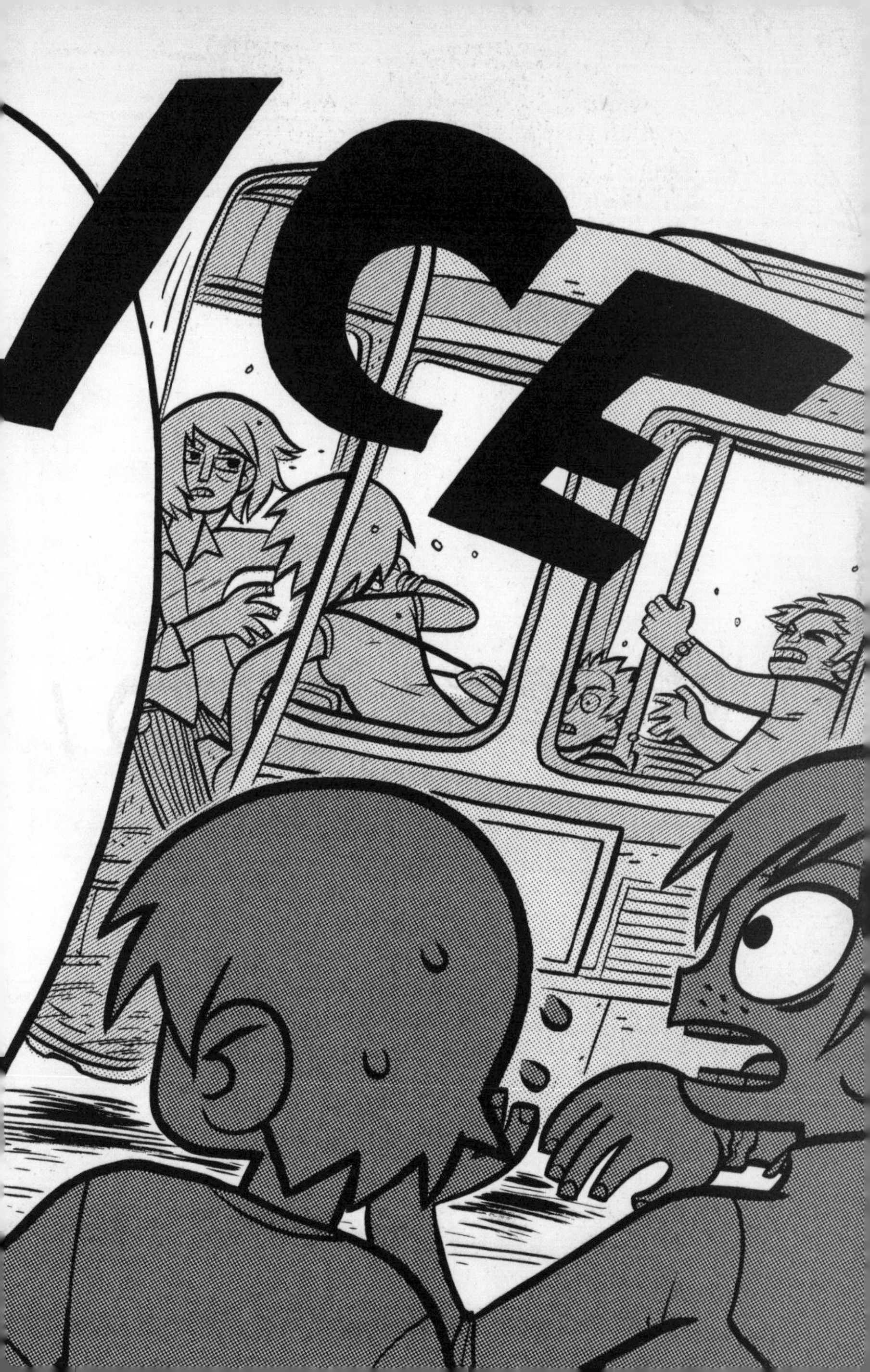

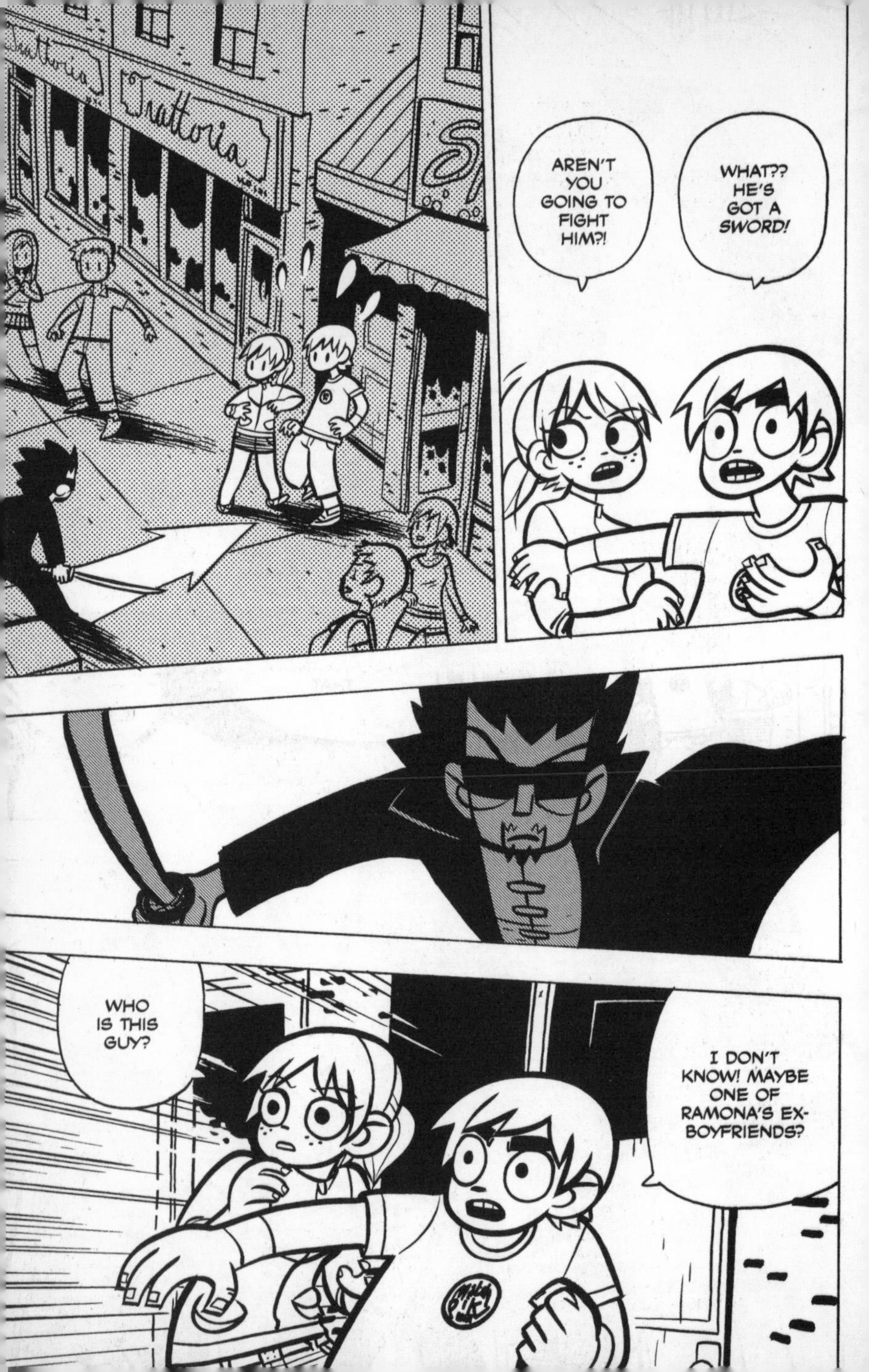
Trattoria
ARE'N'T YOU GOING TO FIGHT HIM?!
WHAT?? HE'S GOT A SWORD!
WHO IS THIS GUY?
I DON'T KNOW! MAYBE ONE OF RAMONA'S EX-BOYFRIENDS?

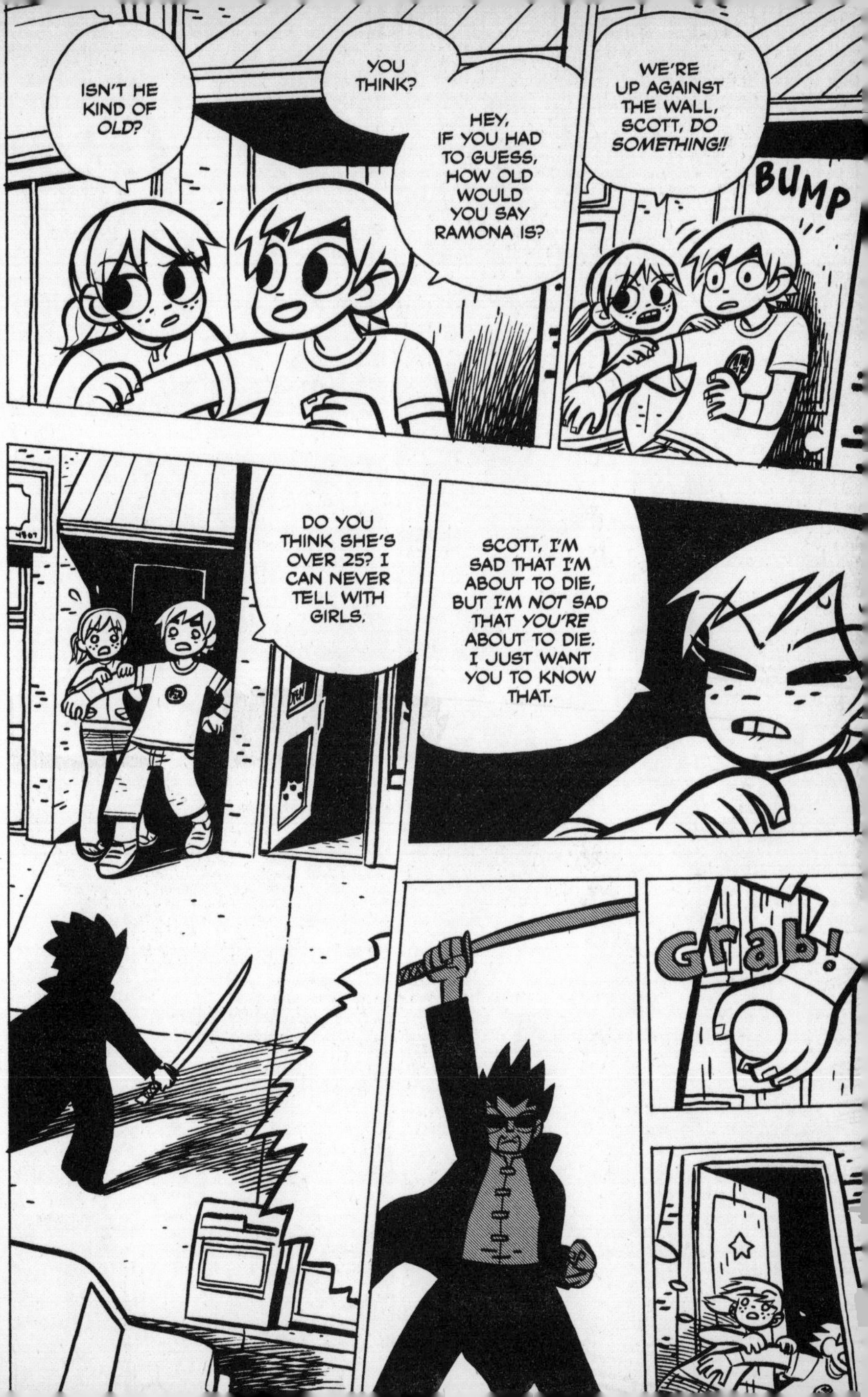

ISN'T HE KIND OF *OLD?*
YOU THINK?
HEY, IF YOU HAD TO GUESS, HOW OLD WOULD YOU SAY RAMONA IS?
WE'RE UP AGAINST THE WALL, SCOTT, *DO SOMETHING!!*
BUMP
DO YOU THINK SHE'S OVER 25? I CAN NEVER TELL WITH GIRLS.
SCOTT, I'M SAD THAT I'M ABOUT TO DIE, BUT I'M *NOT* SAD THAT *YOU'RE* ABOUT TO DIE. I JUST WANT YOU TO KNOW THAT.
Grab!

GRIP

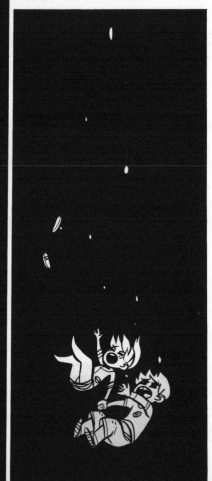

Subspace
Ramona works here.

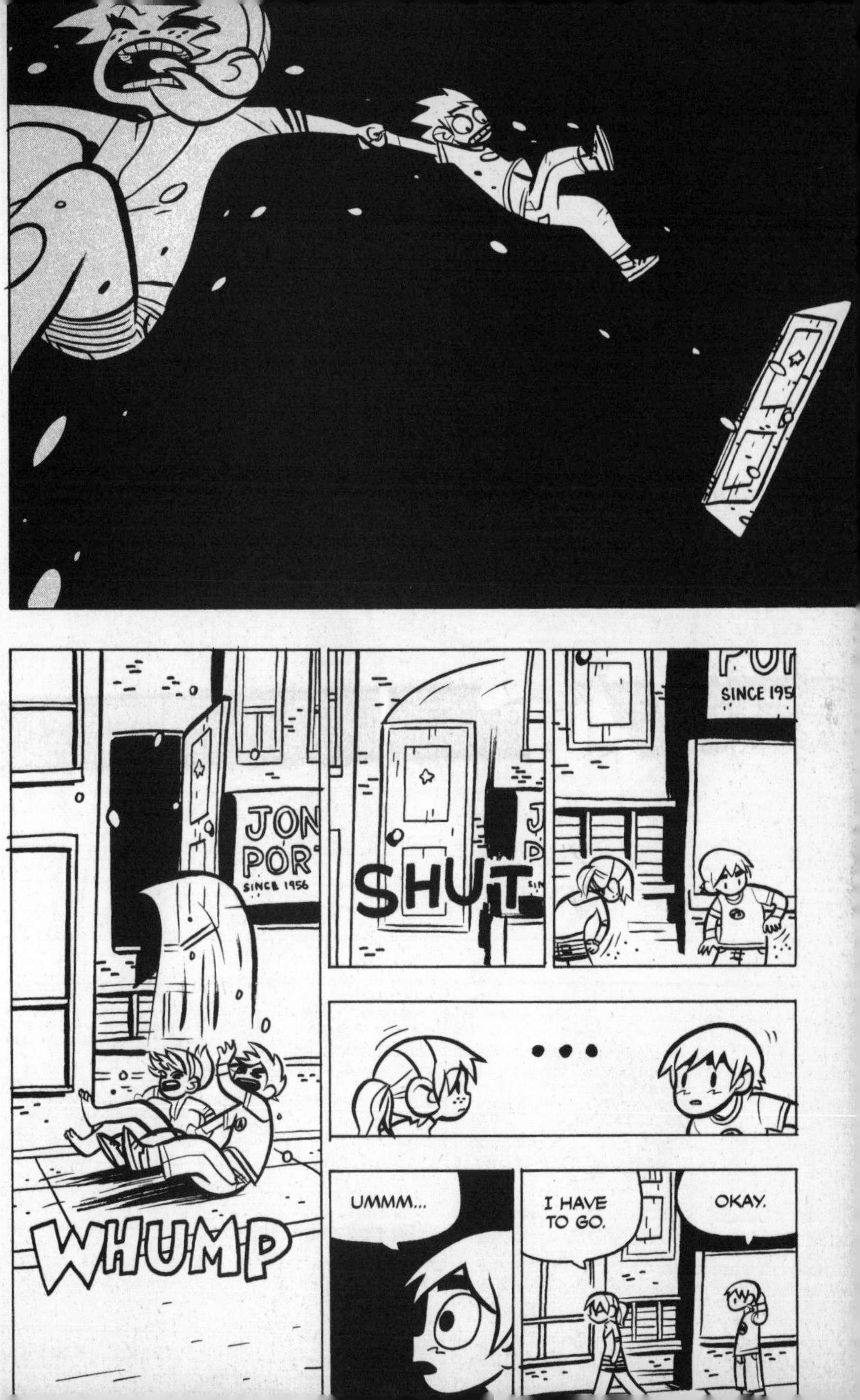
JON
POR
SINCE 1956
WHUMP
SHUT
SINCE 195
• • •
UMMM...
I HAVE TO GO.
OKAY.

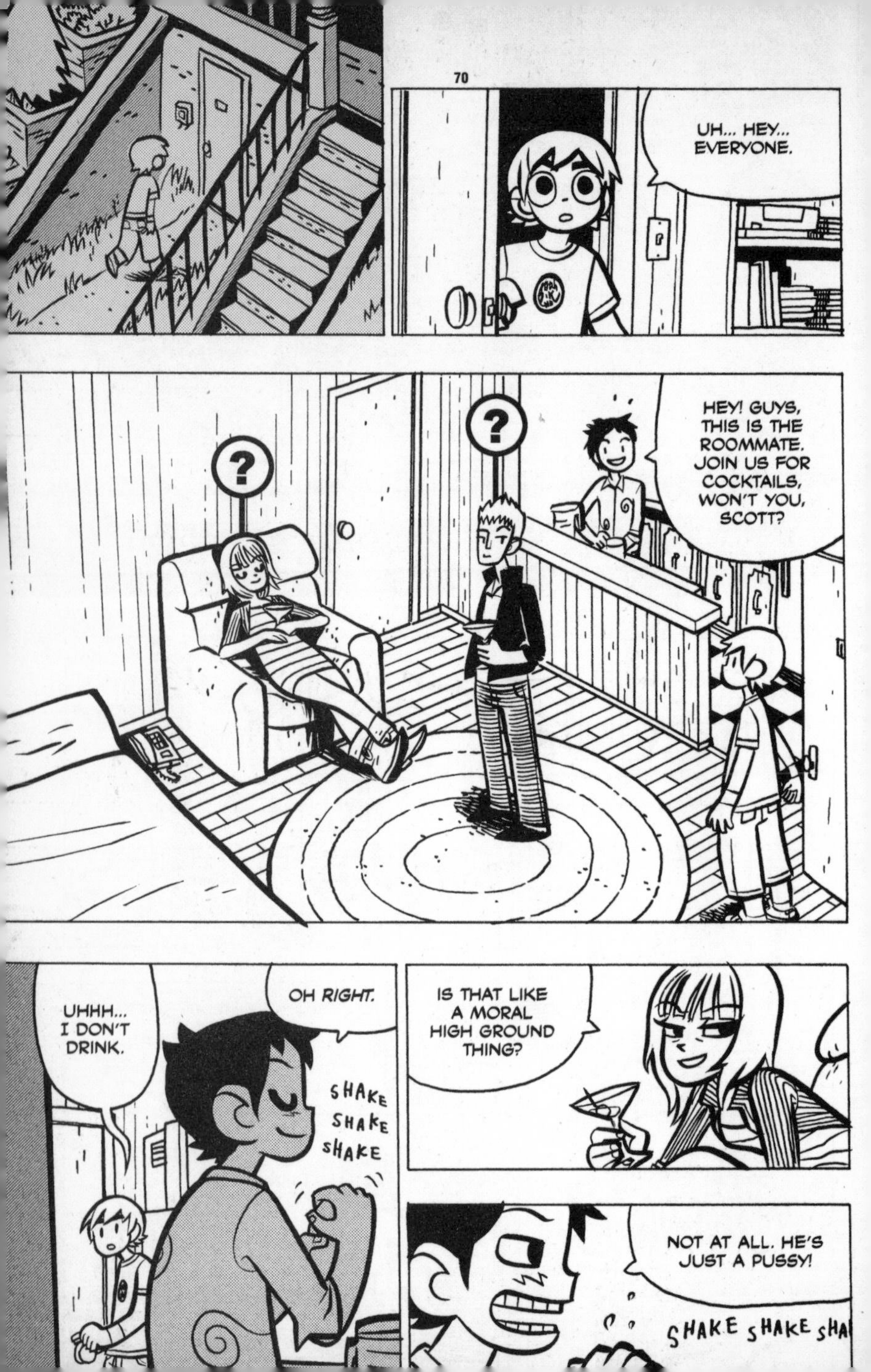

UH... HEY... EVERYONE.
HEY! GUYS, THIS IS THE ROOMMATE. JOIN US FOR COCKTAILS, WON'T YOU, SCOTT?
UHHH... I DON'T DRINK.
OH *RIGHT.*
SHAKE SHAKE SHAKE
IS THAT LIKE A MORAL HIGH GROUND THING?
NOT AT ALL. HE'S JUST A PUSSY!
SHAKE SHAKE SHA

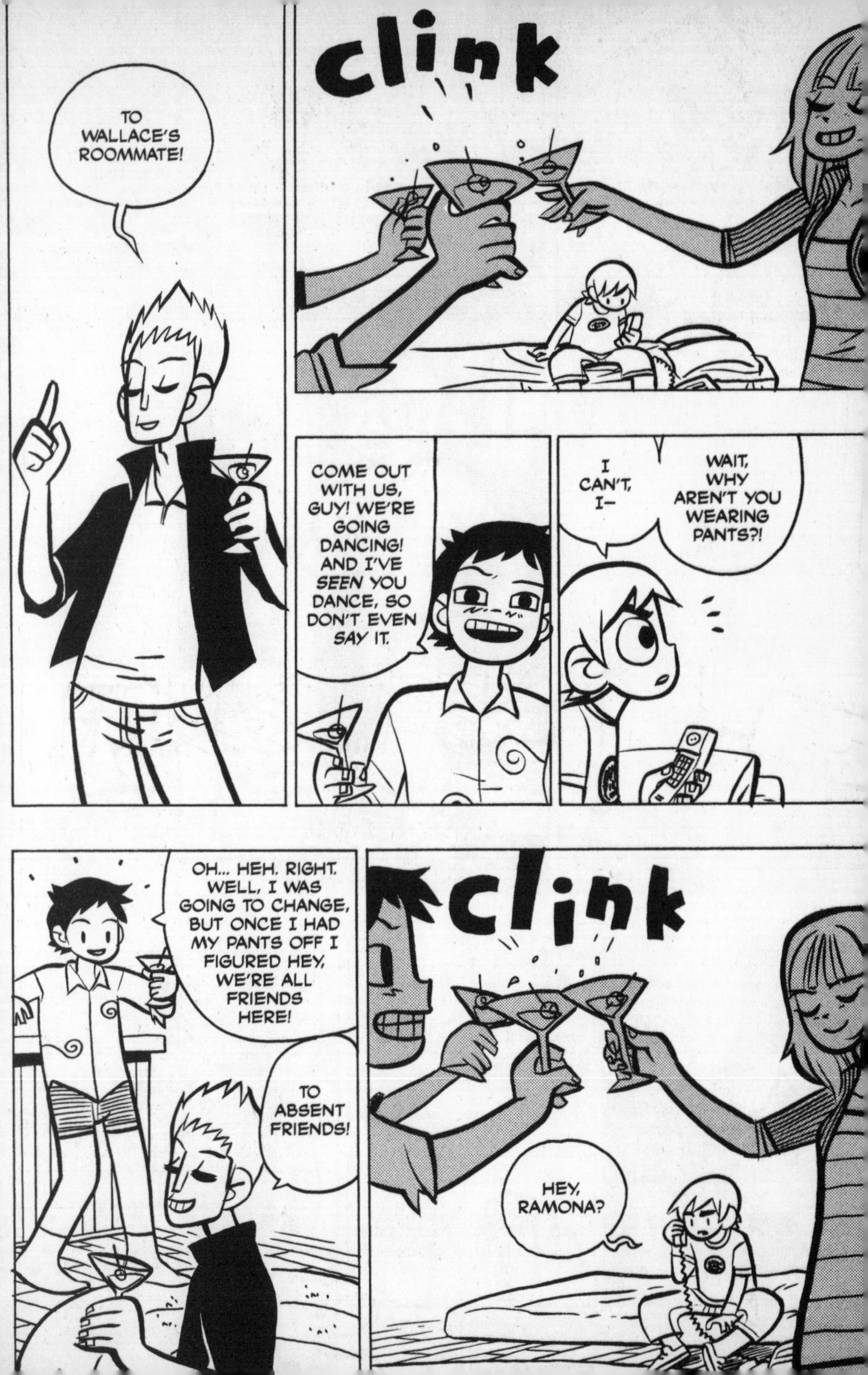
TO WALLACE'S ROOMMATE!
clink
COME OUT WITH US, GUY! WE'RE GOING DANCING! AND I'VE *SEEN* YOU DANCE, SO DON'T EVEN *SAY* IT.
I CAN'T, I–
WAIT, WHY AREN'T YOU WEARING PANTS?!
OH... HEH. RIGHT. WELL, I WAS GOING TO CHANGE, BUT ONCE I HAD MY PANTS OFF I FIGURED HEY, WE'RE ALL FRIENDS HERE!
TO ABSENT FRIENDS!
clink
HEY, RAMONA?

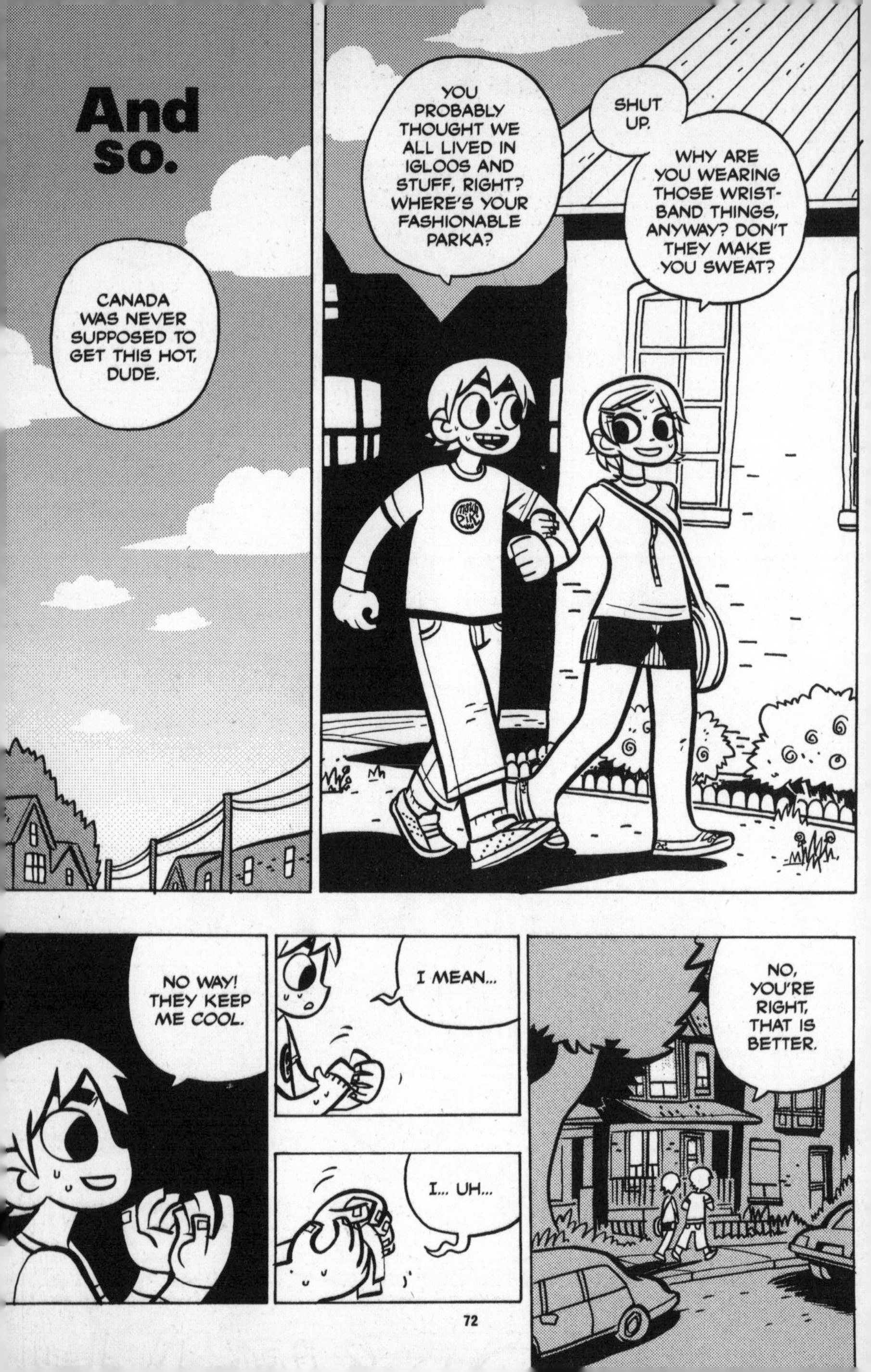
And so.
CANADA WAS NEVER SUPPOSED TO GET THIS HOT, DUDE.
YOU PROBABLY THOUGHT WE ALL LIVED IN IGLOOS AND STUFF, RIGHT? WHERE'S YOUR FASHIONABLE PARKA?
SHUT UP.
WHY ARE YOU WEARING THOSE WRIST-BAND THINGS, ANYWAY? DON'T THEY MAKE YOU SWEAT?
NO WAY! THEY KEEP ME *COOL*.
I MEAN...
I... UH...
NO, YOU'RE RIGHT, THAT IS BETTER.

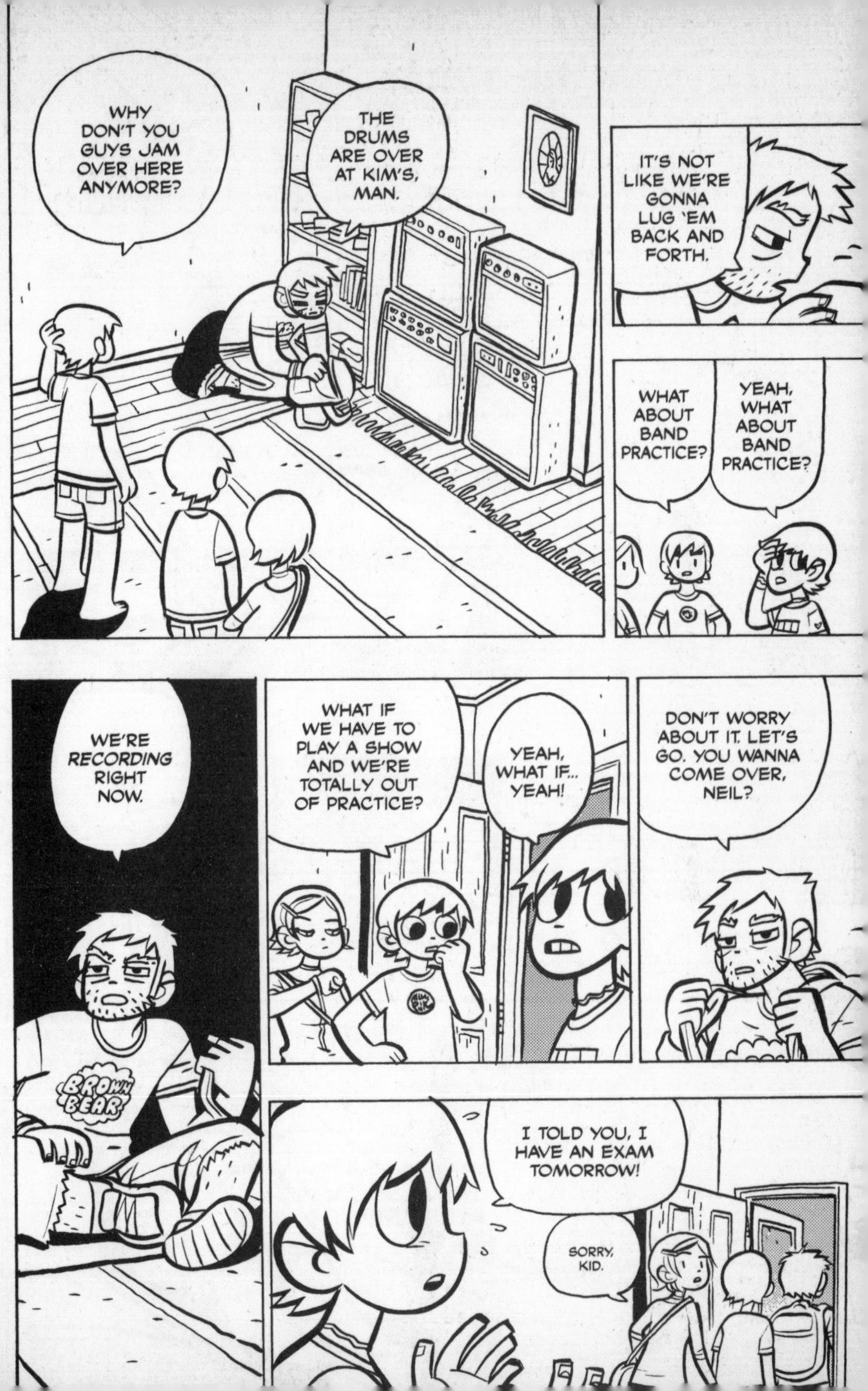
WHY DON'T YOU GUYS JAM OVER HERE ANYMORE?
THE DRUMS ARE OVER AT KIM'S, MAN.
IT'S NOT LIKE WE'RE GONNA LUG 'EM BACK AND FORTH.
WHAT ABOUT BAND PRACTICE?
YEAH, WHAT ABOUT BAND PRACTICE?
WE'RE *RECORDING* RIGHT NOW.
WHAT IF WE HAVE TO PLAY A SHOW AND WE'RE TOTALLY OUT OF PRACTICE?
YEAH, WHAT IF... YEAH!
DON'T WORRY ABOUT IT. LET'S GO. YOU WANNA COME OVER, NEIL?
BROWN BEAR
I TOLD YOU, I HAVE AN EXAM TOMORROW!
SORRY, KID.

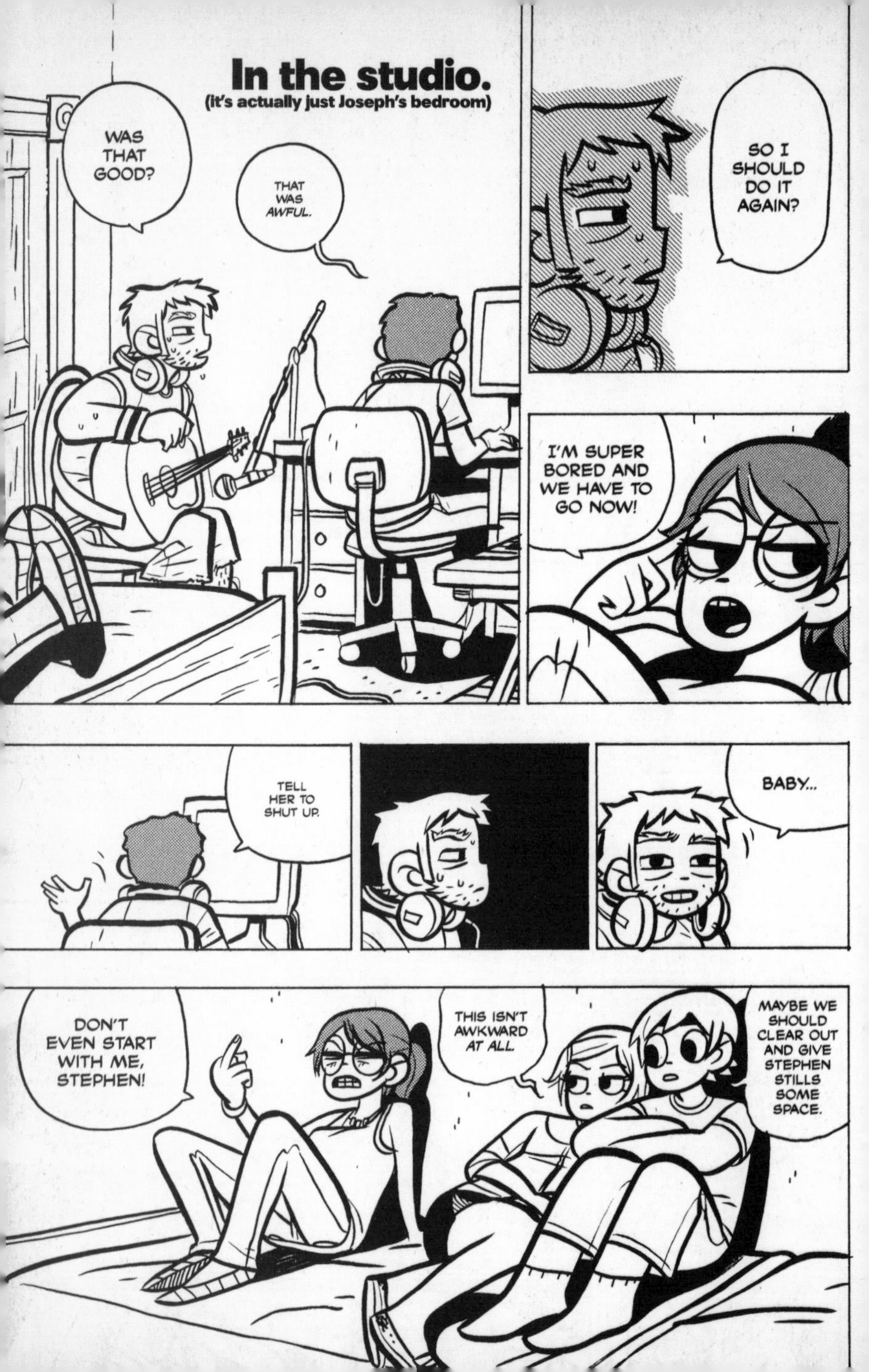

In the studio.
(it's actually just Joseph's bedroom)
WAS THAT GOOD?
THAT WAS AWFUL.
SO I SHOULD DO IT AGAIN?
I'M SUPER BORED AND WE HAVE TO GO NOW!
TELL HER TO SHUT UP.
BABY...
DON'T EVEN START WITH ME, STEPHEN!
THIS ISN'T AWKWARD AT ALL.
MAYBE WE SHOULD CLEAR OUT AND GIVE STEPHEN STILLS SOME SPACE.

Sneaky Dee's (again)

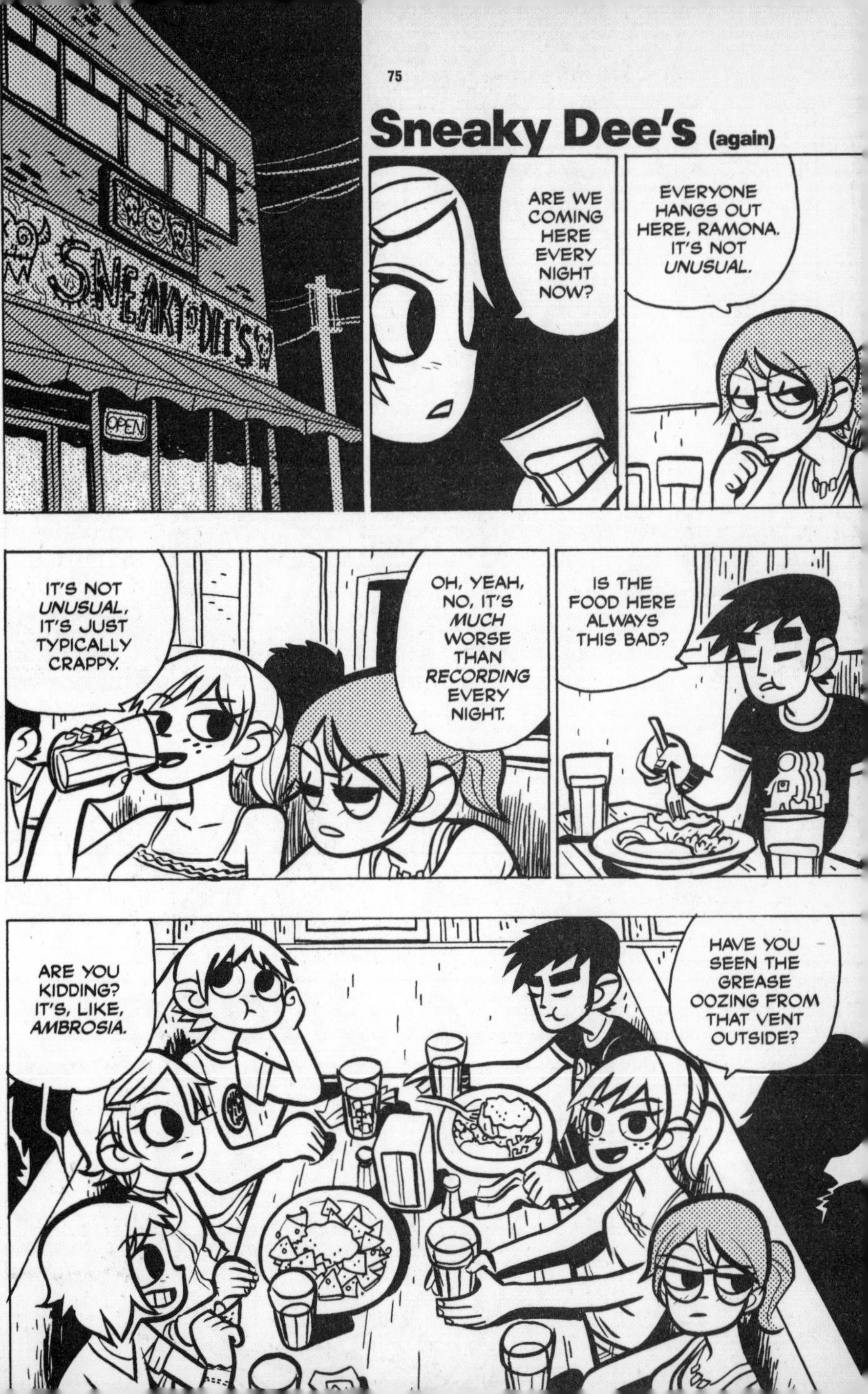
SNEAKY DEE'S
OPEN
ARE WE COMING HERE EVERY NIGHT NOW?
EVERYONE HANGS OUT HERE, RAMONA. IT'S NOT *UNUSUAL*.
IT'S NOT *UNUSUAL*, IT'S JUST TYPICALLY CRAPPY.
OH, YEAH, NO, IT'S *MUCH* WORSE THAN *RECORDING* EVERY NIGHT.
IS THE FOOD HERE ALWAYS THIS BAD?
ARE YOU KIDDING? IT'S, LIKE, *AMBROSIA*.
HAVE YOU SEEN THE GREASE OOZING FROM THAT VENT OUTSIDE?

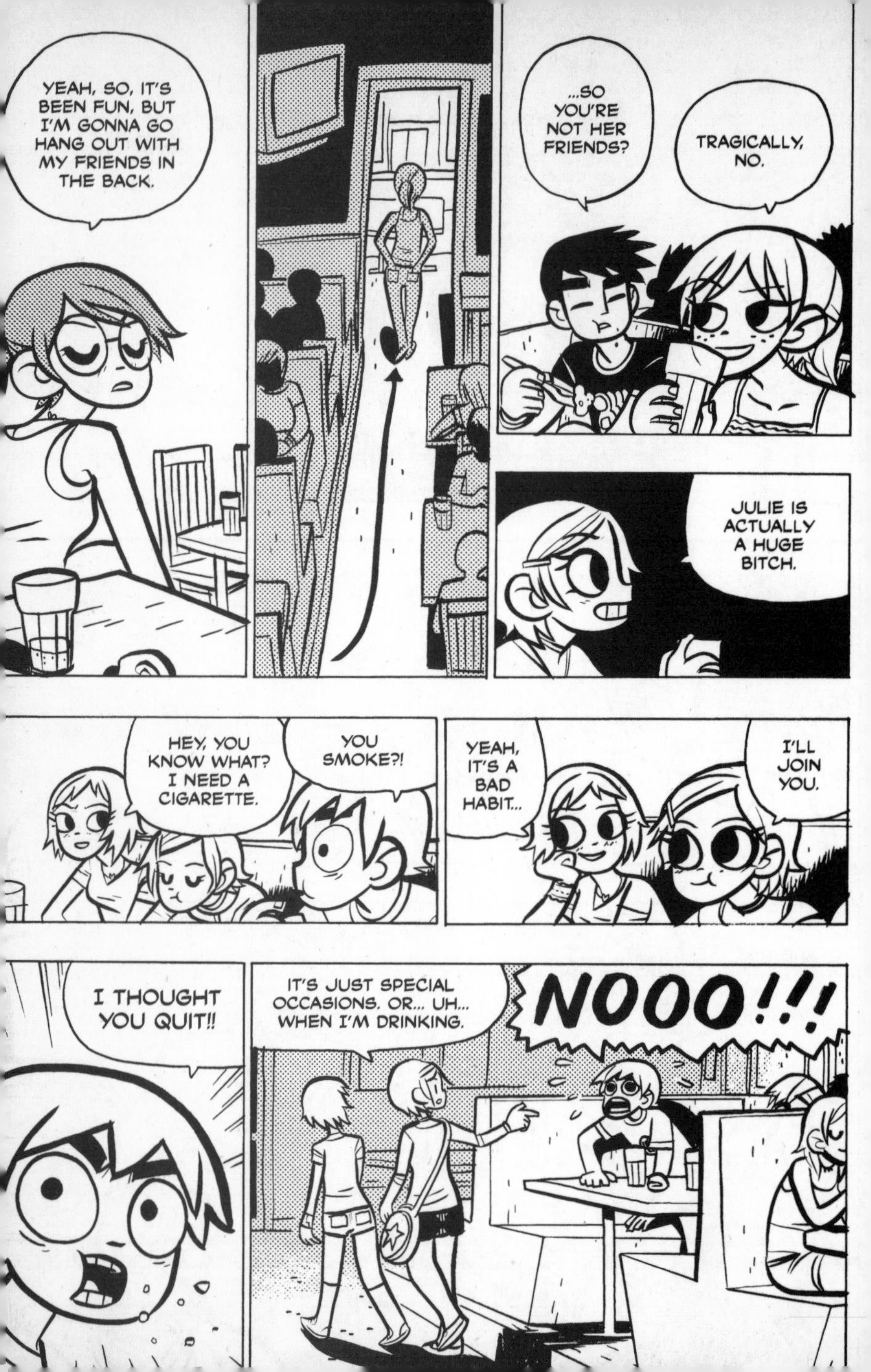
YEAH, SO, IT'S BEEN FUN, BUT I'M GONNA GO HANG OUT WITH MY FRIENDS IN THE BACK.
...SO YOU'RE NOT HER FRIENDS?
TRAGICALLY, NO.
JULIE IS ACTUALLY A HUGE BITCH.
HEY, YOU KNOW WHAT? I NEED A CIGARETTE.
YOU SMOKE?!
YEAH, IT'S A BAD HABIT...
I'LL JOIN YOU.
I THOUGHT YOU QUIT!!
IT'S JUST SPECIAL OCCASIONS. OR... UH... WHEN I'M DRINKING.
NOOO!!!

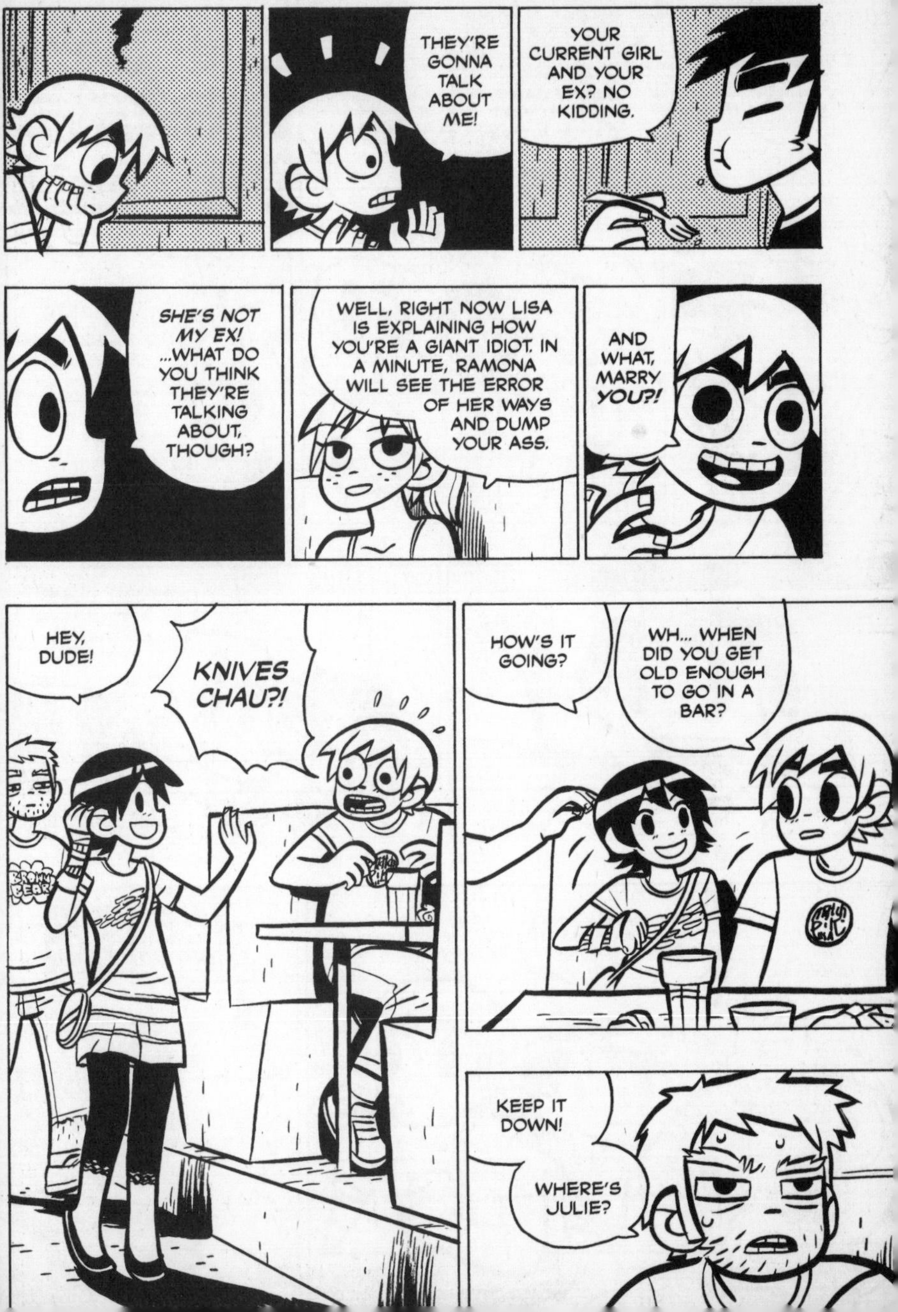
THEY'RE GONNA TALK ABOUT ME!
YOUR CURRENT GIRL AND YOUR EX? NO KIDDING.
SHE'S NOT MY EX! ...WHAT DO YOU THINK THEY'RE TALKING ABOUT, THOUGH?
WELL, RIGHT NOW LISA IS EXPLAINING HOW YOU'RE A GIANT IDIOT. IN A MINUTE, RAMONA WILL SEE THE ERROR OF HER WAYS AND DUMP YOUR ASS.
AND WHAT, MARRY YOU?!
HEY, DUDE!
KNIVES CHAU?!
HOW'S IT GOING?
WH... WHEN DID YOU GET OLD ENOUGH TO GO IN A BAR?
KEEP IT DOWN!
WHERE'S JULIE?

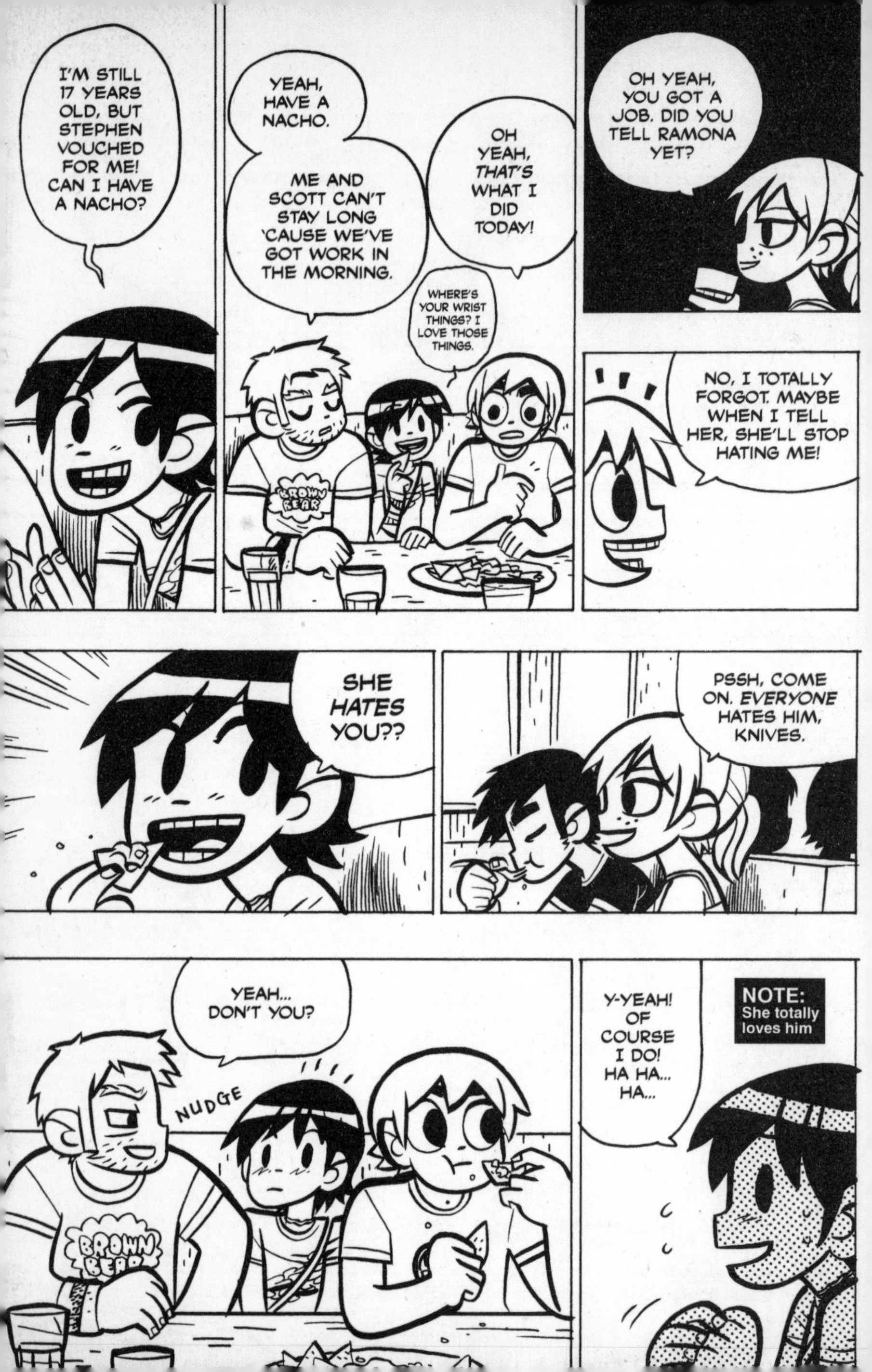
I'M STILL 17 YEARS OLD, BUT STEPHEN VOUCHED FOR ME! CAN I HAVE A NACHO?
YEAH, HAVE A NACHO.
ME AND SCOTT CAN'T STAY LONG 'CAUSE WE'VE GOT WORK IN THE MORNING.
OH YEAH, THAT'S WHAT I DID TODAY!
WHERE'S YOUR WRIST THINGS? I LOVE THOSE THINGS.
BROWN BEAR
OH YEAH, YOU GOT A JOB. DID YOU TELL RAMONA YET?
NO, I TOTALLY FORGOT. MAYBE WHEN I TELL HER, SHE'LL STOP HATING ME!
SHE HATES YOU??
PSSH, COME ON. EVERYONE HATES HIM, KNIVES.
YEAH... DON'T YOU?
NUDGE
BROWN BEAR
Y-YEAH! OF COURSE I DO! HA HA... HA...
NOTE: She totally loves him

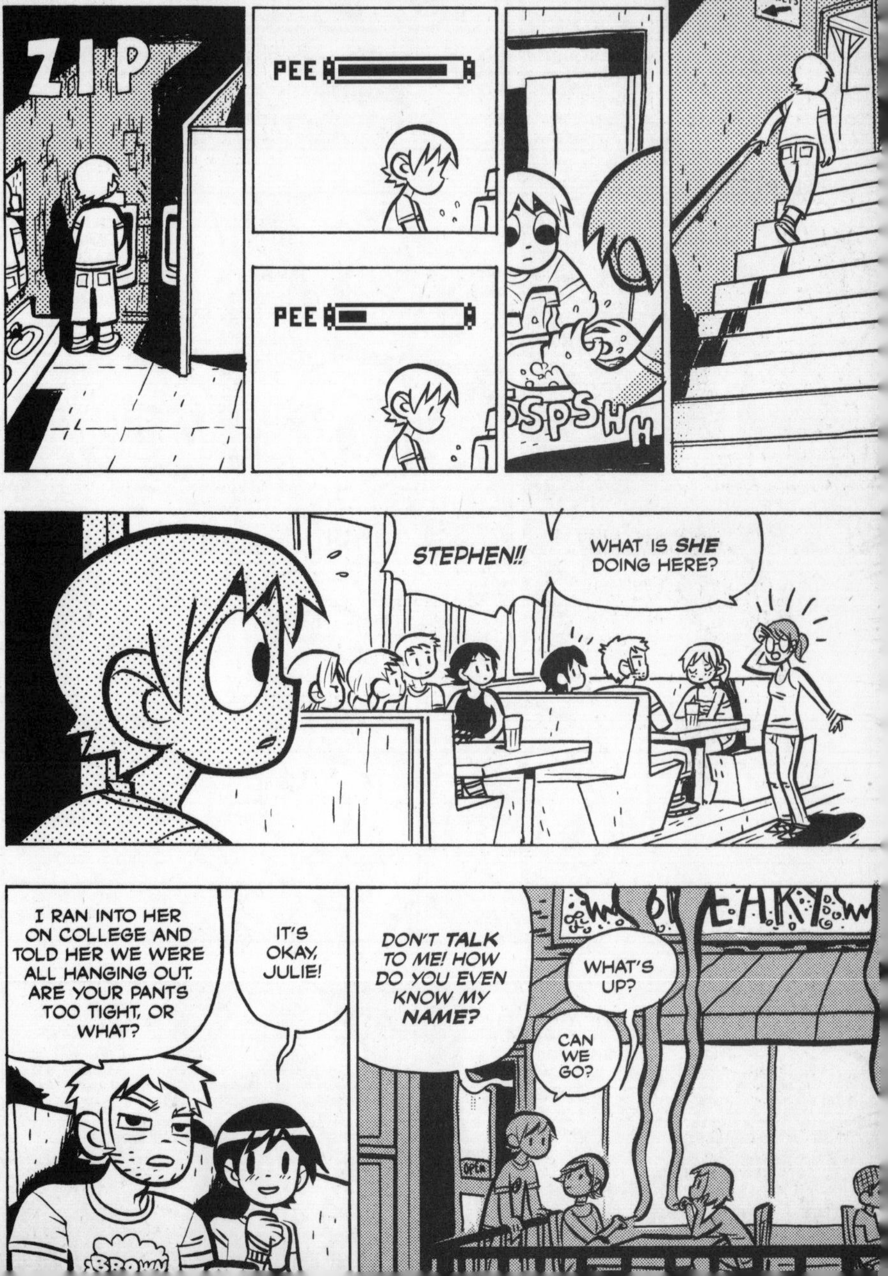
ZIP
PEE
PEE
SPSHH
TOILETS
STEPHEN!!
WHAT IS *SHE* DOING HERE?
I RAN INTO HER ON COLLEGE AND TOLD HER WE WERE ALL HANGING OUT. ARE YOUR PANTS TOO TIGHT, OR WHAT?
IT'S OKAY, JULIE!
DON'T **TALK** *TO ME! HOW DO YOU EVEN KNOW MY* **NAME?**
WHAT'S UP?
CAN WE GO?

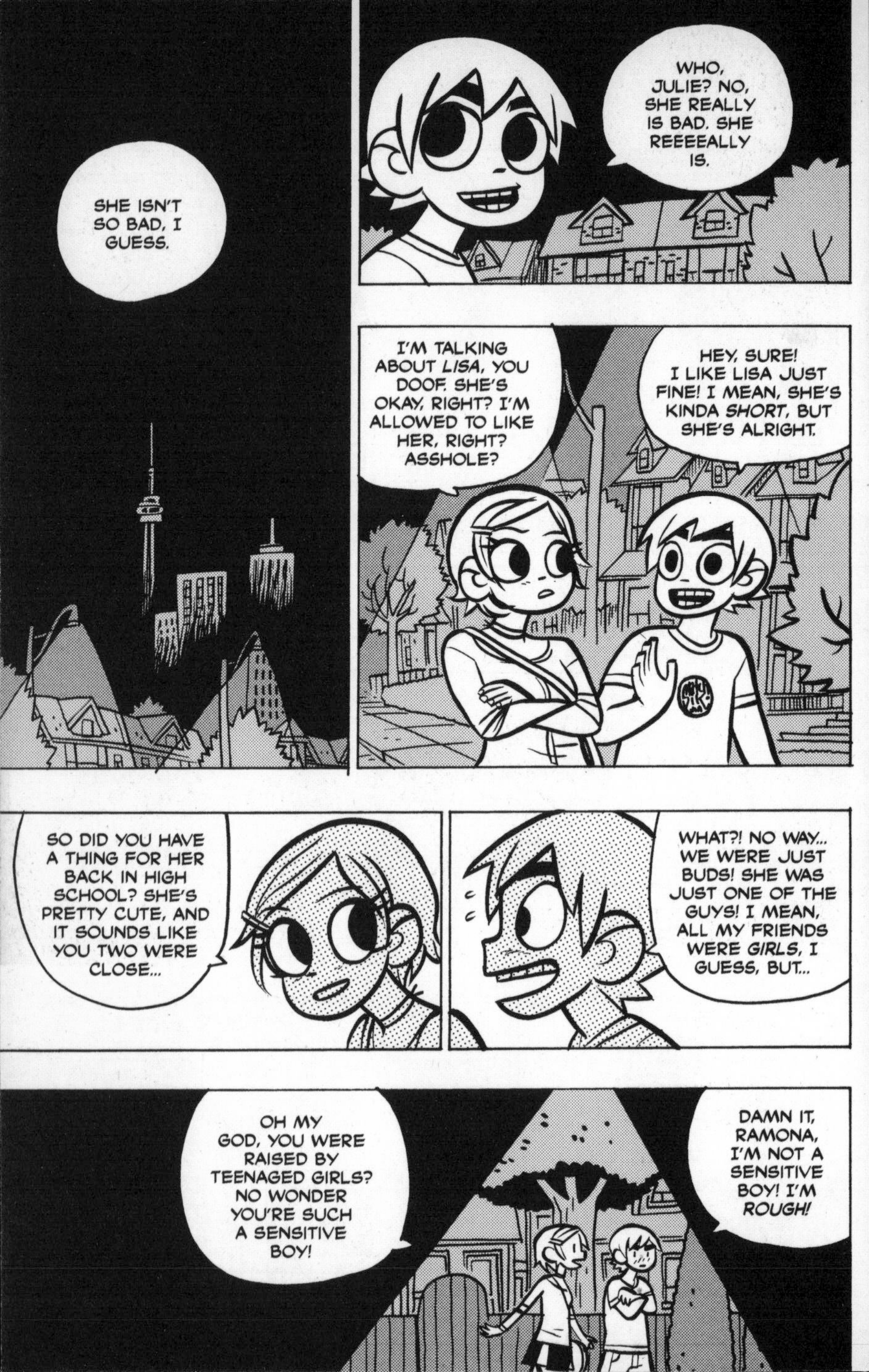
SHE ISN'T SO BAD, I GUESS.
WHO, JULIE? NO, SHE REALLY IS BAD. SHE REEEEALLY IS.
I'M TALKING ABOUT *LISA*, YOU DOOF. SHE'S OKAY, RIGHT? I'M ALLOWED TO LIKE HER, RIGHT? ASSHOLE?
HEY, SURE! I LIKE LISA JUST FINE! I MEAN, SHE'S KINDA *SHORT*, BUT SHE'S ALRIGHT.
SO DID YOU HAVE A THING FOR HER BACK IN HIGH SCHOOL? SHE'S PRETTY CUTE, AND IT SOUNDS LIKE YOU TWO WERE CLOSE...
WHAT?! NO WAY... WE WERE JUST BUDS! SHE WAS JUST ONE OF THE GUYS! I MEAN, ALL MY FRIENDS WERE *GIRLS*, I GUESS, BUT...
OH MY GOD, YOU WERE RAISED BY TEENAGED GIRLS? NO WONDER YOU'RE SUCH A SENSITIVE BOY!
DAMN IT, RAMONA, I'M NOT A SENSITIVE BOY! I'M *ROUGH!*

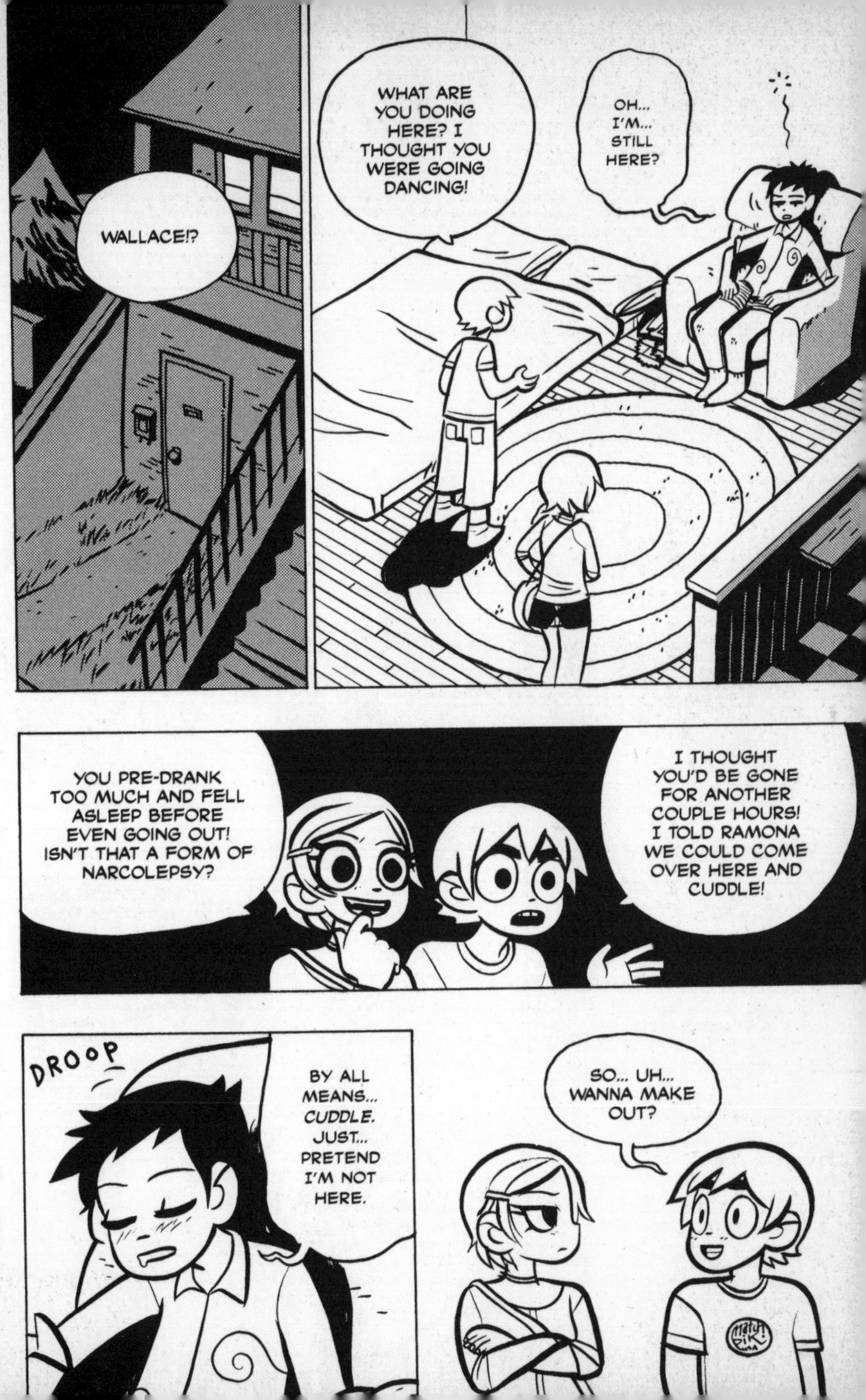
WALLACE!?
WHAT ARE YOU DOING HERE? I THOUGHT YOU WERE GOING DANCING!
OH... I'M... STILL HERE?
YOU PRE-DRANK TOO MUCH AND FELL ASLEEP BEFORE EVEN GOING OUT! ISN'T THAT A FORM OF NARCOLEPSY?
I THOUGHT YOU'D BE GONE FOR ANOTHER COUPLE HOURS! I TOLD RAMONA WE COULD COME OVER HERE AND CUDDLE!
DROOP
BY ALL MEANS... CUDDLE. JUST... PRETEND I'M NOT HERE.
SO... UH... WANNA MAKE OUT?

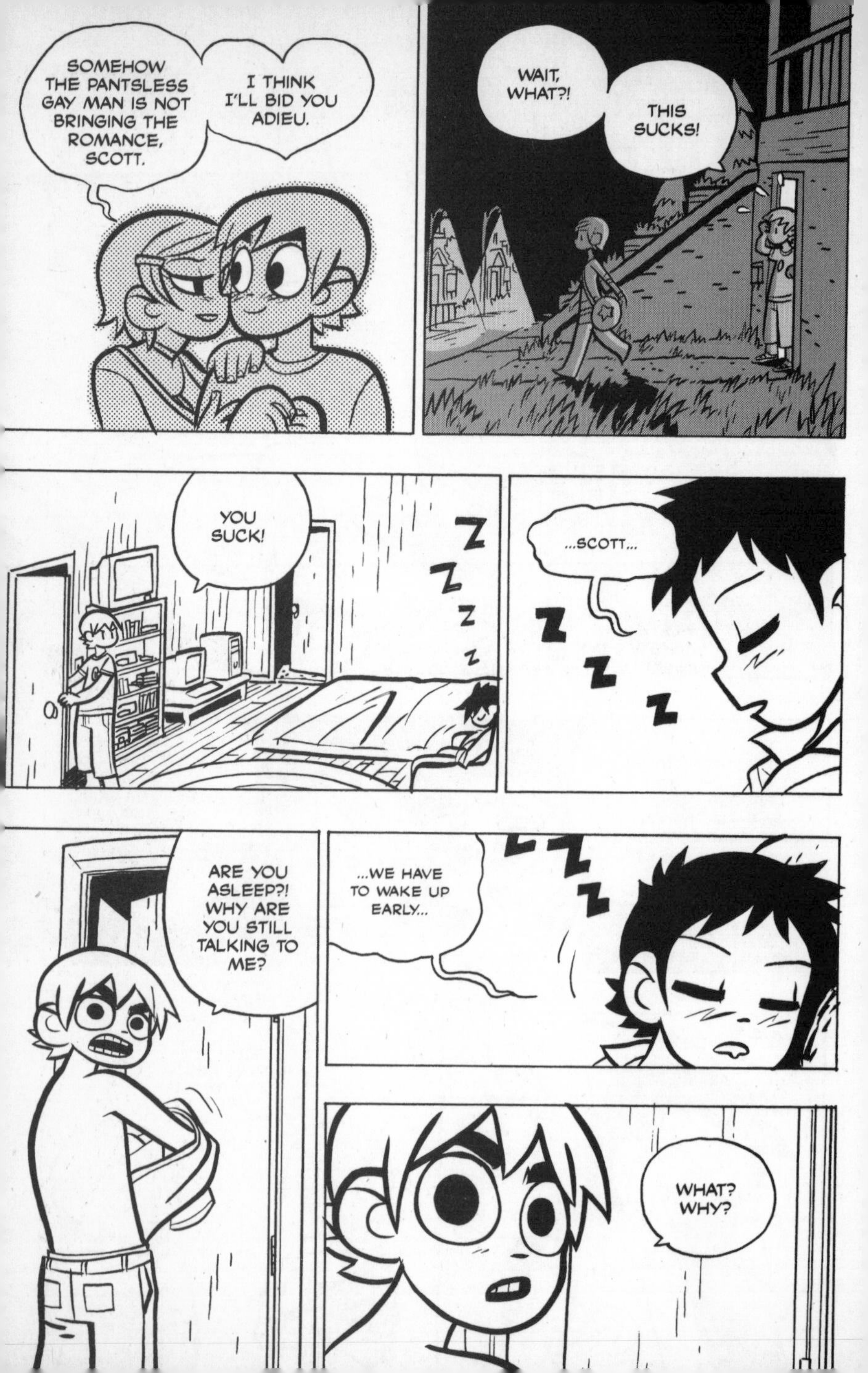
SOMEHOW THE PANTSLESS GAY MAN IS NOT BRINGING THE ROMANCE, SCOTT.
I THINK I'LL BID YOU ADIEU.
WAIT, WHAT?!
THIS SUCKS!
YOU SUCK!
Z Z Z Z
...SCOTT...
Z Z Z
ARE YOU ASLEEP?! WHY ARE YOU STILL TALKING TO ME?
...WE HAVE TO WAKE UP EARLY...
Z Z Z
WHAT? WHY?

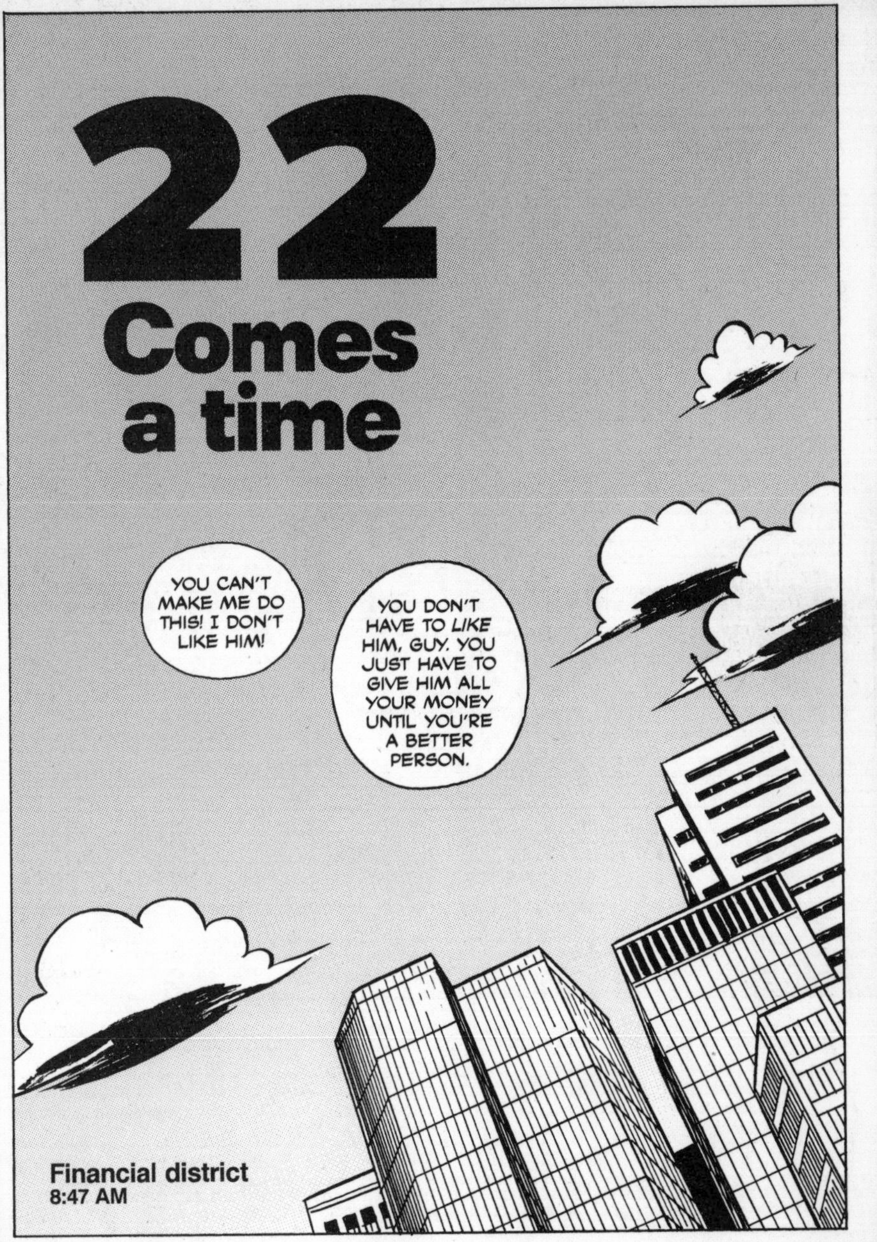
22
Comes a time
YOU CAN'T MAKE ME DO THIS! I DON'T LIKE HIM!
YOU DON'T HAVE TO *LIKE* HIM, GUY. YOU JUST HAVE TO GIVE HIM ALL YOUR MONEY UNTIL YOU'RE A BETTER PERSON.
Financial district
8:47 AM

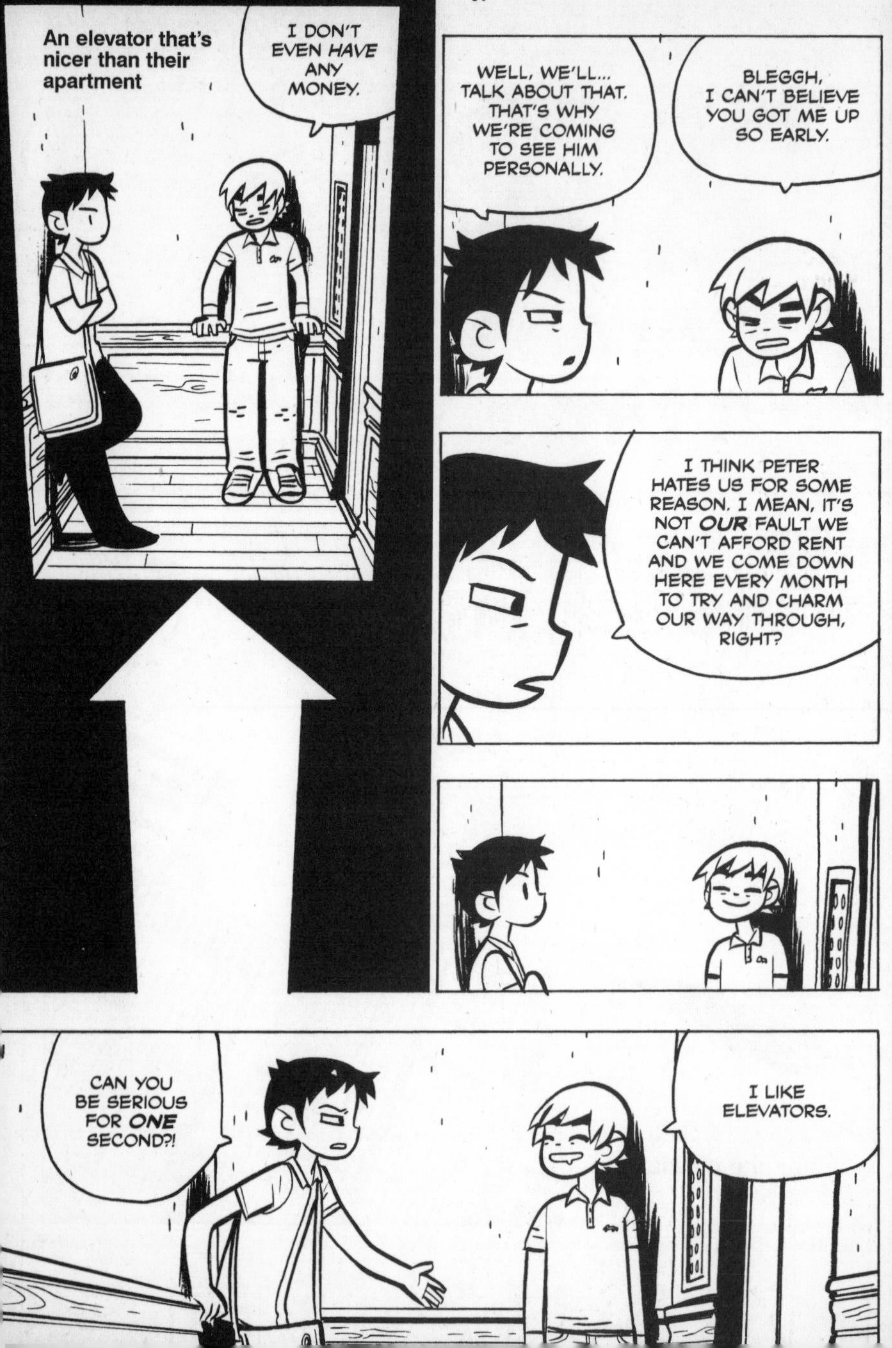
An elevator that's nicer than their apartment
I DON'T EVEN *HAVE* ANY MONEY.
WELL, WE'LL... TALK ABOUT THAT. THAT'S WHY WE'RE COMING TO SEE HIM PERSONALLY.
BLEGGH, I CAN'T BELIEVE YOU GOT ME UP SO EARLY.
I THINK PETER HATES US FOR SOME REASON. I MEAN, IT'S NOT ***OUR*** FAULT WE CAN'T AFFORD RENT AND WE COME DOWN HERE EVERY MONTH TO TRY AND CHARM OUR WAY THROUGH, RIGHT?
CAN YOU BE SERIOUS FOR ***ONE*** SECOND?!
I LIKE ELEVATORS.

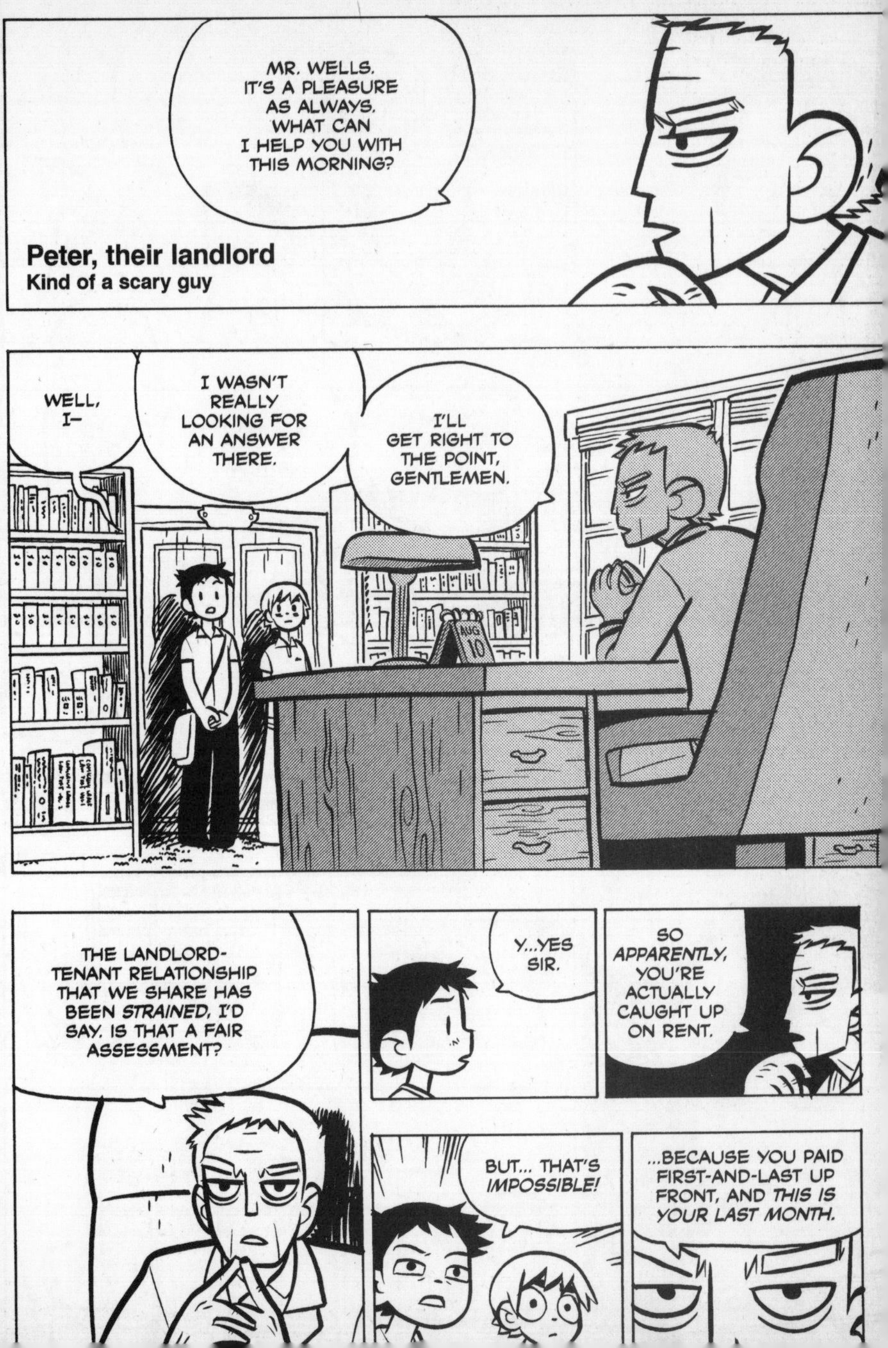
MR. WELLS. IT'S A PLEASURE AS ALWAYS. WHAT CAN I HELP YOU WITH THIS MORNING?
Peter, their landlord
Kind of a scary guy
WELL, I–
I WASN'T REALLY LOOKING FOR AN ANSWER THERE.
I'LL GET RIGHT TO THE POINT, GENTLEMEN.
AUG 10
THE LANDLORD-TENANT RELATIONSHIP THAT WE SHARE HAS BEEN *STRAINED,* I'D SAY. IS THAT A FAIR ASSESSMENT?
Y...YES SIR.
SO *APPARENTLY,* YOU'RE ACTUALLY CAUGHT UP ON RENT.
BUT... THAT'S *IMPOSSIBLE!*
...BECAUSE YOU PAID FIRST-AND-LAST UP FRONT, AND *THIS IS YOUR LAST MONTH.*

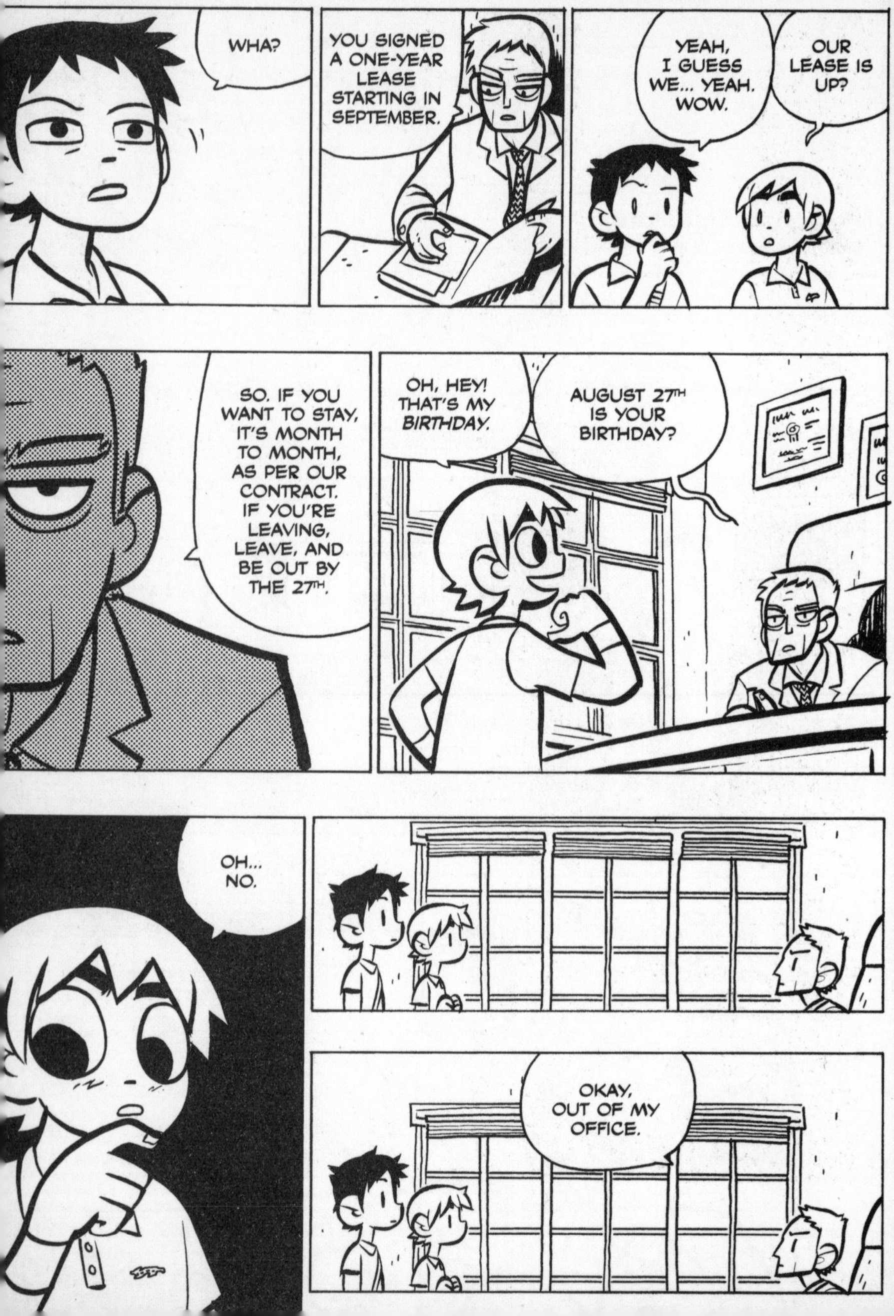
WHA?
YOU SIGNED A ONE-YEAR LEASE STARTING IN SEPTEMBER.
OUR LEASE IS UP?
YEAH, I GUESS WE... YEAH. WOW.
SO. IF YOU WANT TO STAY, IT'S MONTH TO MONTH, AS PER OUR CONTRACT. IF YOU'RE LEAVING, LEAVE, AND BE OUT BY THE 27TH.
OH, HEY! THAT'S MY BIRTHDAY.
AUGUST 27TH IS YOUR BIRTHDAY?
OH... NO.
OKAY, OUT OF MY OFFICE.

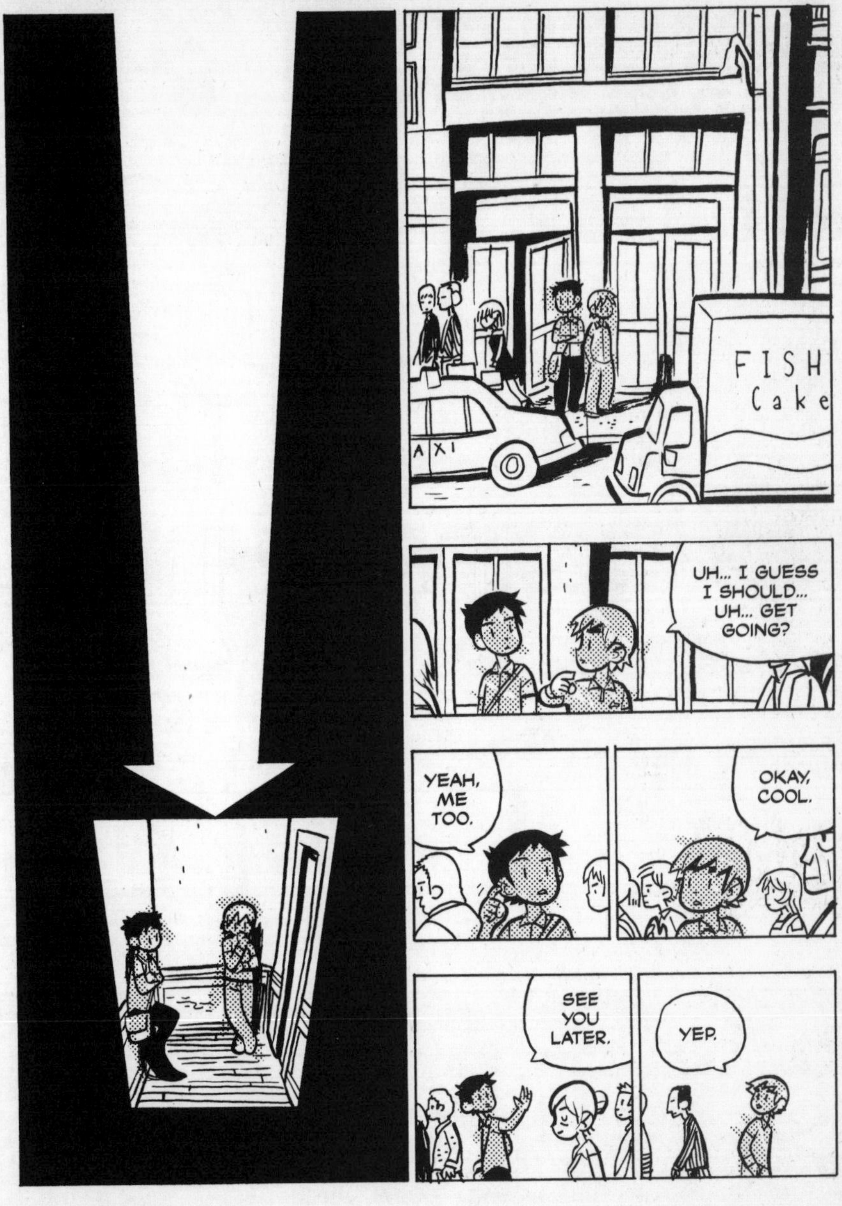
FISH
Cake
AXI
UH... I GUESS I SHOULD... UH... GET GOING?
YEAH, ME TOO.
OKAY, COOL.
SEE YOU LATER.
YEP.

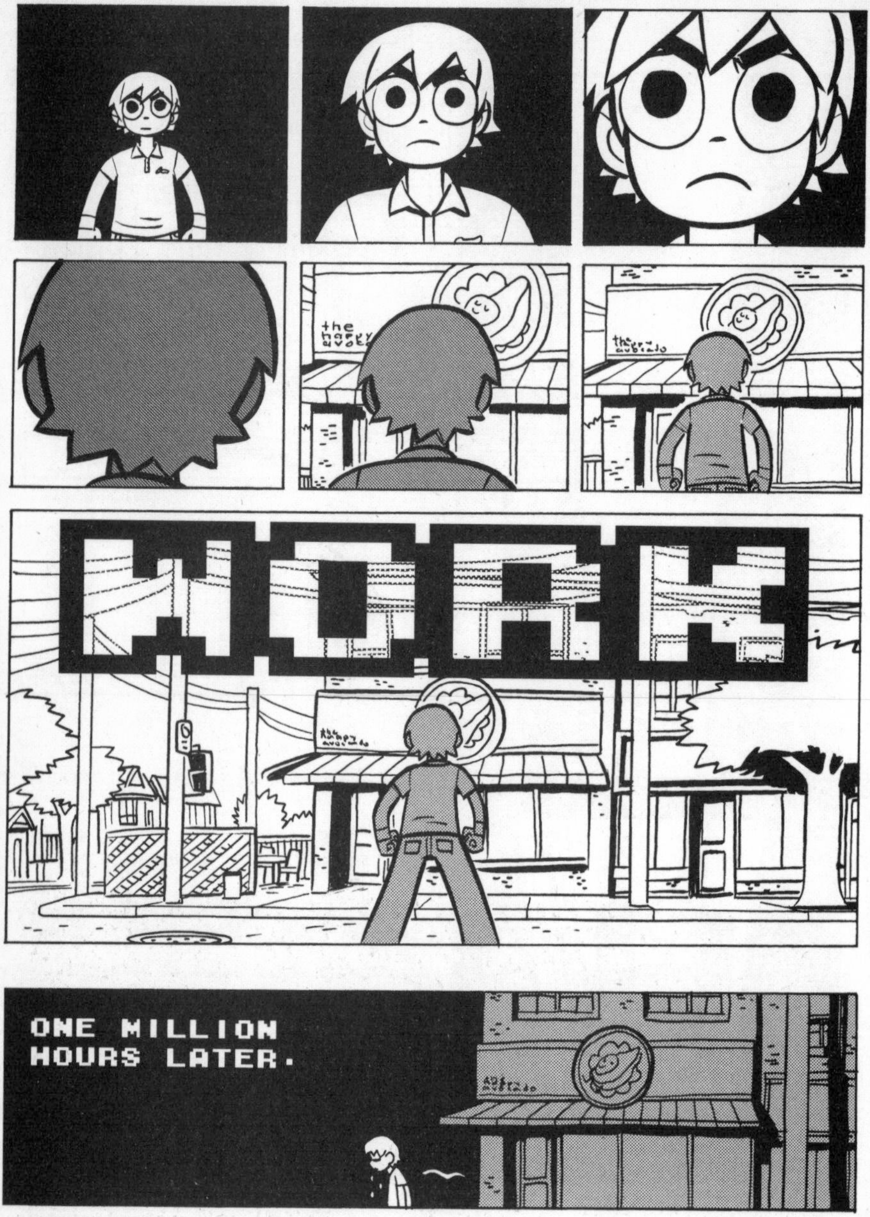
WORK
ONE MILLION
HOURS LATER.

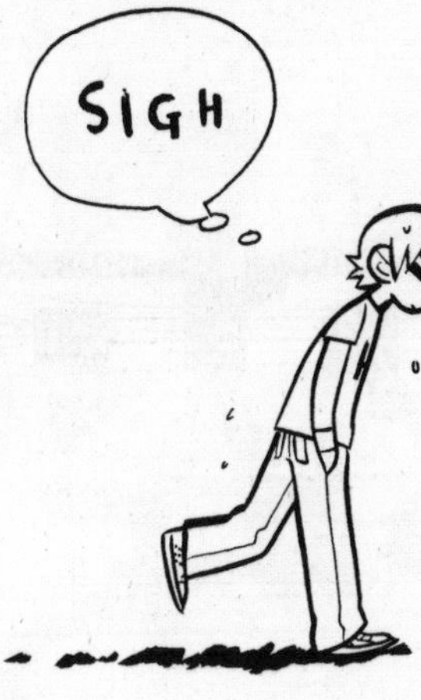
SIGH

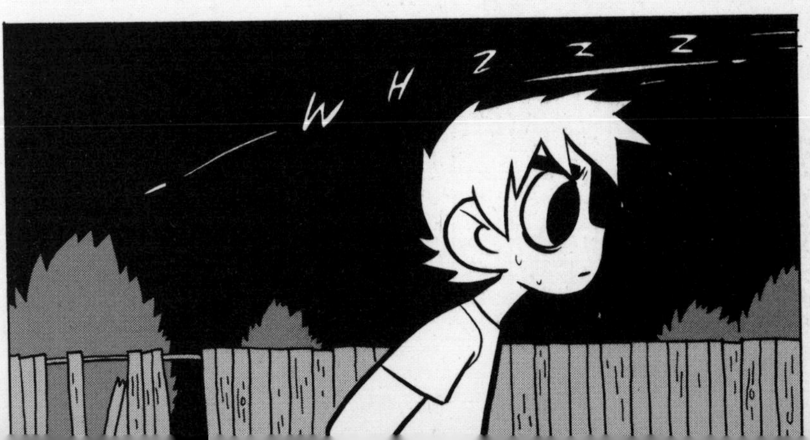
WHZZZ

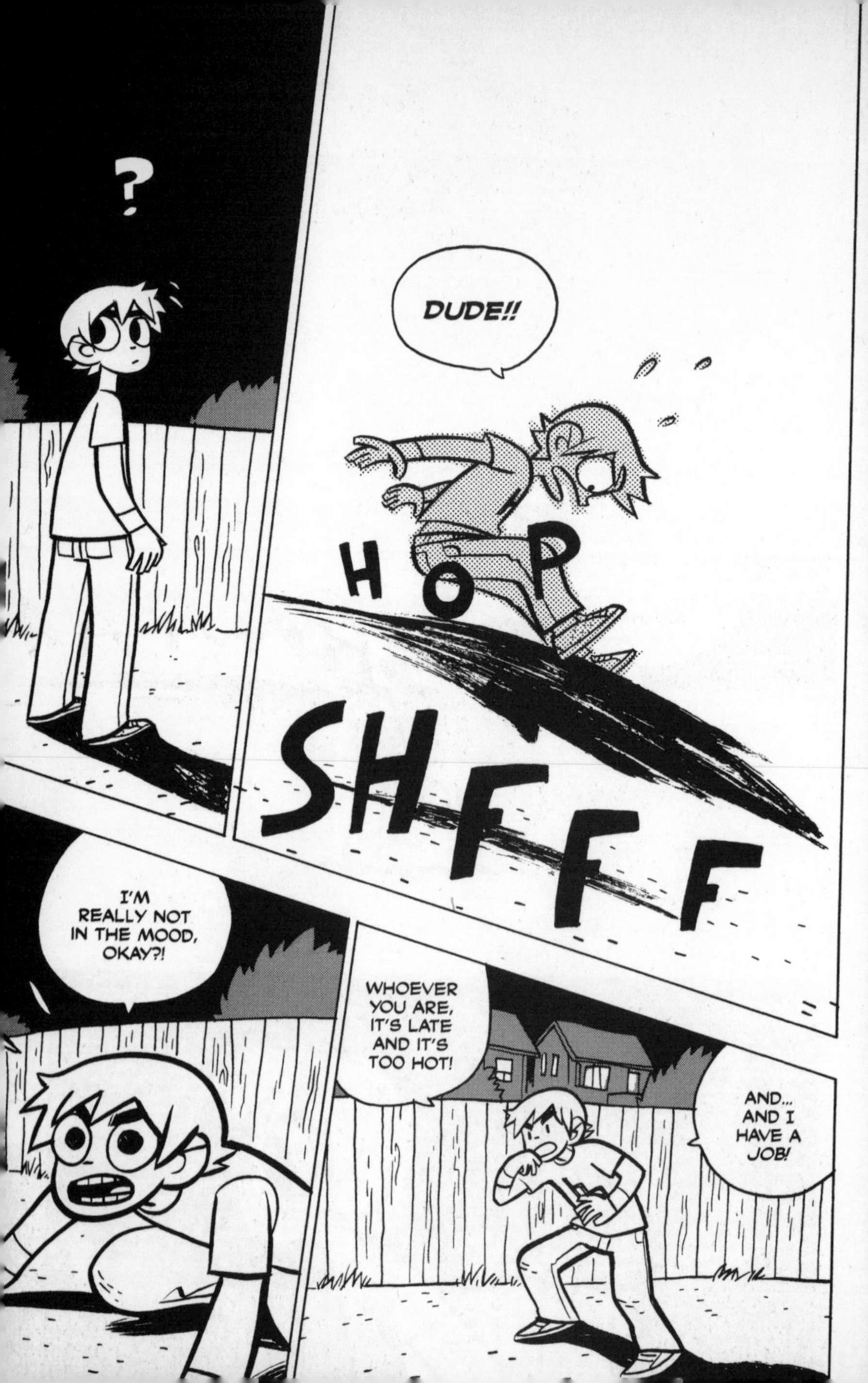
?
DUDE!!
HOP
SHFFF
I'M REALLY NOT IN THE MOOD, OKAY?!
WHOEVER YOU ARE, IT'S LATE AND IT'S TOO HOT!
AND... AND I HAVE A JOB!

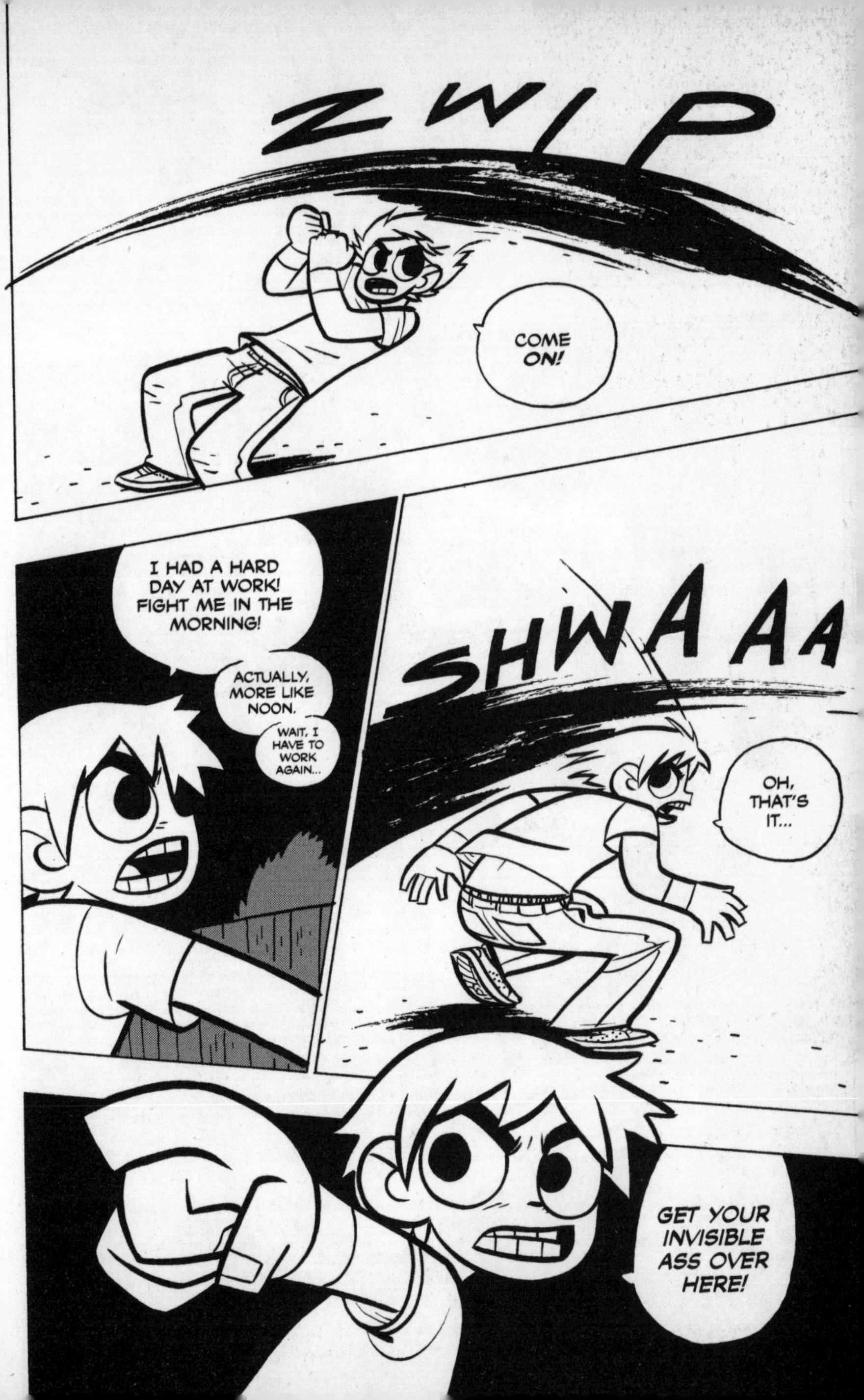
ZWIP
COME ON!
I HAD A HARD DAY AT WORK! FIGHT ME IN THE MORNING!
ACTUALLY, MORE LIKE NOON.
WAIT, I HAVE TO WORK AGAIN...
SHWAAAA
OH, THAT'S IT...
GET YOUR INVISIBLE ASS OVER HERE!

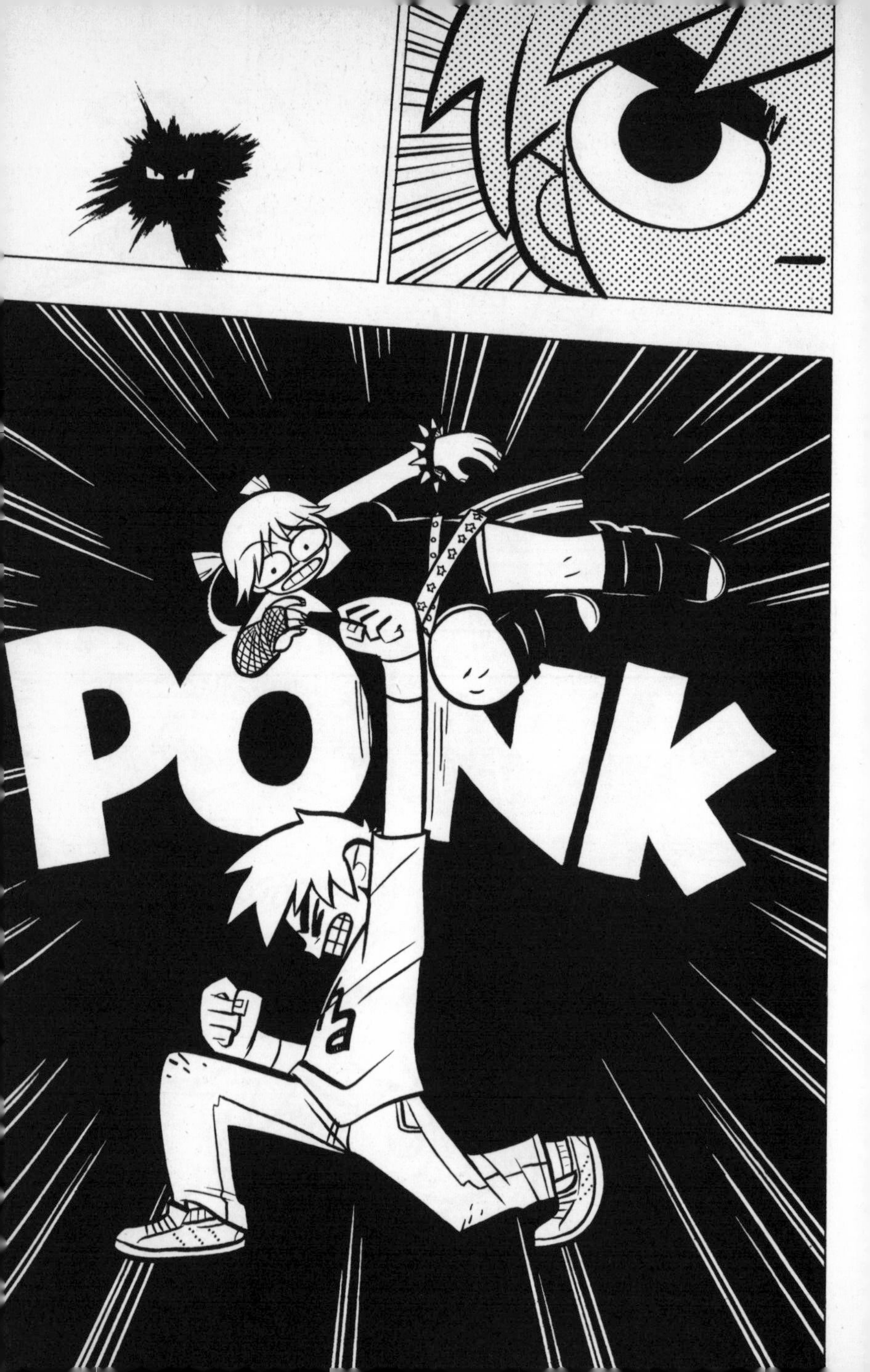
POINK

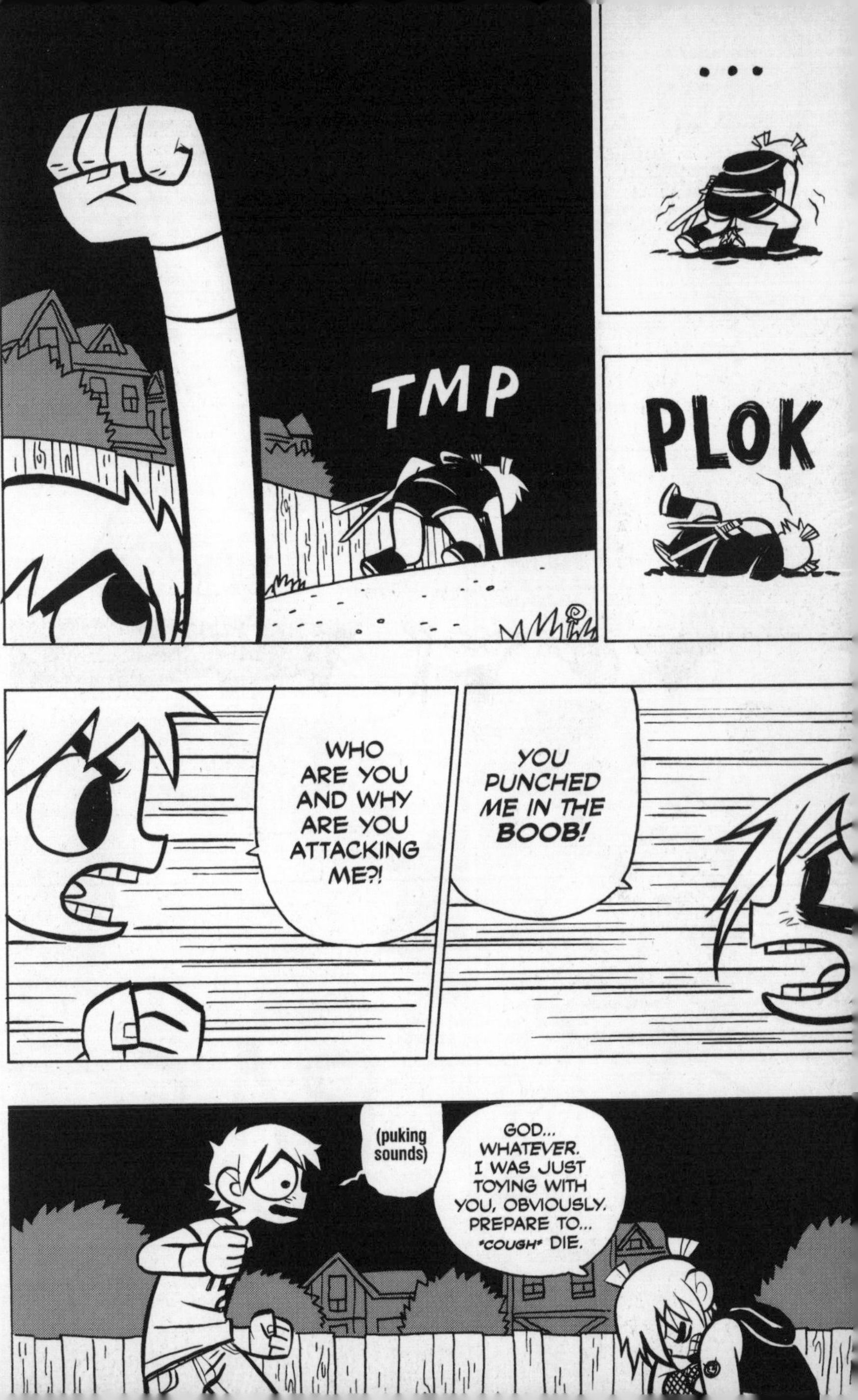
...
TMP
PLOK
WHO ARE YOU AND WHY ARE YOU ATTACKING ME?!
YOU PUNCHED ME IN THE BOOB!
(puking sounds)
GOD... WHATEVER. I WAS JUST TOYING WITH YOU, OBVIOUSLY. PREPARE TO... *COUGH* DIE.

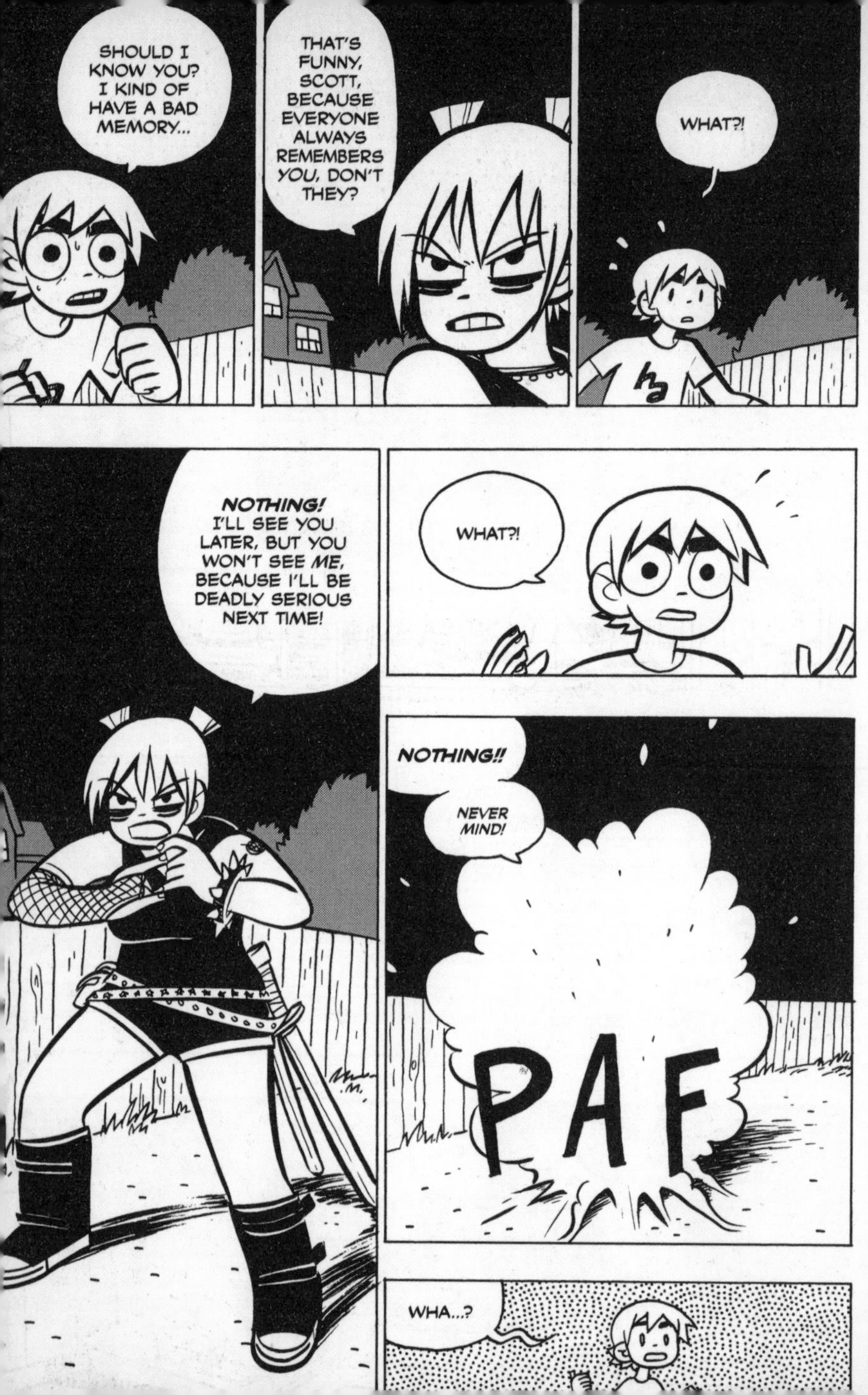
SHOULD I KNOW YOU? I KIND OF HAVE A BAD MEMORY...
THAT'S FUNNY, SCOTT, BECAUSE EVERYONE ALWAYS REMEMBERS *YOU*, DON'T THEY?
WHAT?!
NOTHING! I'LL SEE YOU LATER, BUT YOU WON'T SEE *ME*, BECAUSE I'LL BE DEADLY SERIOUS NEXT TIME!
WHAT?!
NOTHING!!
NEVER MIND!
PAF
WHA...?

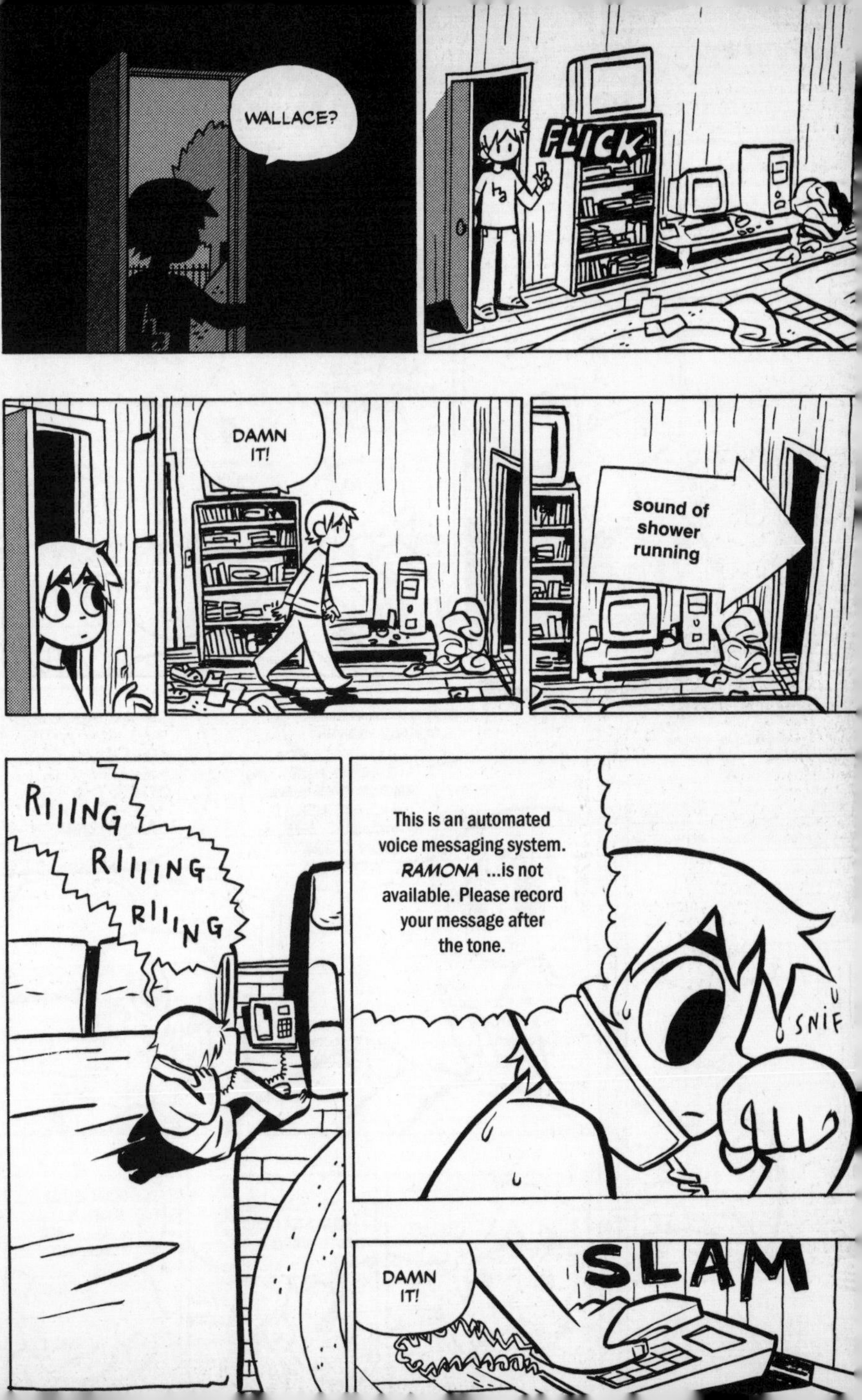
WALLACE?
FLICK
DAMN IT!
sound of shower running
RIIING
RIIIING
RIIING
This is an automated voice messaging system. RAMONA ...is not available. Please record your message after the tone.
SNIF
DAMN IT!
SLAM

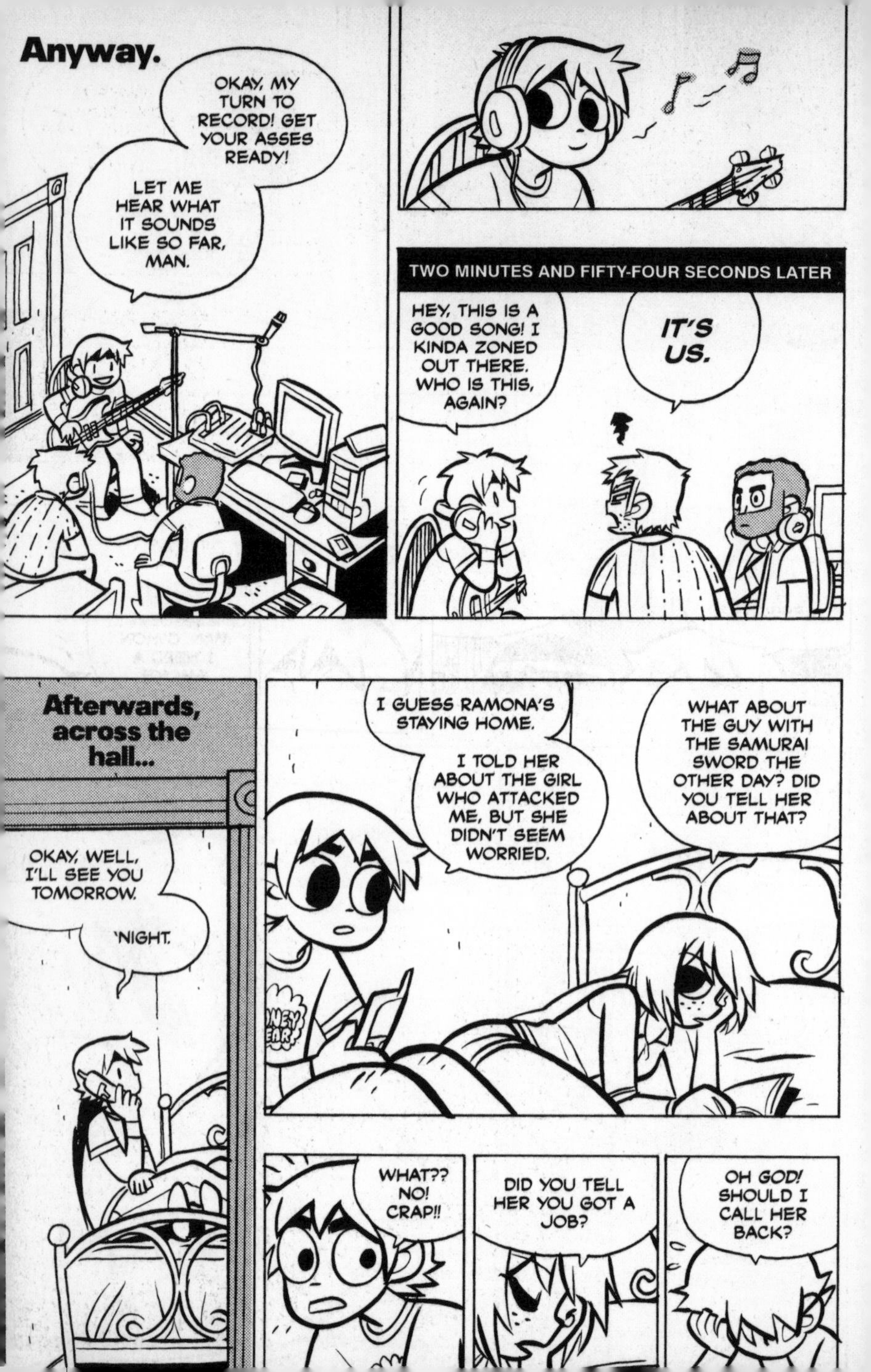
Anyway.
OKAY, MY TURN TO RECORD! GET YOUR ASSES READY!
LET ME HEAR WHAT IT SOUNDS LIKE SO FAR, MAN.
TWO MINUTES AND FIFTY-FOUR SECONDS LATER
HEY, THIS IS A GOOD SONG! I KINDA ZONED OUT THERE. WHO IS THIS, AGAIN?
IT'S US.
Afterwards, across the hall...
OKAY, WELL, I'LL SEE YOU TOMORROW.
'NIGHT.
I GUESS RAMONA'S STAYING HOME.
I TOLD HER ABOUT THE GIRL WHO ATTACKED ME, BUT SHE DIDN'T SEEM WORRIED.
WHAT ABOUT THE GUY WITH THE SAMURAI SWORD THE OTHER DAY? DID YOU TELL HER ABOUT THAT?
WHAT?? NO! CRAP!!
DID YOU TELL HER YOU GOT A JOB?
OH GOD! SHOULD I CALL HER BACK?

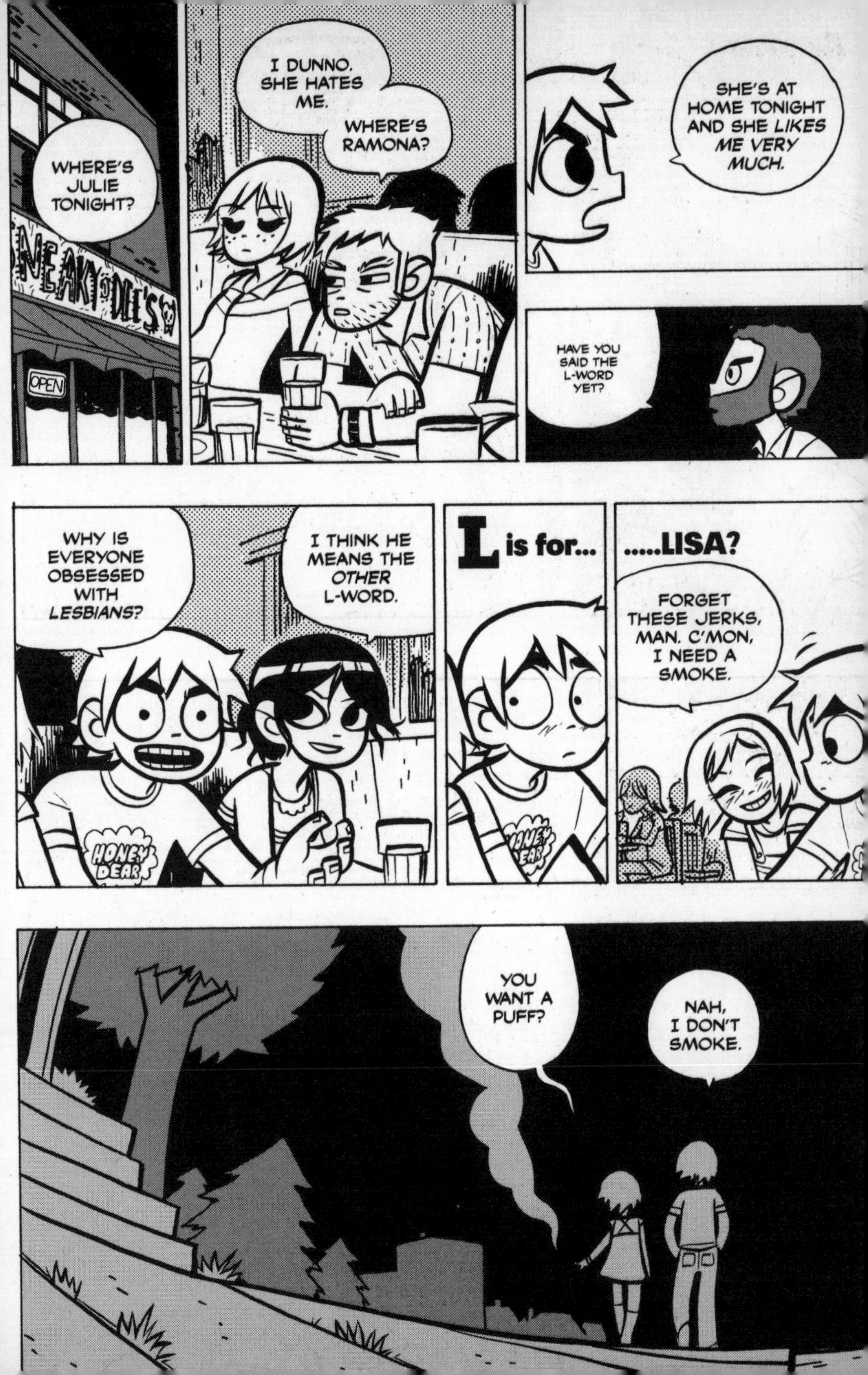
WHERE'S JULIE TONIGHT?
SNEAKY DEE'S
OPEN
I DUNNO. SHE HATES ME.
WHERE'S RAMONA?
SHE'S AT HOME TONIGHT AND SHE *LIKES ME VERY MUCH.*
HAVE YOU SAID THE L-WORD YET?
WHY IS EVERYONE OBSESSED WITH *LESBIANS?*
I THINK HE MEANS THE *OTHER* L-WORD.
HONEY DEAR
L is for...
.....LISA?
FORGET THESE JERKS, MAN. C'MON, I NEED A SMOKE.
YOU WANT A PUFF?
NAH, I DON'T SMOKE.

IS THAT LIKE A MORAL HIGH GROUND THING, OR ARE YOU JUST A PUSSY?

SMOKING IS... IT'S EVIL, RIGHT?

WHO SMOKES?

SO RAMONA STAYED HOME, EH? YOU DON'T THINK THAT'S A BAD SIGN?

SHE'S ALLOWED.

YOU WANT A PUFF?

HUH? UH... NO. I *SAID* NO, DIDN'T I?

St. Larson Catholic Primary School

St. Hope Larson Catholic Primary School

SCOTT...

YEAH?

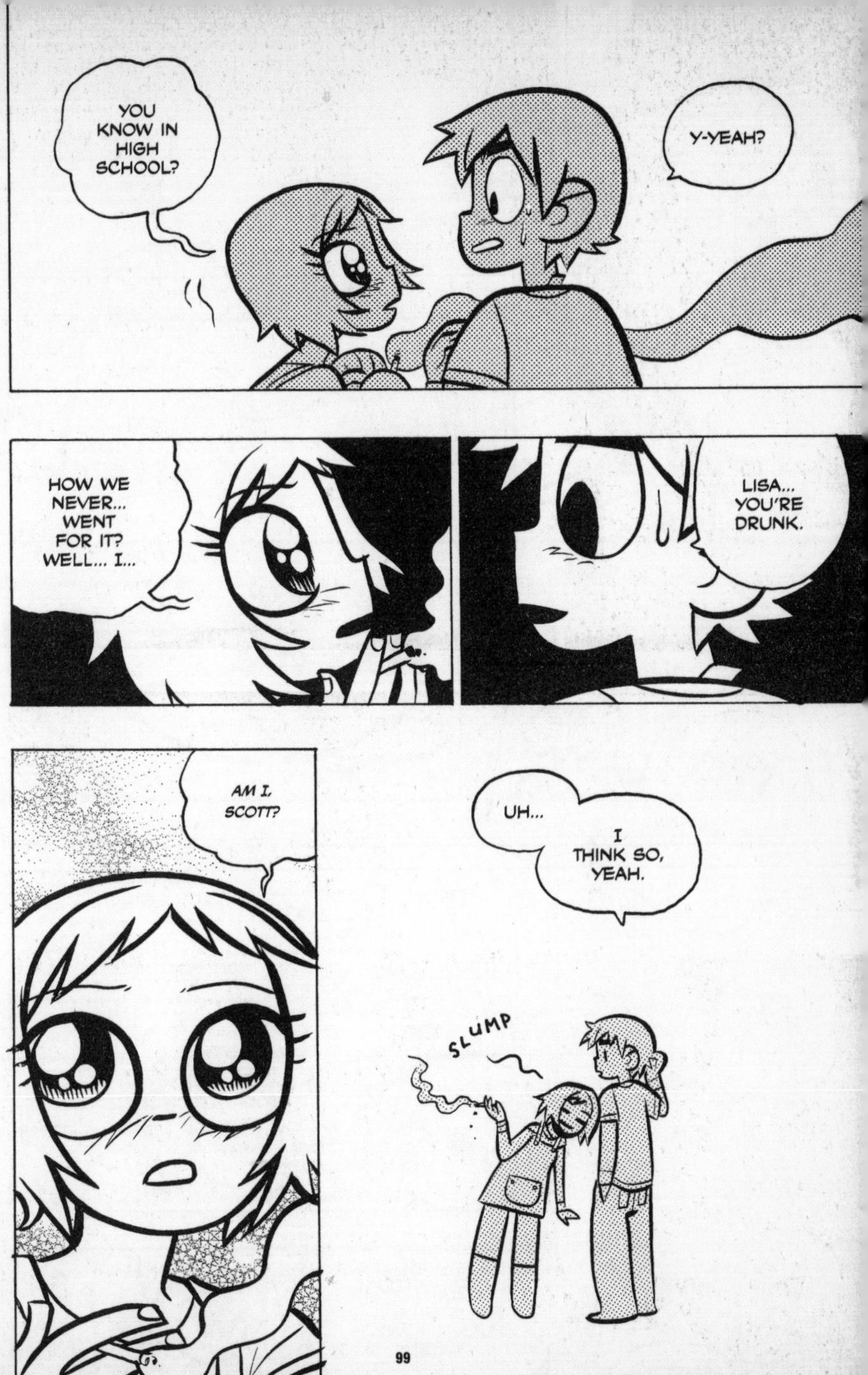
YOU KNOW IN HIGH SCHOOL?
Y-YEAH?
HOW WE NEVER... WENT FOR IT? WELL... I...
LISA... YOU'RE DRUNK.
AM I, SCOTT?
UH...
I THINK SO, YEAH.
SLUMP

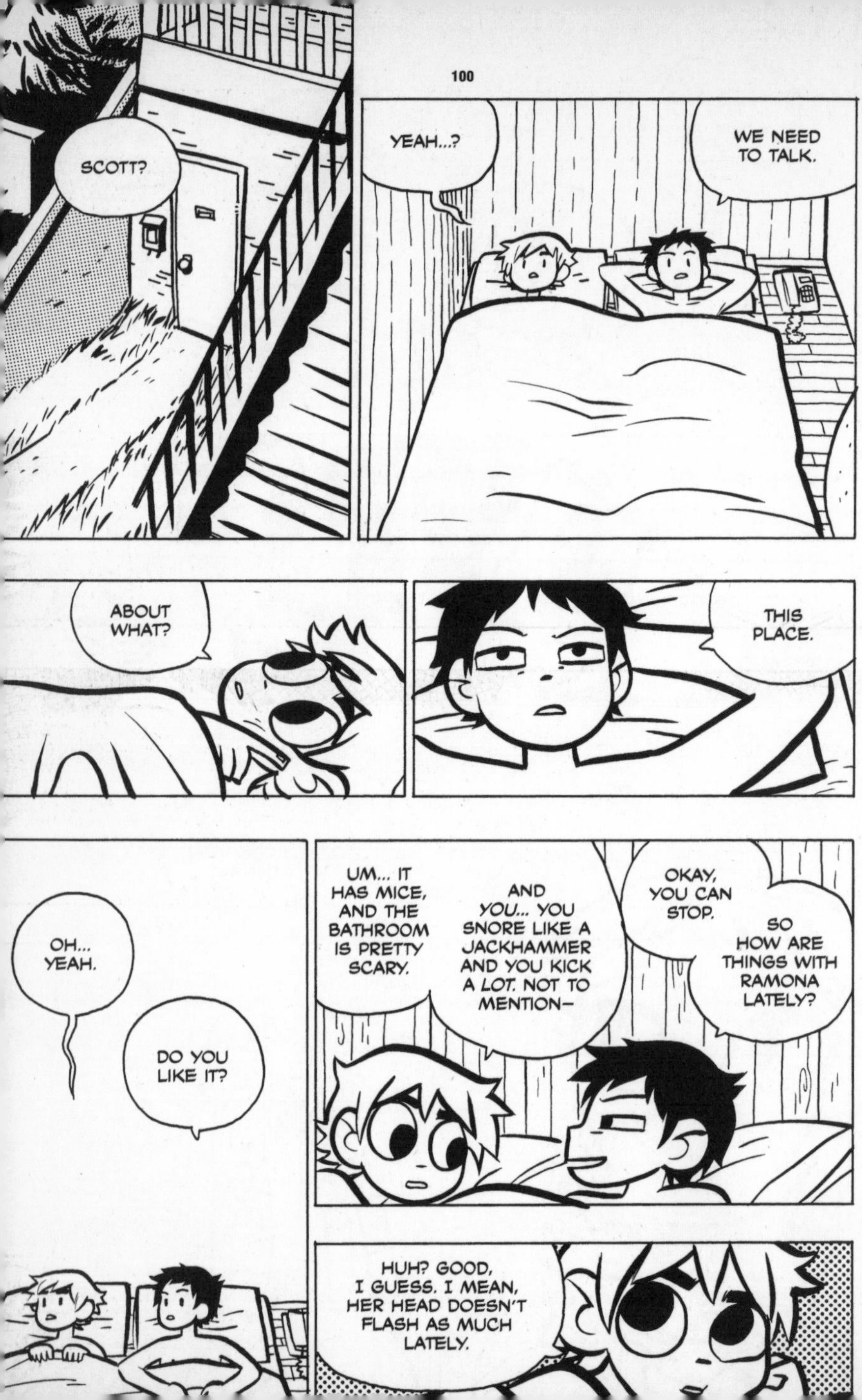
SCOTT?
YEAH...?
WE NEED TO TALK.
ABOUT WHAT?
THIS PLACE.
OH... YEAH.
DO YOU LIKE IT?
UM... IT HAS MICE, AND THE BATHROOM IS PRETTY SCARY.
AND YOU... YOU SNORE LIKE A JACKHAMMER AND YOU KICK A LOT. NOT TO MENTION–
OKAY, YOU CAN STOP.
SO HOW ARE THINGS WITH RAMONA LATELY?
HUH? GOOD, I GUESS. I MEAN, HER HEAD DOESN'T FLASH AS MUCH LATELY.

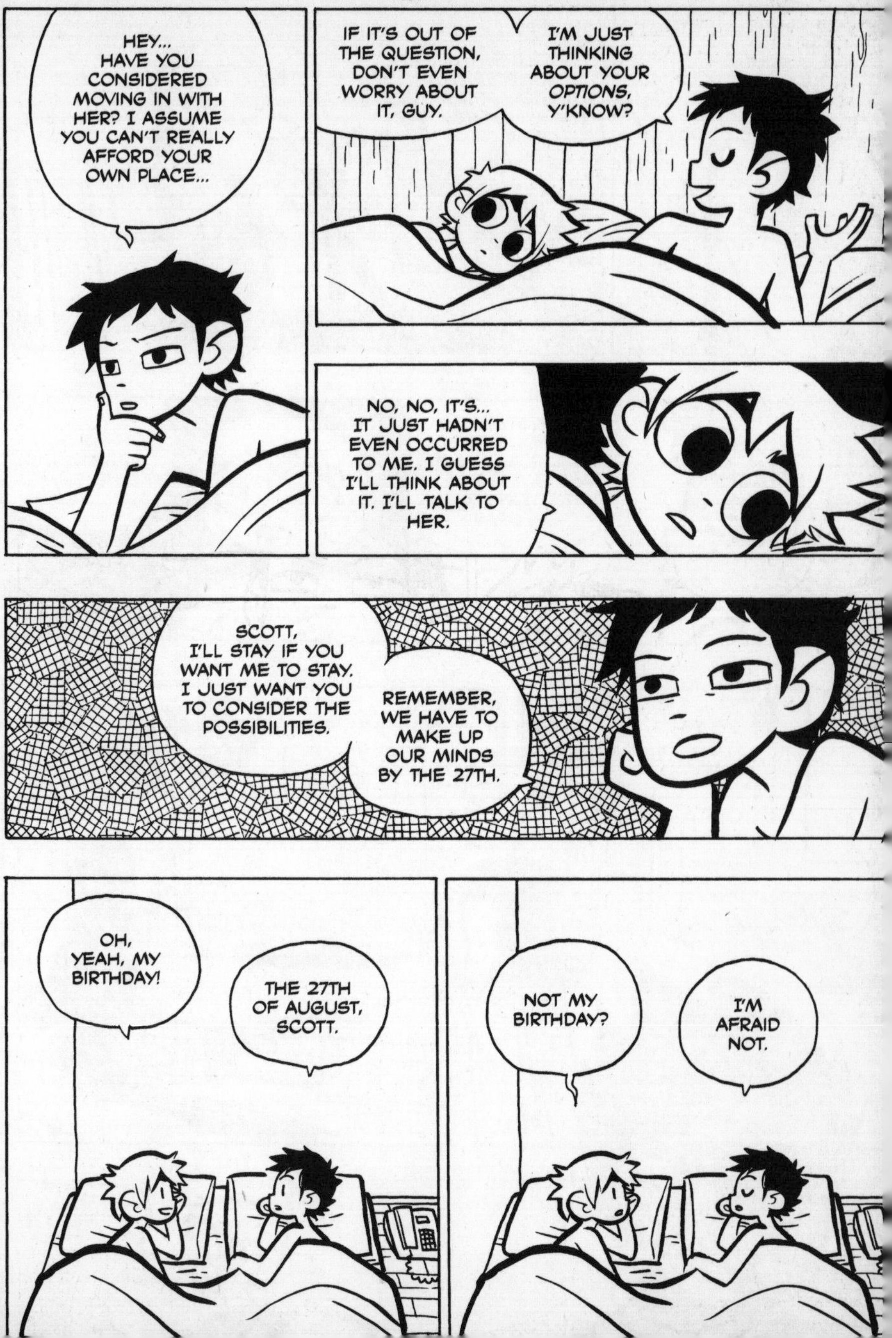
HEY... HAVE YOU CONSIDERED MOVING IN WITH HER? I ASSUME YOU CAN'T REALLY AFFORD YOUR OWN PLACE...
IF IT'S OUT OF THE QUESTION, DON'T EVEN WORRY ABOUT IT, GUY.
I'M JUST THINKING ABOUT YOUR *OPTIONS*, Y'KNOW?
NO, NO, IT'S... IT JUST HADN'T EVEN OCCURRED TO ME. I GUESS I'LL THINK ABOUT IT. I'LL TALK TO HER.
SCOTT, I'LL STAY IF YOU WANT ME TO STAY. I JUST WANT YOU TO CONSIDER THE POSSIBILITIES.
REMEMBER, WE HAVE TO MAKE UP OUR MINDS BY THE 27TH.
OH, YEAH, MY BIRTHDAY!
THE 27TH OF AUGUST, SCOTT.
NOT MY BIRTHDAY?
I'M AFRAID NOT.

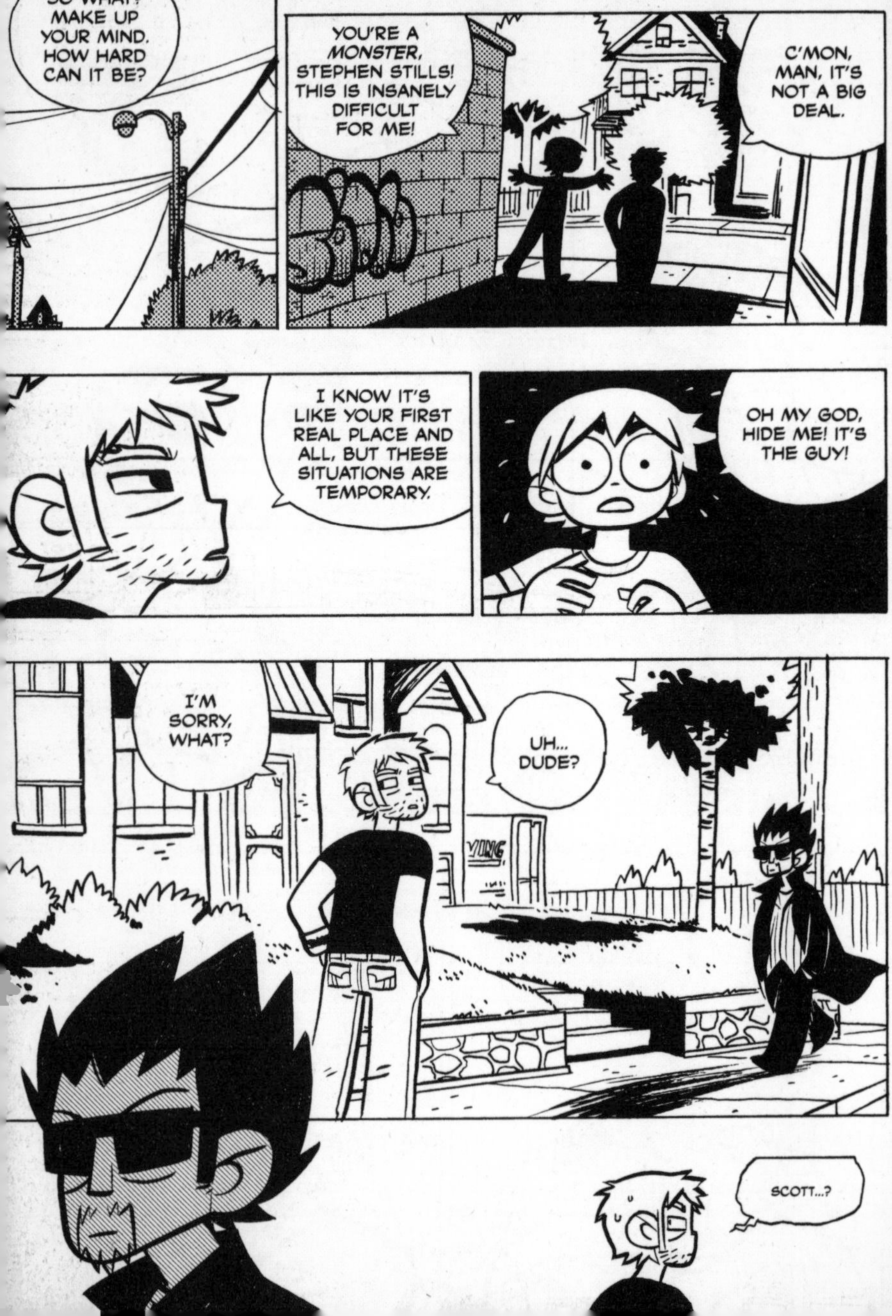
SO WHAT? MAKE UP YOUR MIND. HOW HARD CAN IT BE?
YOU'RE A *MONSTER*, STEPHEN STILLS! THIS IS INSANELY DIFFICULT FOR ME!
C'MON, MAN, IT'S NOT A BIG DEAL.
I KNOW IT'S LIKE YOUR FIRST REAL PLACE AND ALL, BUT THESE SITUATIONS ARE TEMPORARY.
OH MY GOD, HIDE ME! IT'S THE GUY!
I'M SORRY, WHAT?
UH... DUDE?
SCOTT...?

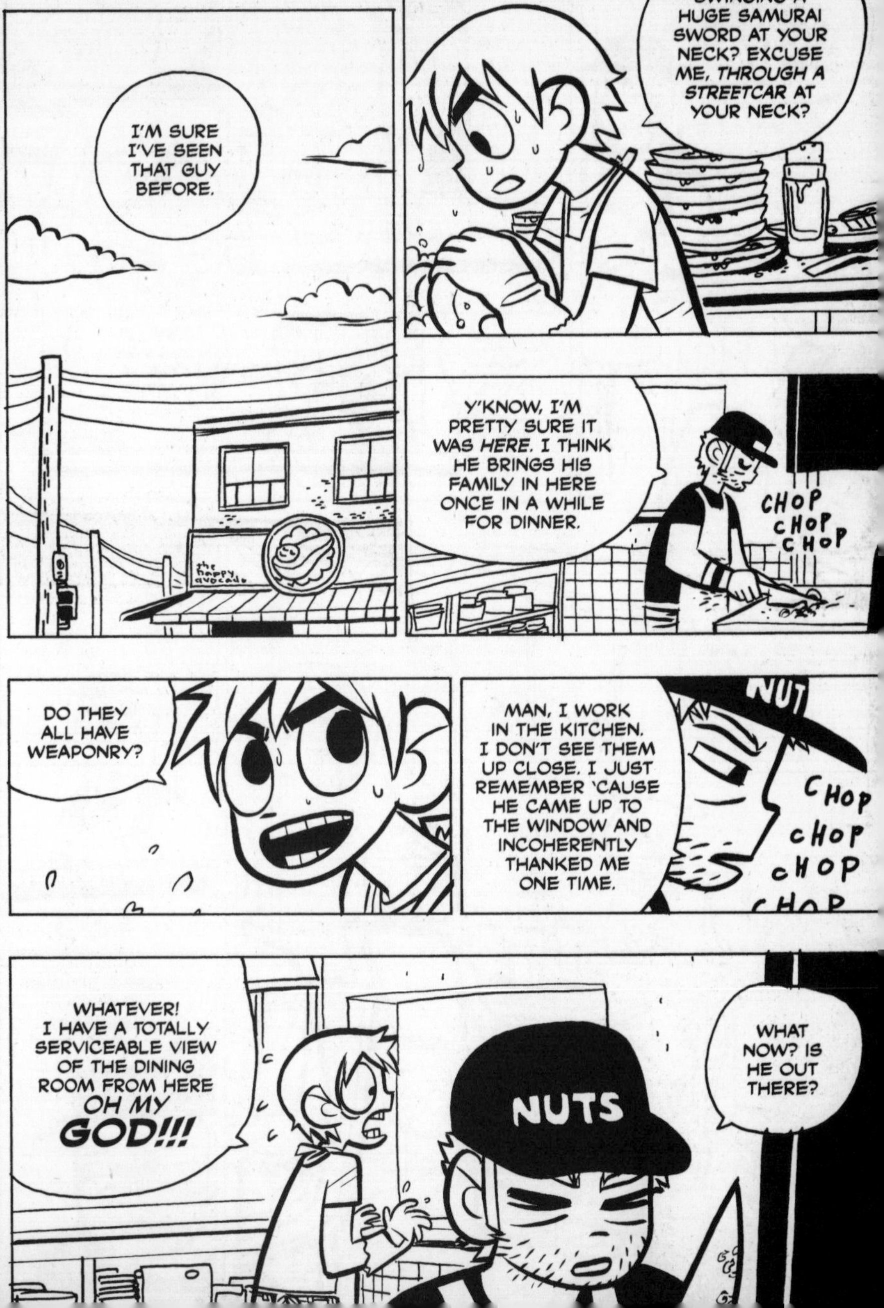

I'M SURE I'VE SEEN THAT GUY BEFORE.
the happy avocado
WAS HE SWINGING A HUGE SAMURAI SWORD AT YOUR NECK? EXCUSE ME, *THROUGH A STREETCAR* AT YOUR NECK?
Y'KNOW, I'M PRETTY SURE IT WAS *HERE*. I THINK HE BRINGS HIS FAMILY IN HERE ONCE IN A WHILE FOR DINNER.
CHOP CHOP CHOP
DO THEY ALL HAVE WEAPONRY?
MAN, I WORK IN THE KITCHEN. I DON'T SEE THEM UP CLOSE. I JUST REMEMBER 'CAUSE HE CAME UP TO THE WINDOW AND INCOHERENTLY THANKED ME ONE TIME.
CHOP CHOP CHOP
WHATEVER! I HAVE A TOTALLY SERVICEABLE VIEW OF THE DINING ROOM FROM HERE *OH MY* ***GOD!!!***
NUTS
WHAT NOW? IS HE OUT THERE?

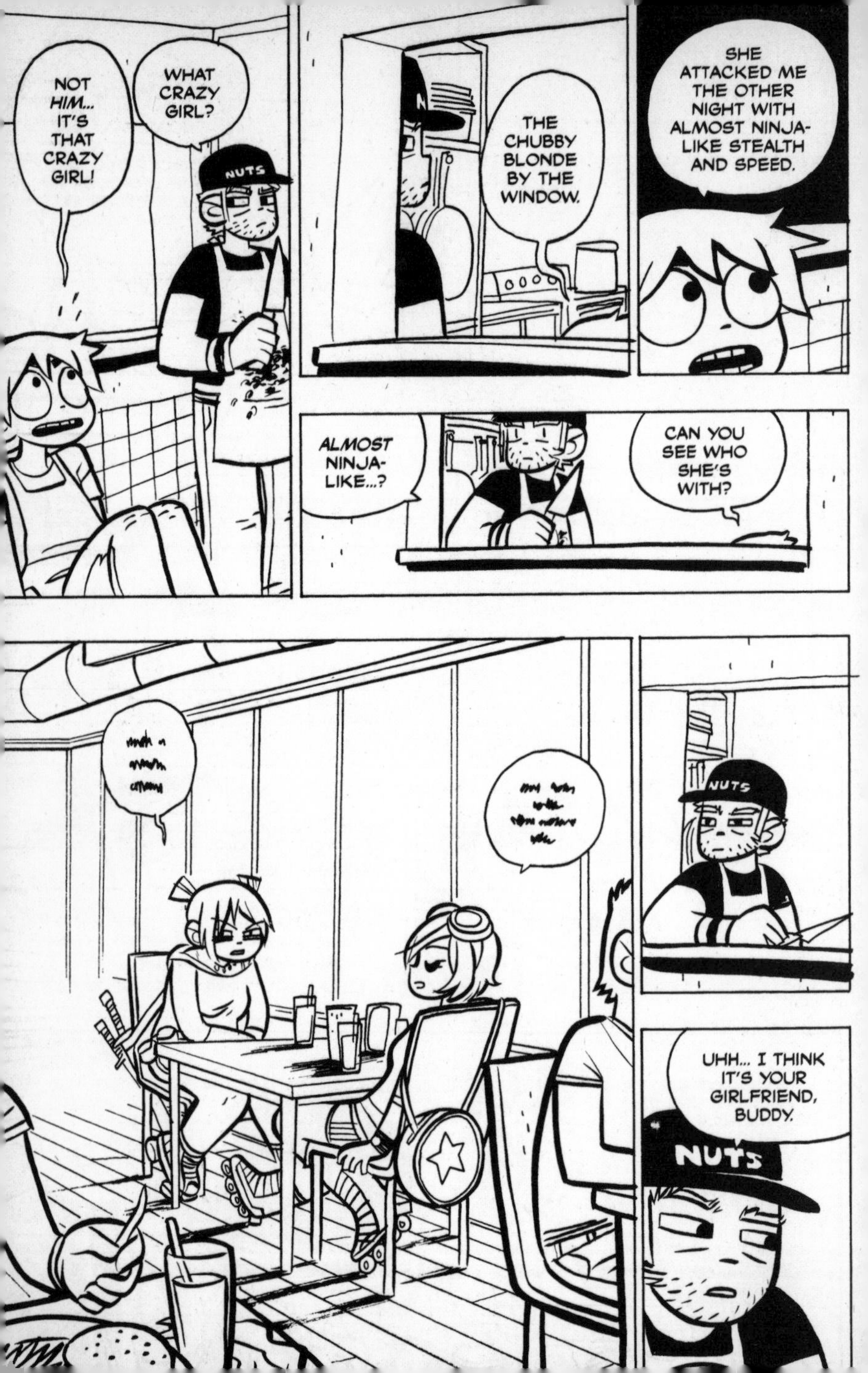
NOT *HIM*... IT'S THAT CRAZY GIRL!
WHAT CRAZY GIRL?
NUTS
THE CHUBBY BLONDE BY THE WINDOW.
SHE ATTACKED ME THE OTHER NIGHT WITH ALMOST NINJA-LIKE STEALTH AND SPEED.
ALMOST NINJA-LIKE...?
CAN YOU SEE WHO SHE'S WITH?
NUTS
UHH... I THINK IT'S YOUR GIRLFRIEND, BUDDY.
NUTS

We now join their conversation, already in progress...

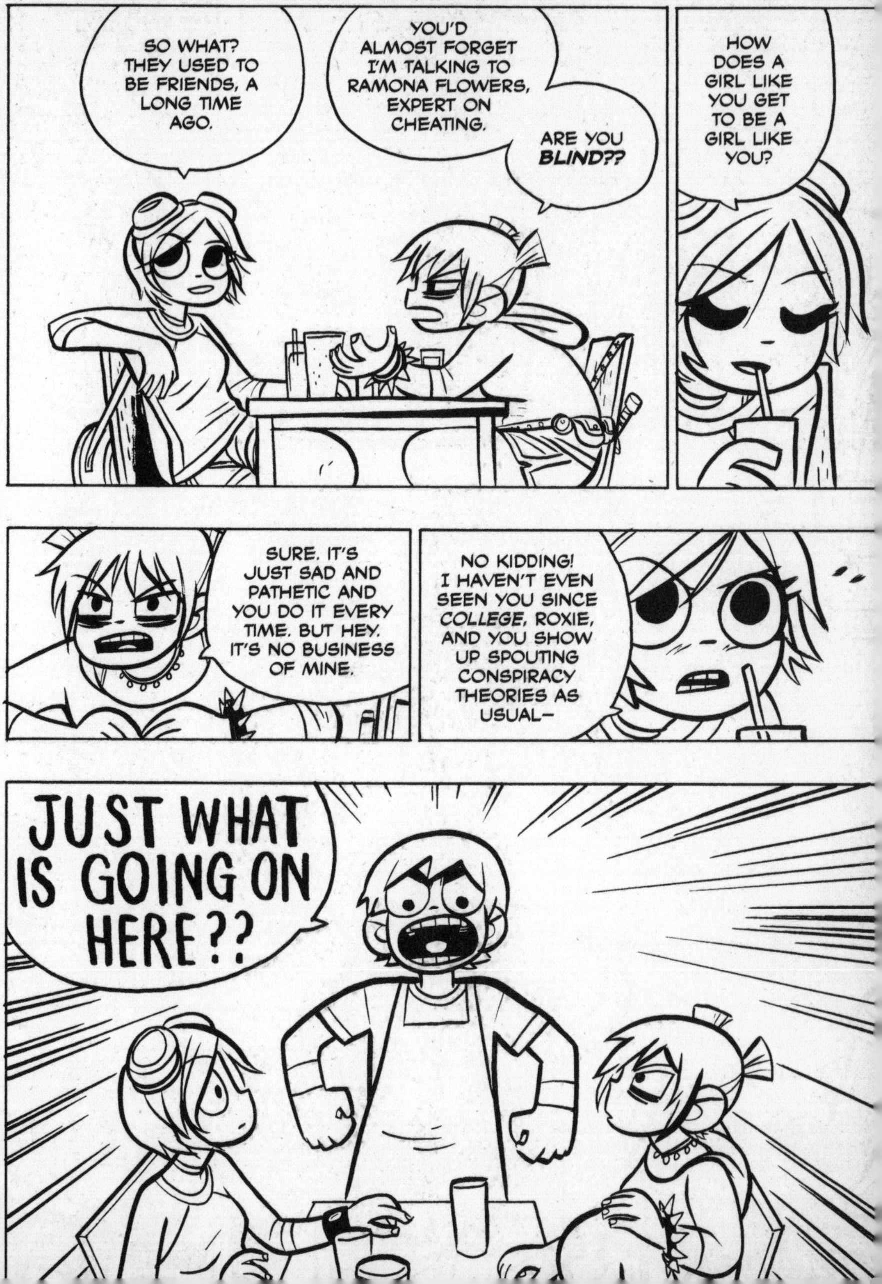
SO WHAT? THEY USED TO BE FRIENDS, A LONG TIME AGO.
YOU'D ALMOST FORGET I'M TALKING TO RAMONA FLOWERS, EXPERT ON CHEATING.
ARE YOU *BLIND??*
HOW DOES A GIRL LIKE YOU GET TO BE A GIRL LIKE YOU?
SURE. IT'S JUST SAD AND PATHETIC AND YOU DO IT EVERY TIME. BUT HEY. IT'S NO BUSINESS OF MINE.
NO KIDDING! I HAVEN'T EVEN SEEN YOU SINCE *COLLEGE*, ROXIE, AND YOU SHOW UP SPOUTING CONSPIRACY THEORIES AS USUAL–
JUST WHAT IS GOING ON HERE??

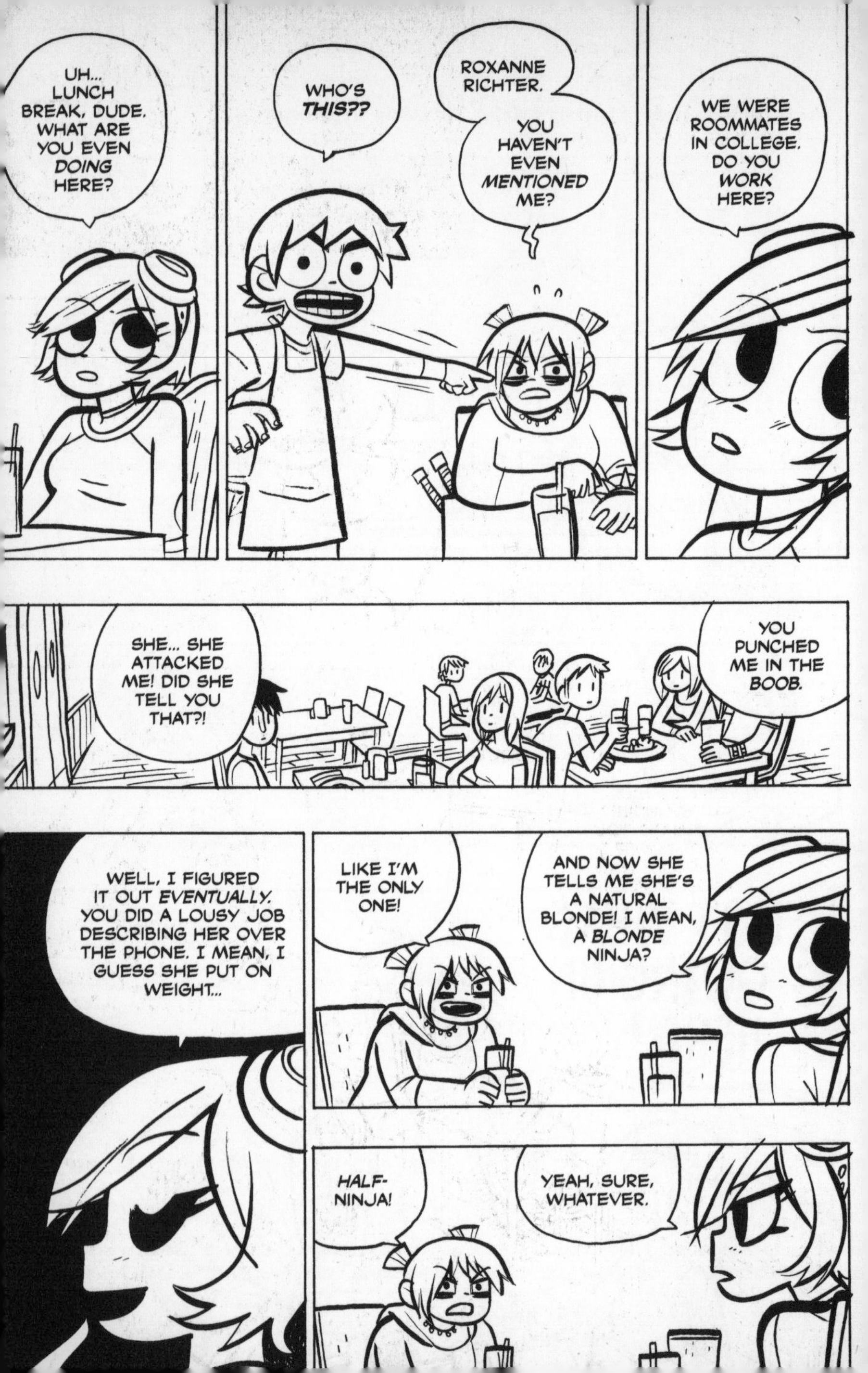
UH... LUNCH BREAK, DUDE. WHAT ARE YOU EVEN *DOING* HERE?
WHO'S *THIS??*
ROXANNE RICHTER.
YOU HAVEN'T EVEN *MENTIONED* ME?
WE WERE ROOMMATES IN COLLEGE. DO YOU *WORK* HERE?
SHE... SHE ATTACKED ME! DID SHE TELL YOU THAT?!
YOU PUNCHED ME IN THE *BOOB.*
WELL, I FIGURED IT OUT *EVENTUALLY.* YOU DID A LOUSY JOB DESCRIBING HER OVER THE PHONE. I MEAN, I GUESS SHE PUT ON WEIGHT...
LIKE I'M THE ONLY ONE!
AND NOW SHE TELLS ME SHE'S A NATURAL BLONDE! I MEAN, A *BLONDE* NINJA?
HALF- NINJA!
YEAH, SURE, WHATEVER.

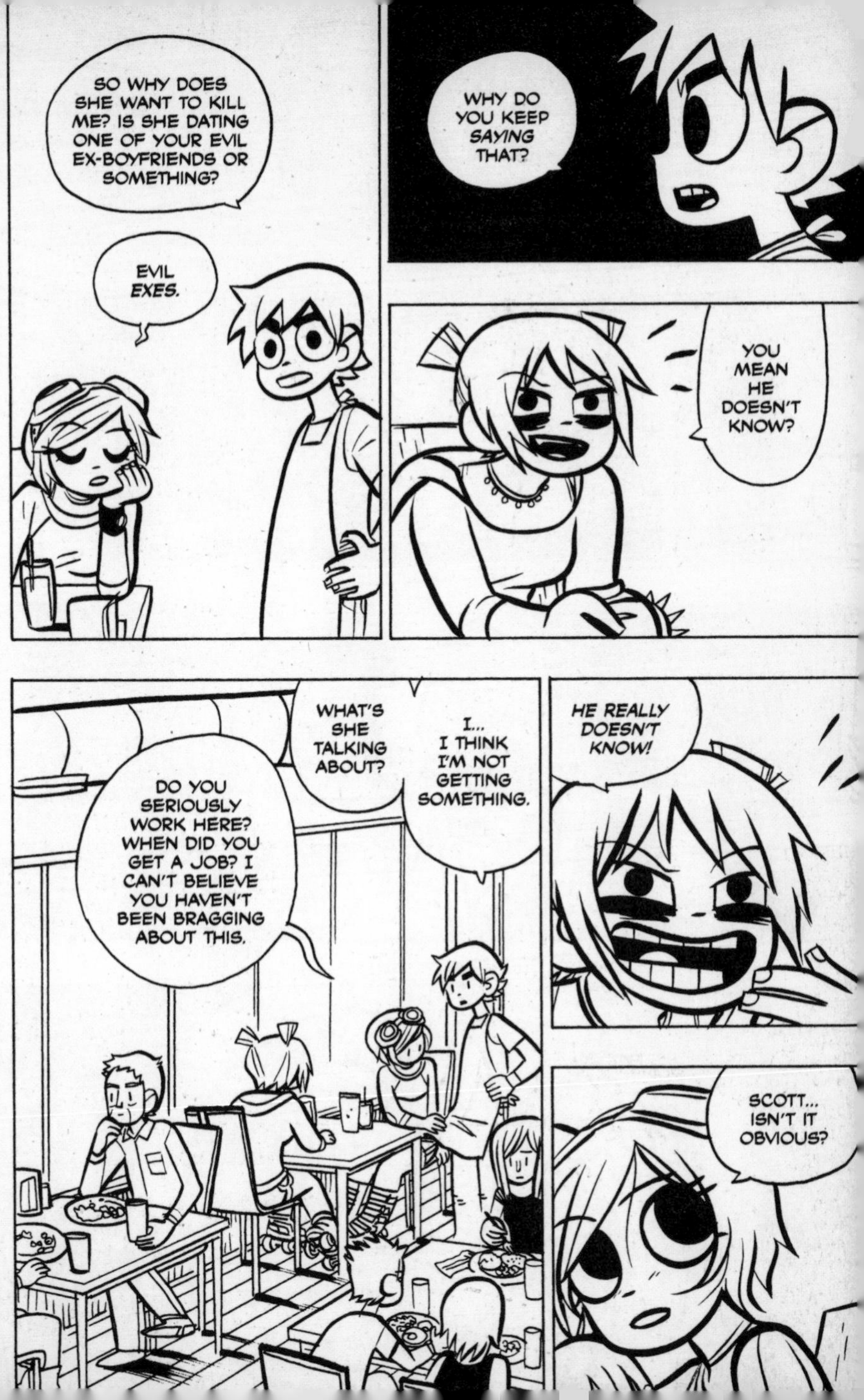
SO WHY DOES SHE WANT TO KILL ME? IS SHE DATING ONE OF YOUR EVIL EX-BOYFRIENDS OR SOMETHING?
EVIL *EXES.*
WHY DO YOU KEEP *SAYING* THAT?
YOU MEAN HE DOESN'T KNOW?
DO YOU SERIOUSLY WORK HERE? WHEN DID YOU GET A JOB? I CAN'T BELIEVE YOU HAVEN'T BEEN BRAGGING ABOUT THIS.
WHAT'S SHE TALKING ABOUT?
I... I THINK I'M NOT GETTING SOMETHING.
HE REALLY DOESN'T KNOW!
SCOTT... ISN'T IT OBVIOUS?

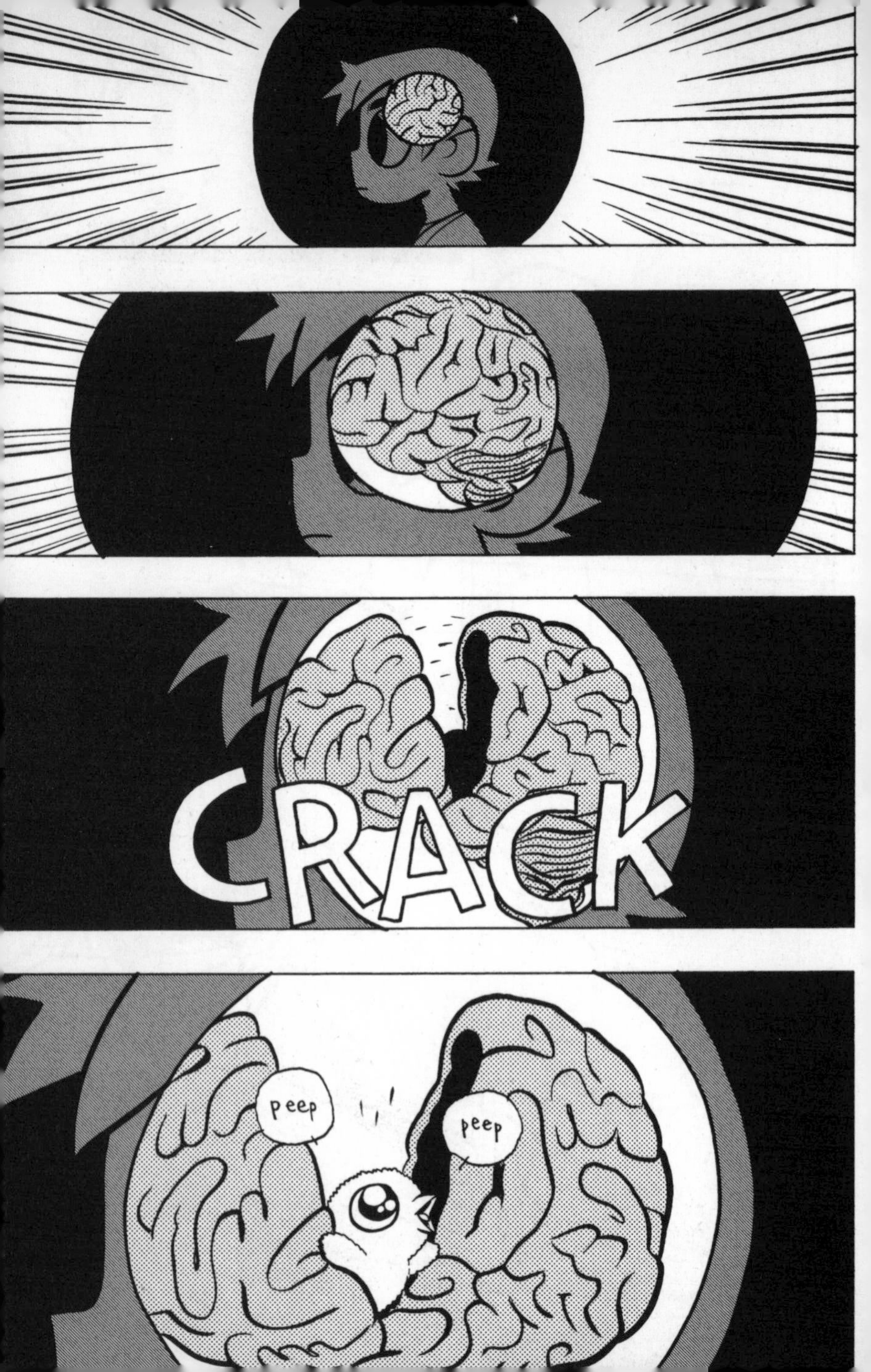
CRACK
peep
peep

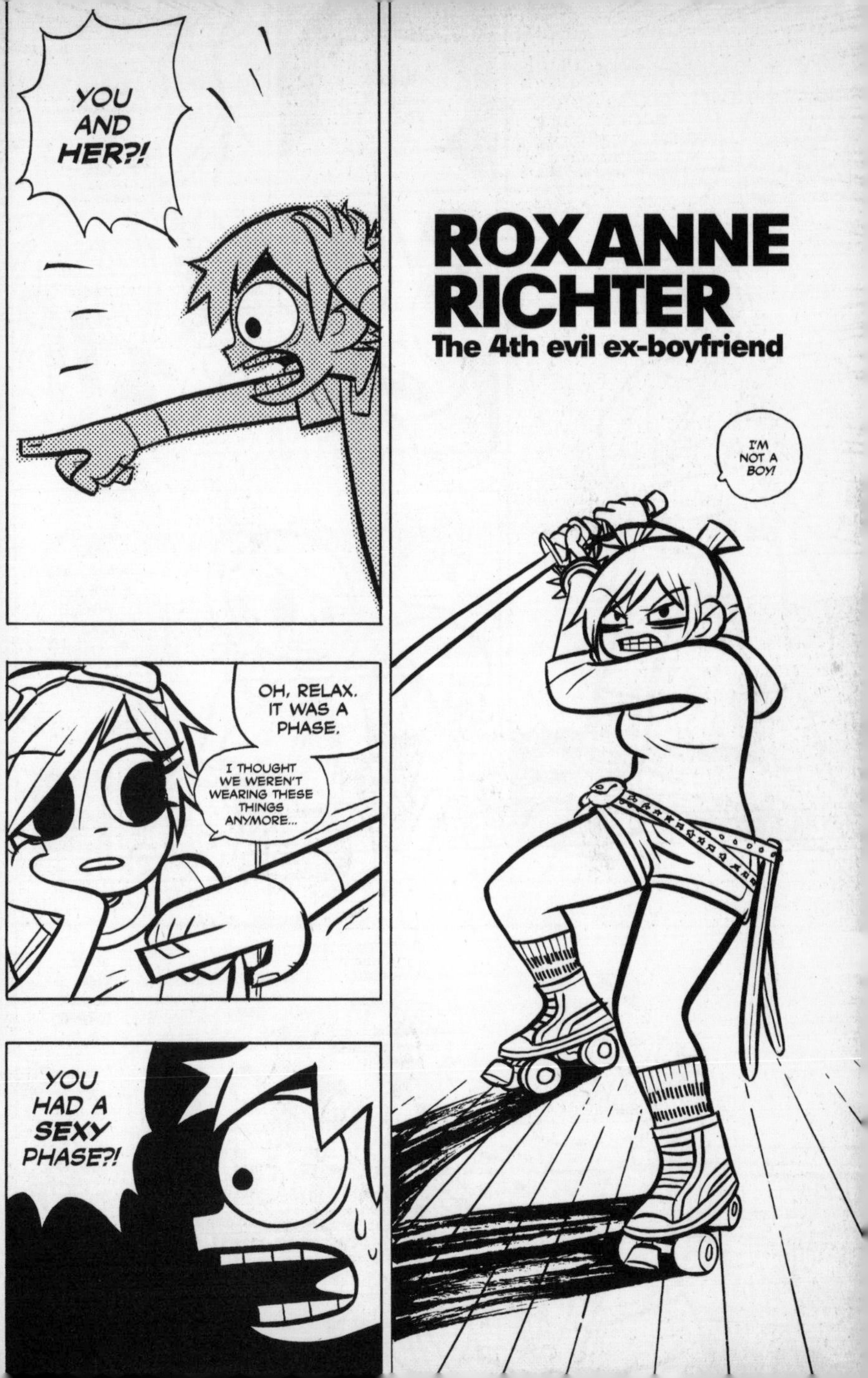

YOU AND HER?!
OH, RELAX. IT WAS A PHASE.
I THOUGHT WE WEREN'T WEARING THESE THINGS ANYMORE...
YOU HAD A SEXY PHASE?!
ROXANNE RICHTER
The 4th evil ex-boyfriend
I'M NOT A BOY!

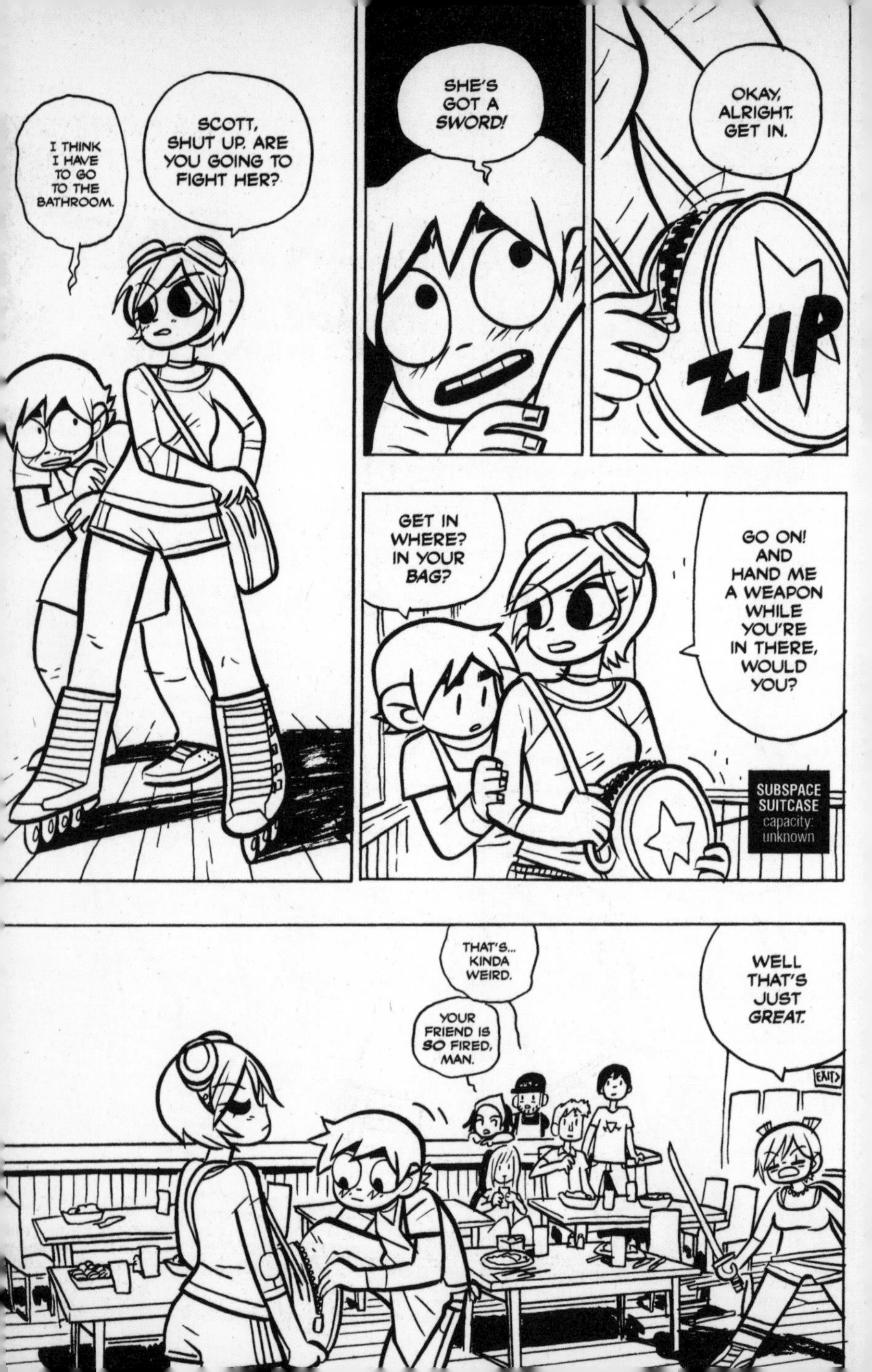
I THINK I HAVE TO GO TO THE BATHROOM.
SCOTT, SHUT UP. ARE YOU GOING TO FIGHT HER?
SHE'S GOT A SWORD!
OKAY, ALRIGHT. GET IN.
ZIP
GET IN WHERE? IN YOUR BAG?
GO ON! AND HAND ME A WEAPON WHILE YOU'RE IN THERE, WOULD YOU?
SUBSPACE SUITCASE capacity: unknown
THAT'S... KINDA WEIRD.
YOUR FRIEND IS SO FIRED, MAN.
WELL THAT'S JUST GREAT.
EXIT

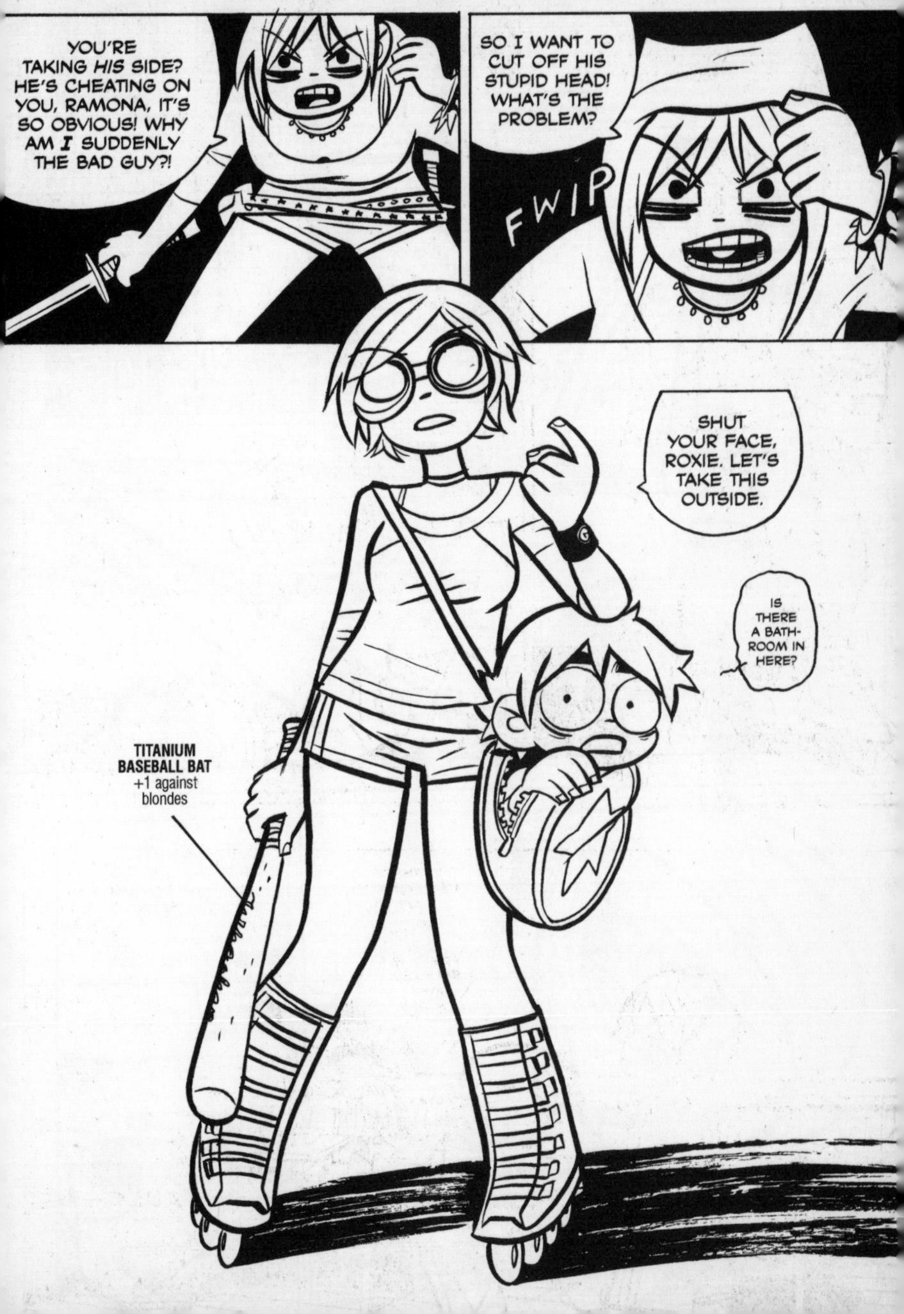
YOU'RE TAKING *HIS* SIDE? HE'S CHEATING ON YOU, RAMONA, IT'S SO OBVIOUS! WHY AM *I* SUDDENLY THE BAD GUY?!
SO I WANT TO CUT OFF HIS STUPID HEAD! WHAT'S THE PROBLEM?
FWIP
SHUT YOUR FACE, ROXIE. LET'S TAKE THIS OUTSIDE.
IS THERE A BATH-ROOM IN HERE?
TITANIUM BASEBALL BAT
+1 against blondes

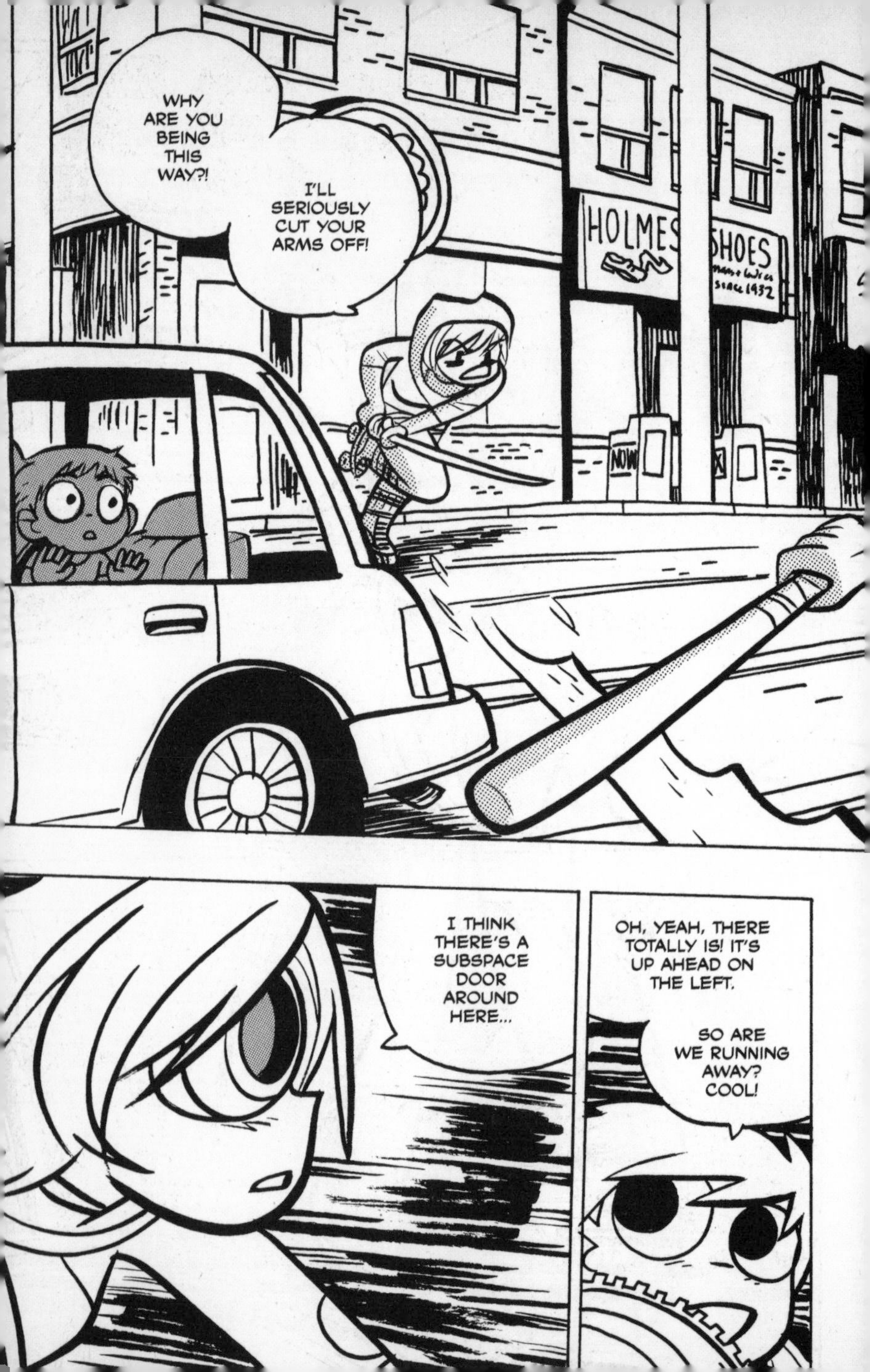
WHY ARE YOU BEING THIS WAY?!
I'LL SERIOUSLY CUT YOUR ARMS OFF!
HOLMES SHOES
SINCE 1932
NOW
I THINK THERE'S A SUBSPACE DOOR AROUND HERE...
OH, YEAH, THERE TOTALLY IS! IT'S UP AHEAD ON THE LEFT.
SO ARE WE RUNNING AWAY? COOL!

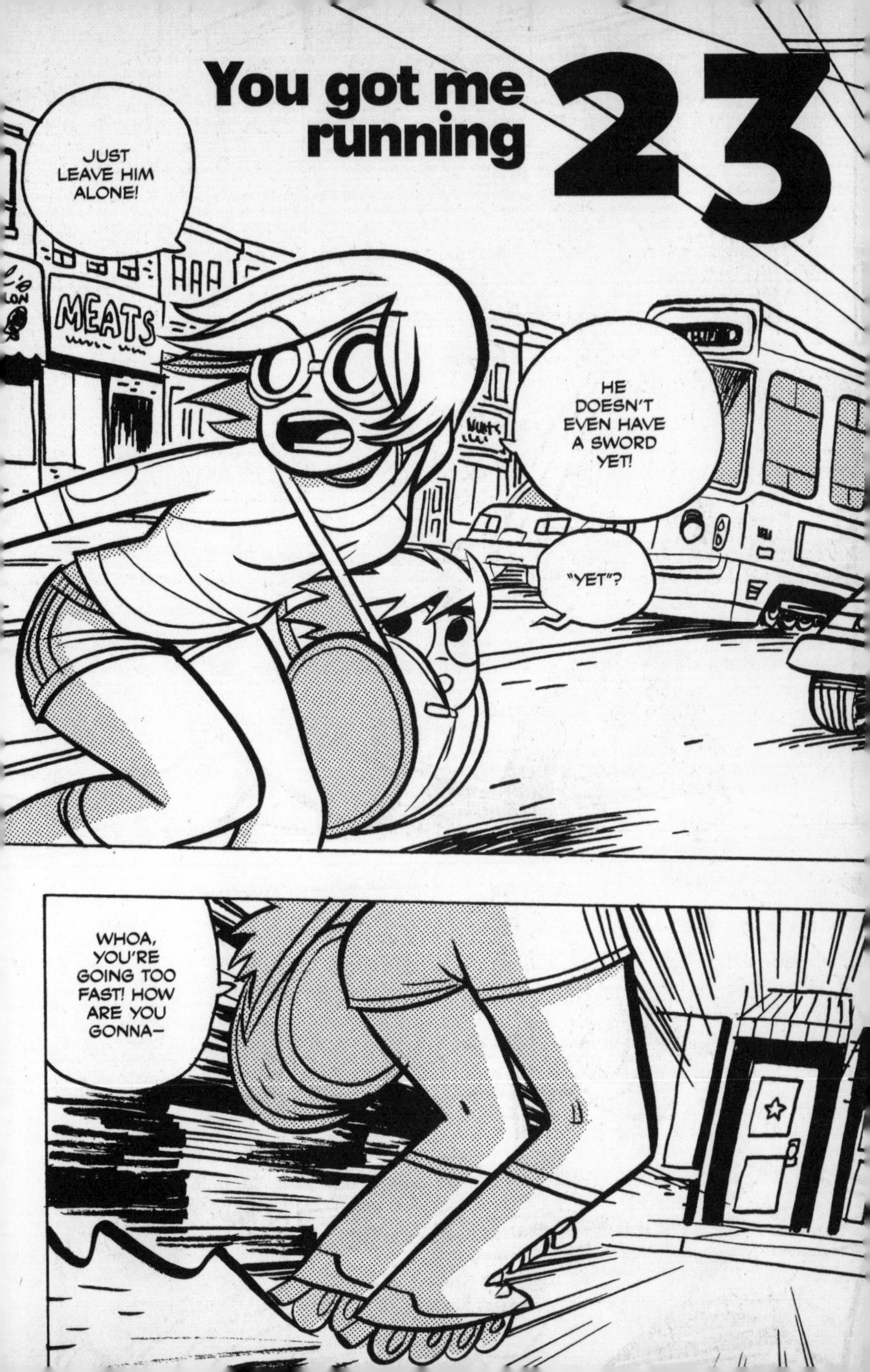
You got me running
23
JUST LEAVE HIM ALONE!
HE DOESN'T EVEN HAVE A SWORD YET!
"YET"?
MEATS
WHOA, YOU'RE GOING TOO FAST! HOW ARE YOU GONNA–

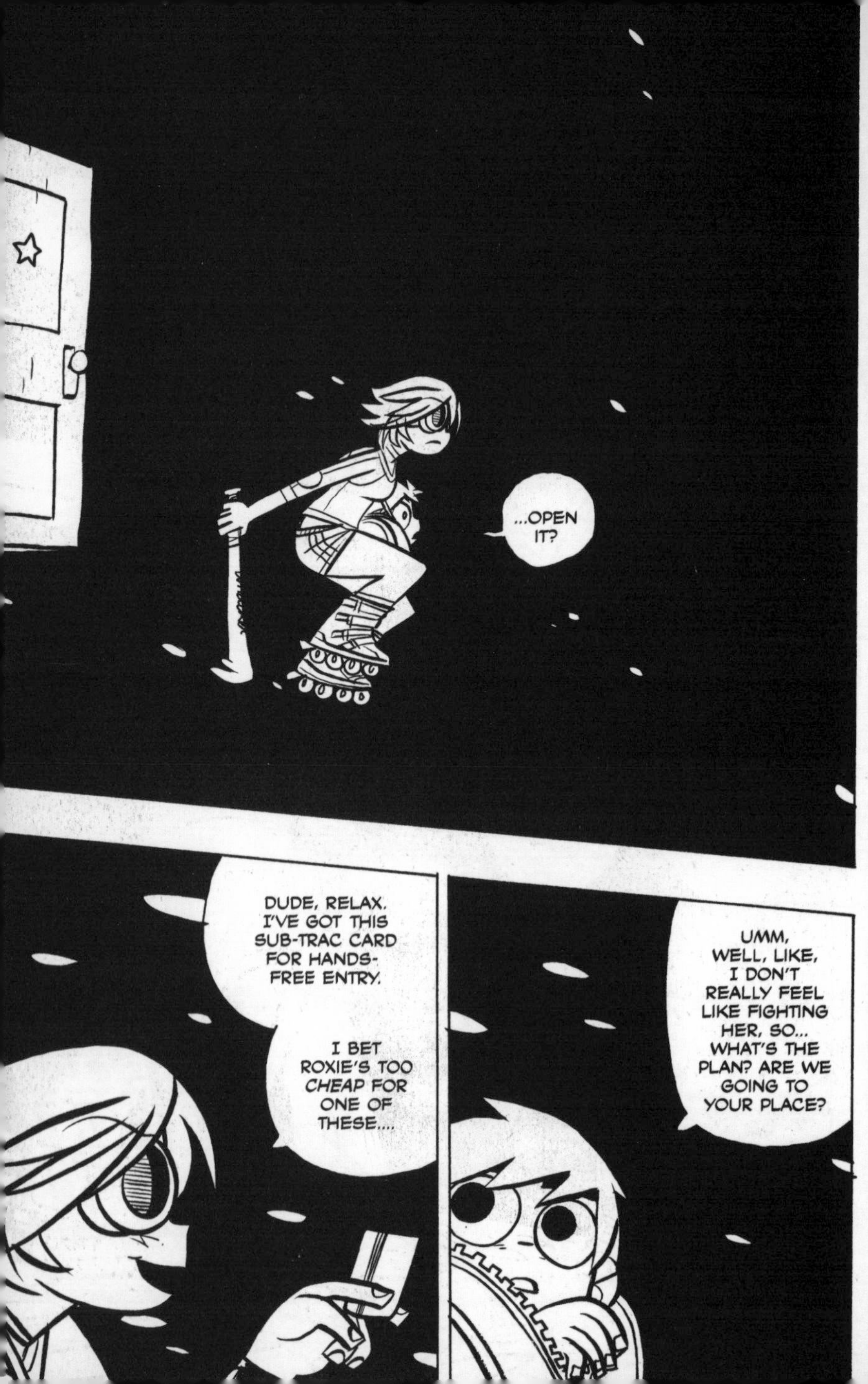
...OPEN IT?
DUDE, RELAX. I'VE GOT THIS SUB-TRAC CARD FOR HANDS-FREE ENTRY.
I BET ROXIE'S TOO *CHEAP* FOR ONE OF THESE....
UMM, WELL, LIKE, I DON'T REALLY FEEL LIKE FIGHTING HER, SO... WHAT'S THE PLAN? ARE WE GOING TO YOUR PLACE?

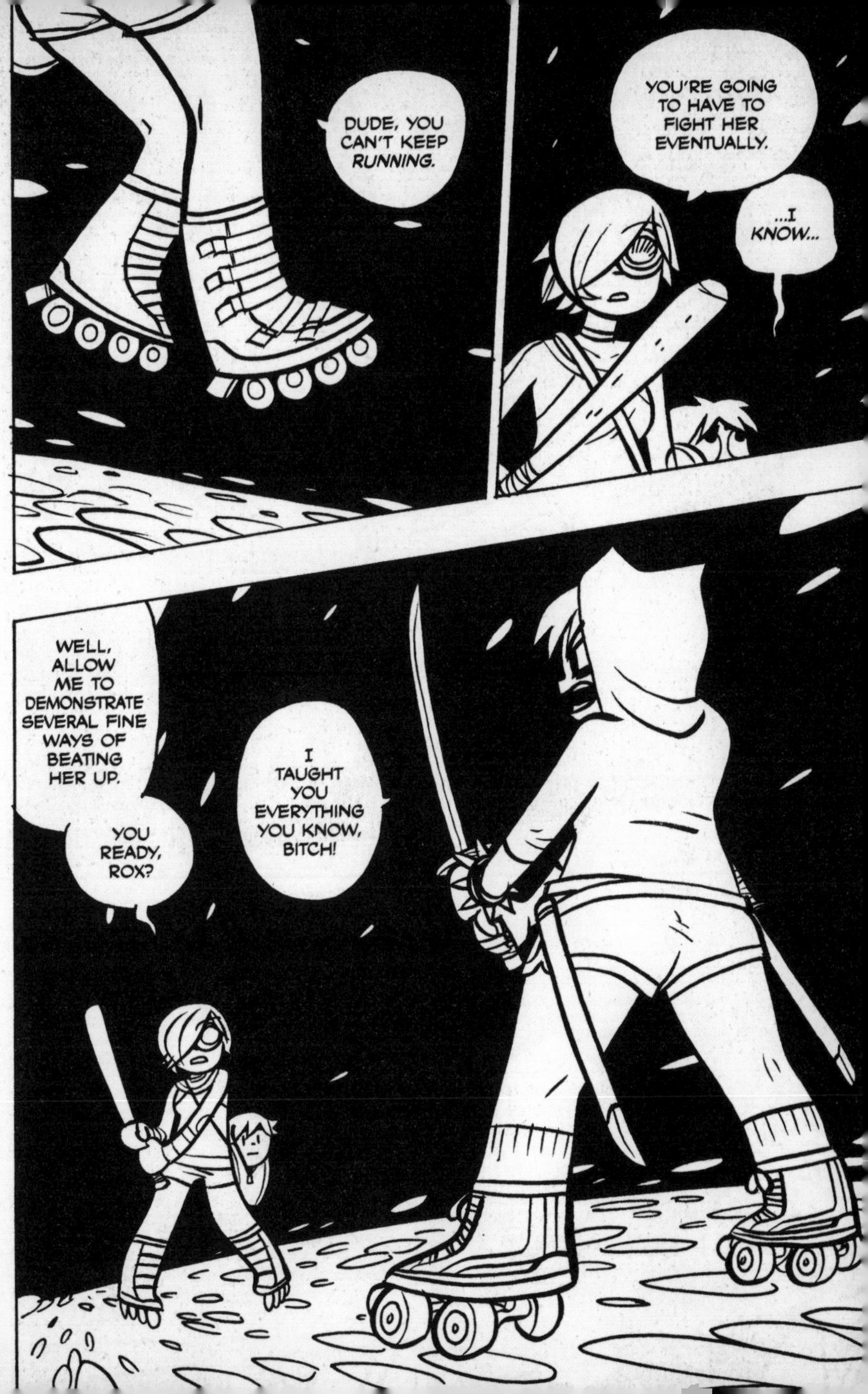
DUDE, YOU CAN'T KEEP *RUNNING.*
YOU'RE GOING TO HAVE TO FIGHT HER EVENTUALLY.
...I KNOW...
WELL, ALLOW ME TO DEMONSTRATE SEVERAL FINE WAYS OF BEATING HER UP.
YOU READY, ROX?
I TAUGHT YOU EVERYTHING YOU KNOW, BITCH!

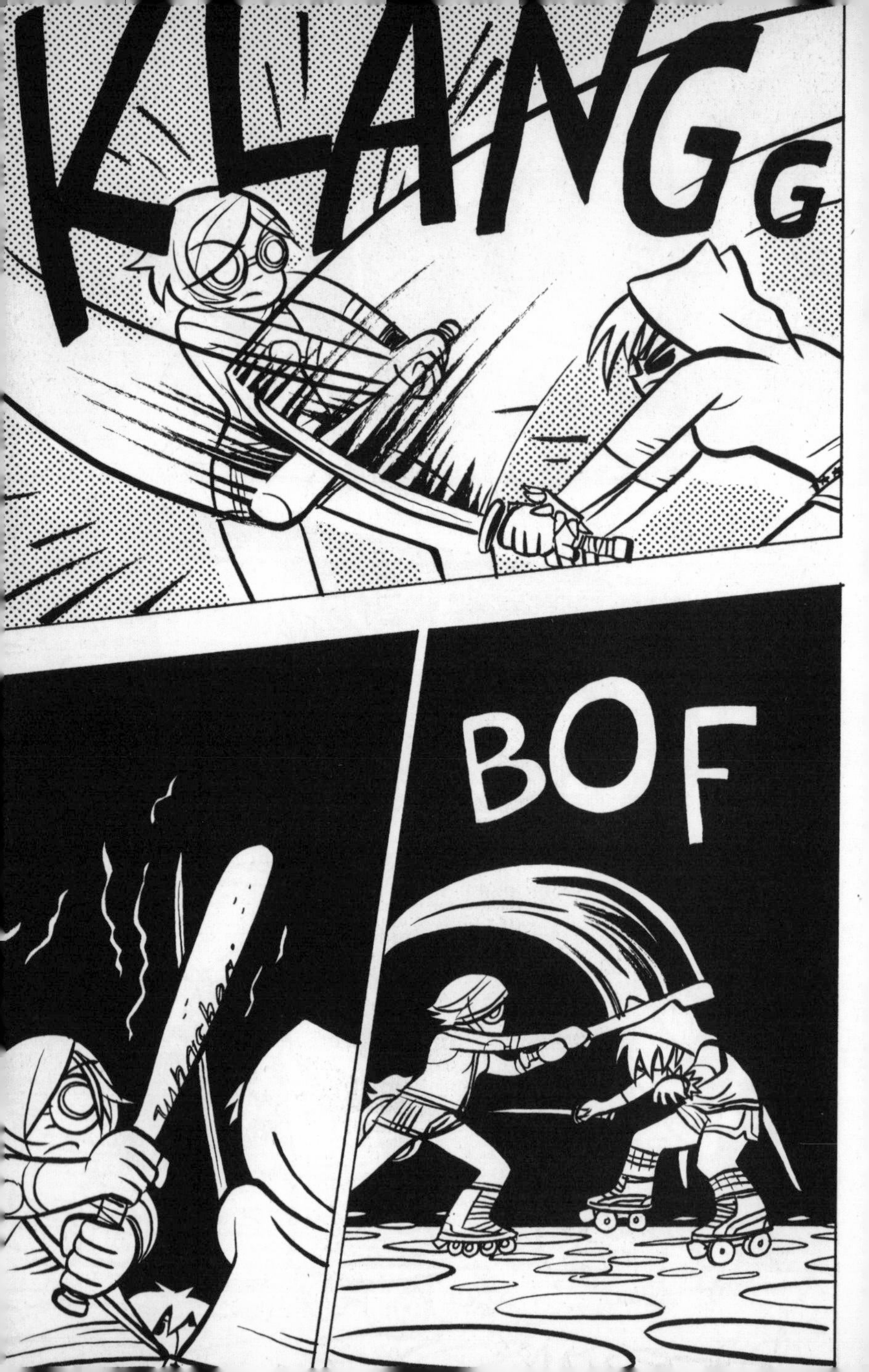
KLANGG
BOF

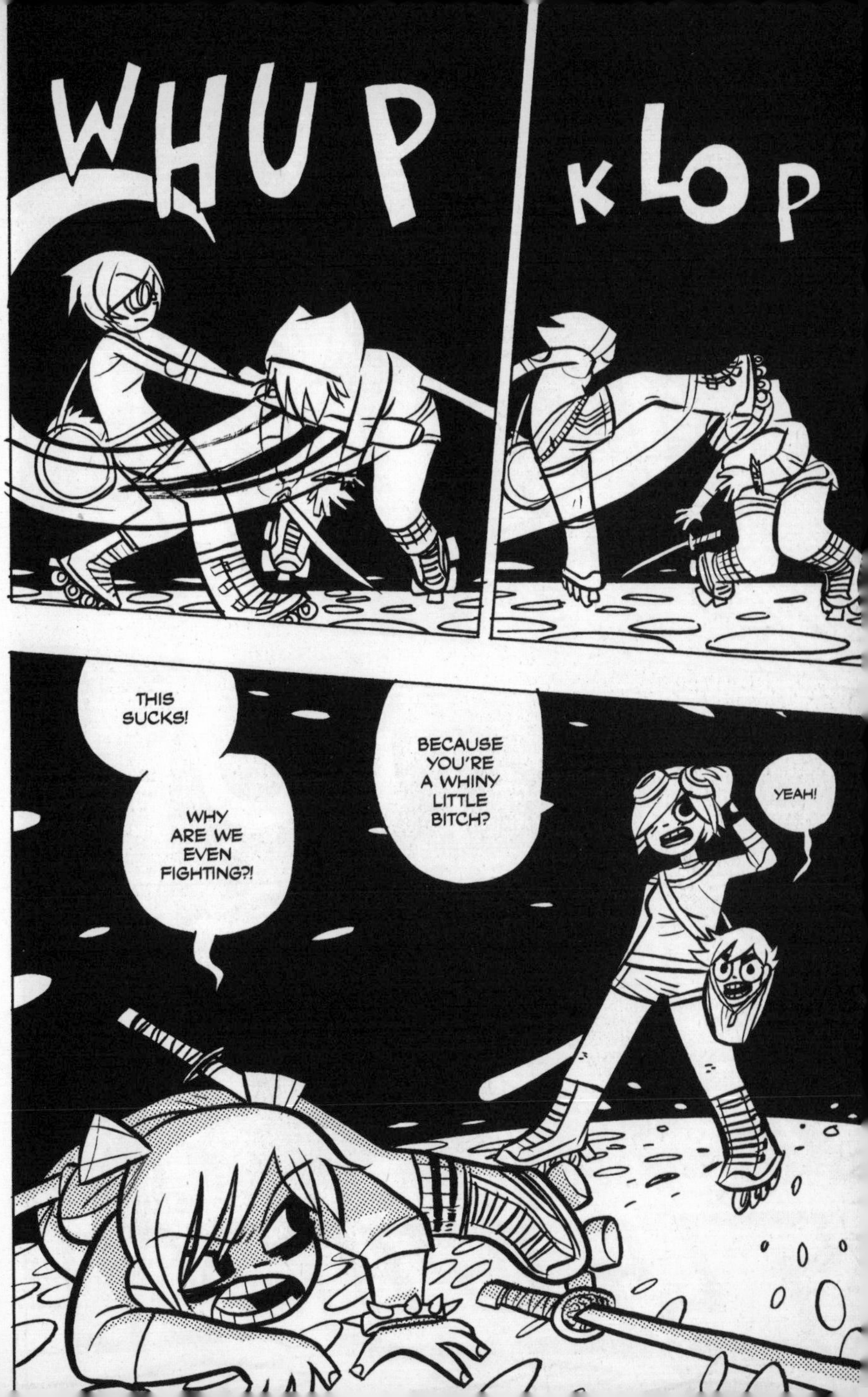
WHUP
KLOP
THIS SUCKS!
WHY ARE WE EVEN FIGHTING?!
BECAUSE YOU'RE A WHINY LITTLE BITCH?
YEAH!

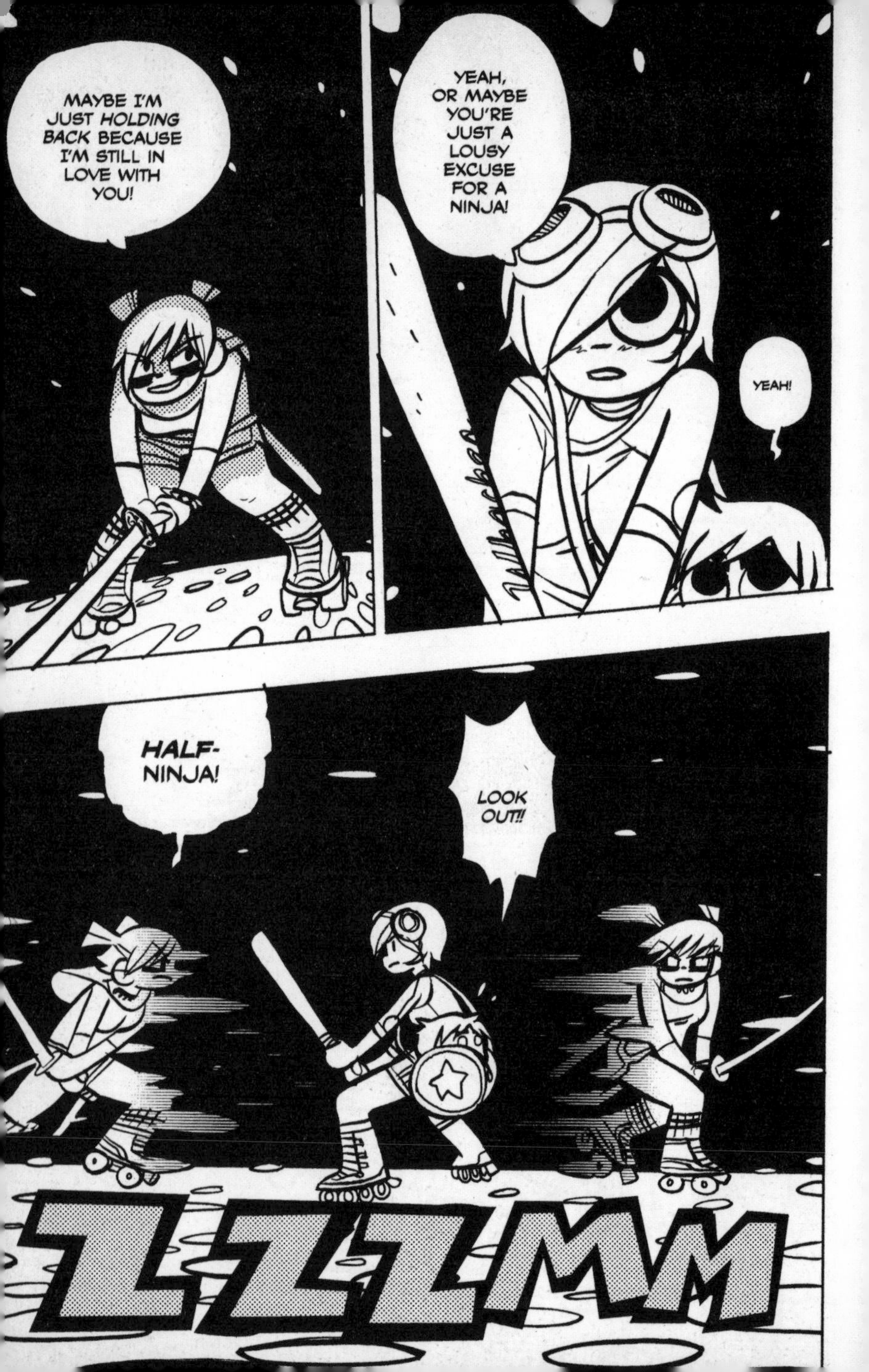
MAYBE I'M JUST *HOLDING* BACK BECAUSE I'M STILL IN LOVE WITH YOU!
YEAH, OR MAYBE YOU'RE JUST A LOUSY EXCUSE FOR A NINJA!
YEAH!
HALF-NINJA!
LOOK OUT!!
ZZZMM

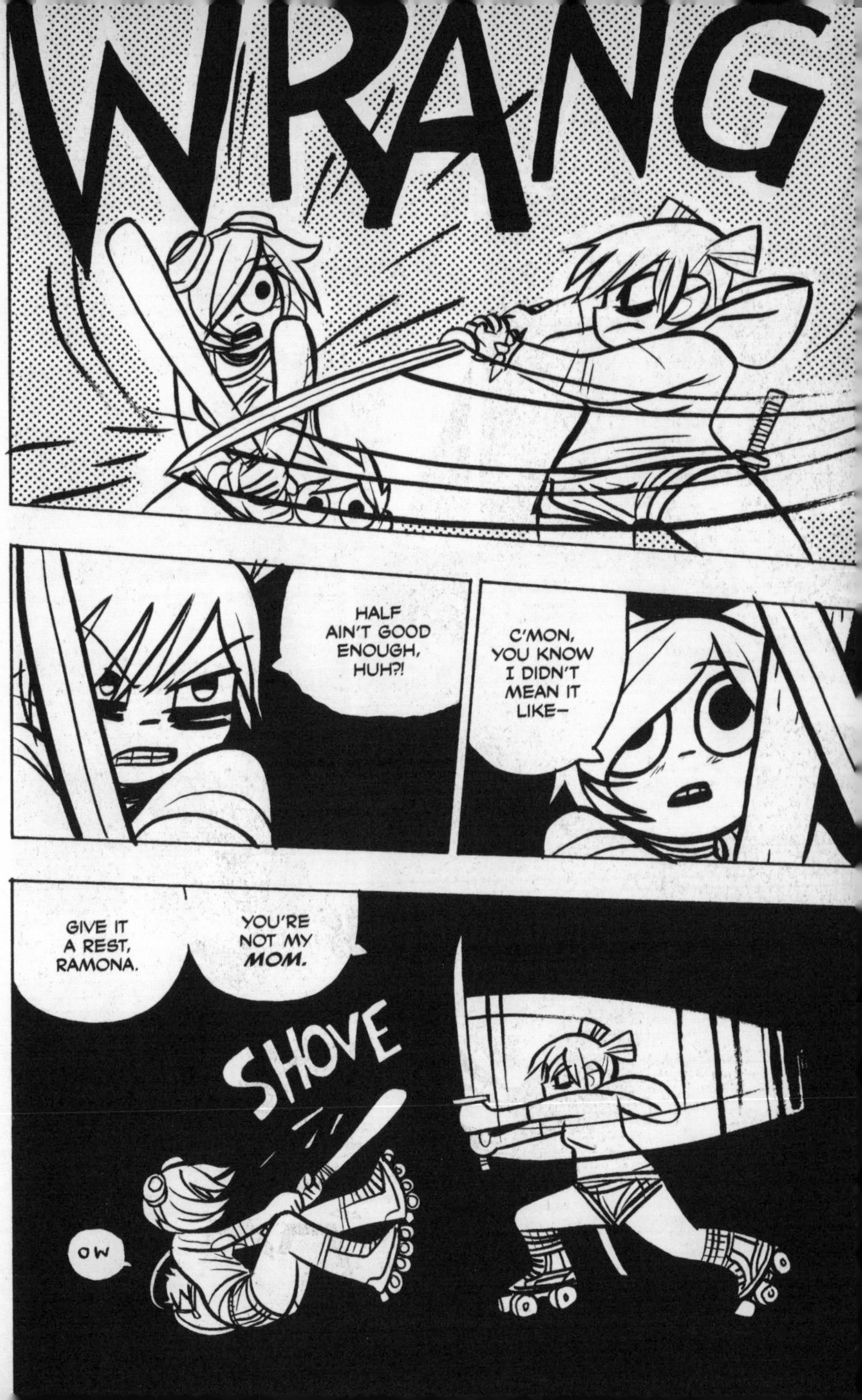
WRANG
HALF AIN'T GOOD ENOUGH, HUH?!
C'MON, YOU KNOW I DIDN'T MEAN IT LIKE–
GIVE IT A REST, RAMONA.
YOU'RE NOT MY *MOM.*
SHOVE
OW

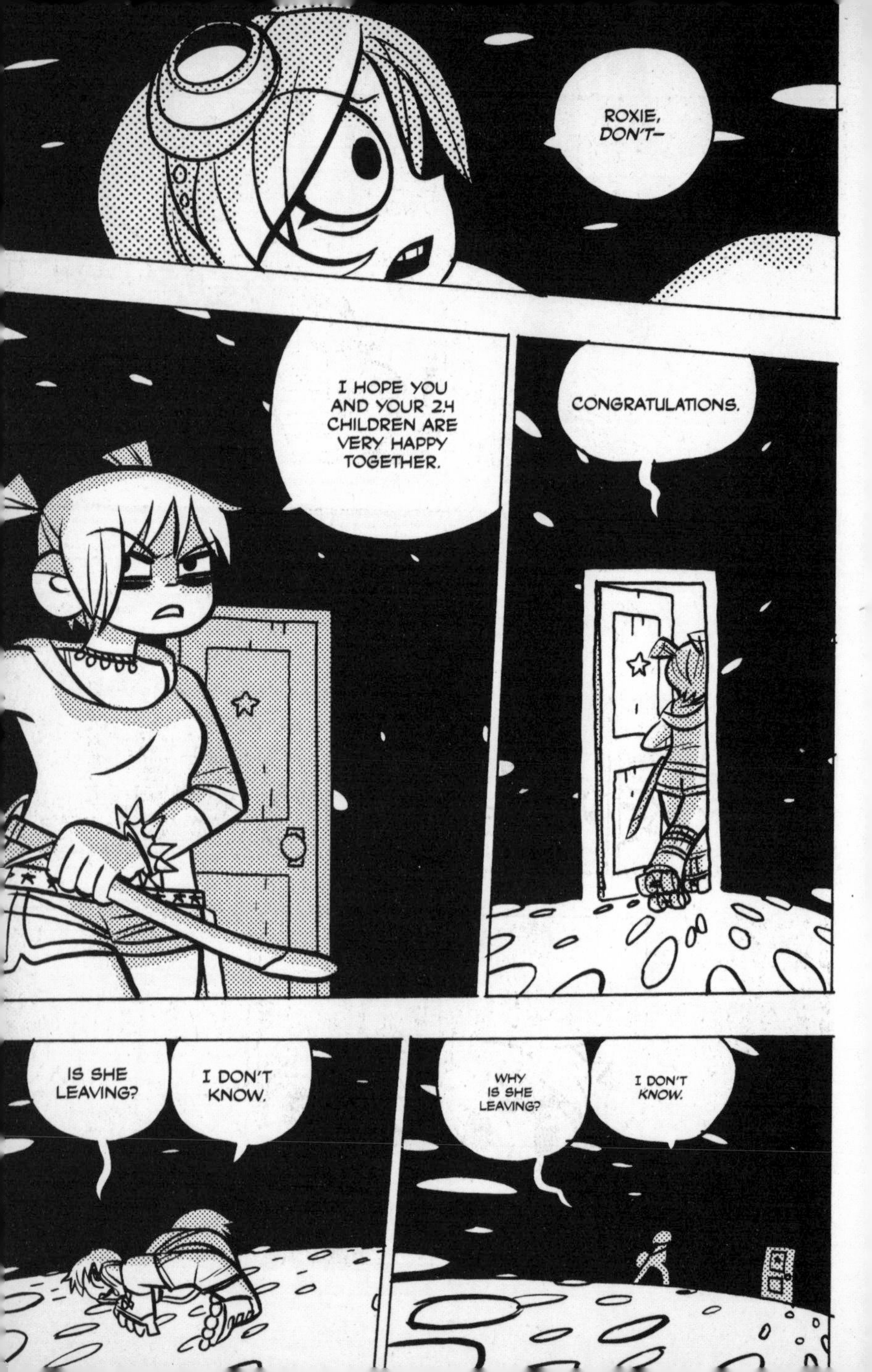
ROXIE, DON'T—
I HOPE YOU AND YOUR 2.4 CHILDREN ARE VERY HAPPY TOGETHER.
CONGRATULATIONS.
IS SHE LEAVING?
I DON'T KNOW.
WHY IS SHE LEAVING?
I DON'T KNOW.

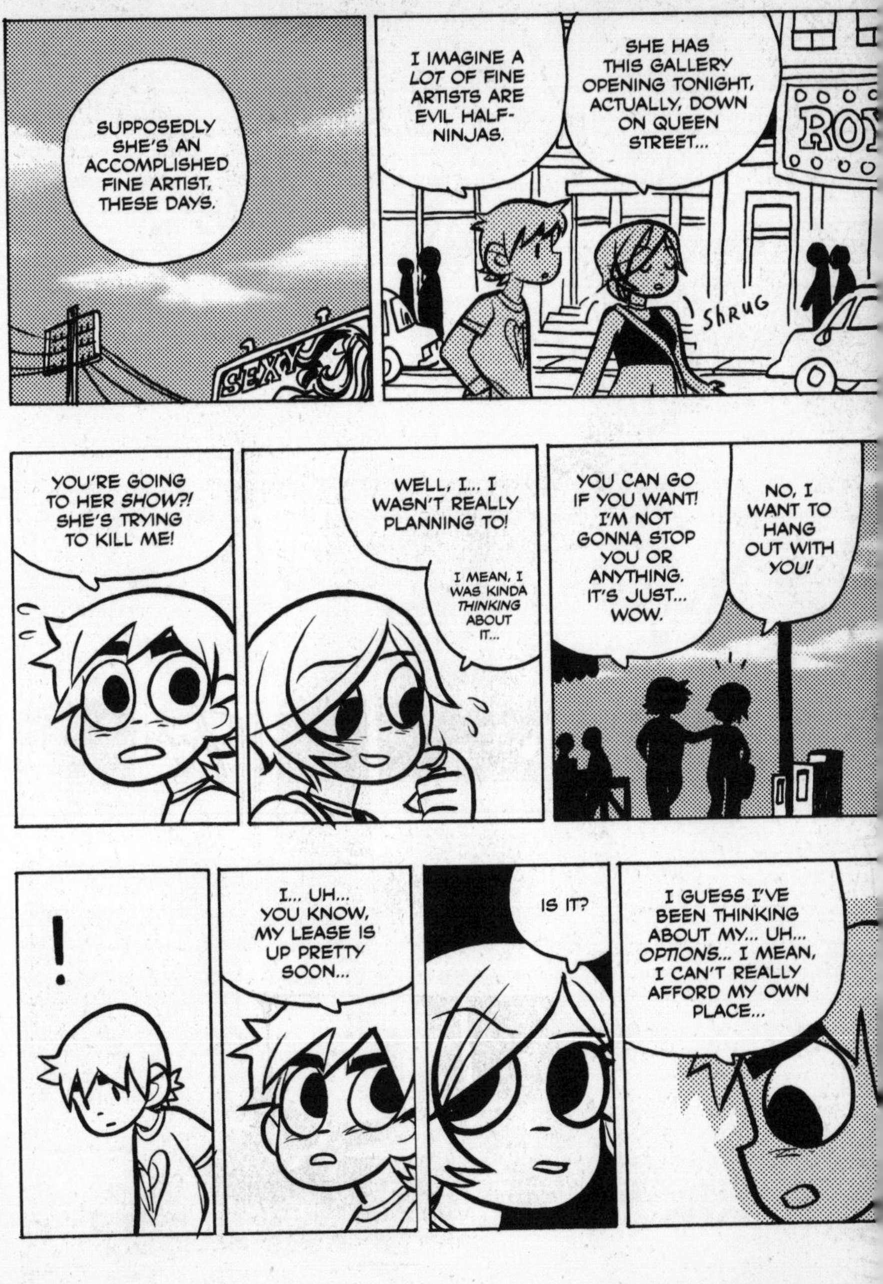
SUPPOSEDLY SHE'S AN ACCOMPLISHED FINE ARTIST, THESE DAYS.
SEXY
I IMAGINE A LOT OF FINE ARTISTS ARE EVIL HALF-NINJAS.
SHE HAS THIS GALLERY OPENING TONIGHT, ACTUALLY, DOWN ON QUEEN STREET...
SHRUG
YOU'RE GOING TO HER SHOW?! SHE'S TRYING TO KILL ME!
WELL, I... I WASN'T REALLY PLANNING TO!
I MEAN, I WAS KINDA THINKING ABOUT IT...
YOU CAN GO IF YOU WANT! I'M NOT GONNA STOP YOU OR ANYTHING. IT'S JUST... WOW.
NO, I WANT TO HANG OUT WITH YOU!
!
I... UH... YOU KNOW, MY LEASE IS UP PRETTY SOON...
IS IT?
I GUESS I'VE BEEN THINKING ABOUT MY... UH... OPTIONS... I MEAN, I CAN'T REALLY AFFORD MY OWN PLACE...

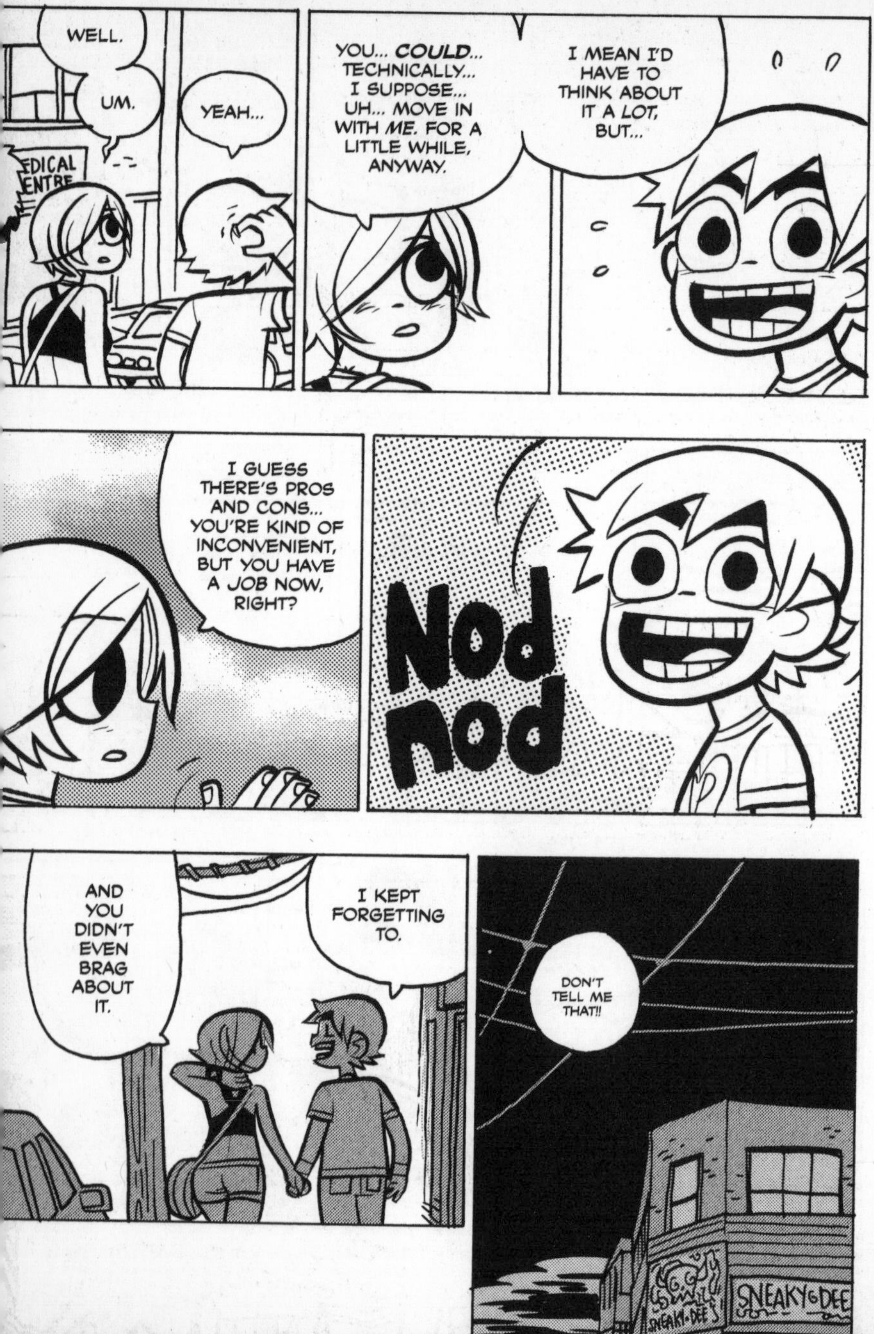

WELL.
UM.
YEAH...
EDICAL ENTRE
YOU... COULD... TECHNICALLY... I SUPPOSE... UH... MOVE IN WITH ME. FOR A LITTLE WHILE, ANYWAY.
I MEAN I'D HAVE TO THINK ABOUT IT A LOT, BUT...
I GUESS THERE'S PROS AND CONS... YOU'RE KIND OF INCONVENIENT, BUT YOU HAVE A JOB NOW, RIGHT?
Nod nod
AND YOU DIDN'T EVEN BRAG ABOUT IT.
I KEPT FORGETTING TO.
DON'T TELL ME THAT!!
SNEAKY DEE
SNEAKY DEE'S

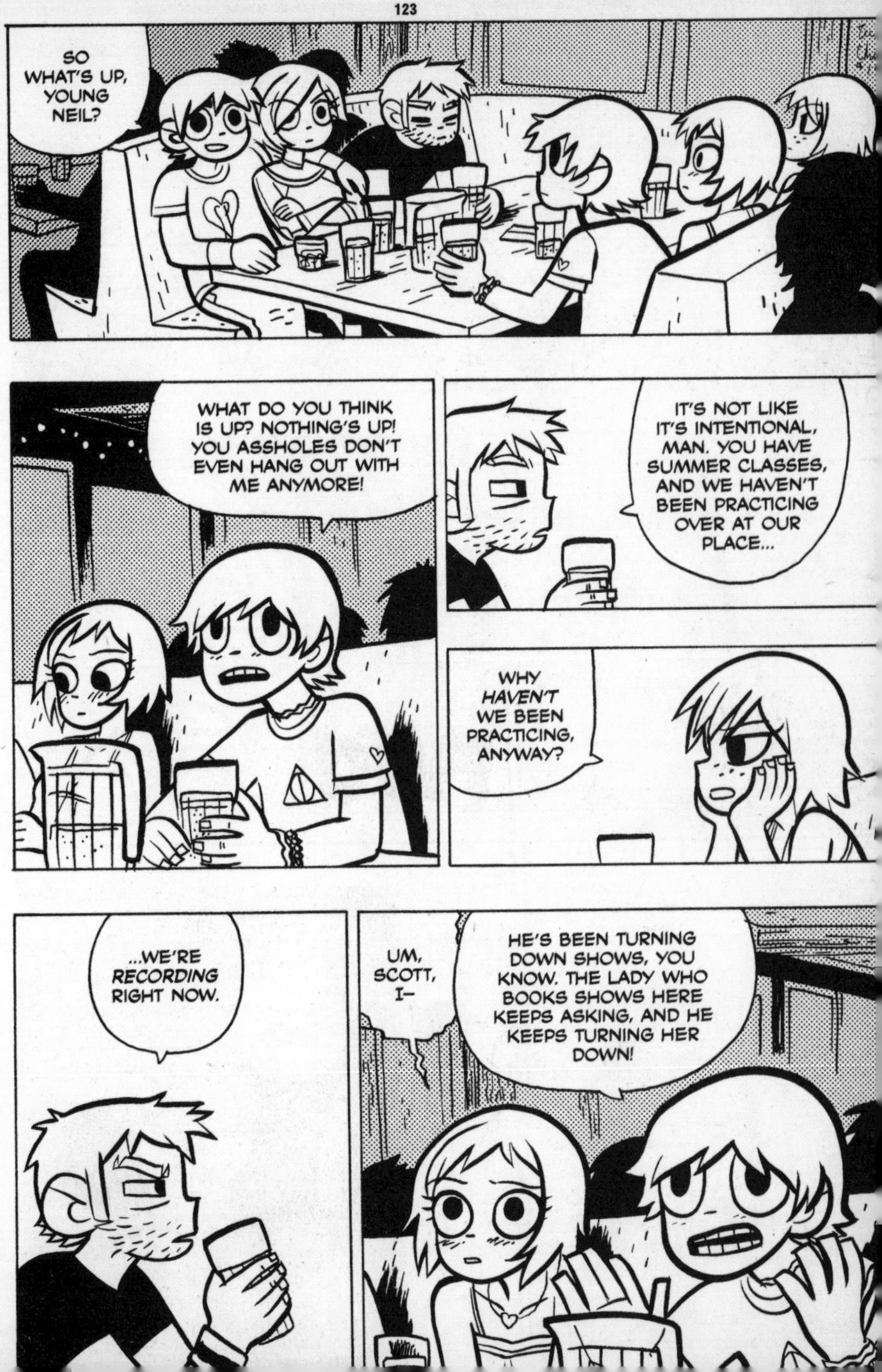
SO WHAT'S UP, YOUNG NEIL?
WHAT DO YOU THINK IS UP? NOTHING'S UP! YOU ASSHOLES DON'T EVEN HANG OUT WITH ME ANYMORE!
IT'S NOT LIKE IT'S INTENTIONAL, MAN. YOU HAVE SUMMER CLASSES, AND WE HAVEN'T BEEN PRACTICING OVER AT OUR PLACE...
WHY *HAVEN'T* WE BEEN PRACTICING, ANYWAY?
...WE'RE *RECORDING* RIGHT NOW.
UM, SCOTT, I–
HE'S BEEN TURNING DOWN SHOWS, YOU KNOW. THE LADY WHO BOOKS SHOWS HERE KEEPS ASKING, AND HE KEEPS TURNING HER DOWN!

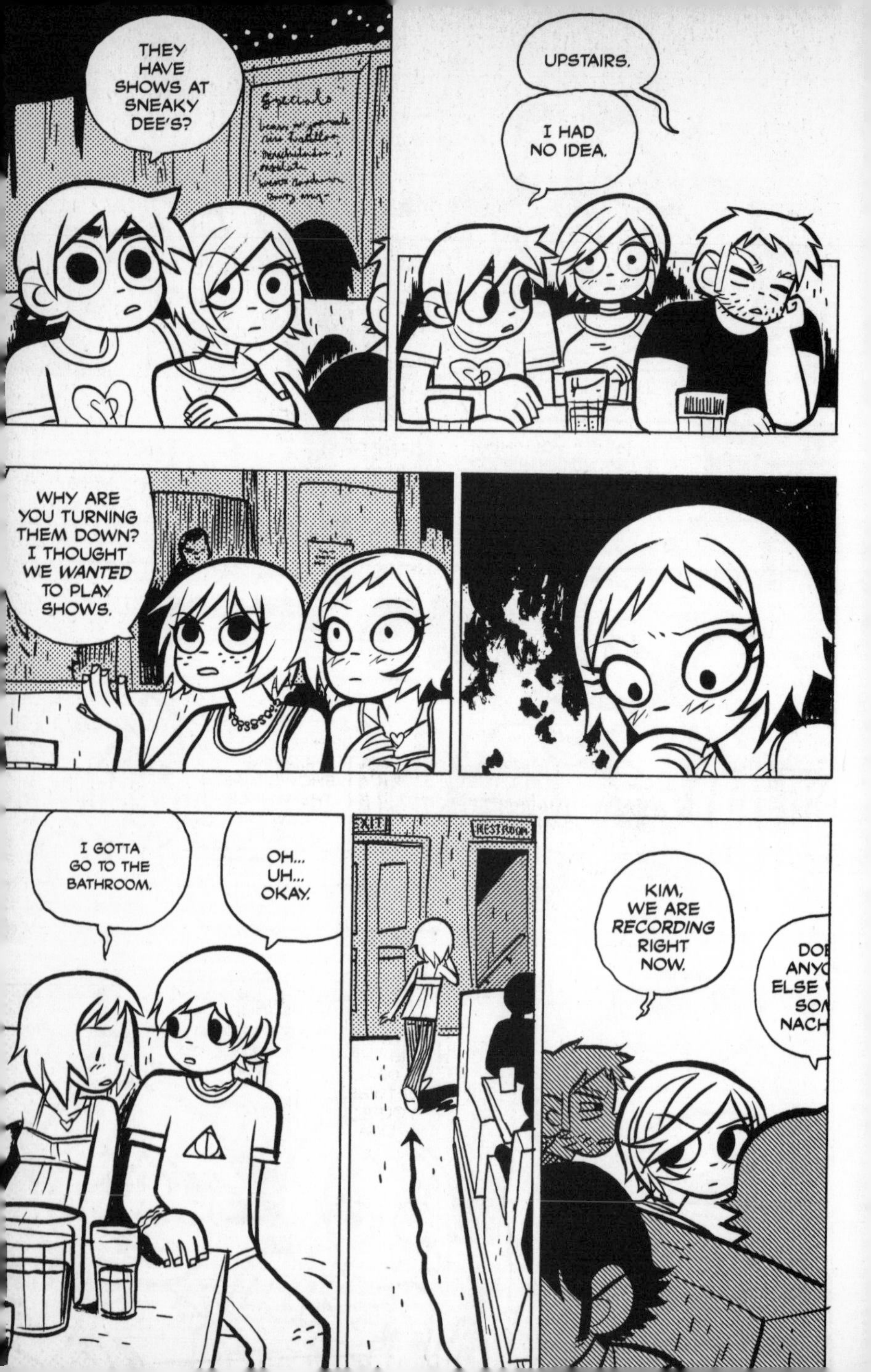
THEY HAVE SHOWS AT SNEAKY DEE'S?
UPSTAIRS.
I HAD NO IDEA.
WHY ARE YOU TURNING THEM DOWN? I THOUGHT WE *WANTED* TO PLAY SHOWS.
I GOTTA GO TO THE BATHROOM.
OH... UH... OKAY.
EXIT
RESTROOM
KIM, WE ARE *RECORDING* RIGHT NOW.
DOE ANYO ELSE SOM NACH

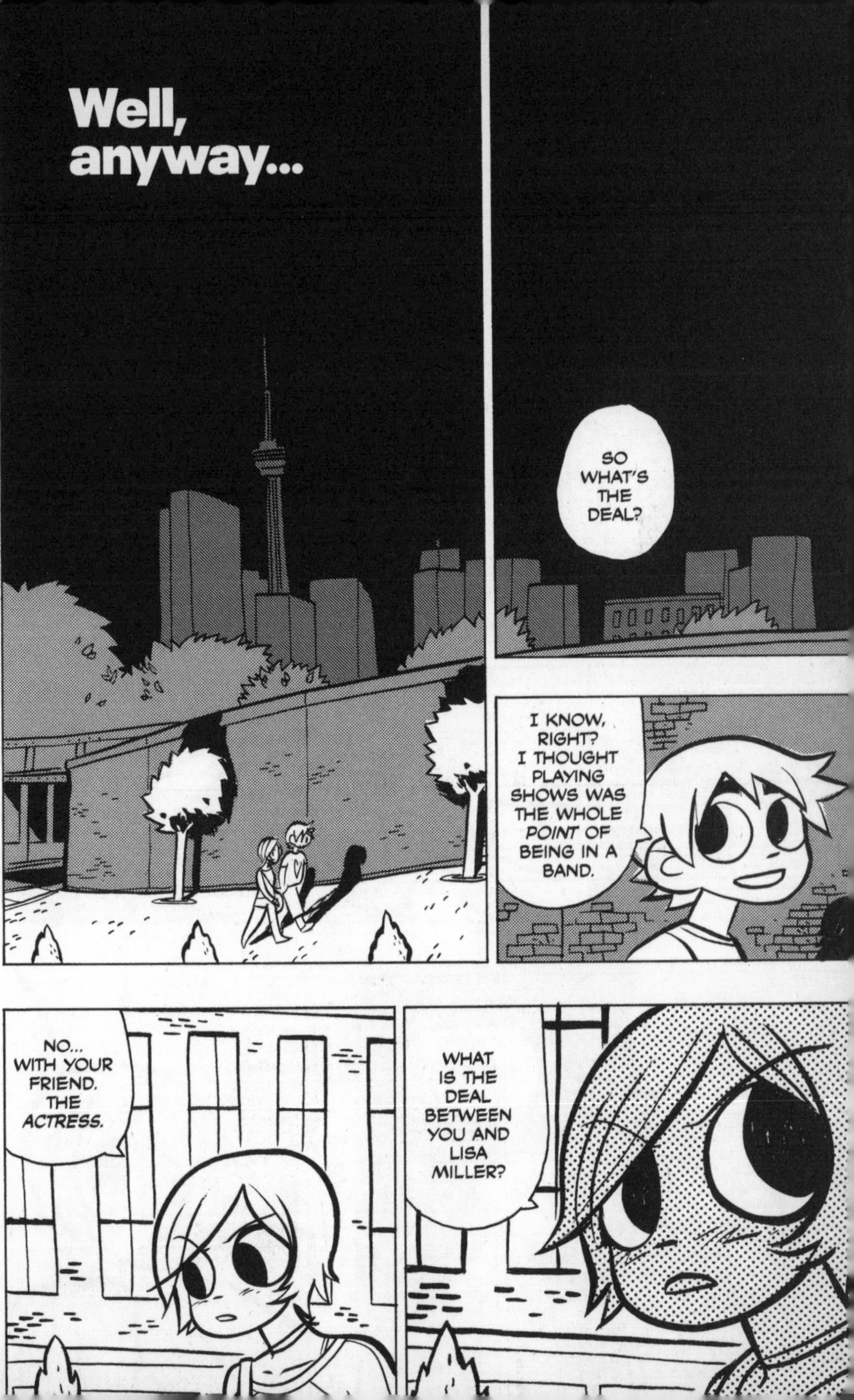
Well, anyway...
SO WHAT'S THE DEAL?
I KNOW, RIGHT? I THOUGHT PLAYING SHOWS WAS THE WHOLE *POINT* OF BEING IN A BAND.
NO... WITH YOUR FRIEND. THE *ACTRESS.*
WHAT IS THE DEAL BETWEEN YOU AND LISA MILLER?

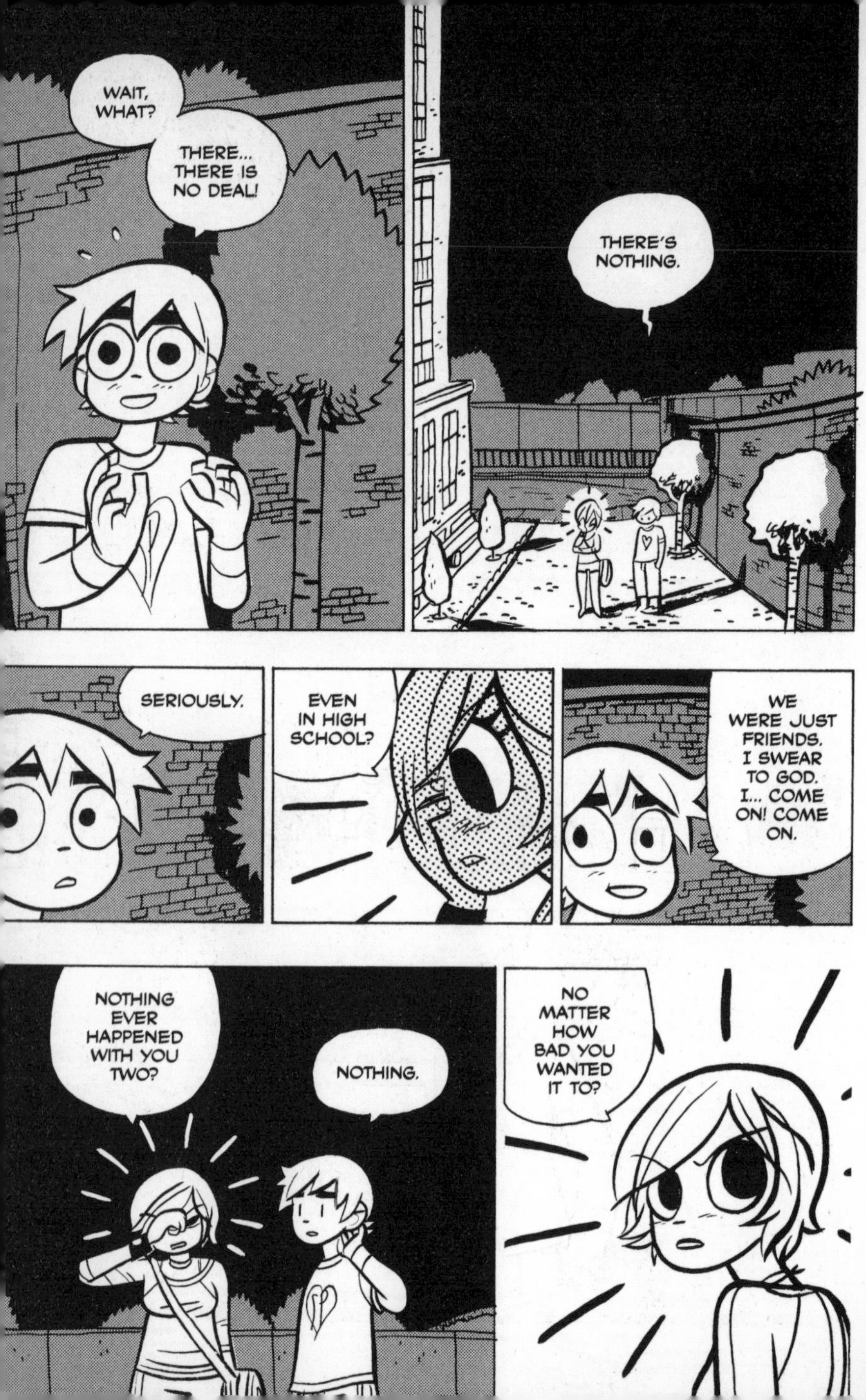
WAIT, WHAT?
THERE... THERE IS NO DEAL!
THERE'S NOTHING.
SERIOUSLY.
EVEN IN HIGH SCHOOL?
WE WERE JUST FRIENDS. I SWEAR TO GOD. I... COME ON! COME ON.
NOTHING EVER HAPPENED WITH YOU TWO?
NOTHING.
NO MATTER HOW BAD YOU WANTED IT TO?

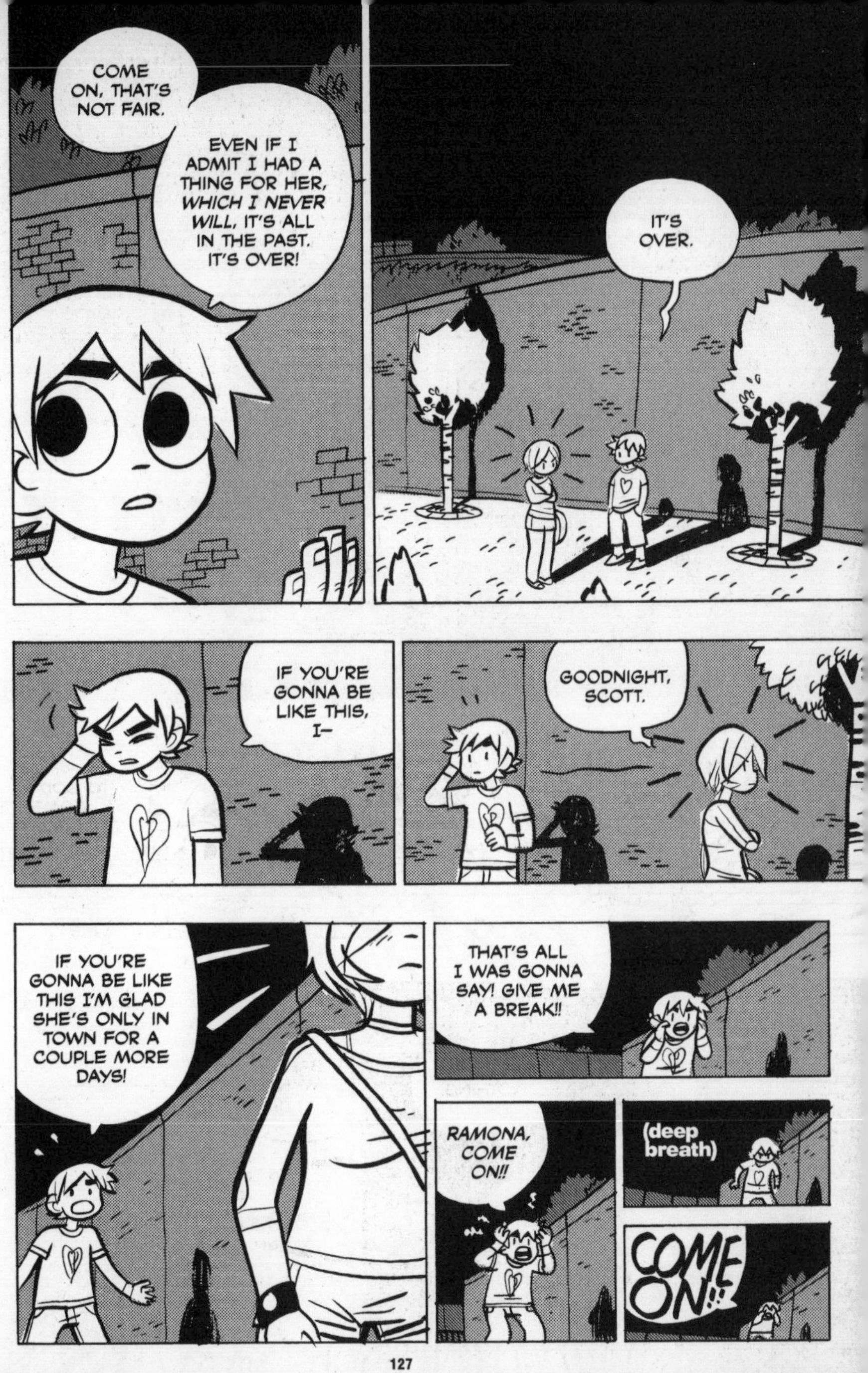
COME ON, THAT'S NOT FAIR.
EVEN IF I ADMIT I HAD A THING FOR HER, *WHICH I NEVER WILL*, IT'S ALL IN THE PAST. IT'S OVER!
IT'S OVER.
IF YOU'RE GONNA BE LIKE THIS, I—
GOODNIGHT, SCOTT.
IF YOU'RE GONNA BE LIKE THIS I'M GLAD SHE'S ONLY IN TOWN FOR A COUPLE MORE DAYS!
THAT'S ALL I WAS GONNA SAY! GIVE ME A BREAK!!
RAMONA, COME ON!!
(deep breath)
COME ON!!

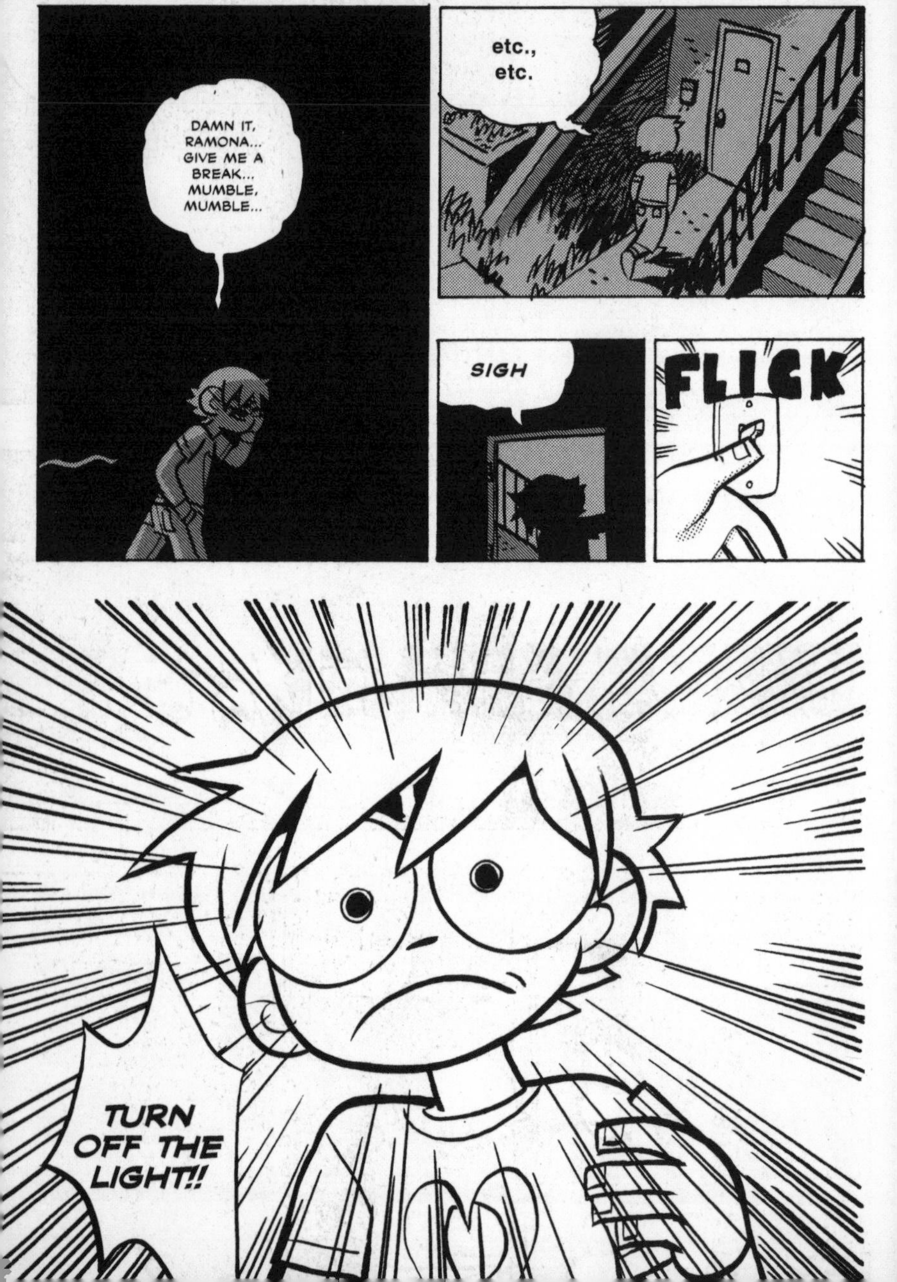
DAMN IT, RAMONA... GIVE ME A BREAK... MUMBLE, MUMBLE...
etc., etc.
SIGH
FLICK
TURN OFF THE LIGHT!!

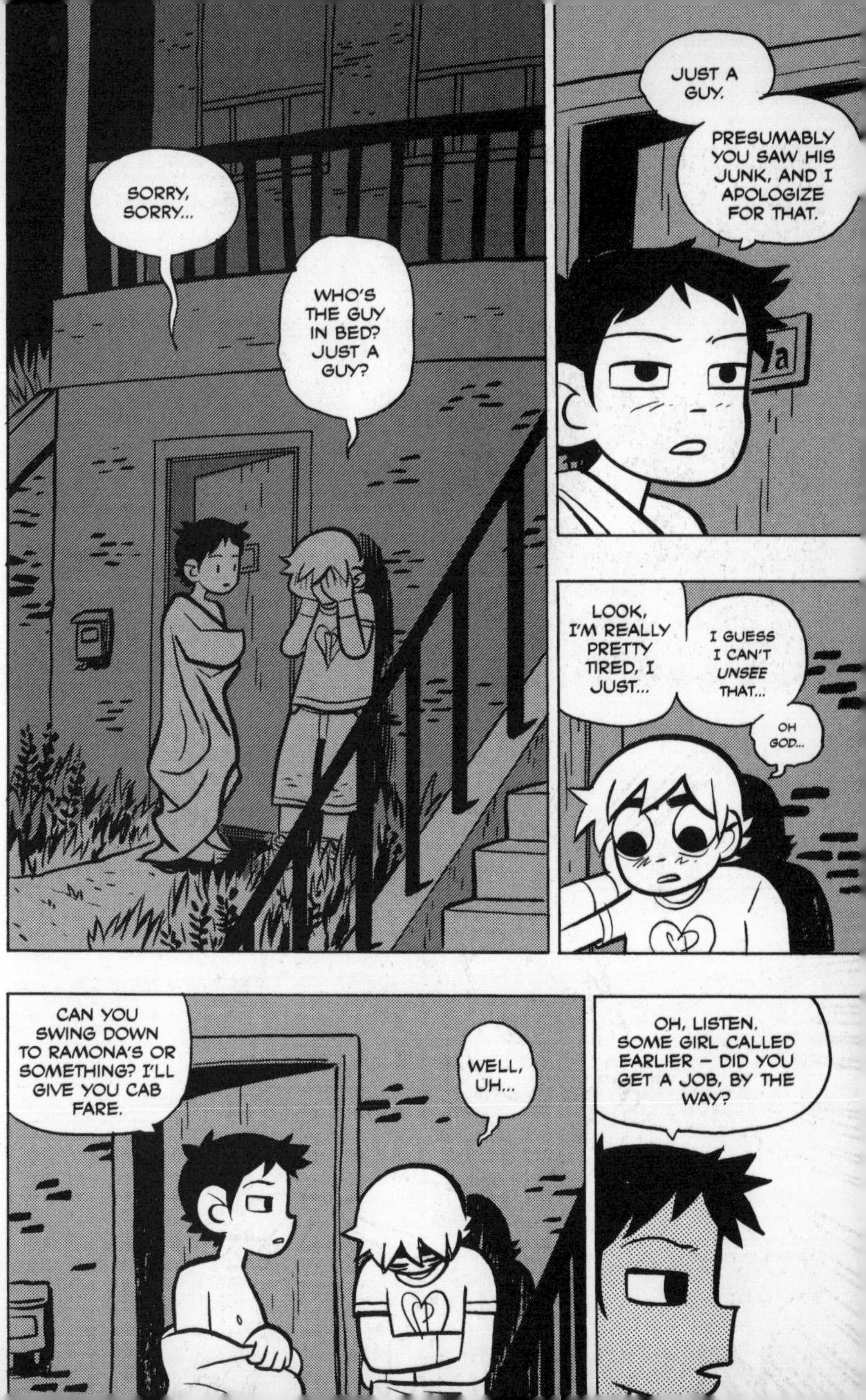
SORRY, SORRY...
WHO'S THE GUY IN BED? JUST A GUY?
JUST A GUY.
PRESUMABLY YOU SAW HIS JUNK, AND I APOLOGIZE FOR THAT.
LOOK, I'M REALLY PRETTY TIRED, I JUST...
I GUESS I CAN'T *UNSEE* THAT...
OH GOD...
CAN YOU SWING DOWN TO RAMONA'S OR SOMETHING? I'LL GIVE YOU CAB FARE.
WELL, UH...
OH, LISTEN. SOME GIRL CALLED EARLIER – DID YOU GET A JOB, BY THE WAY?

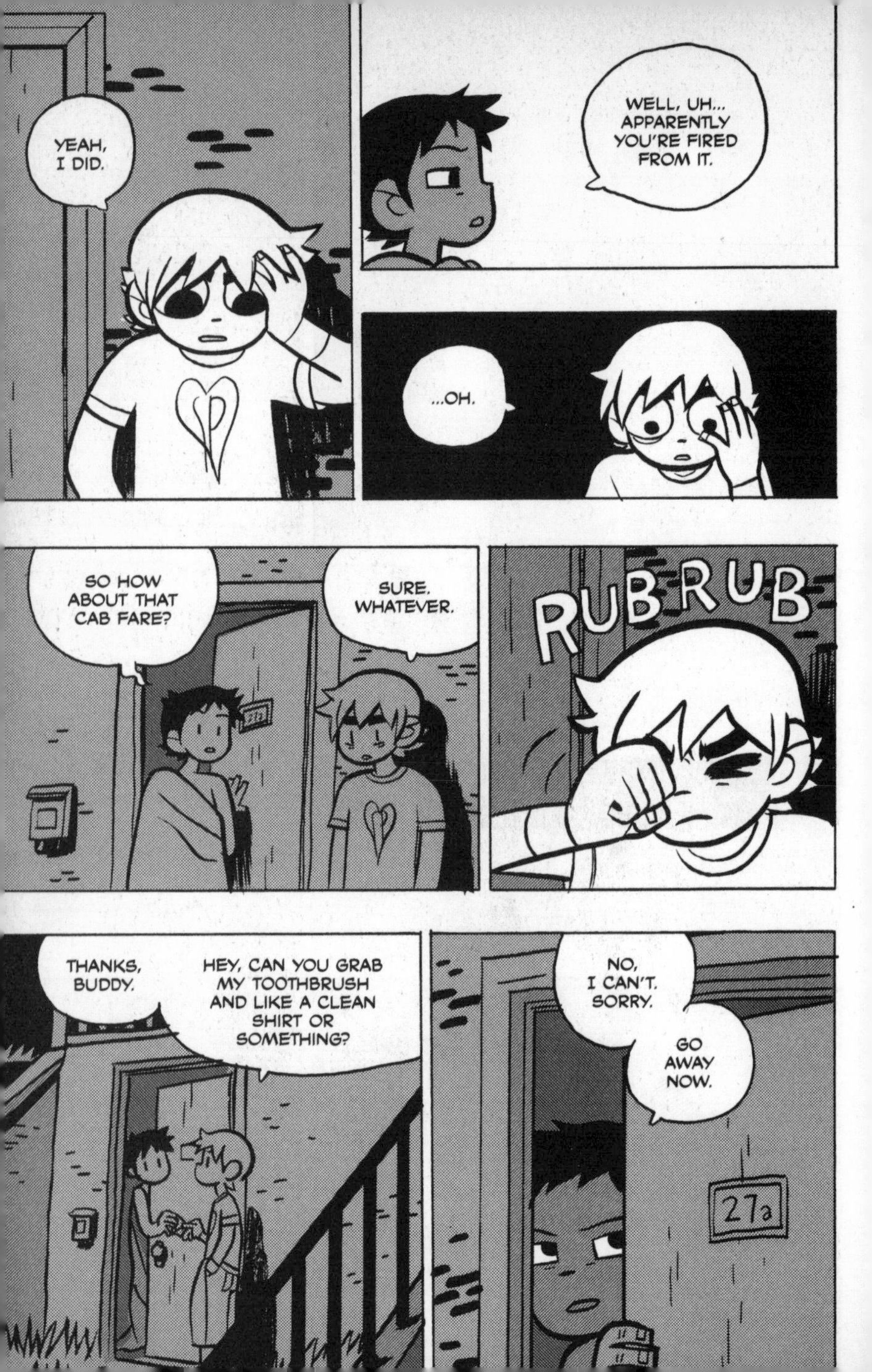
YEAH, I DID.
WELL, UH... APPARENTLY YOU'RE FIRED FROM IT.
...OH.
SO HOW ABOUT THAT CAB FARE?
SURE. WHATEVER.
RUB RUB
THANKS, BUDDY.
HEY, CAN YOU GRAB MY TOOTHBRUSH AND LIKE A CLEAN SHIRT OR SOMETHING?
NO, I CAN'T. SORRY.
GO AWAY NOW.
27a

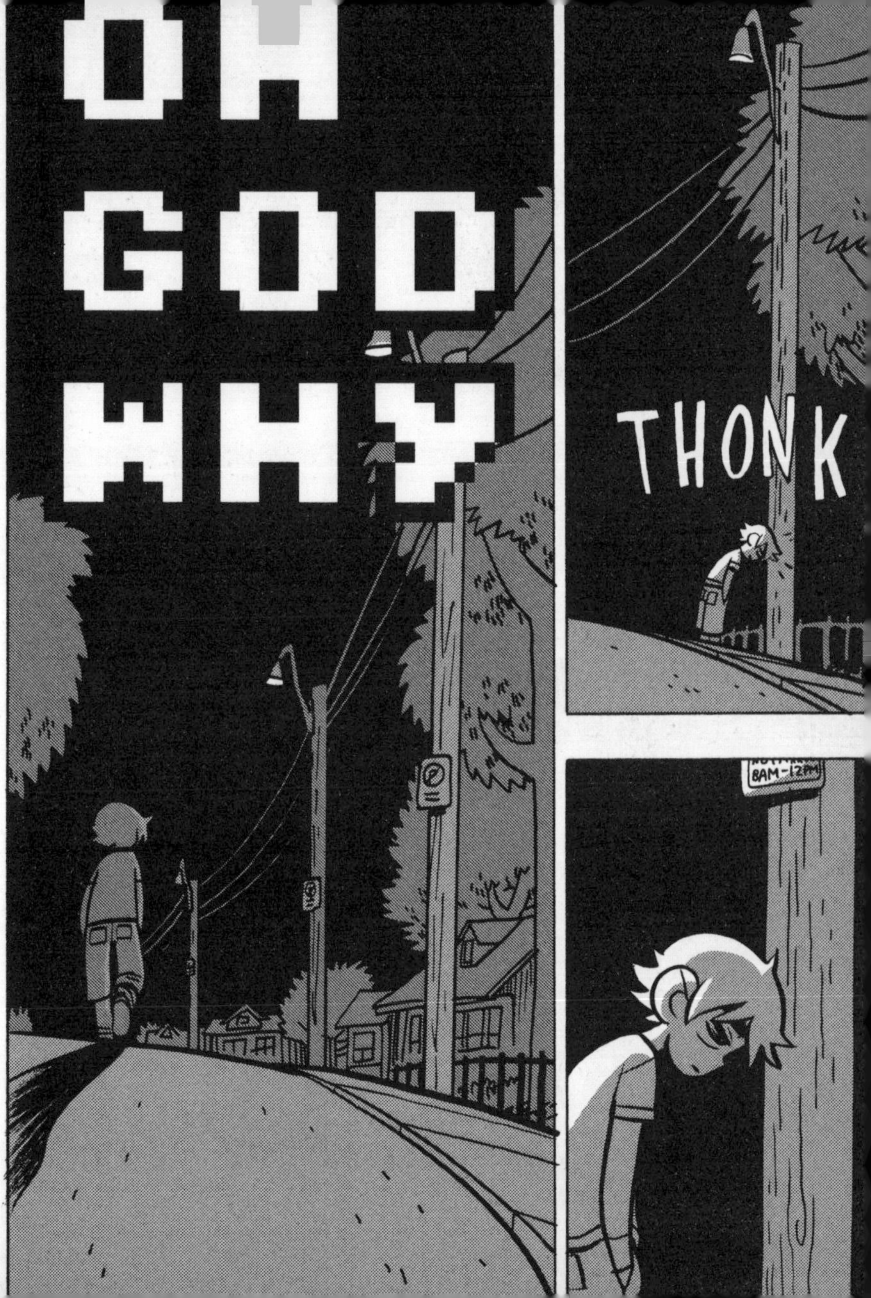
OH
GOD
WHY
THONK
8AM-12PM

THOUGHT
...

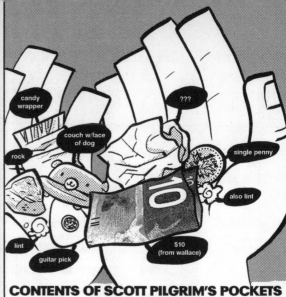

candy wrapper

???

couch w/face of dog

rock

single penny

also lint

lint

guitar pick

$10 (from wallace)

CONTENTS OF SCOTT PILGRIM'S POCKETS

?

(4) 2 277-3490?

Lisa M. ♡

AHAA AAAAA GGHHRR BBLGHRF

(deep breath)

AAAHII EERRGH HHRAAFFGBL

Lisa's sister's apartment

2 AM-ish

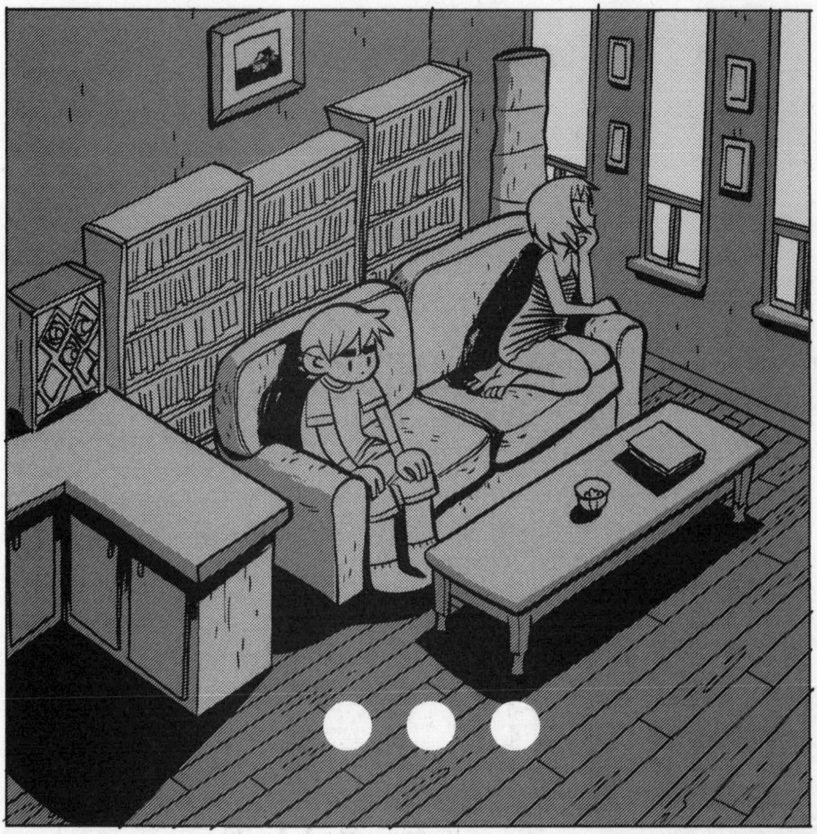

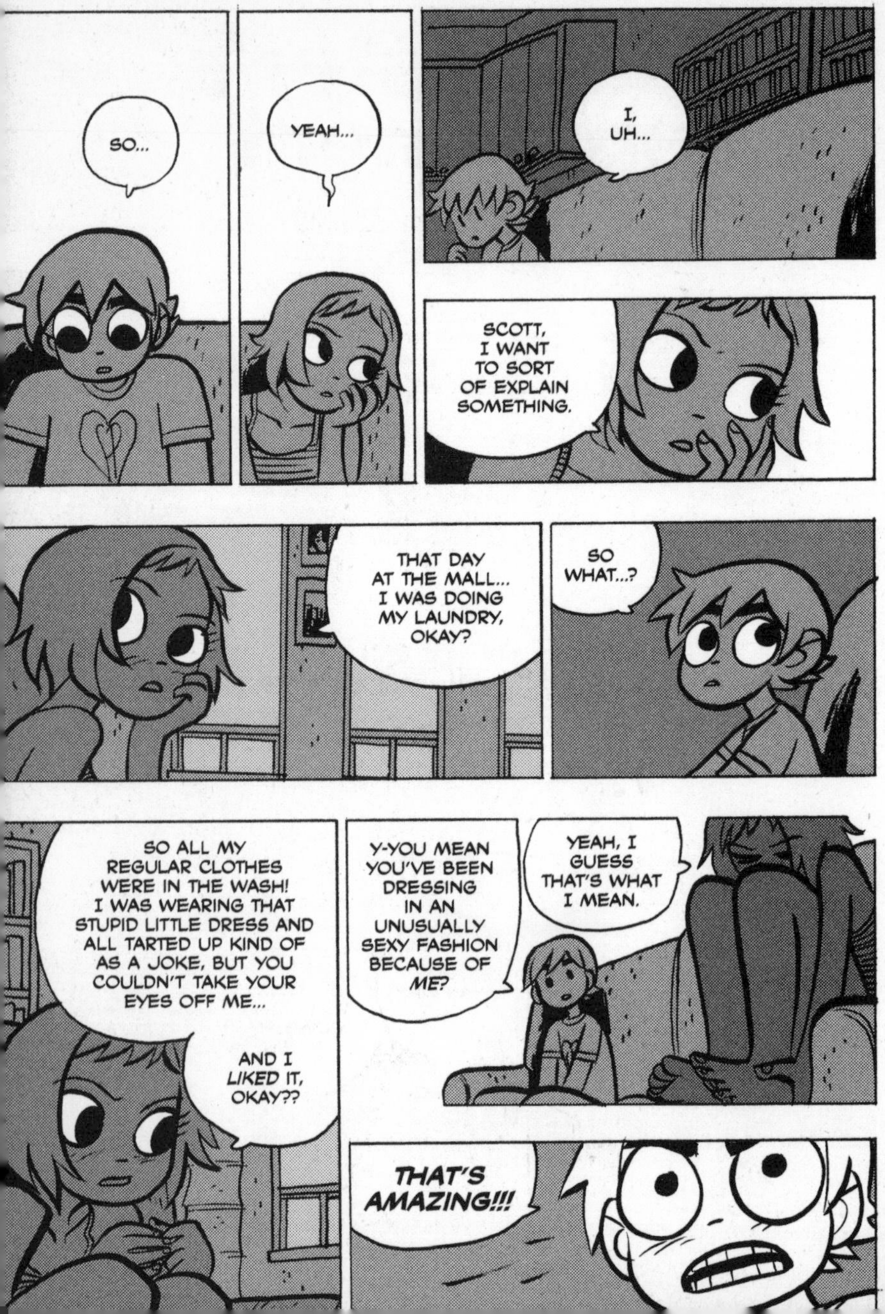
SO...
YEAH...
I, UH...
SCOTT, I WANT TO SORT OF EXPLAIN SOMETHING.
THAT DAY AT THE MALL... I WAS DOING MY LAUNDRY, OKAY?
SO WHAT...?
SO ALL MY REGULAR CLOTHES WERE IN THE WASH! I WAS WEARING THAT STUPID LITTLE DRESS AND ALL TARTED UP KIND OF AS A JOKE, BUT YOU COULDN'T TAKE YOUR EYES OFF ME...
AND I *LIKED* IT, OKAY??
Y-YOU MEAN YOU'VE BEEN DRESSING IN AN UNUSUALLY SEXY FASHION BECAUSE OF *ME*?
YEAH, I GUESS THAT'S WHAT I MEAN.
THAT'S AMAZING!!!

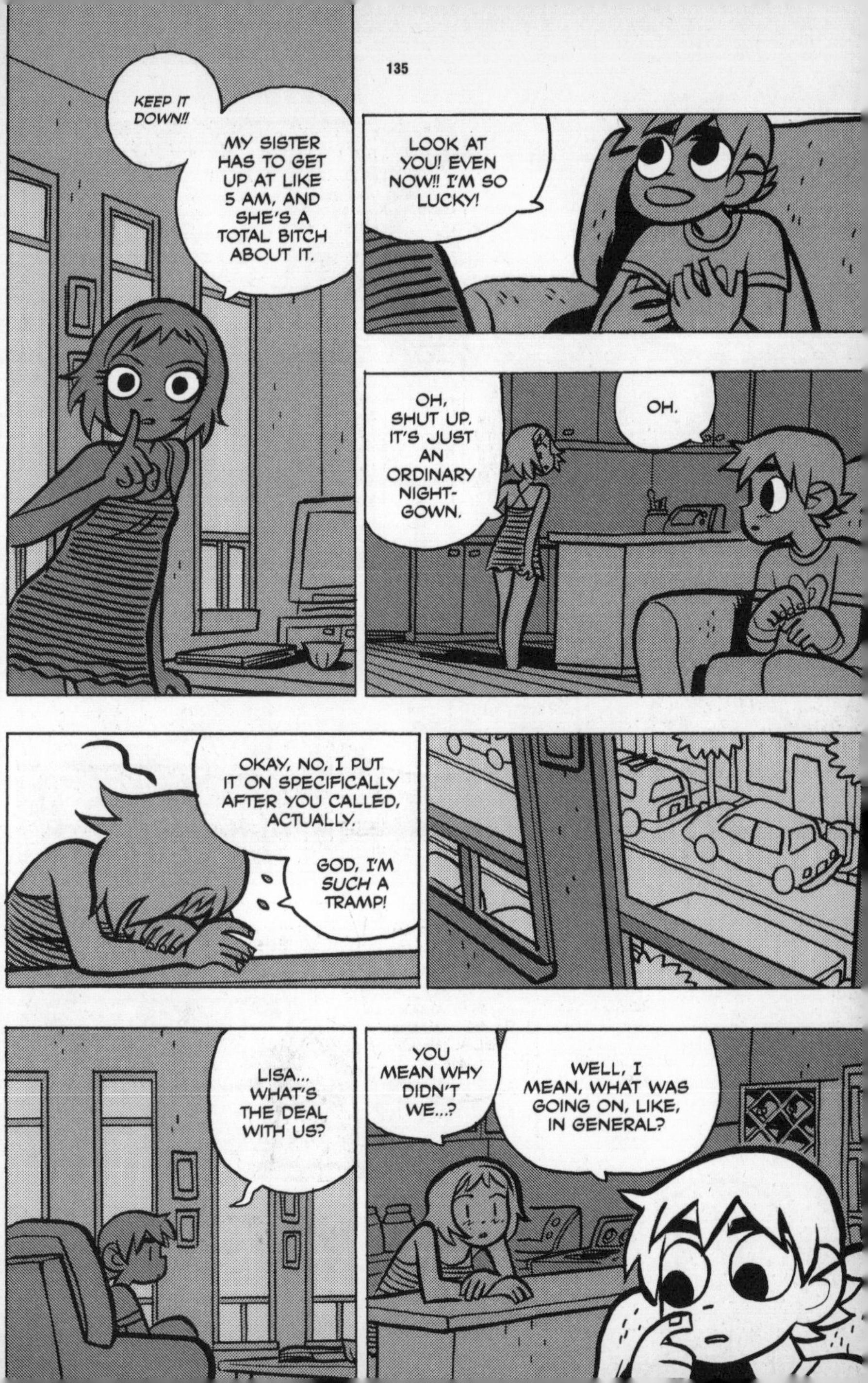
KEEP IT DOWN!!
MY SISTER HAS TO GET UP AT LIKE 5 AM, AND SHE'S A TOTAL BITCH ABOUT IT.
LOOK AT YOU! EVEN NOW!! I'M SO LUCKY!
OH, SHUT UP. IT'S JUST AN ORDINARY NIGHT-GOWN.
OH.
OKAY, NO, I PUT IT ON SPECIFICALLY AFTER YOU CALLED, ACTUALLY.
GOD, I'M *SUCH* A TRAMP!
LISA... WHAT'S THE DEAL WITH US?
YOU MEAN WHY DIDN'T WE...?
WELL, I MEAN, WHAT WAS GOING ON, LIKE, IN GENERAL?

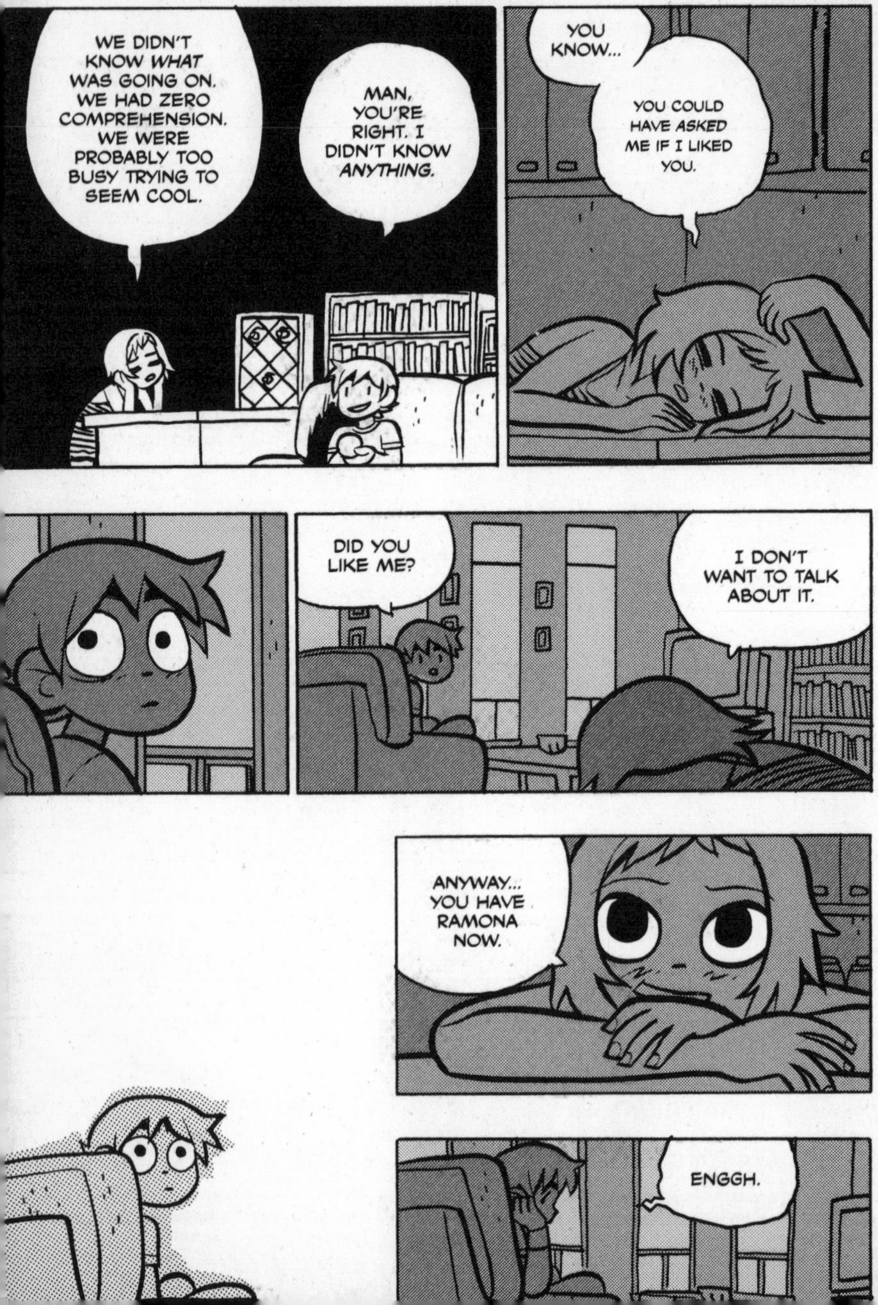
WE DIDN'T KNOW *WHAT* WAS GOING ON. WE HAD ZERO COMPREHENSION. WE WERE PROBABLY TOO BUSY TRYING TO SEEM COOL.
MAN, YOU'RE RIGHT. I DIDN'T KNOW *ANYTHING.*
YOU KNOW...
YOU COULD HAVE *ASKED* ME IF I LIKED YOU.
DID YOU LIKE ME?
I DON'T WANT TO TALK ABOUT IT.
ANYWAY... YOU HAVE RAMONA NOW.
ENGGH.

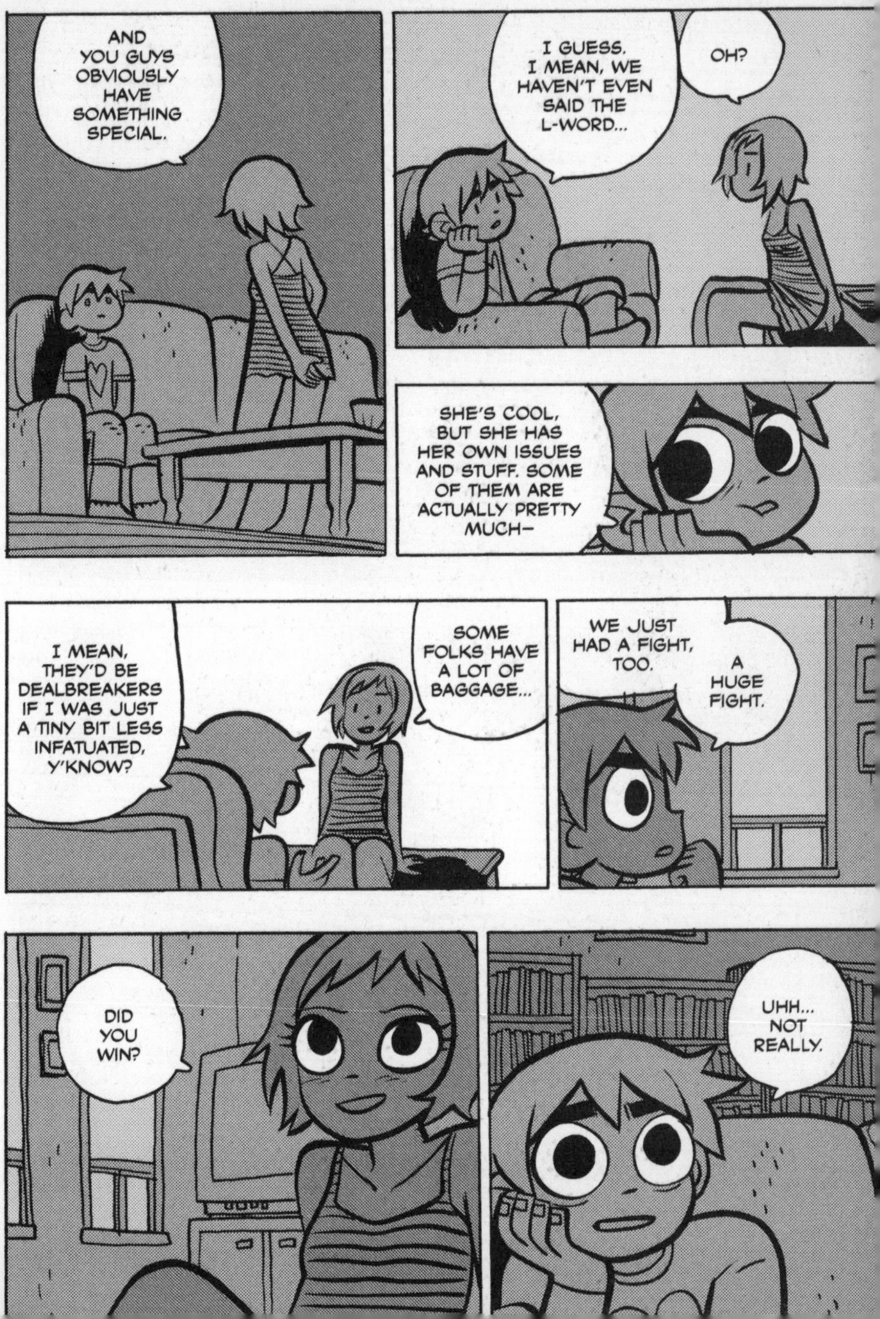
AND YOU GUYS OBVIOUSLY HAVE SOMETHING SPECIAL.
I GUESS. I MEAN, WE HAVEN'T EVEN SAID THE L-WORD...
OH?
SHE'S COOL, BUT SHE HAS HER OWN ISSUES AND STUFF. SOME OF THEM ARE ACTUALLY PRETTY MUCH–
I MEAN, THEY'D BE DEALBREAKERS IF I WAS JUST A TINY BIT LESS INFATUATED, Y'KNOW?
SOME FOLKS HAVE A LOT OF BAGGAGE...
WE JUST HAD A FIGHT, TOO.
A HUGE FIGHT.
DID YOU WIN?
UHH... NOT REALLY.

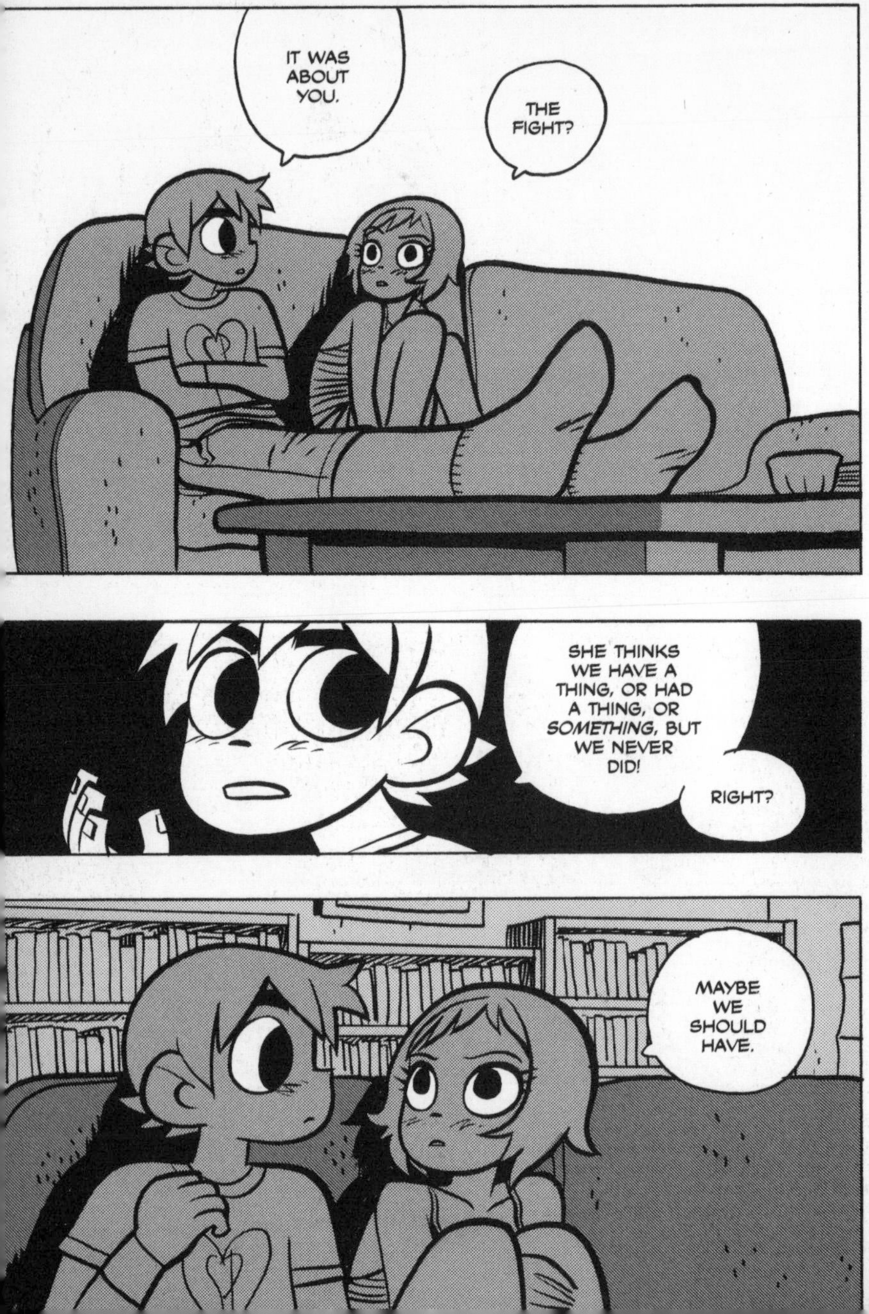
IT WAS ABOUT YOU.
THE FIGHT?
SHE THINKS WE HAVE A THING, OR HAD A THING, OR *SOMETHING*, BUT WE NEVER DID!
RIGHT?
MAYBE WE SHOULD HAVE.

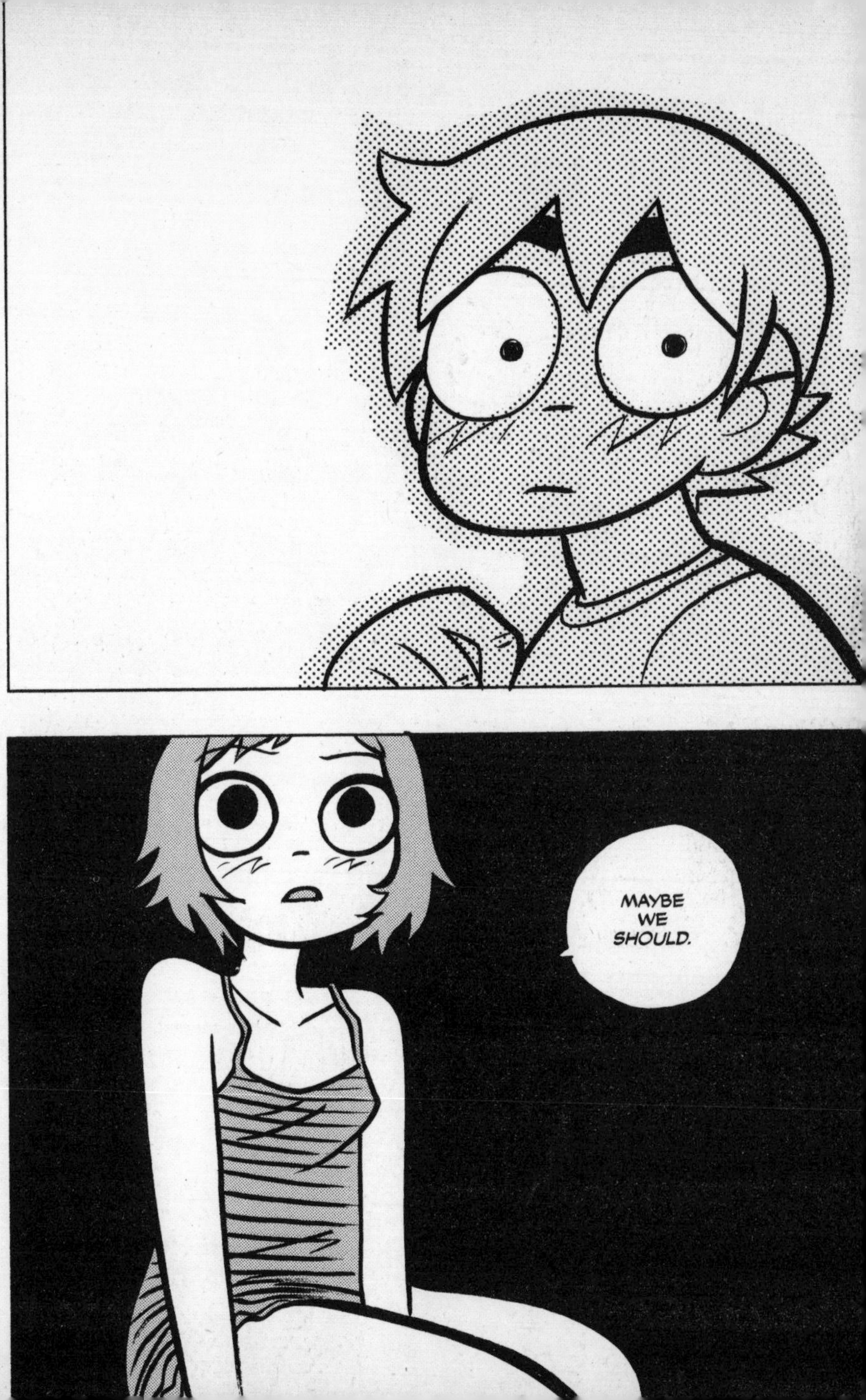
MAYBE WE SHOULD.

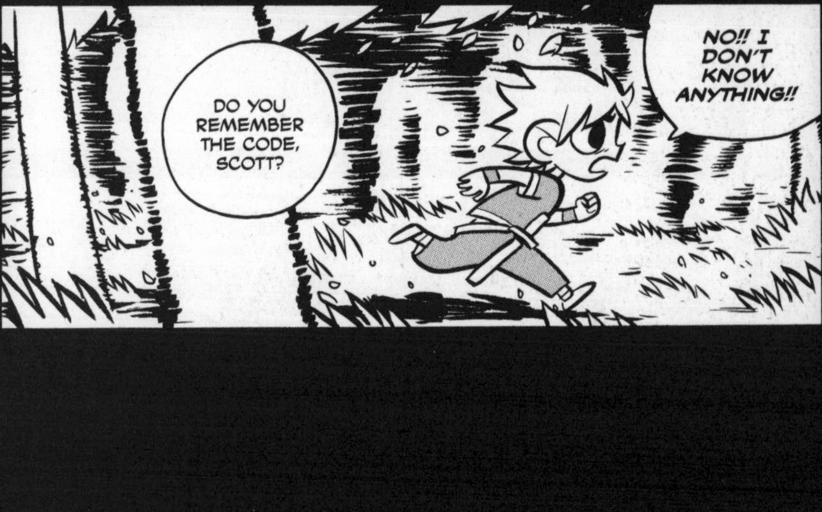
DO YOU REMEMBER THE CODE, SCOTT?
NO!! I DON'T KNOW ANYTHING!!

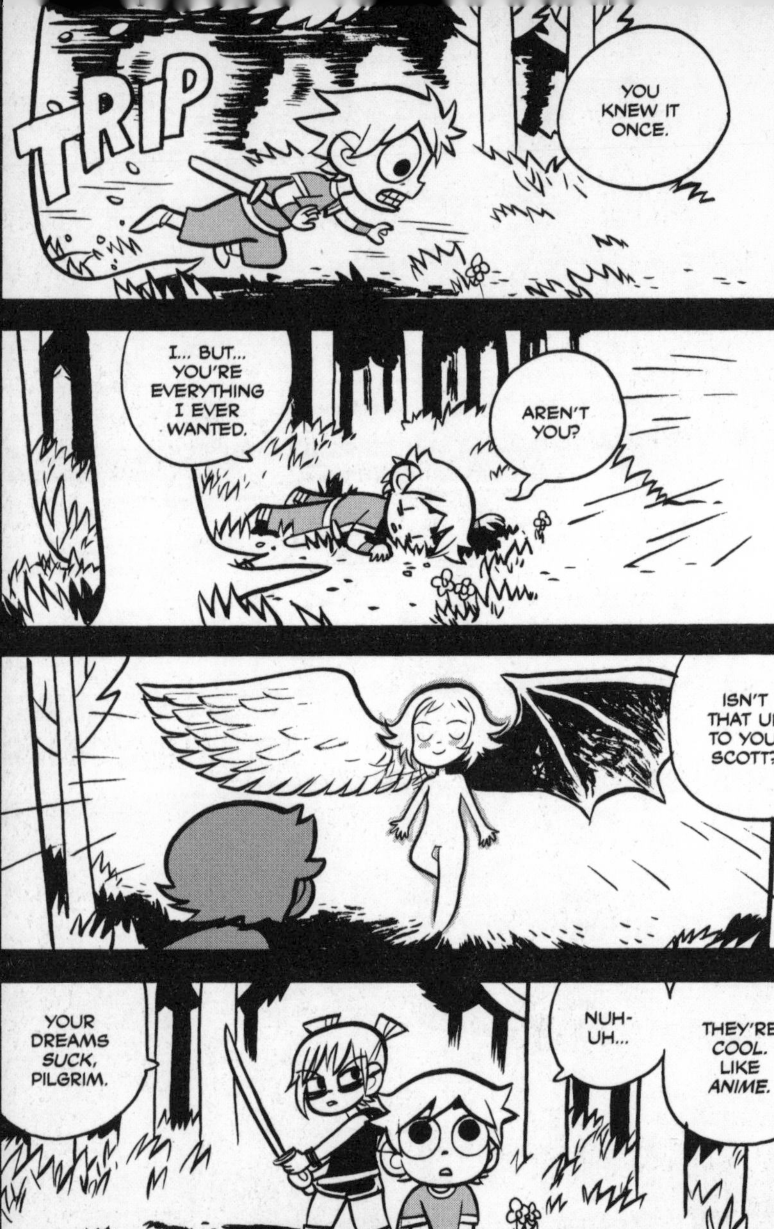
TRIP
YOU KNEW IT ONCE.
I... BUT... YOU'RE EVERYTHING I EVER WANTED.
AREN'T YOU?
ISN'T THAT UP TO YOU, SCOTT?
YOUR DREAMS *SUCK*, PILGRIM.
NUH-UH...
THEY'RE *COOL*. LIKE *ANIME*.

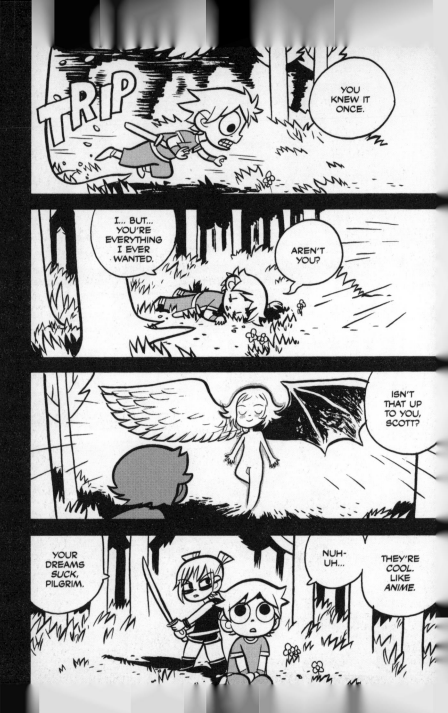

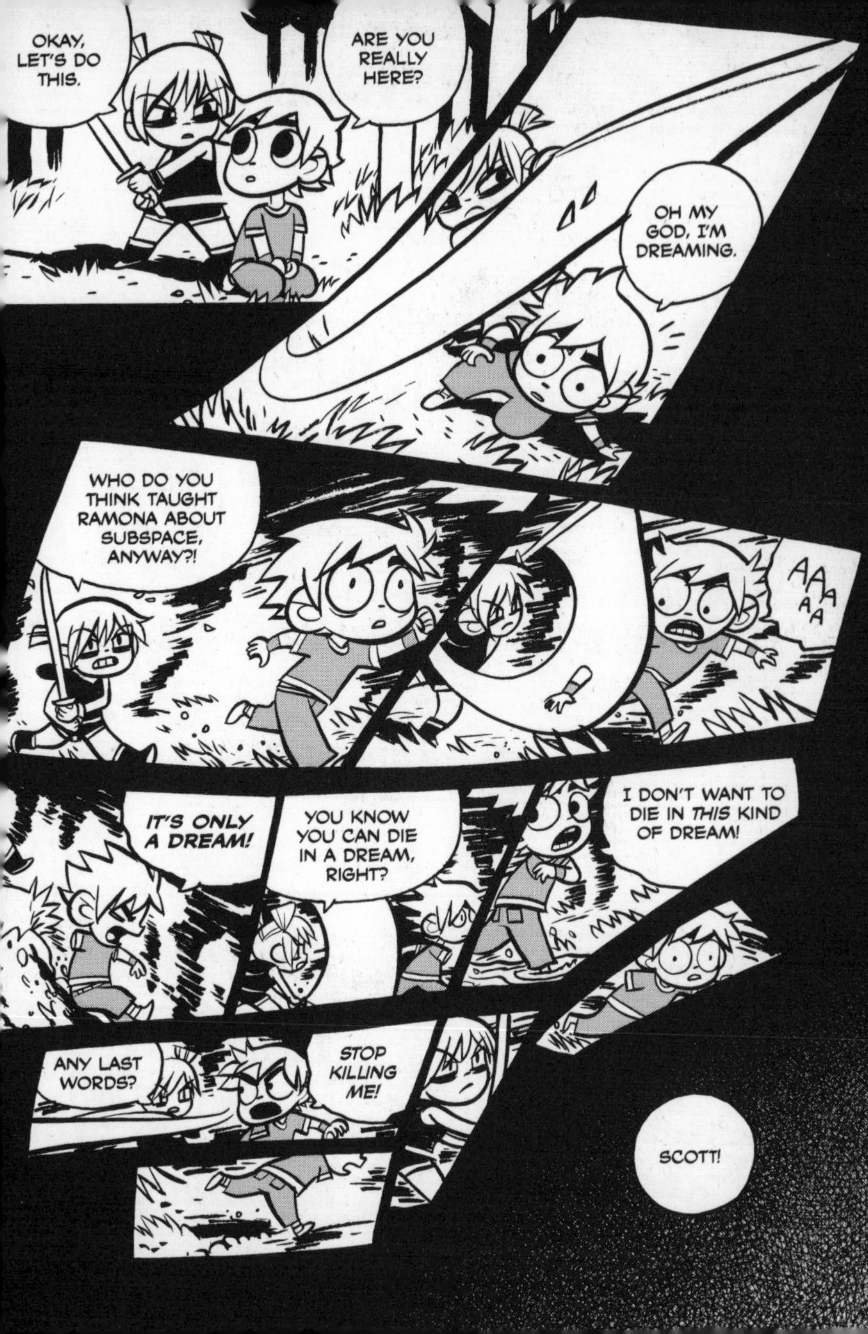
OKAY, LET'S DO THIS.
ARE YOU REALLY HERE?
OH MY GOD, I'M DREAMING.
WHO DO YOU THINK TAUGHT RAMONA ABOUT SUBSPACE, ANYWAY?!
AAAAA
IT'S ONLY A DREAM!
YOU KNOW YOU CAN DIE IN A DREAM, RIGHT?
I DON'T WANT TO DIE IN THIS KIND OF DREAM!
ANY LAST WORDS?
STOP KILLING ME!
SCOTT!

24 Terrible vision

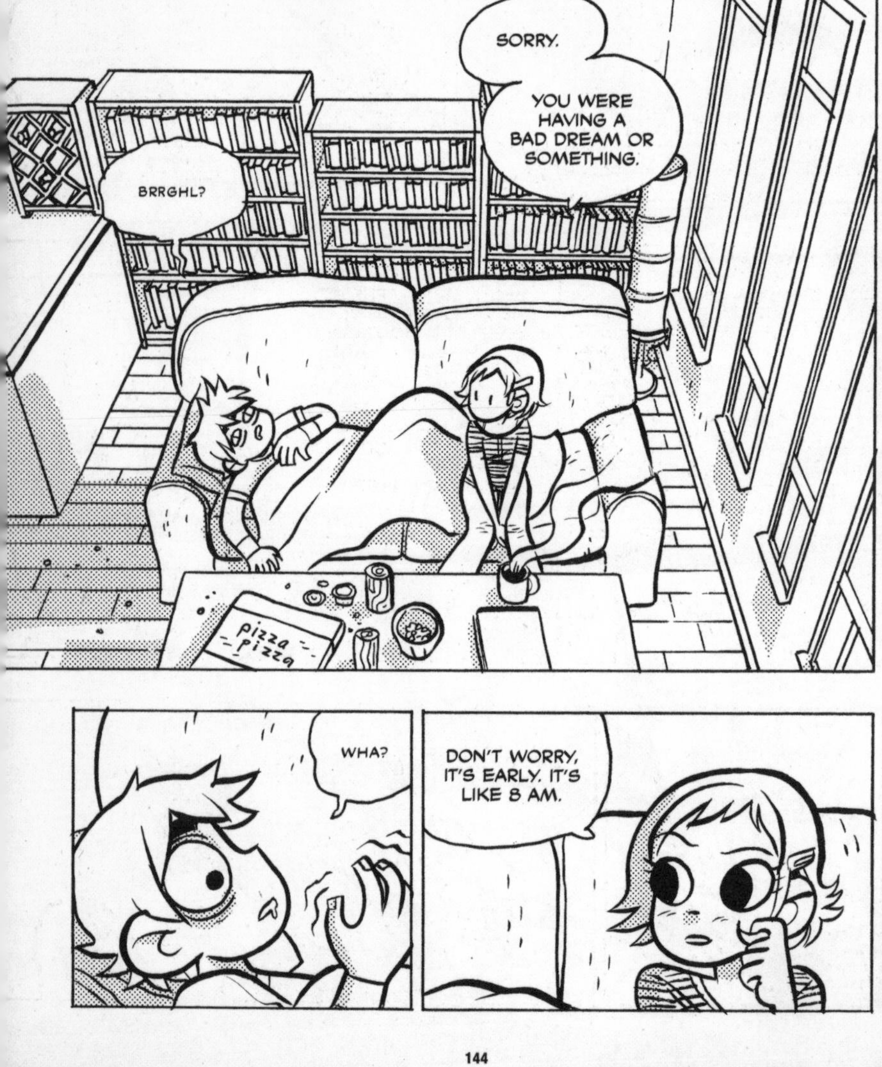
SORRY.
YOU WERE HAVING A BAD DREAM OR SOMETHING.
BRRGHL?
pizza pizza
WHA?
DON'T WORRY, IT'S EARLY. IT'S LIKE 8 AM.

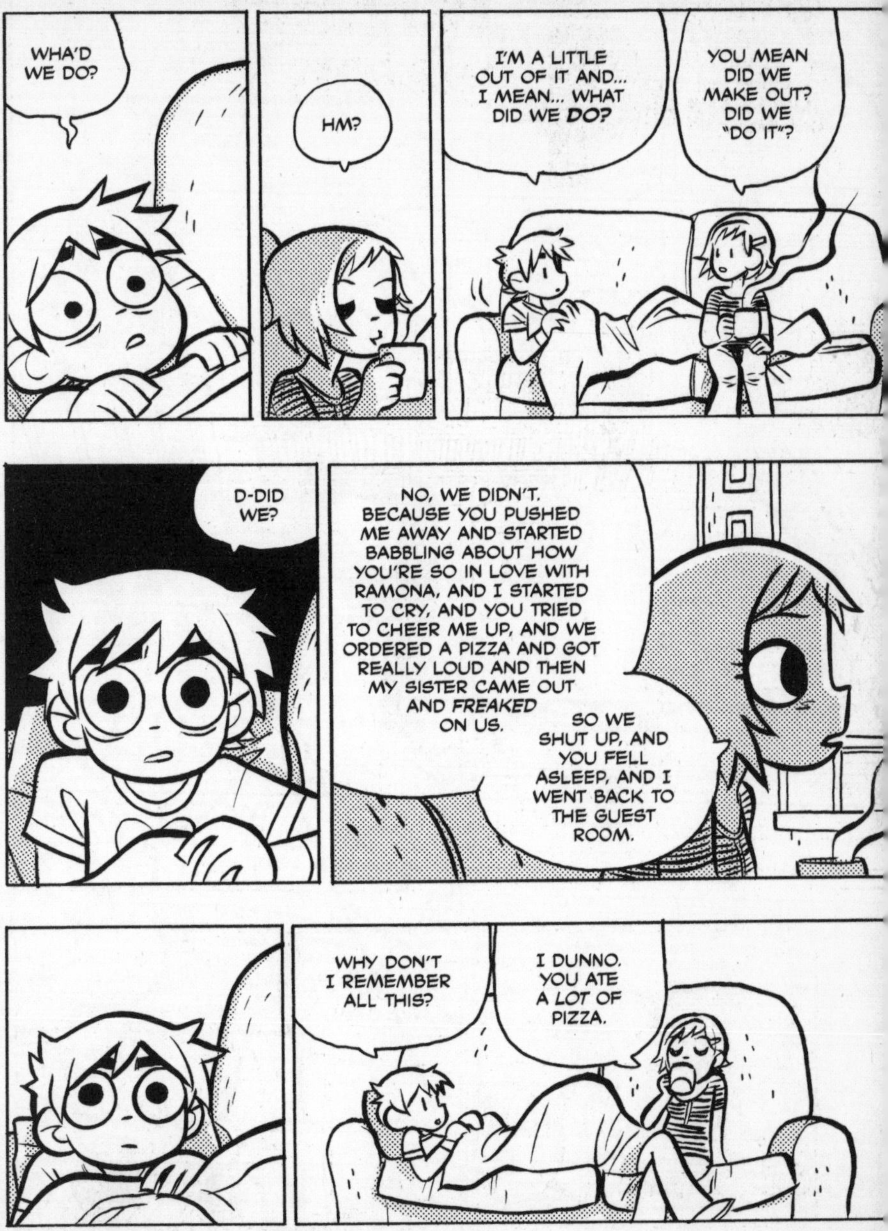
WHA'D WE DO?
HM?
I'M A LITTLE OUT OF IT AND... I MEAN... WHAT DID WE DO?
YOU MEAN DID WE MAKE OUT? DID WE "DO IT"?
D-DID WE?
NO, WE DIDN'T. BECAUSE YOU PUSHED ME AWAY AND STARTED BABBLING ABOUT HOW YOU'RE SO IN LOVE WITH RAMONA, AND I STARTED TO CRY, AND YOU TRIED TO CHEER ME UP, AND WE ORDERED A PIZZA AND GOT REALLY LOUD AND THEN MY SISTER CAME OUT AND FREAKED ON US.
SO WE SHUT UP, AND YOU FELL ASLEEP, AND I WENT BACK TO THE GUEST ROOM.
WHY DON'T I REMEMBER ALL THIS?
I DUNNO. YOU ATE A LOT OF PIZZA.

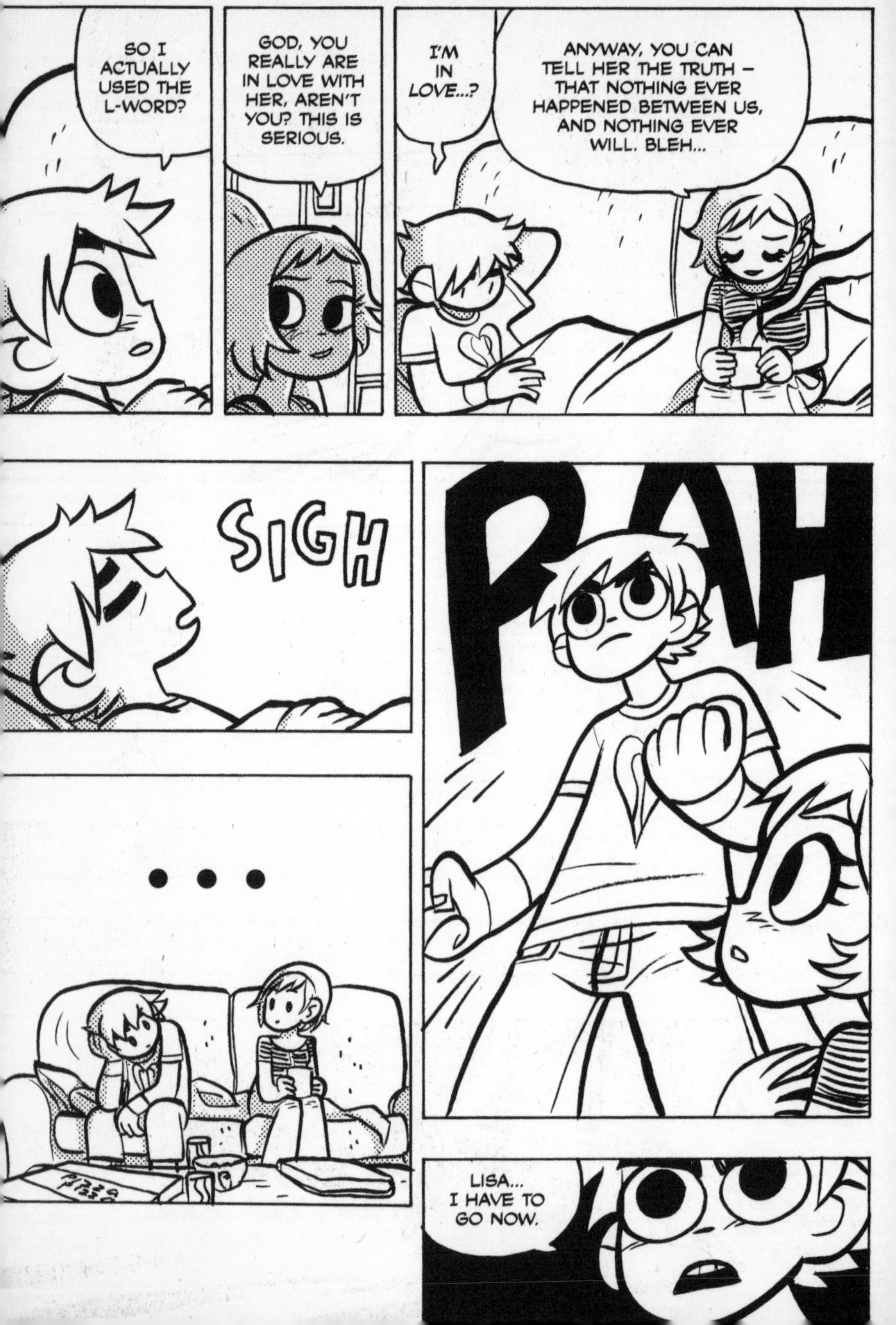
SO I ACTUALLY USED THE L-WORD?
GOD, YOU REALLY ARE IN LOVE WITH HER, AREN'T YOU? THIS IS SERIOUS.
I'M IN *LOVE*...?
ANYWAY, YOU CAN TELL HER THE TRUTH – THAT NOTHING EVER HAPPENED BETWEEN US, AND NOTHING EVER WILL. BLEH...
SIGH
• • •
PAH
LISA... I HAVE TO GO NOW.

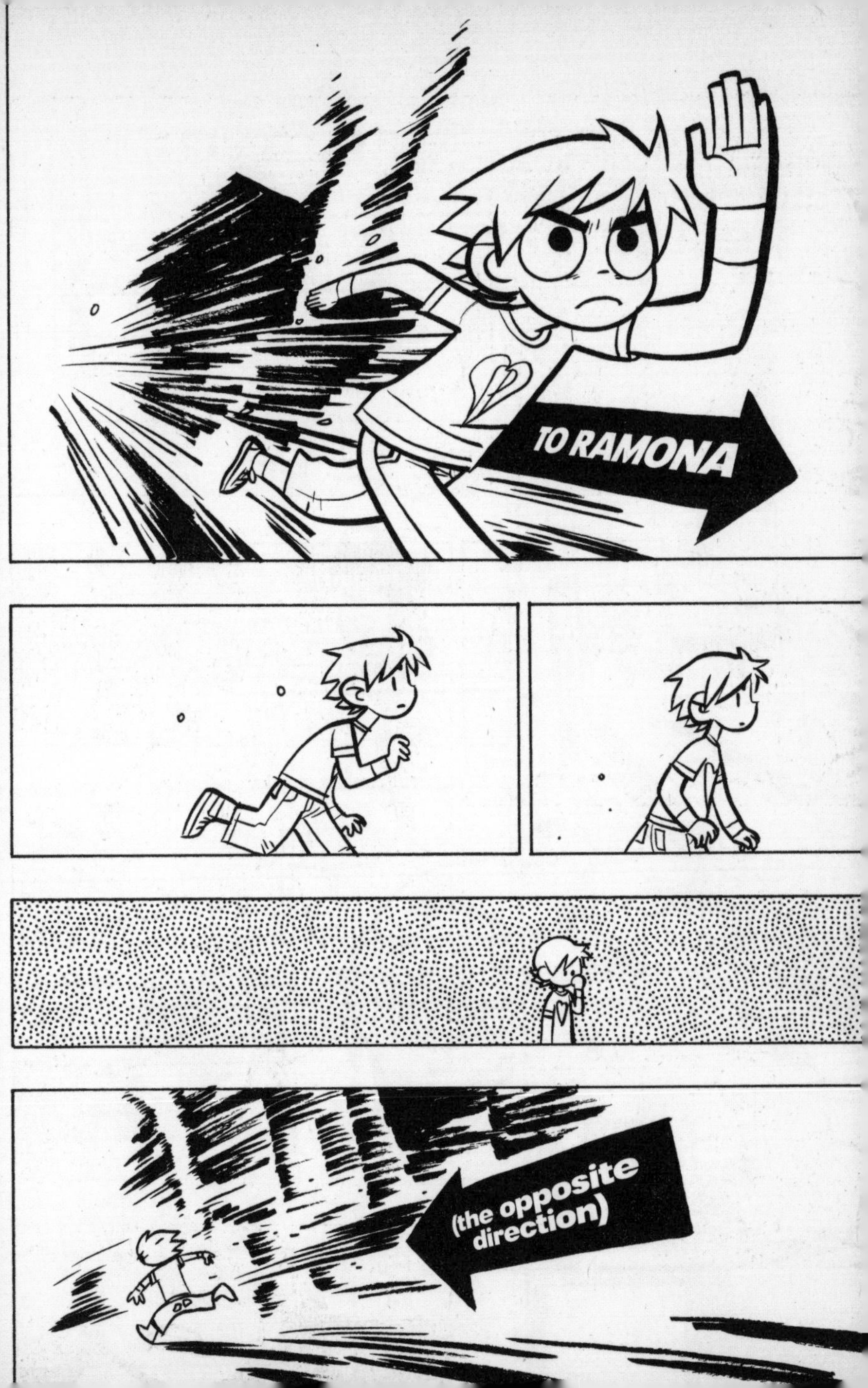
TO RAMONA
(the opposite direction)

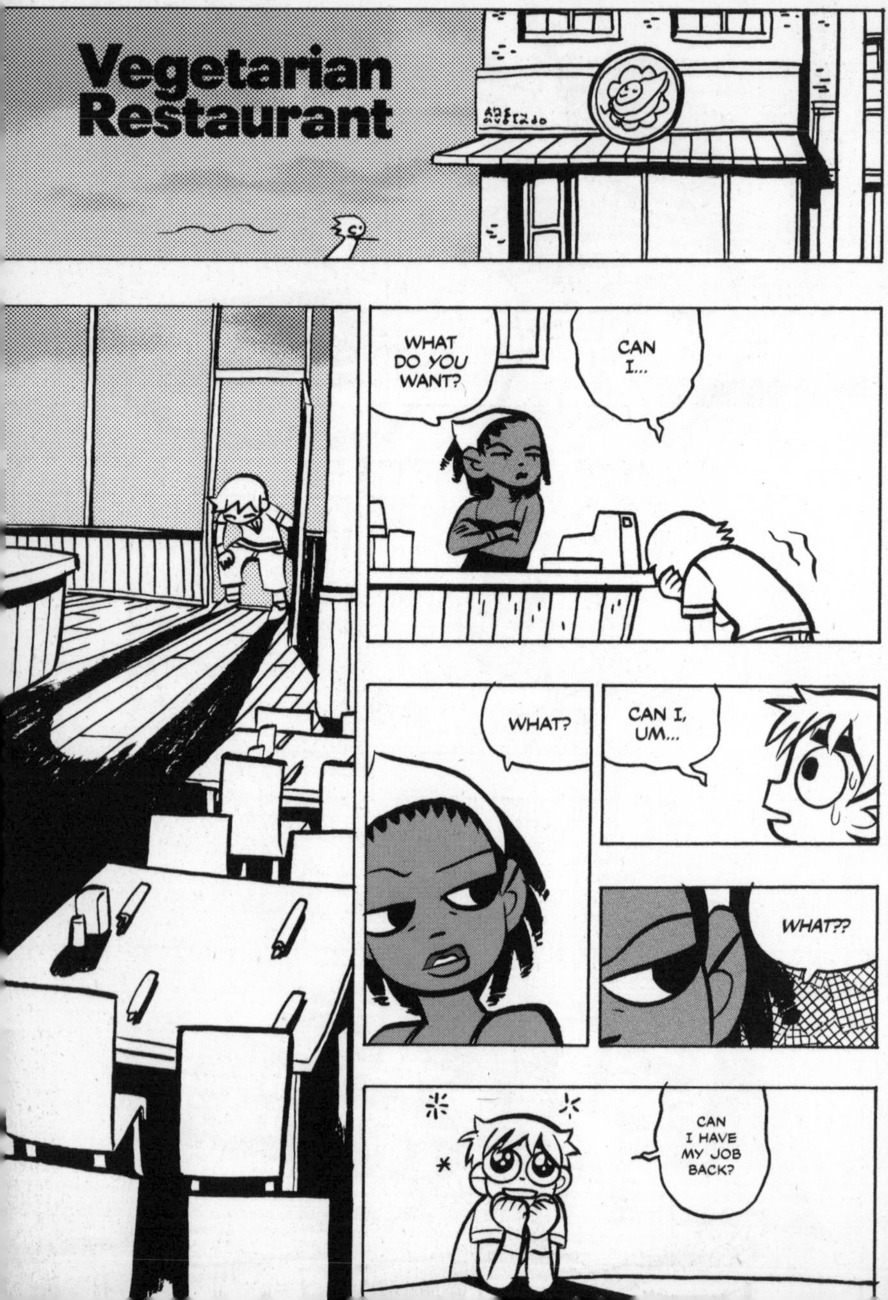
Vegetarian Restaurant
WHAT DO YOU WANT?
CAN I...
WHAT?
CAN I, UM...
WHAT??
CAN I HAVE MY JOB BACK?

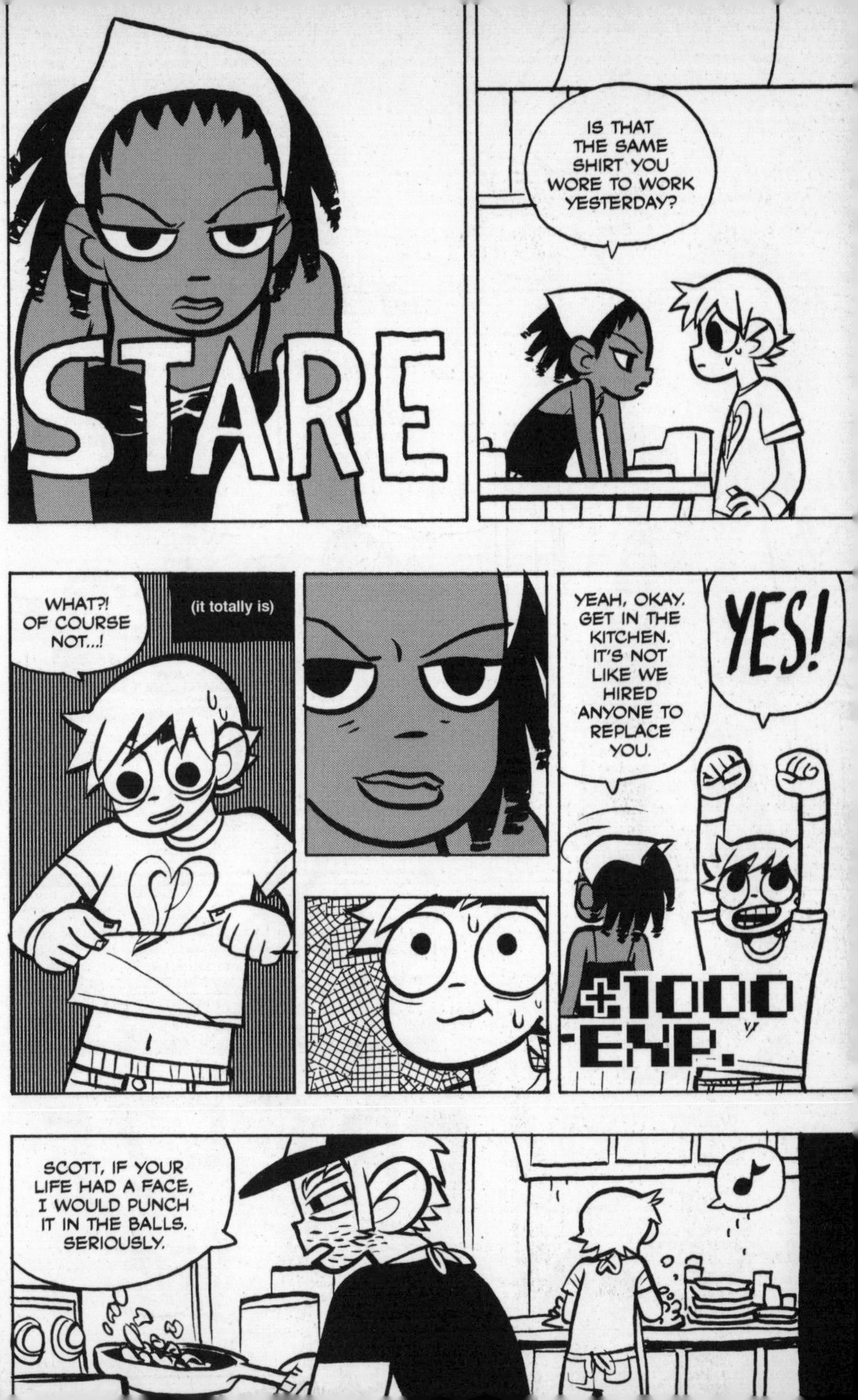
STARE
IS THAT THE SAME SHIRT YOU WORE TO WORK YESTERDAY?
WHAT?! OF COURSE NOT...!
(it totally is)
YEAH, OKAY. GET IN THE KITCHEN. IT'S NOT LIKE WE HIRED ANYONE TO REPLACE YOU.
YES!
+1000 EXP.
SCOTT, IF YOUR LIFE HAD A FACE, I WOULD PUNCH IT IN THE BALLS. SERIOUSLY.

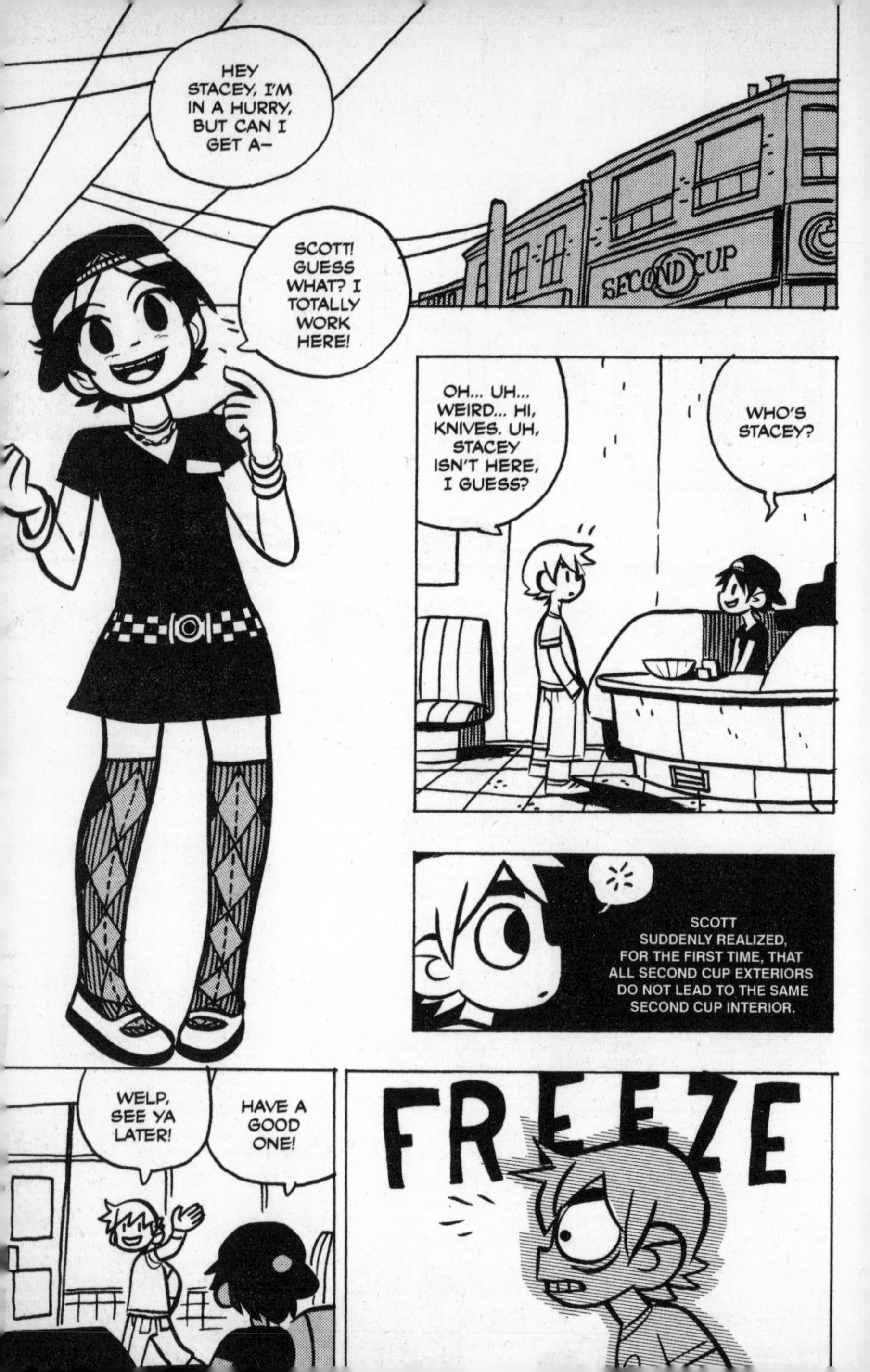
HEY STACEY, I'M IN A HURRY, BUT CAN I GET A–
SECOND CUP
SCOTT! GUESS WHAT? I TOTALLY WORK HERE!
OH... UH... WEIRD... HI, KNIVES. UH, STACEY ISN'T HERE, I GUESS?
WHO'S STACEY?
SCOTT SUDDENLY REALIZED, FOR THE FIRST TIME, THAT ALL SECOND CUP EXTERIORS DO NOT LEAD TO THE SAME SECOND CUP INTERIOR.
WELP, SEE YA LATER!
HAVE A GOOD ONE!
FREEZE

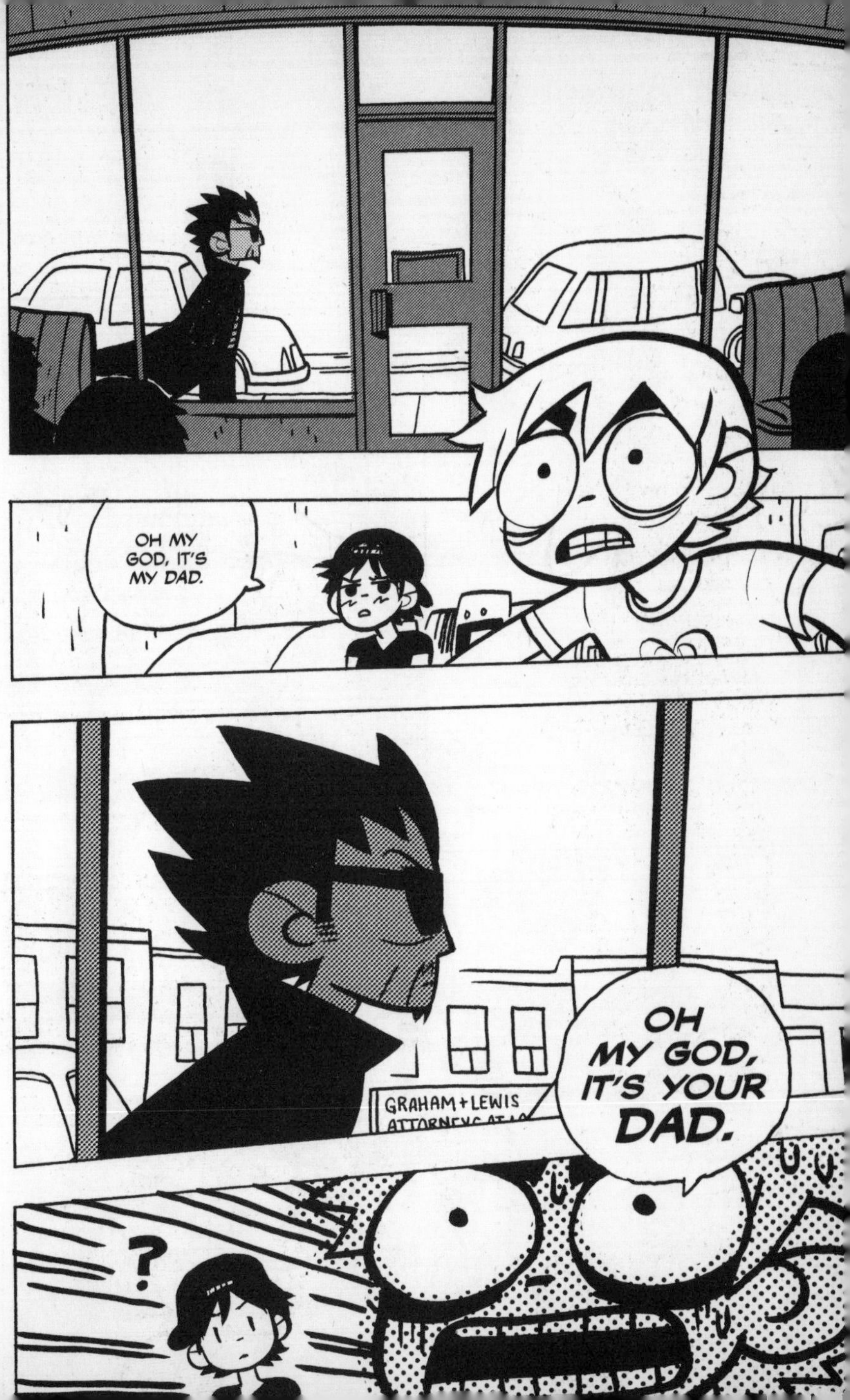
OH MY GOD, IT'S MY DAD.
GRAHAM + LEWIS
OH MY GOD, IT'S YOUR DAD.
?

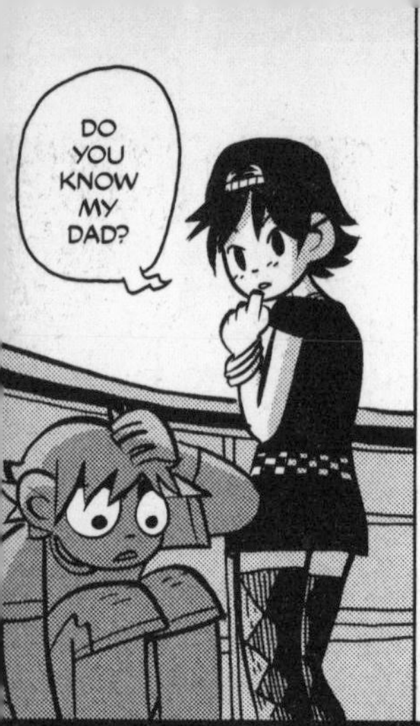
DO YOU KNOW MY DAD?

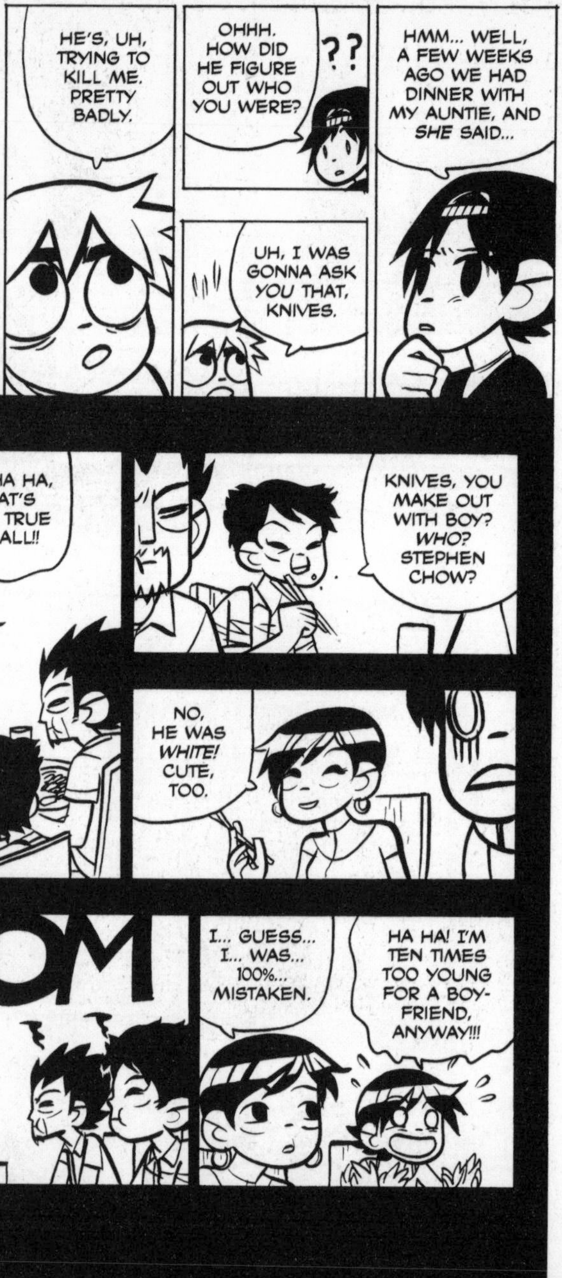
HE'S, UH, TRYING TO KILL ME. PRETTY BADLY.
OHHH. HOW DID HE FIGURE OUT WHO YOU WERE?
??
UH, I WAS GONNA ASK YOU THAT, KNIVES.
HMM... WELL, A FEW WEEKS AGO WE HAD DINNER WITH MY AUNTIE, AND SHE SAID...
I SAW YOU WITH YOUR BOYFRIEND THE OTHER DAY, KNIVES, BUT YOU DIDN'T WAVE BACK.
HA HA HA, THAT'S NOT TRUE AT ALL!!
KNIVES, YOU MAKE OUT WITH BOY? WHO? STEPHEN CHOW?
NO, HE WAS WHITE! CUTE, TOO.
DOOM
?
I... GUESS... I... WAS... 100%... MISTAKEN.
HA HA! I'M TEN TIMES TOO YOUNG FOR A BOY-FRIEND, ANYWAY!!!

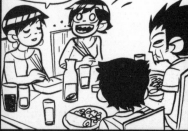

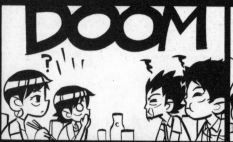

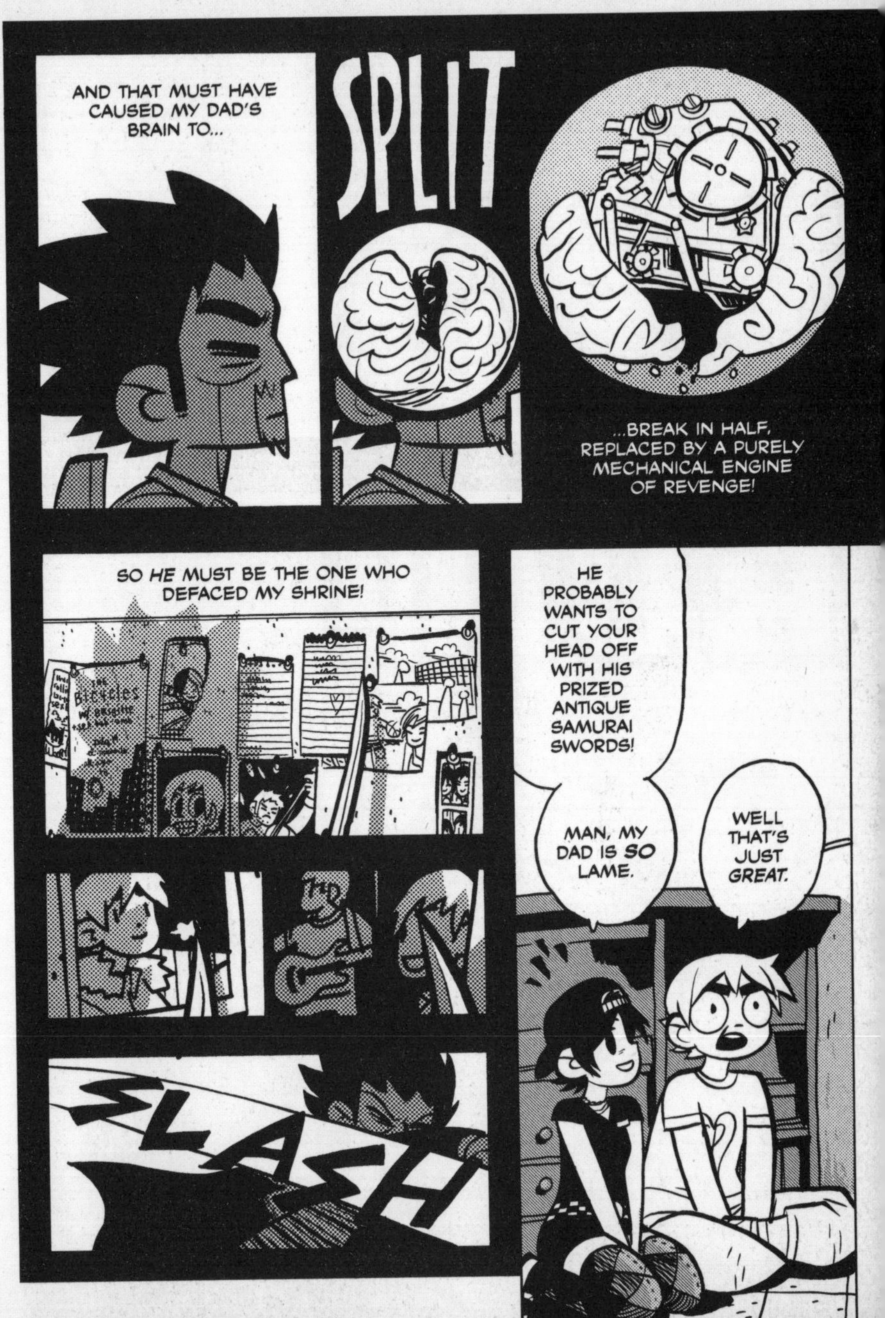
AND THAT MUST HAVE CAUSED MY DAD'S BRAIN TO...
SPLIT
...BREAK IN HALF, REPLACED BY A PURELY MECHANICAL ENGINE OF REVENGE!
SO HE MUST BE THE ONE WHO DEFACED MY SHRINE!
HE PROBABLY WANTS TO CUT YOUR HEAD OFF WITH HIS PRIZED ANTIQUE SAMURAI SWORDS!
MAN, MY DAD IS SO LAME.
WELL THAT'S JUST GREAT.
SLASH

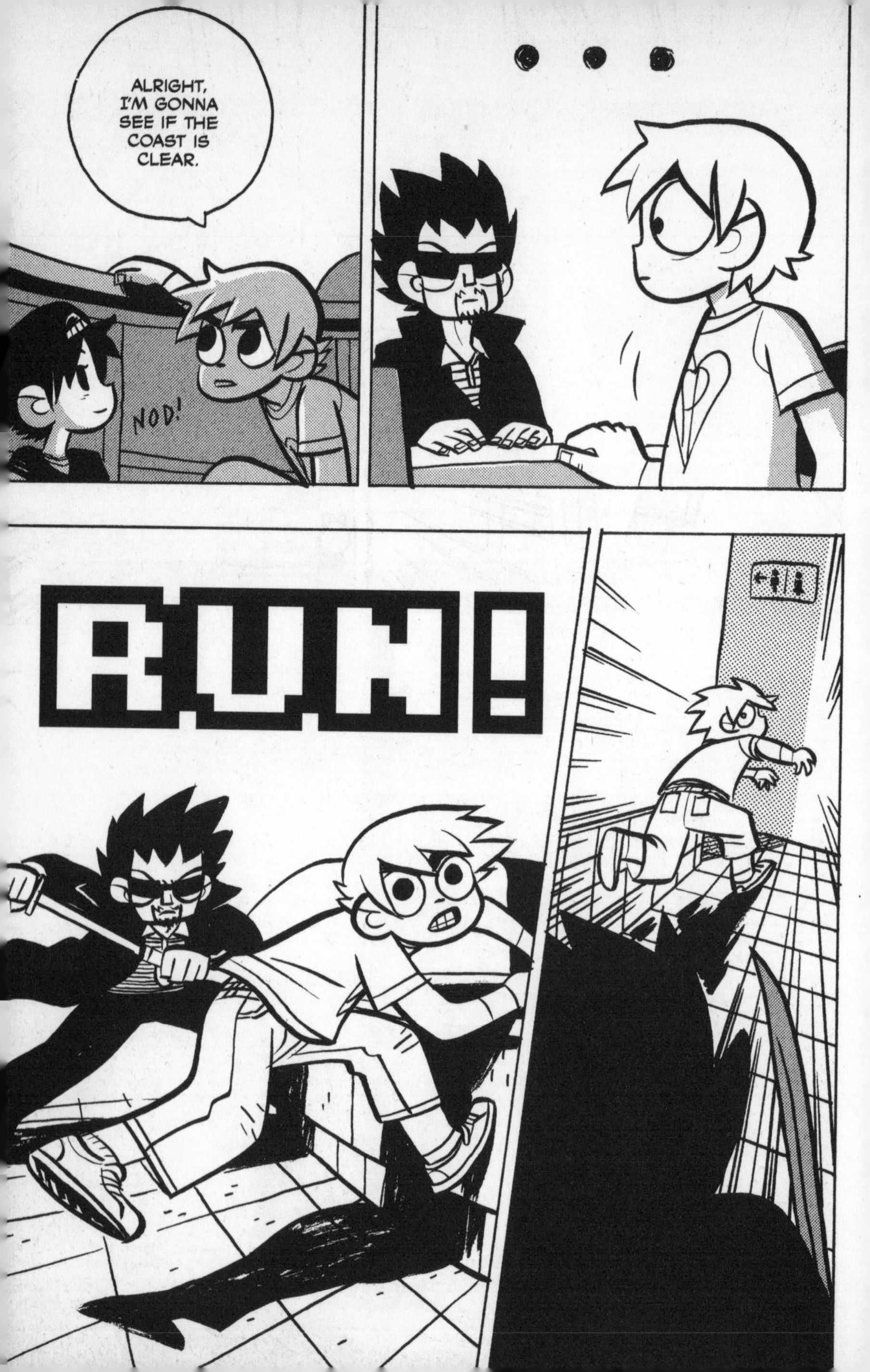
ALRIGHT, I'M GONNA SEE IF THE COAST IS CLEAR.
NOD!
RUN!

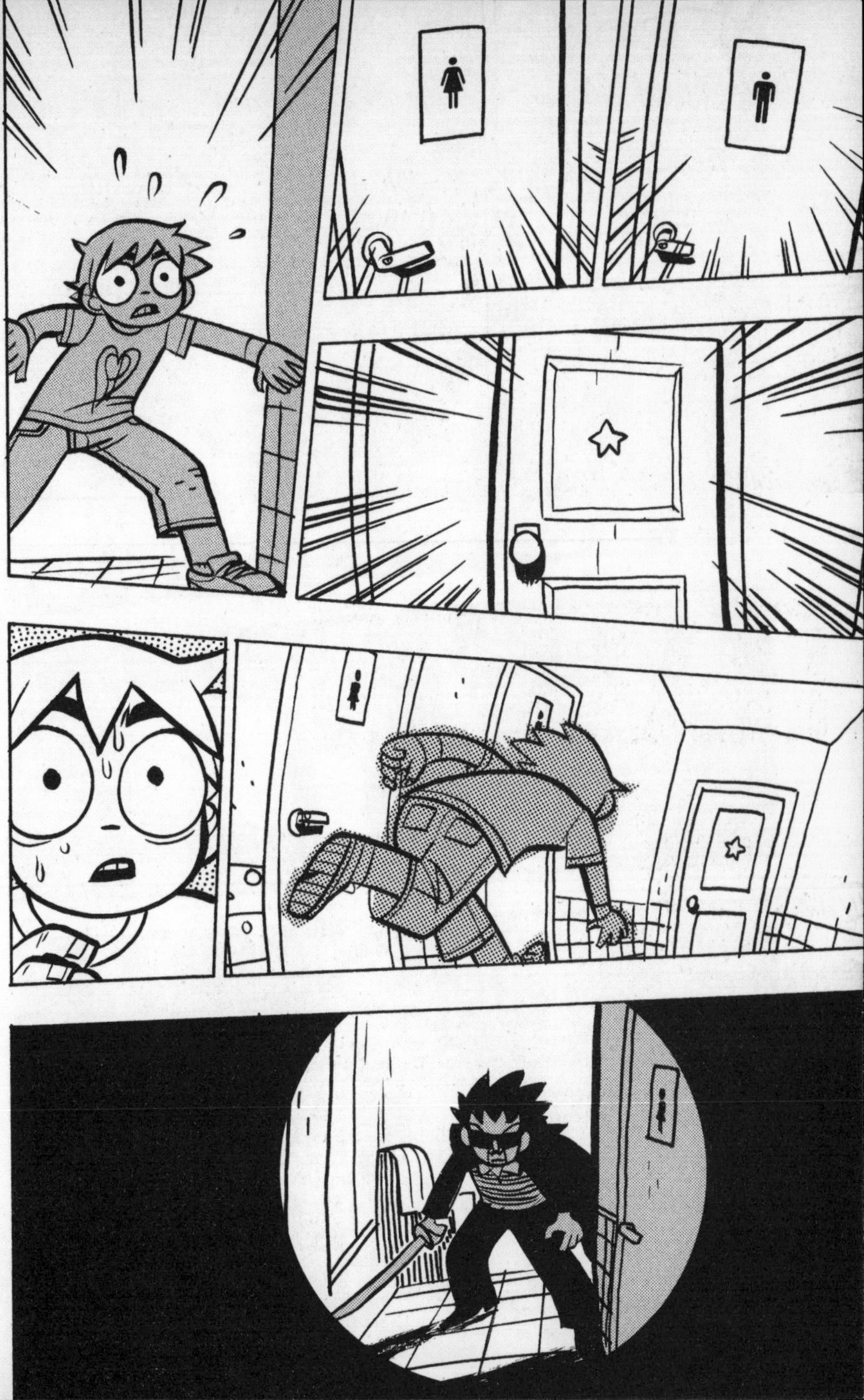

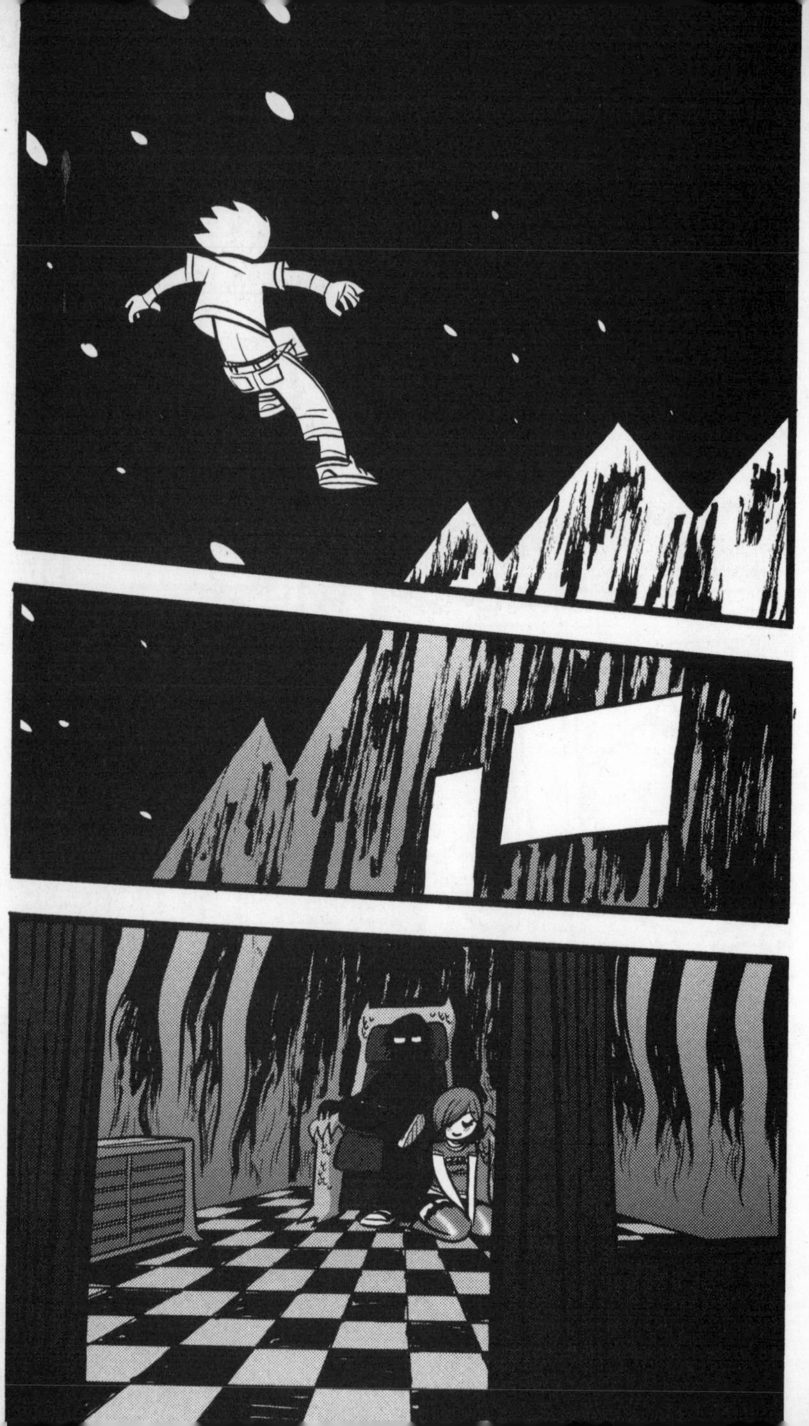

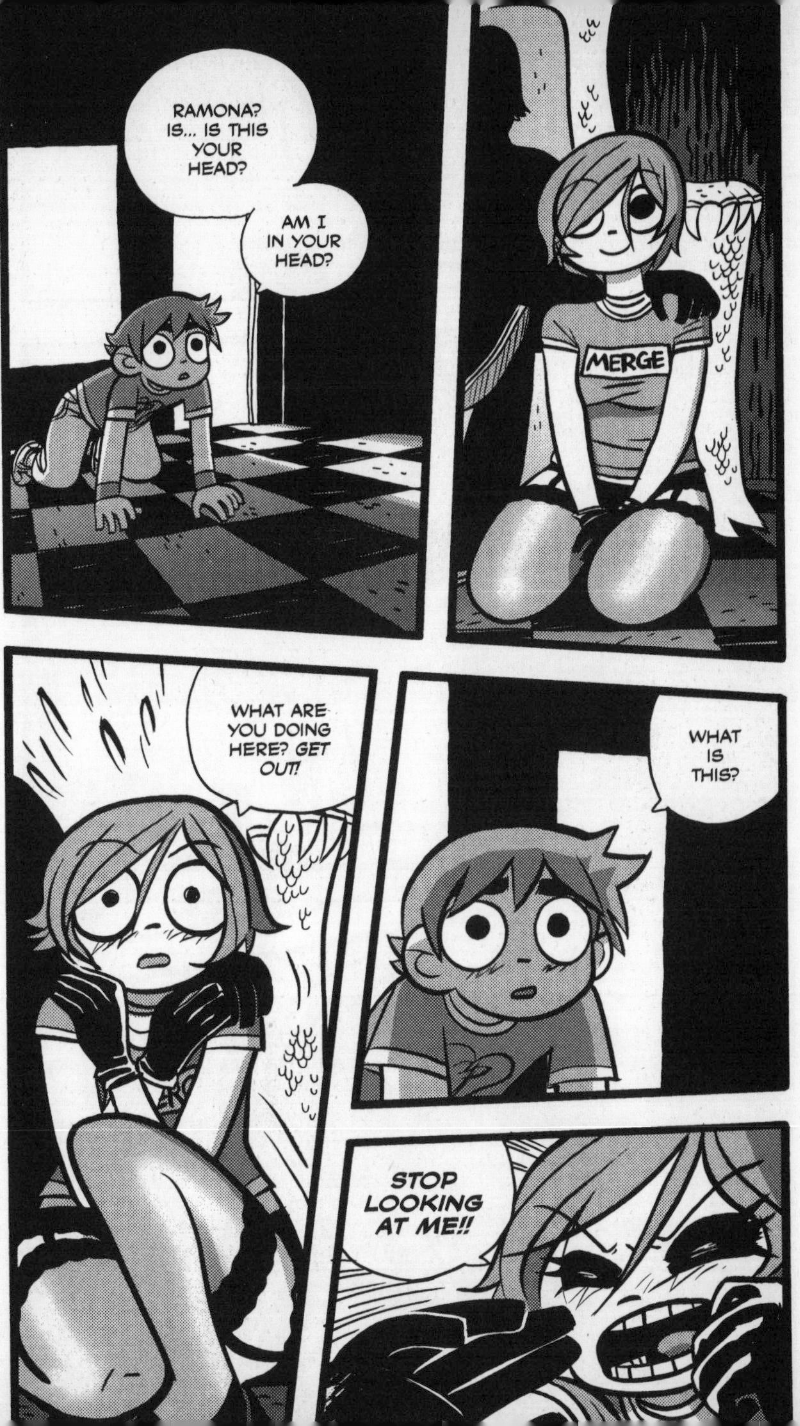
RAMONA? IS... IS THIS YOUR HEAD?
AM I IN YOUR HEAD?
MERGE
WHAT ARE YOU DOING HERE? GET OUT!
WHAT IS THIS?
STOP LOOKING AT ME!!

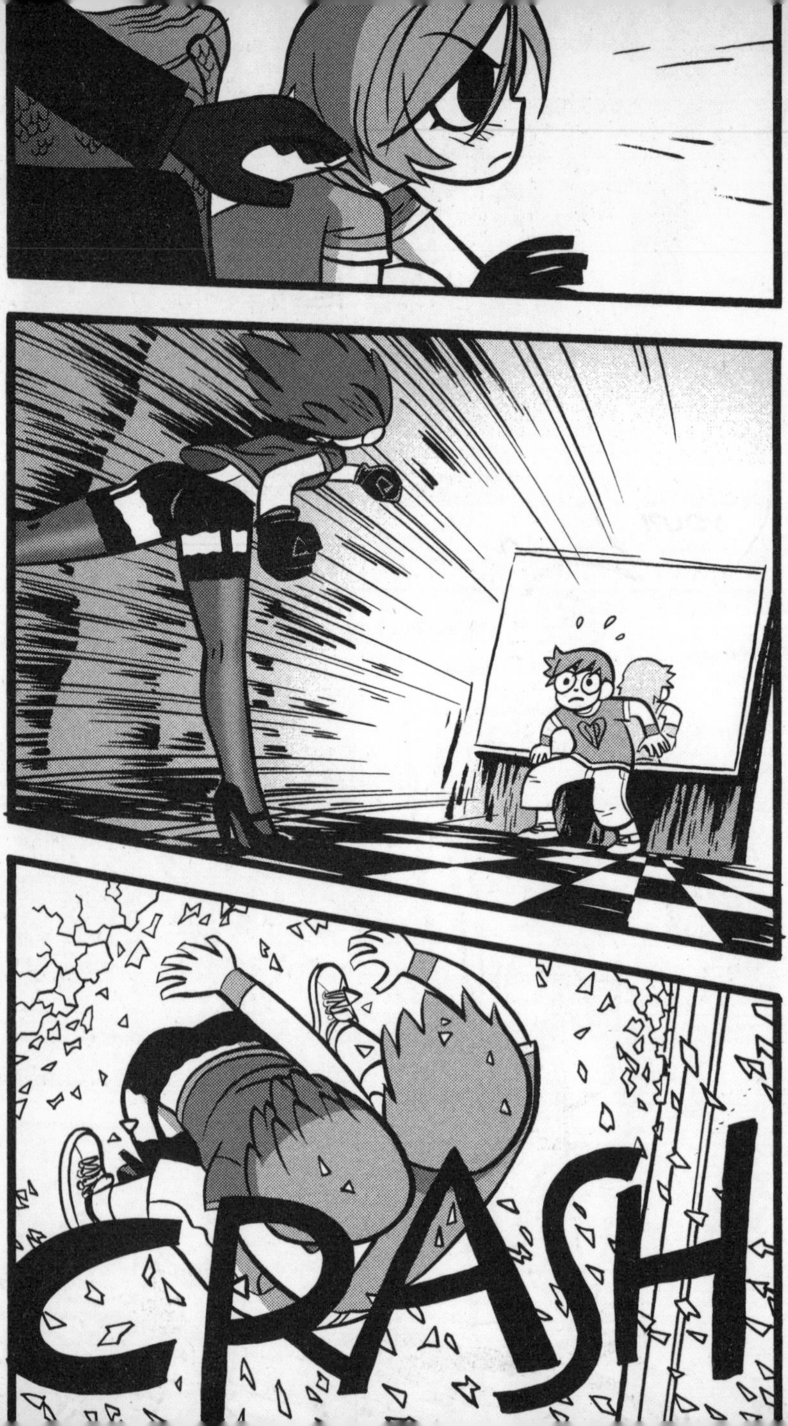
CRASH

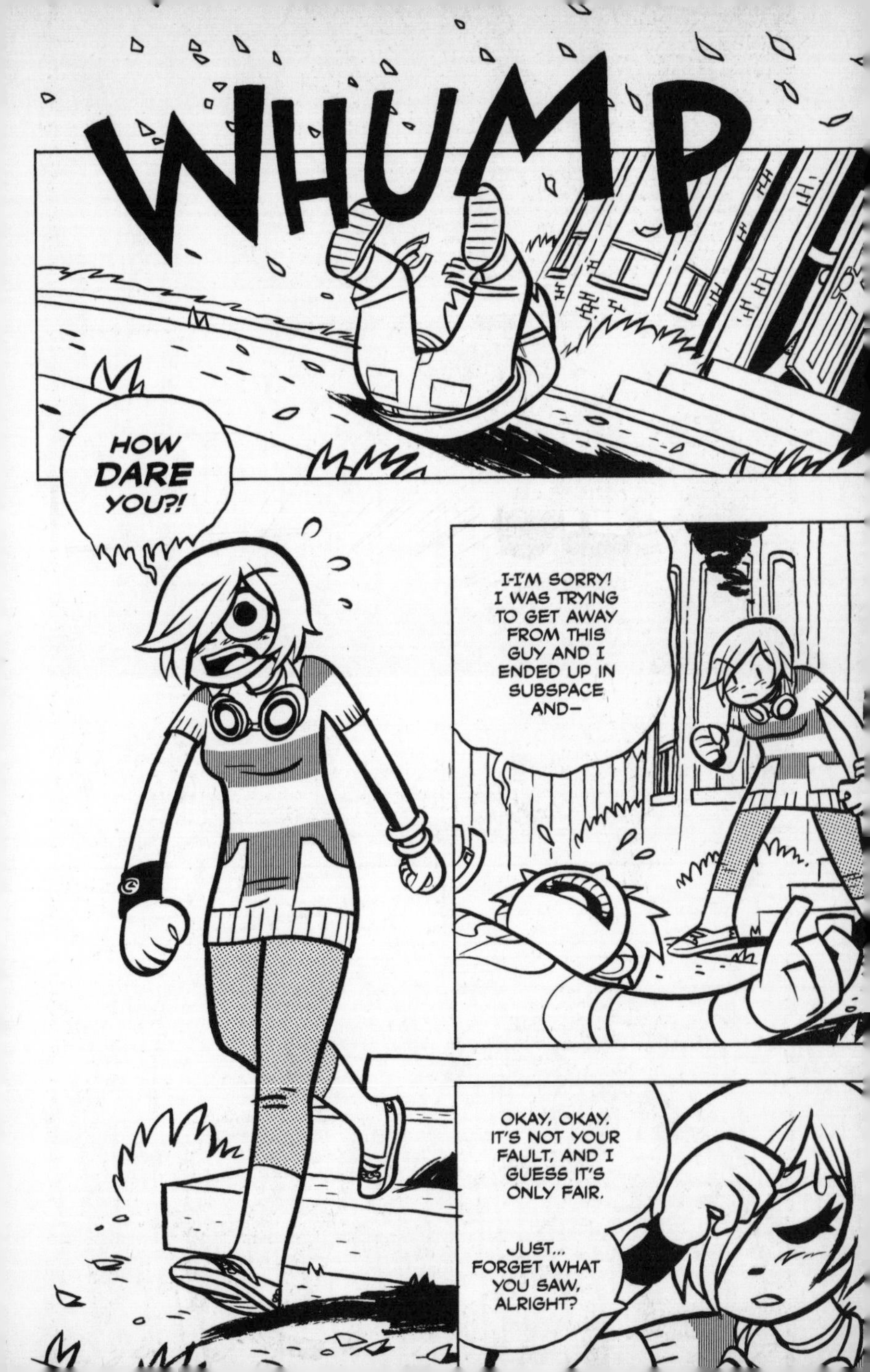
WHUMP
HOW DARE YOU?!
I-I'M SORRY! I WAS TRYING TO GET AWAY FROM THIS GUY AND I ENDED UP IN SUBSPACE AND—
OKAY, OKAY. IT'S NOT YOUR FAULT, AND I GUESS IT'S ONLY FAIR.
JUST... FORGET WHAT YOU SAW, ALRIGHT?

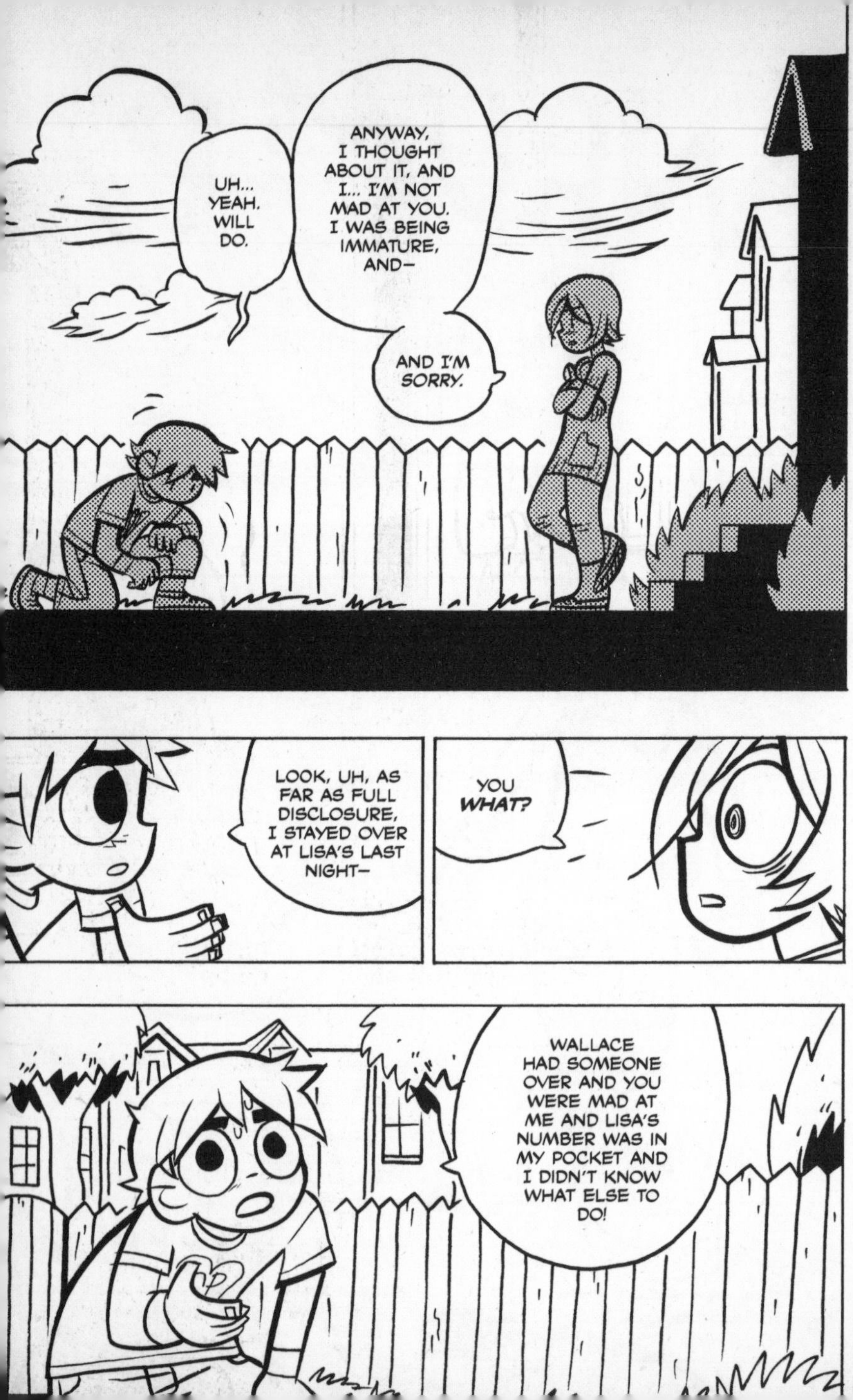
UH... YEAH. WILL DO.
ANYWAY, I THOUGHT ABOUT IT, AND I... I'M NOT MAD AT YOU. I WAS BEING IMMATURE, AND—
AND I'M SORRY.
LOOK, UH, AS FAR AS FULL DISCLOSURE, I STAYED OVER AT LISA'S LAST NIGHT—
YOU WHAT?
WALLACE HAD SOMEONE OVER AND YOU WERE MAD AT ME AND LISA'S NUMBER WAS IN MY POCKET AND I DIDN'T KNOW WHAT ELSE TO DO!

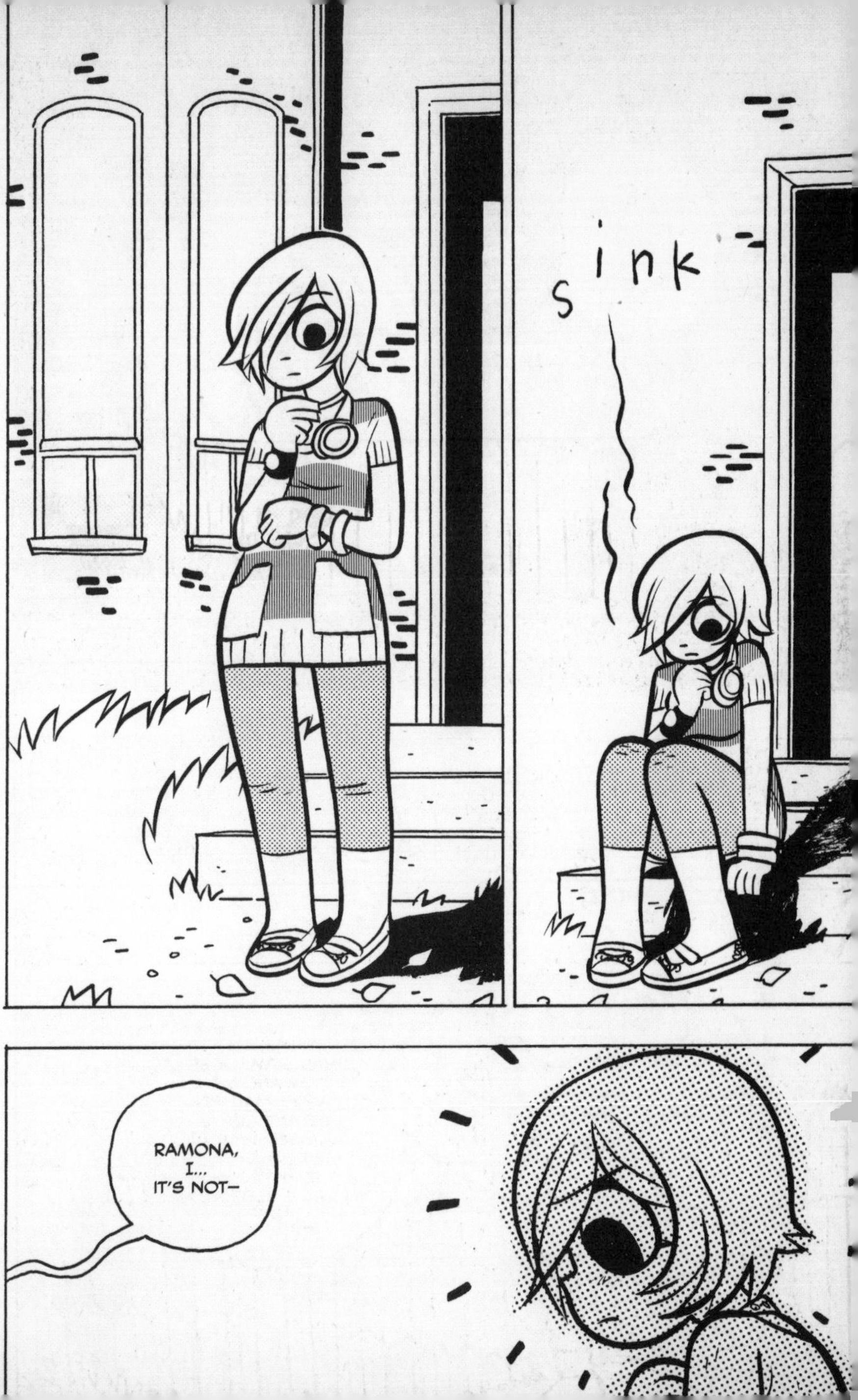

sink
RAMONA, I... IT'S NOT—

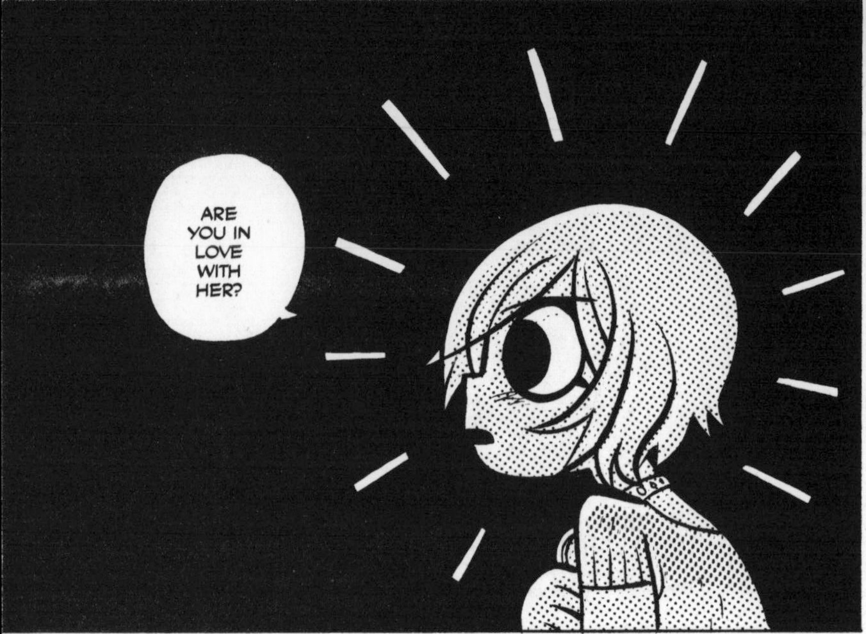
ARE YOU IN LOVE WITH HER?
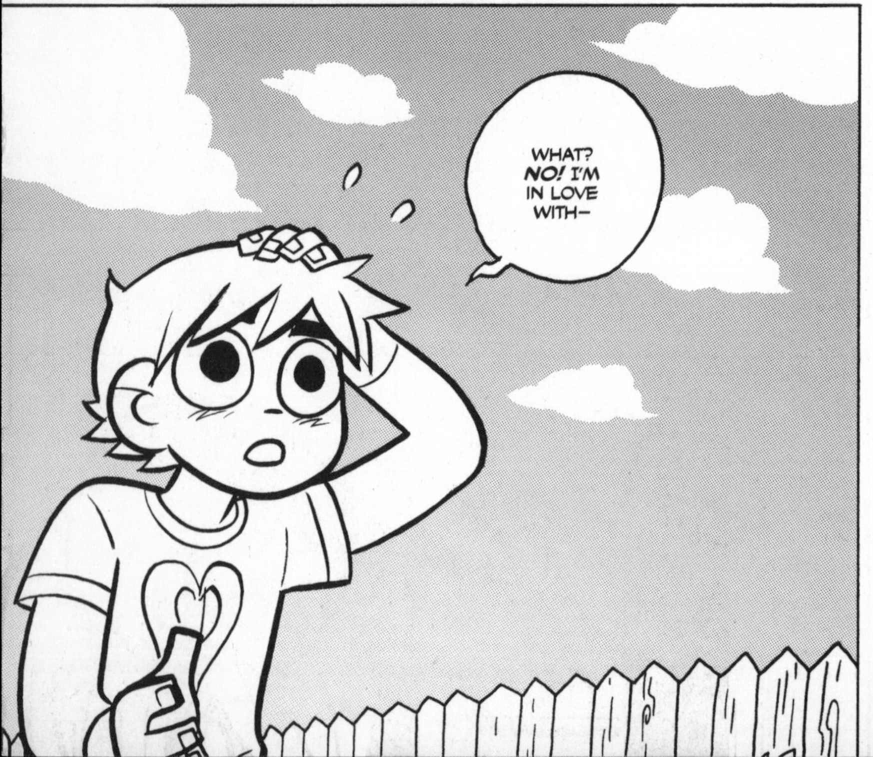
WHAT? NO! I'M IN LOVE WITH–

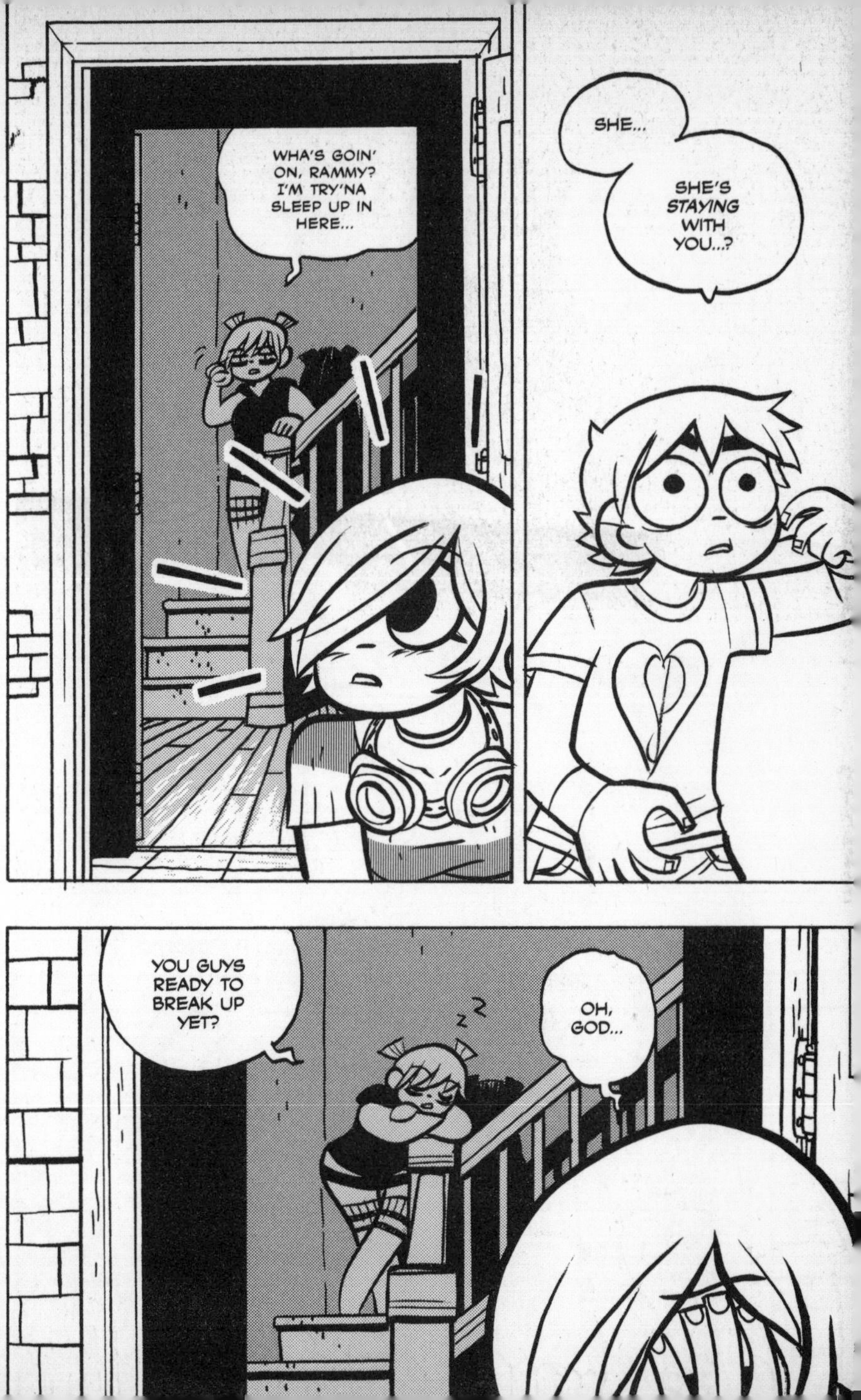
WHA'S GOIN' ON, RAMMY? I'M TRY'NA SLEEP UP IN HERE...
SHE...
SHE'S STAYING WITH YOU...?
YOU GUYS READY TO BREAK UP YET?
Z Z
OH, GOD...

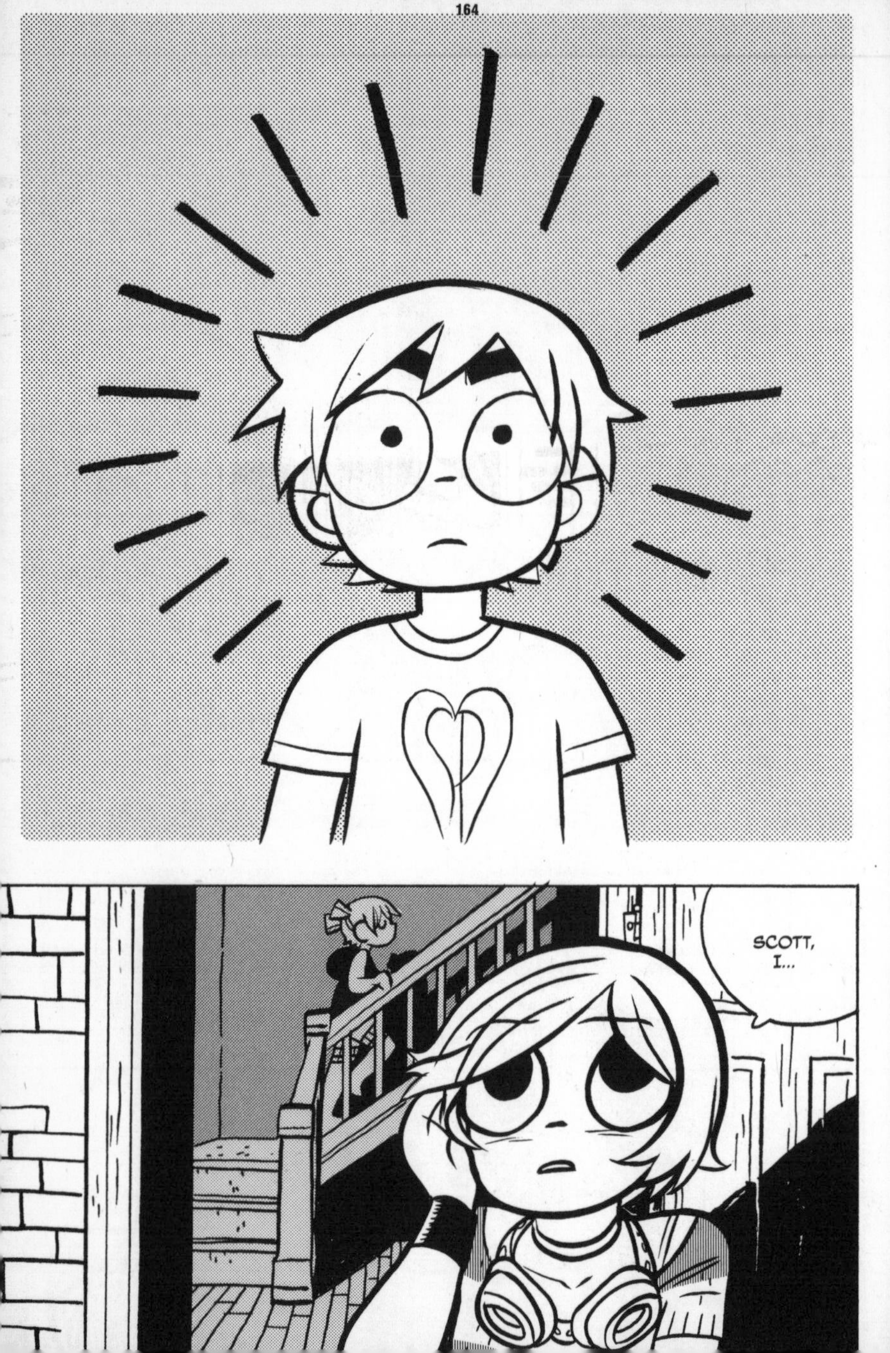
SCOTT,
I...

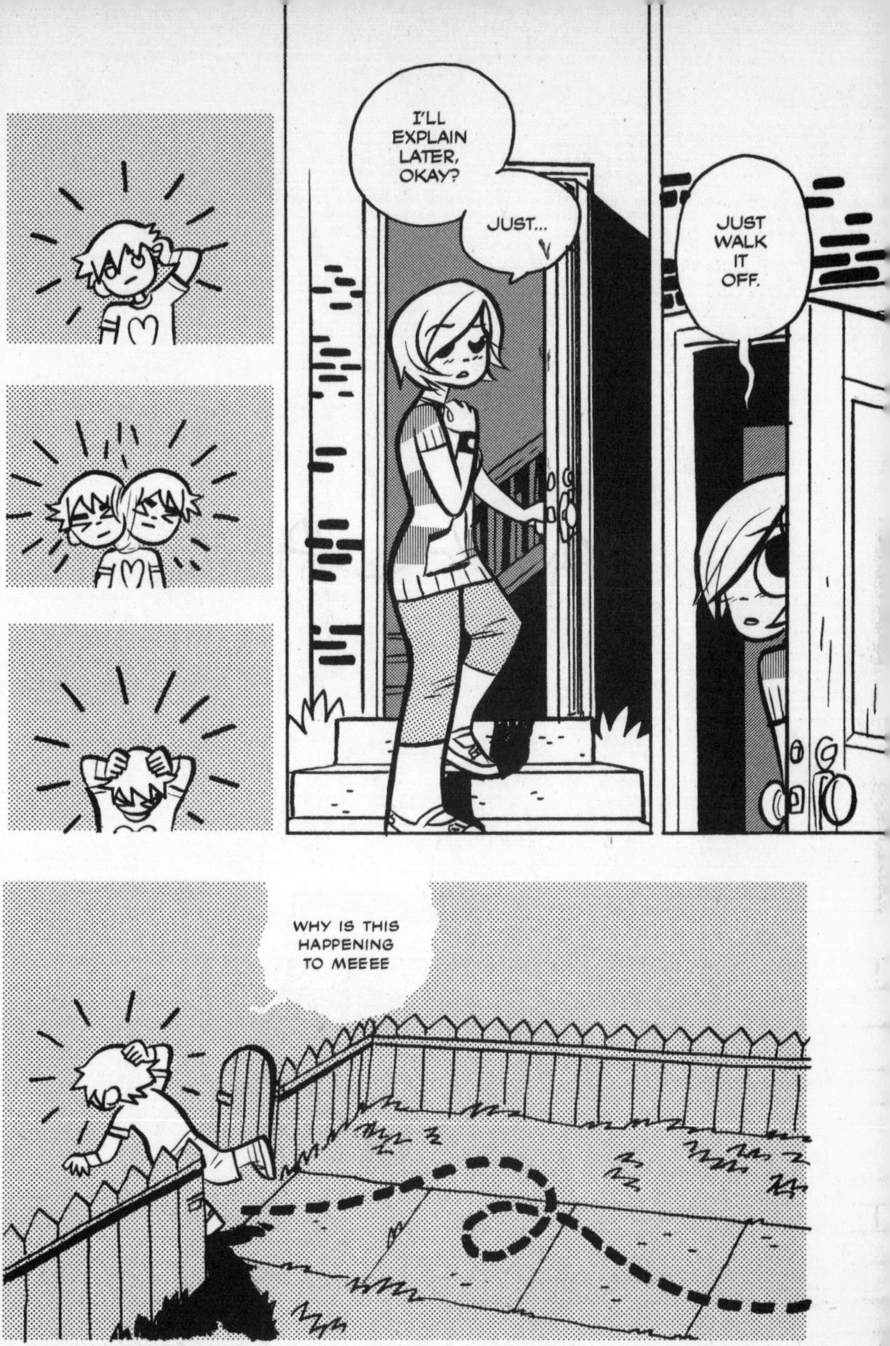
I'LL EXPLAIN LATER, OKAY?
JUST...
JUST WALK IT OFF.
WHY IS THIS HAPPENING TO MEEEE

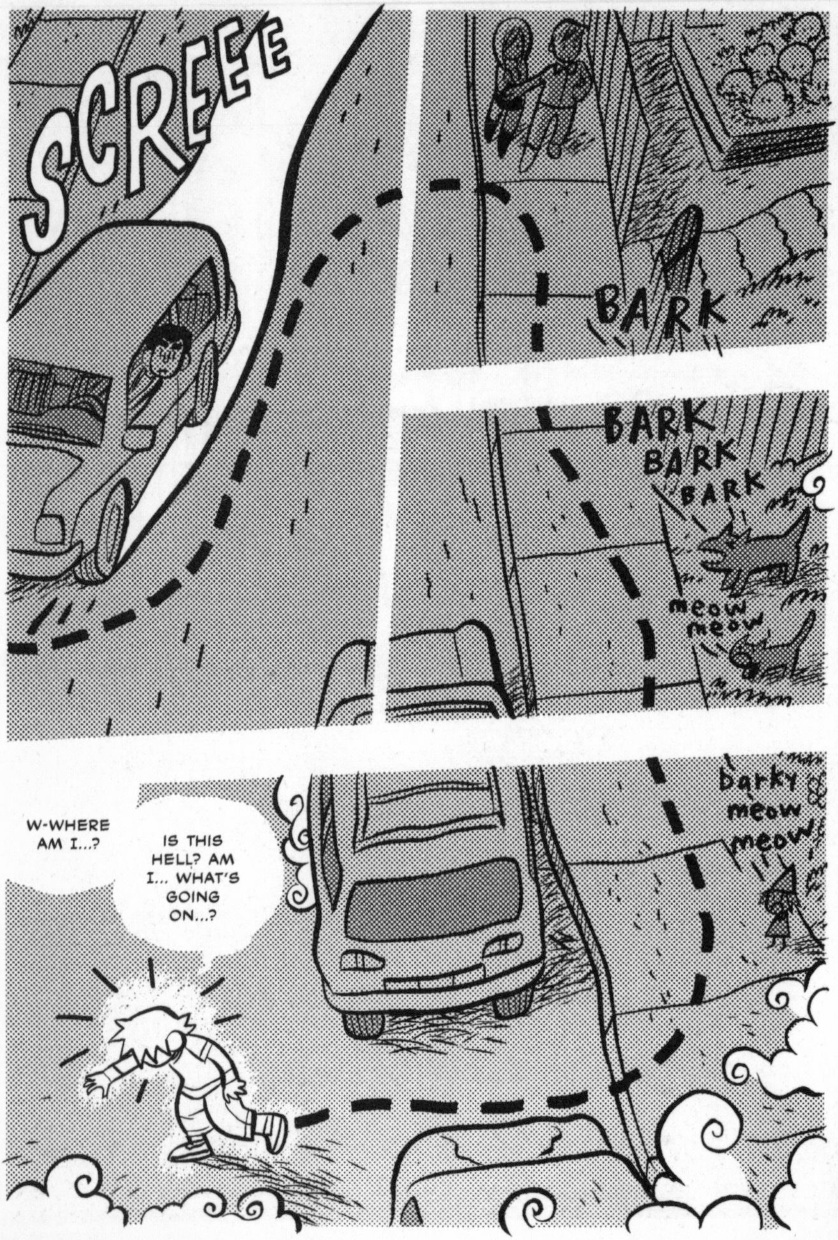
SCREEE
BARK
BARK
BARK
BARK
meow
meow
W-WHERE AM I...?
IS THIS HELL? AM I... WHAT'S GOING ON...?
barky
meow
meow

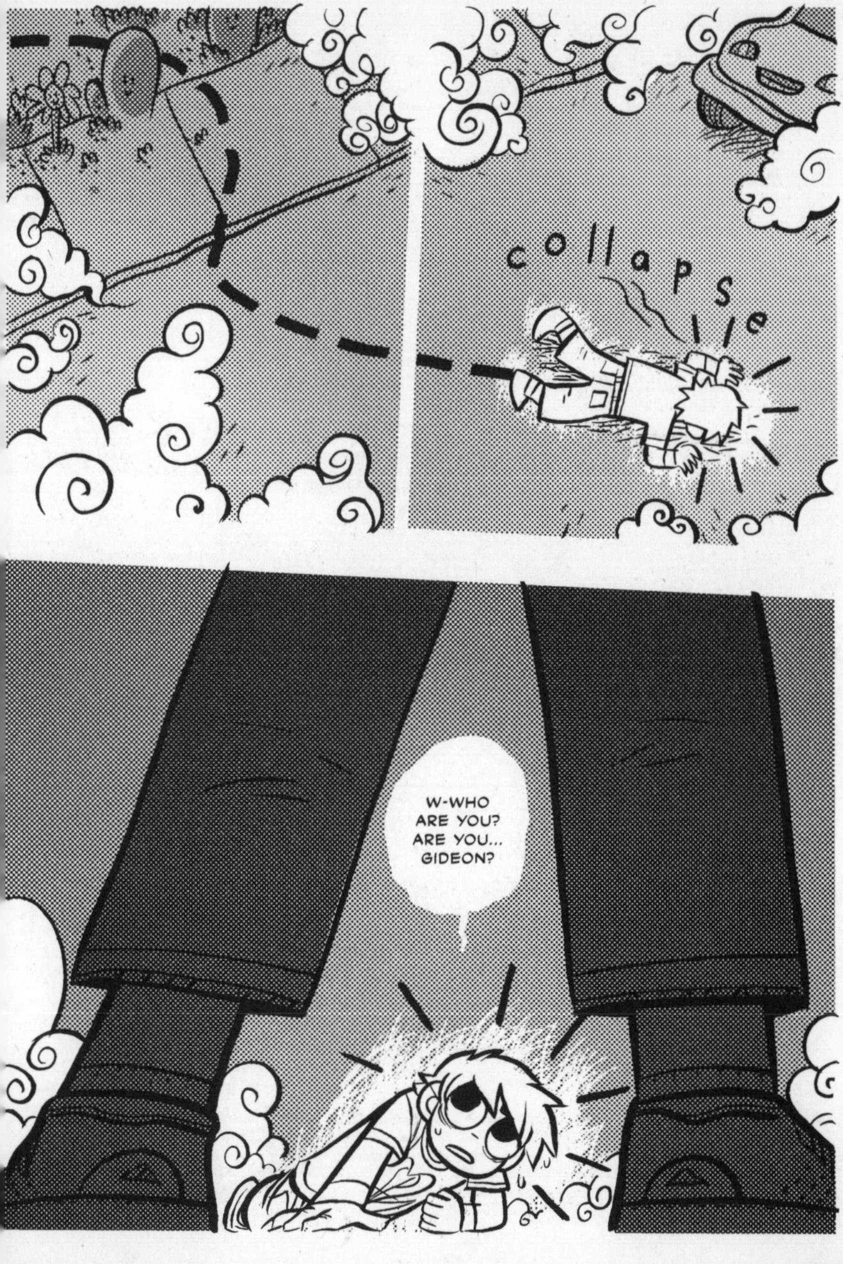
collapse
W-WHO ARE YOU? ARE YOU... GIDEON?

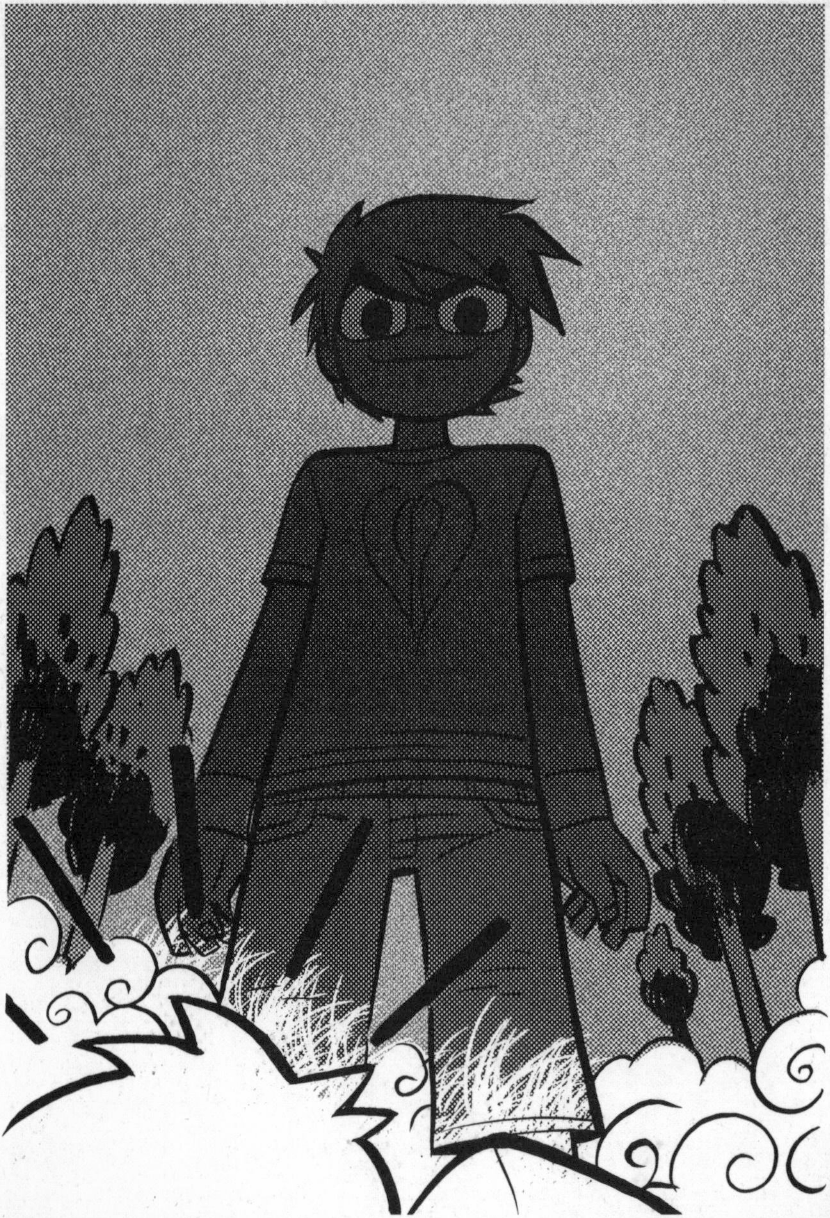

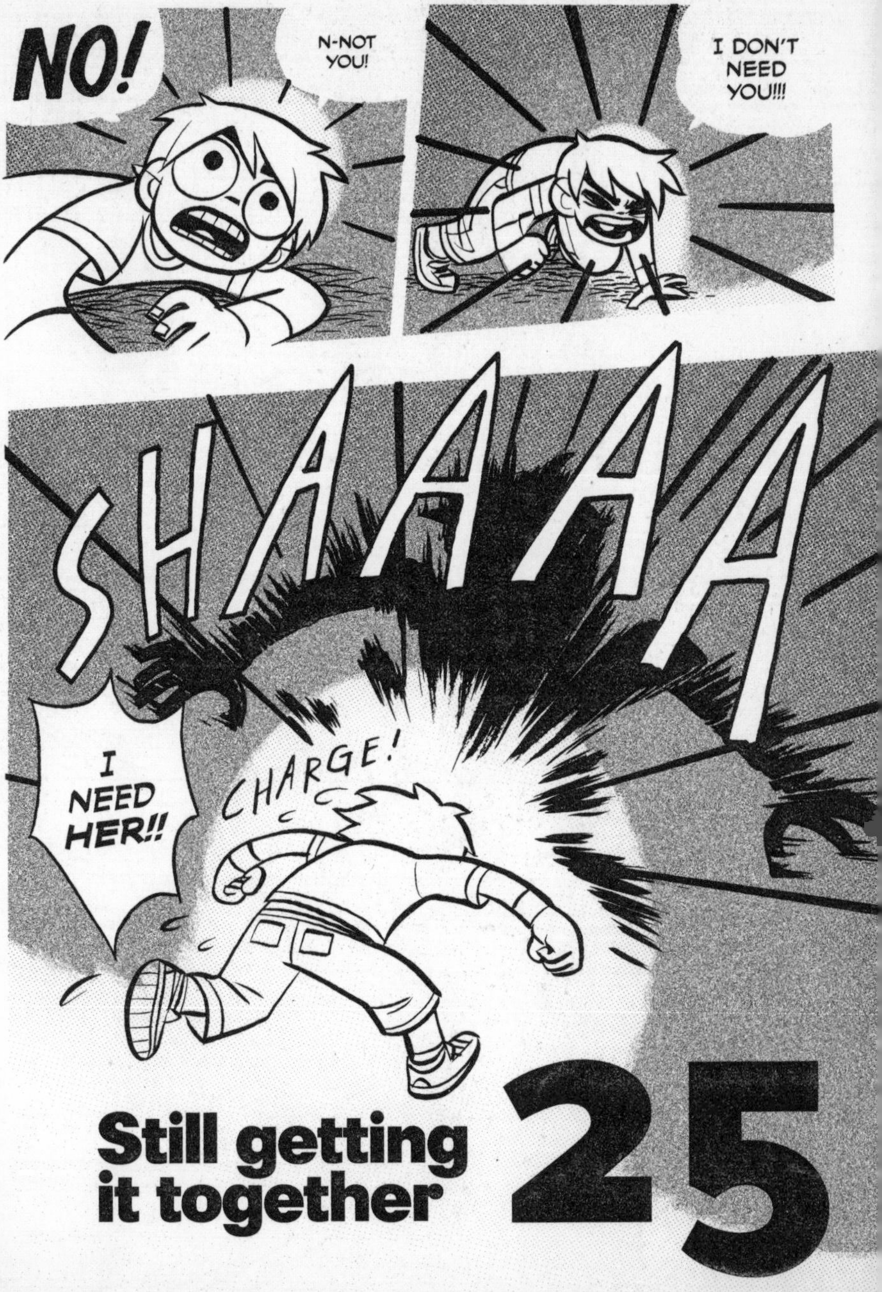
NO!
N-NOT YOU!
I DON'T NEED YOU!!!
SHAAAAA
I NEED HER!!
CHARGE!

Still getting it together 25

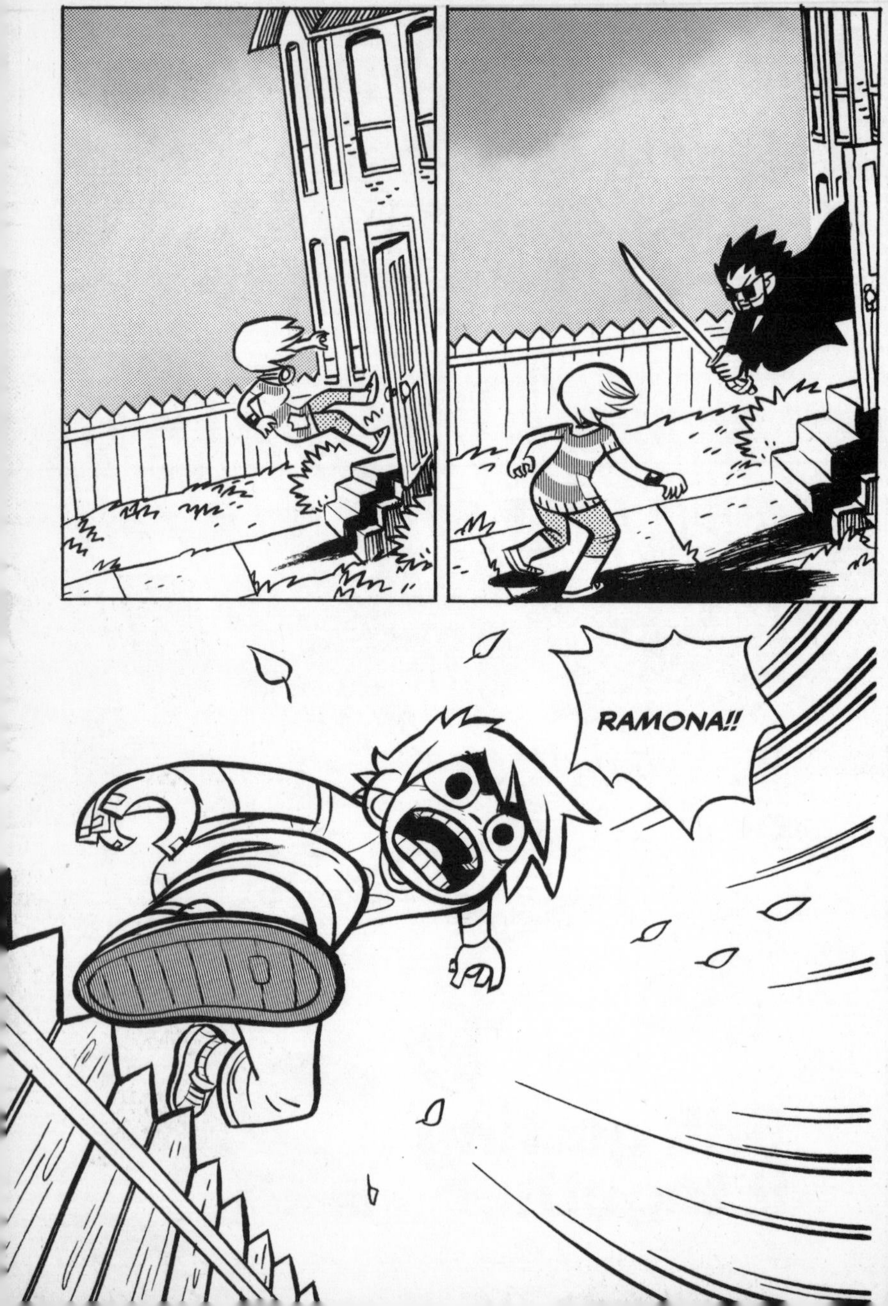
RAMONA!!

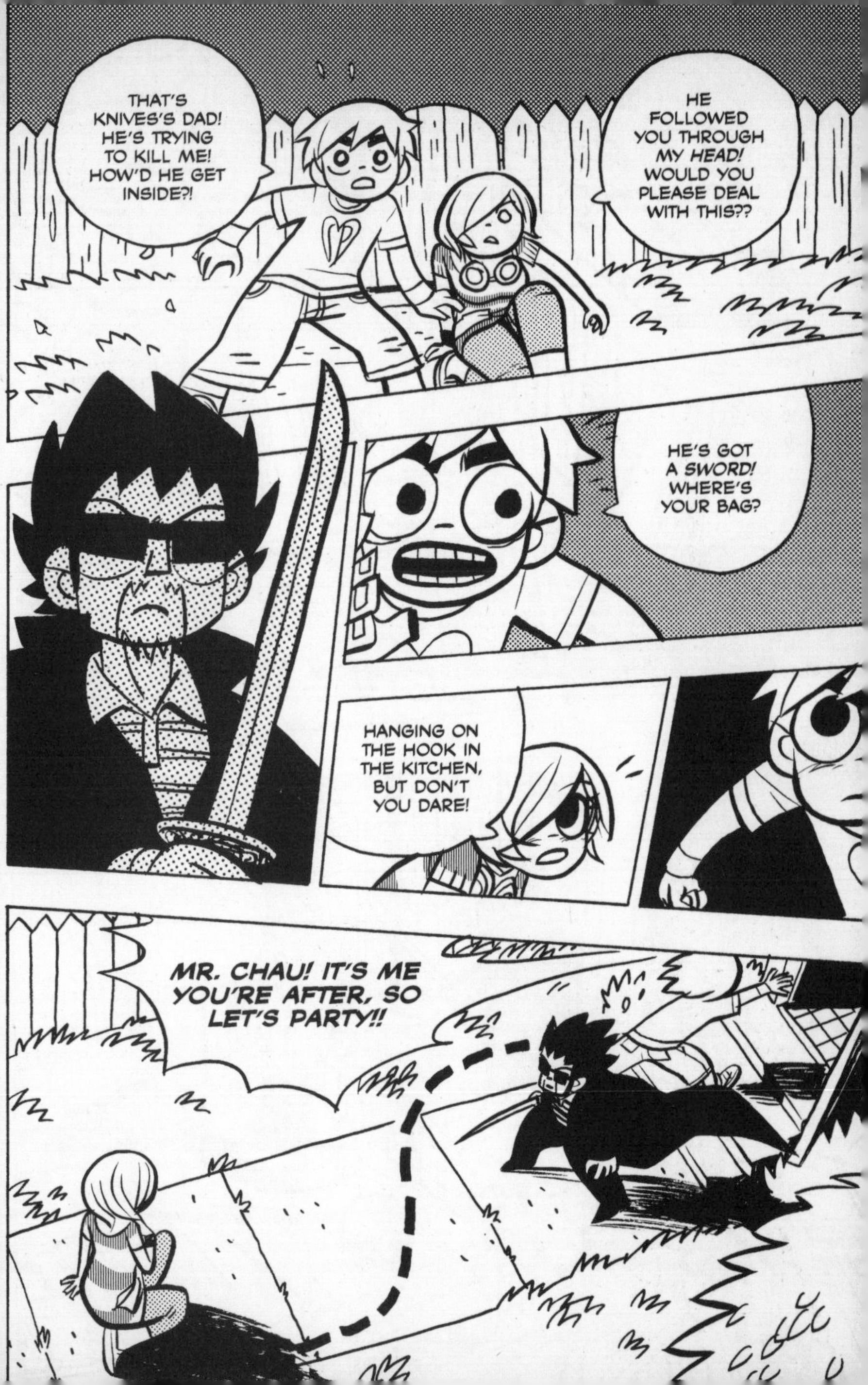
THAT'S KNIVES'S DAD! HE'S TRYING TO KILL ME! HOW'D HE GET INSIDE?!
HE FOLLOWED YOU THROUGH MY *HEAD!* WOULD YOU PLEASE DEAL WITH THIS??
HE'S GOT A *SWORD!* WHERE'S YOUR BAG?
HANGING ON THE HOOK IN THE KITCHEN, BUT DON'T YOU DARE!
MR. CHAU! IT'S ME YOU'RE AFTER, SO LET'S PARTY!!

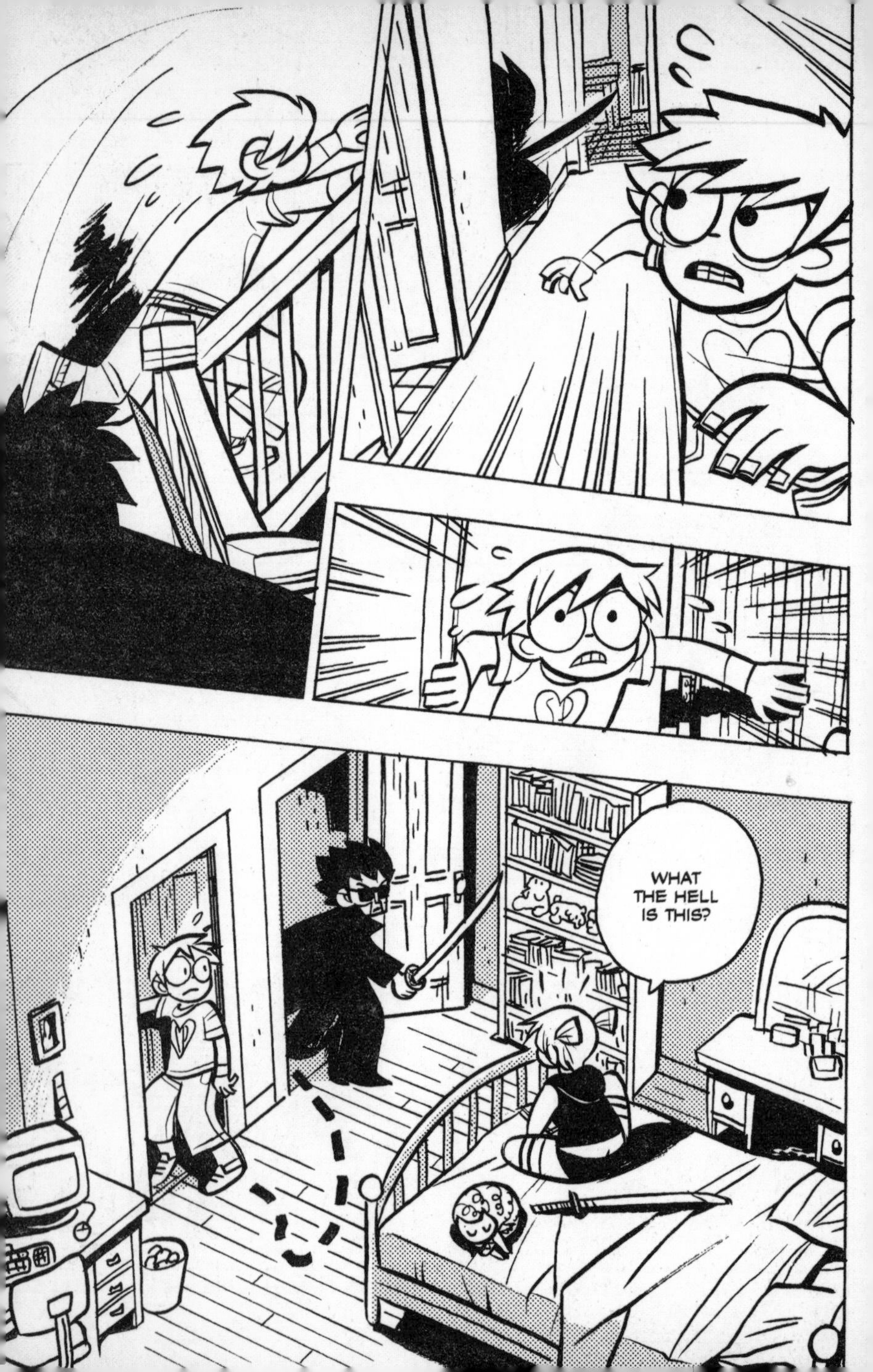
WHAT THE HELL IS THIS?

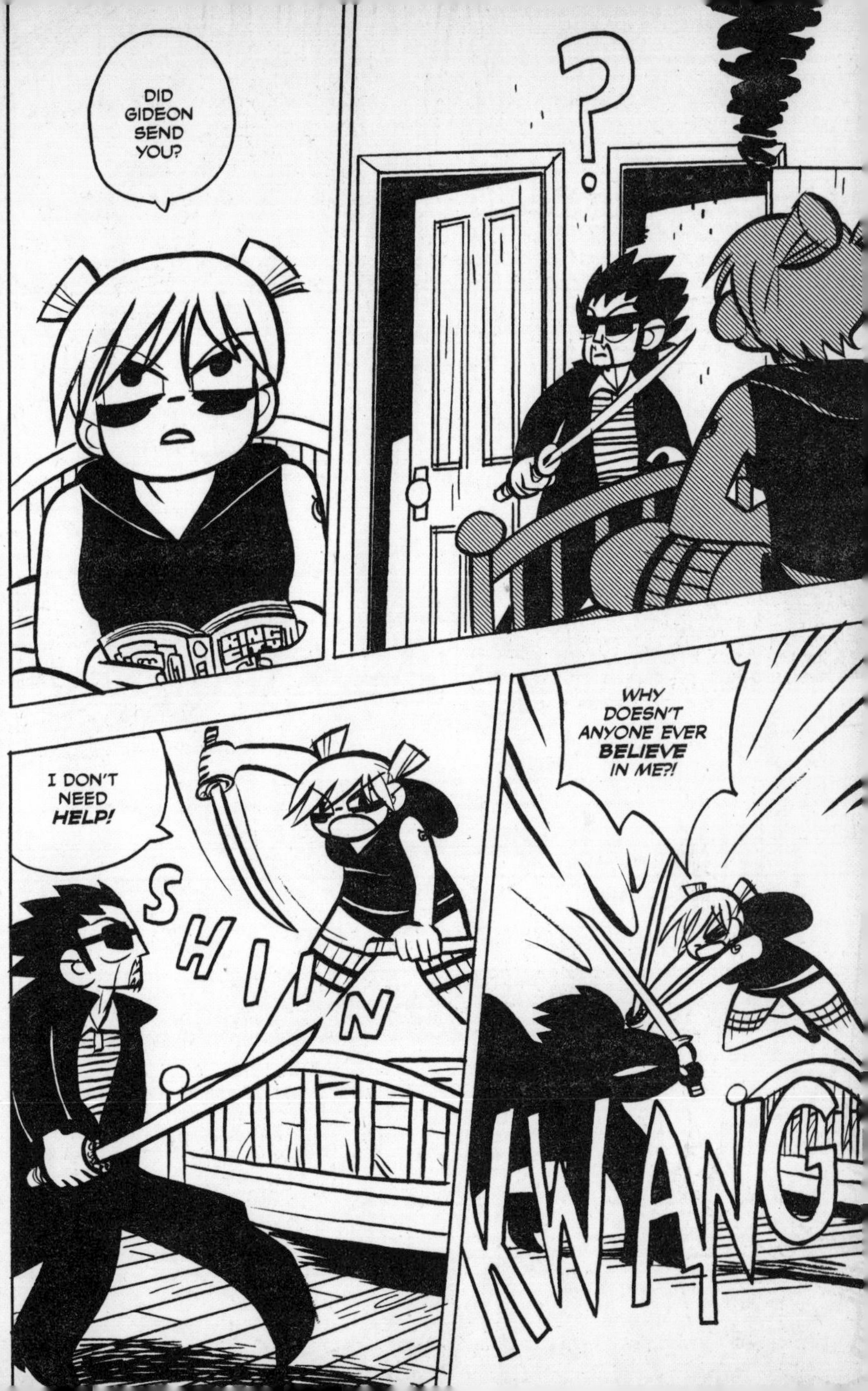
DID GIDEON SEND YOU?
?
I DON'T NEED HELP!
SHIIN
WHY DOESN'T ANYONE EVER BELIEVE IN ME?!
KWANG

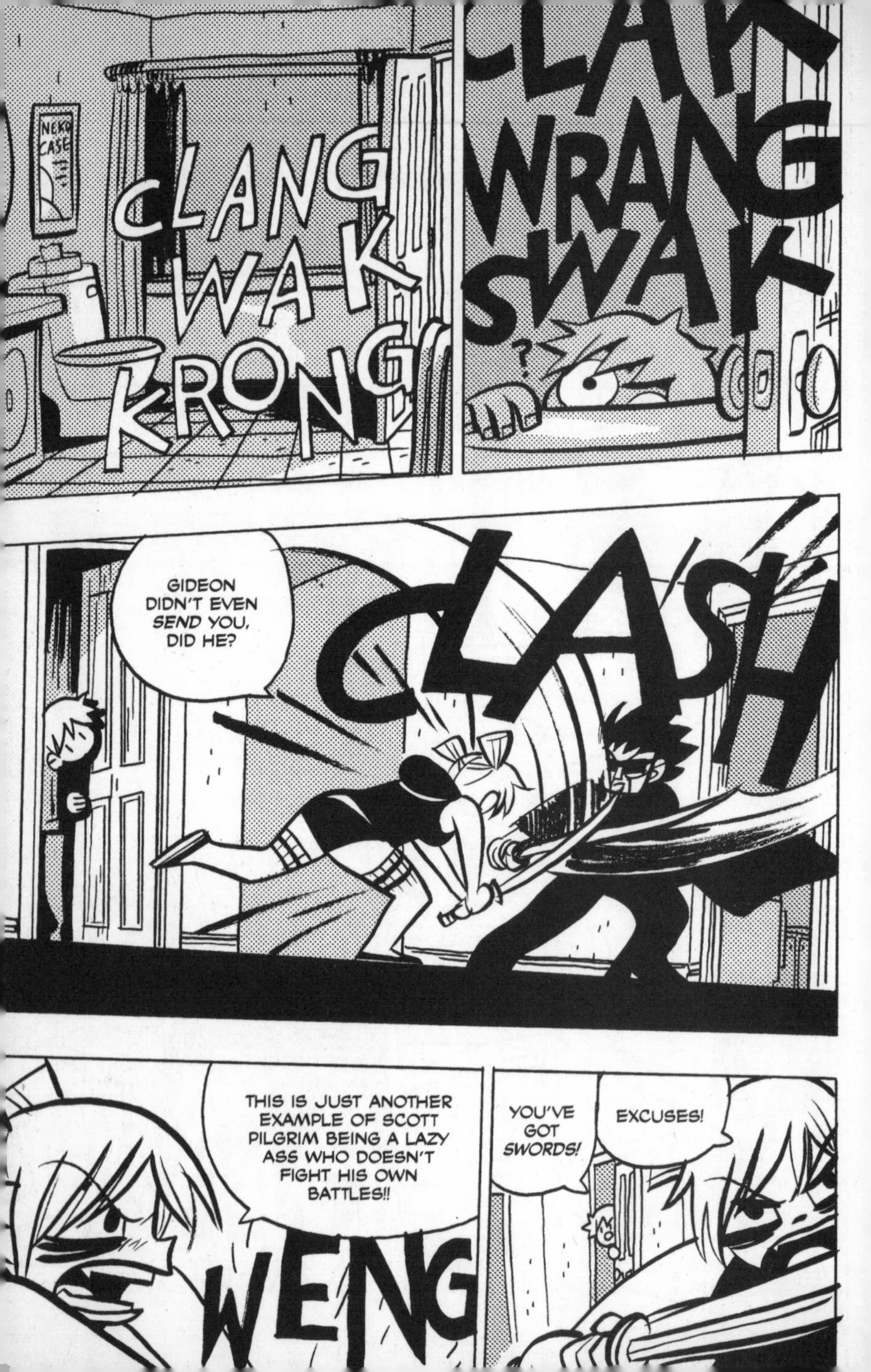
CLANG
WAK
KRONG
CLAK
WRANG
SWAK
?
GIDEON DIDN'T EVEN *SEND* YOU, DID HE?
CLASH
THIS IS JUST ANOTHER EXAMPLE OF SCOTT PILGRIM BEING A LAZY ASS WHO DOESN'T FIGHT HIS OWN BATTLES!!
WENG
YOU'VE GOT *SWORDS!*
EXCUSES!

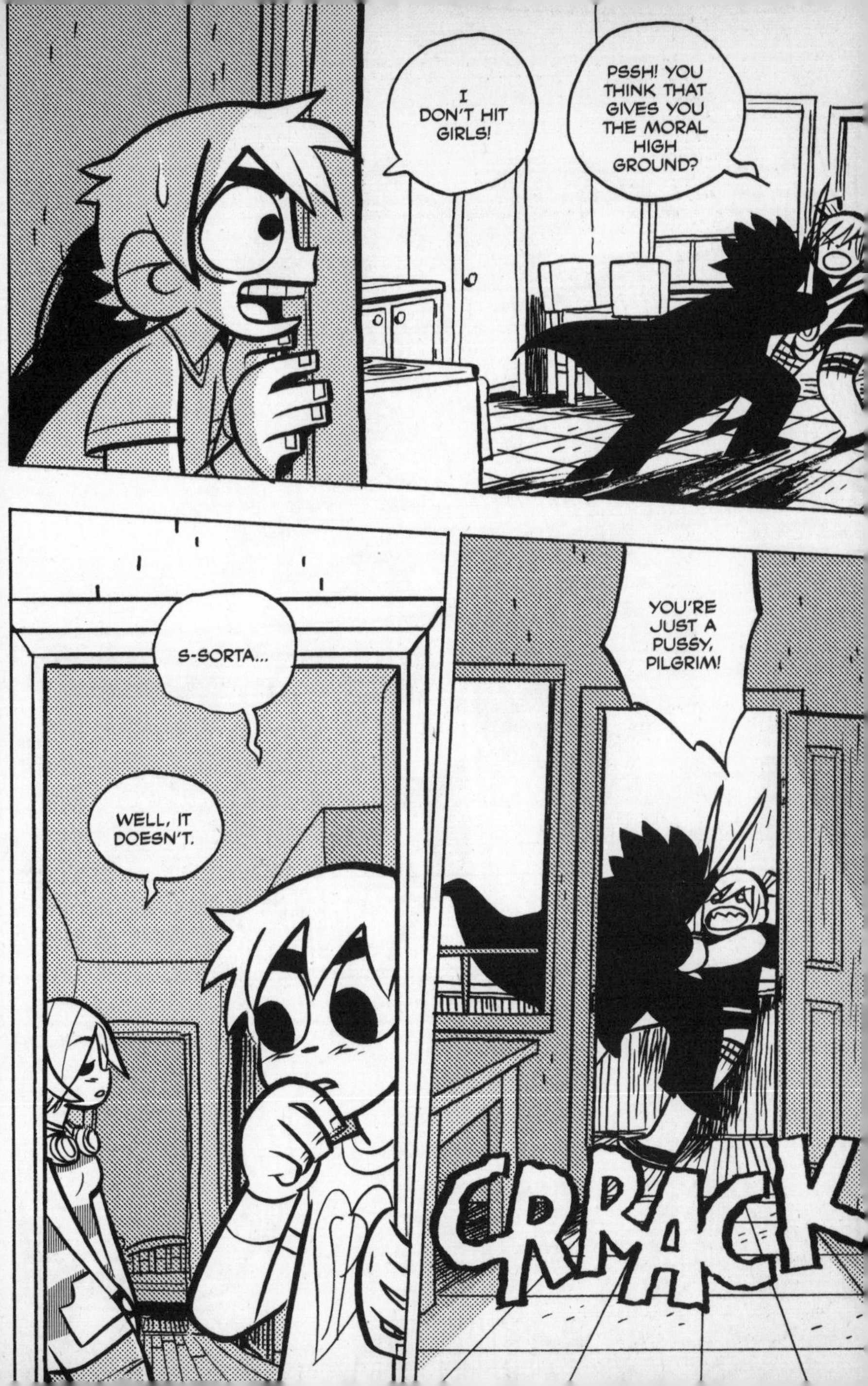

I DON'T HIT GIRLS!
PSSH! YOU THINK THAT GIVES YOU THE MORAL HIGH GROUND?
S-SORTA...
WELL, IT DOESN'T.
YOU'RE JUST A PUSSY, PILGRIM!
CRRACK

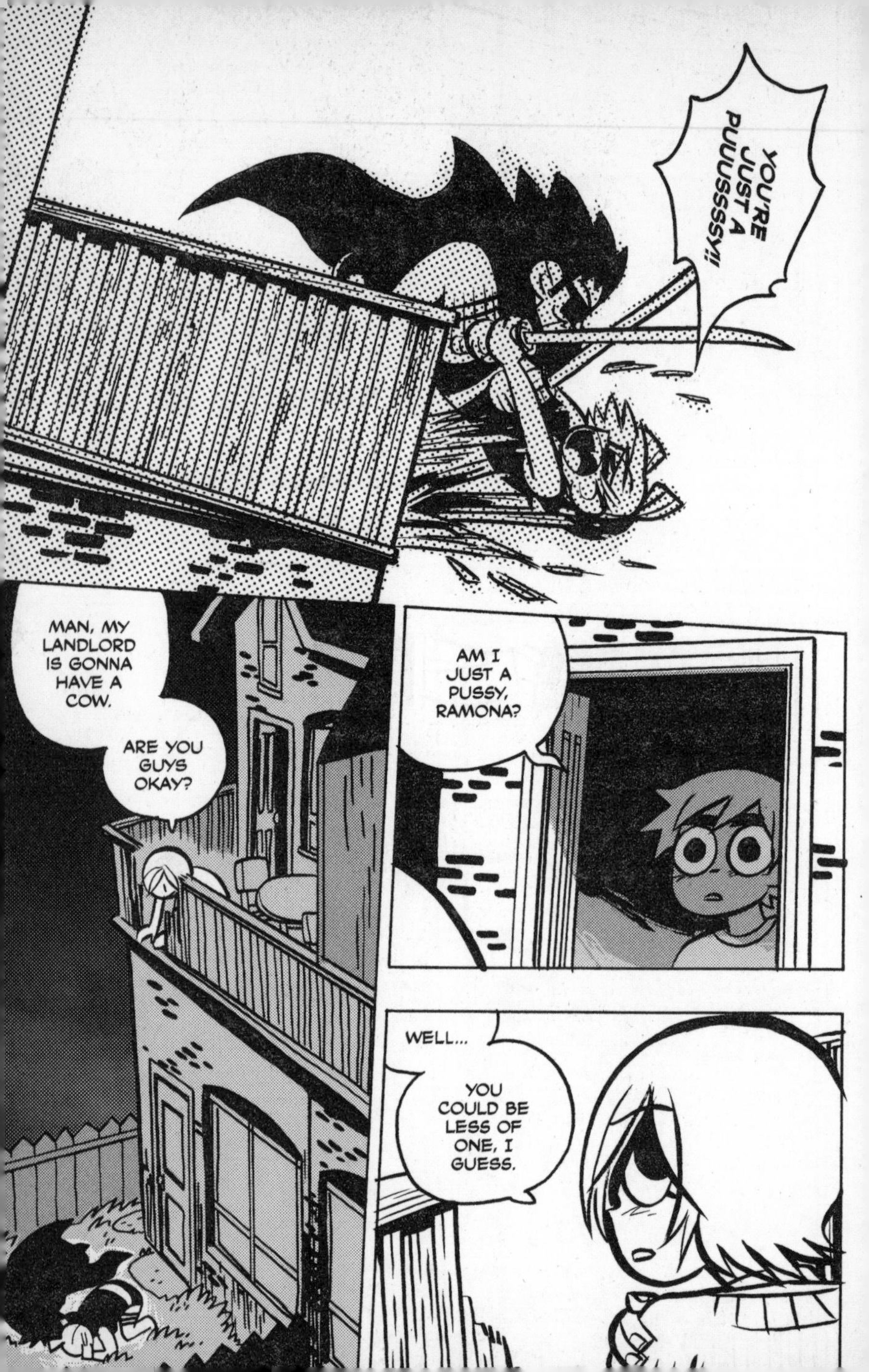
YOU'RE JUST A PUUUSSSY!!
MAN, MY LANDLORD IS GONNA HAVE A COW.
ARE YOU GUYS OKAY?
AM I JUST A PUSSY, RAMONA?
WELL...
YOU COULD BE LESS OF ONE, I GUESS.

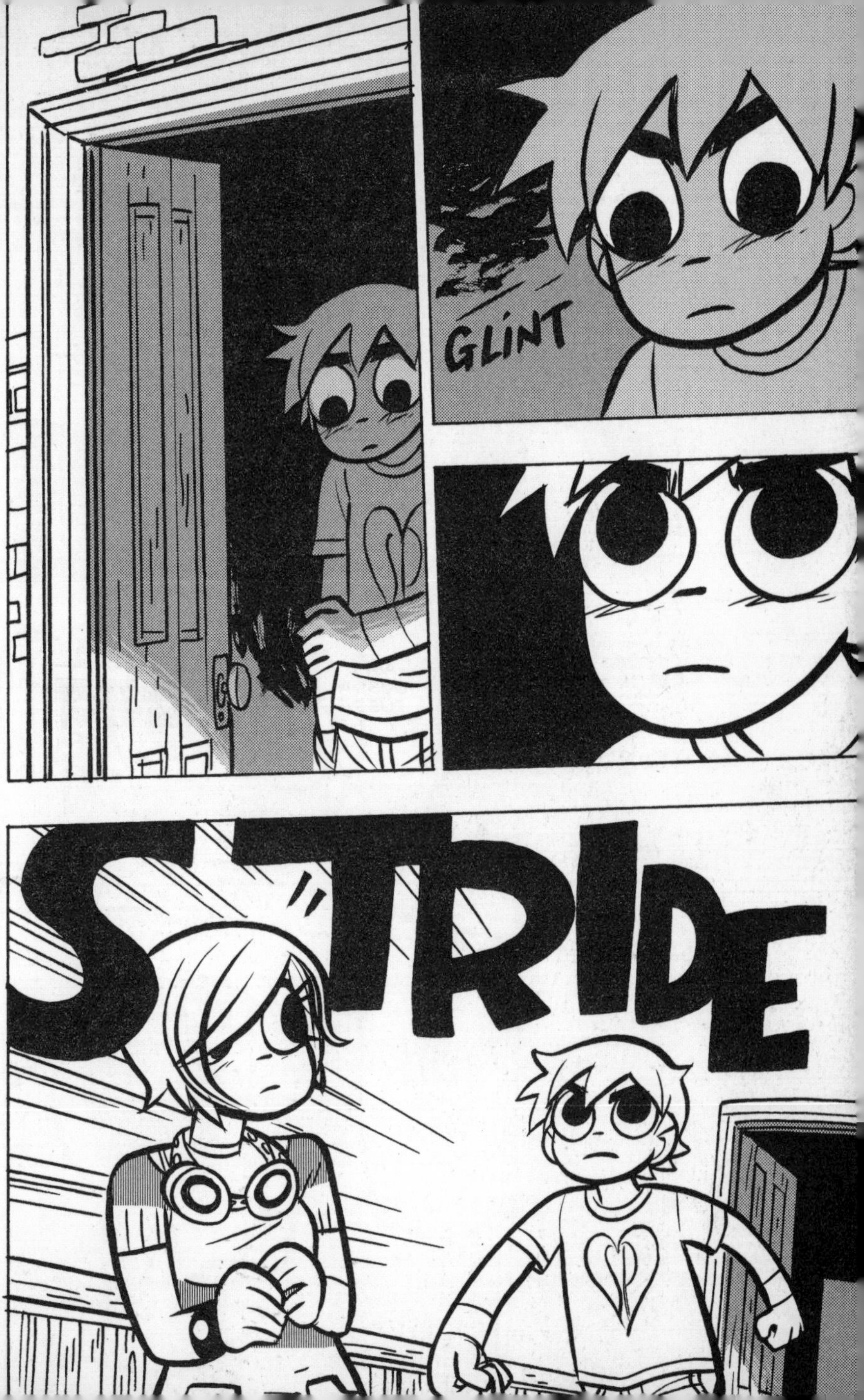
GLINT
STRIDE

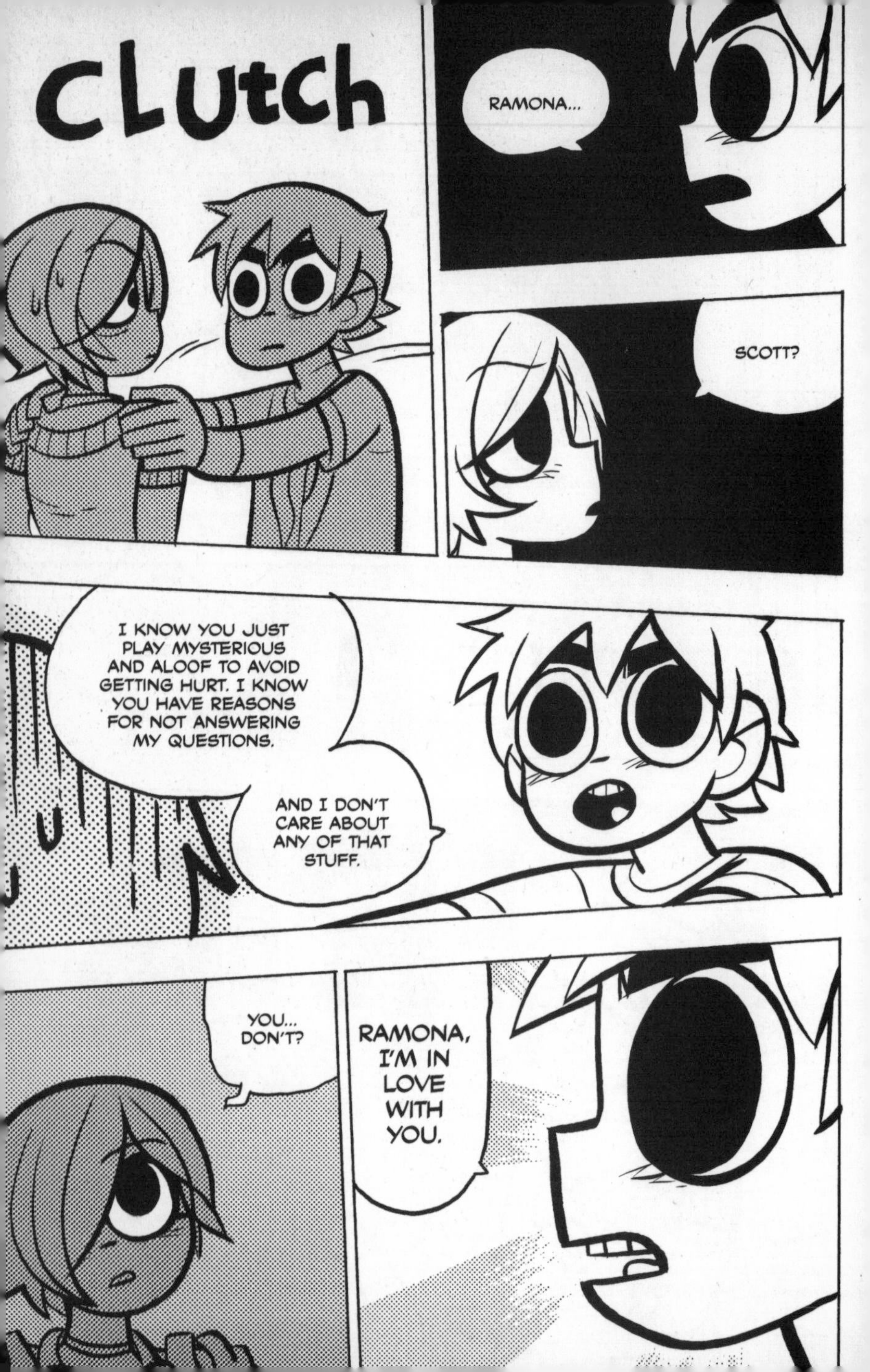
CLUTCH
RAMONA...
SCOTT?
I KNOW YOU JUST PLAY MYSTERIOUS AND ALOOF TO AVOID GETTING HURT. I KNOW YOU HAVE REASONS FOR NOT ANSWERING MY QUESTIONS.
AND I DON'T CARE ABOUT ANY OF THAT STUFF.
YOU... DON'T?
RAMONA, I'M IN LOVE WITH YOU.

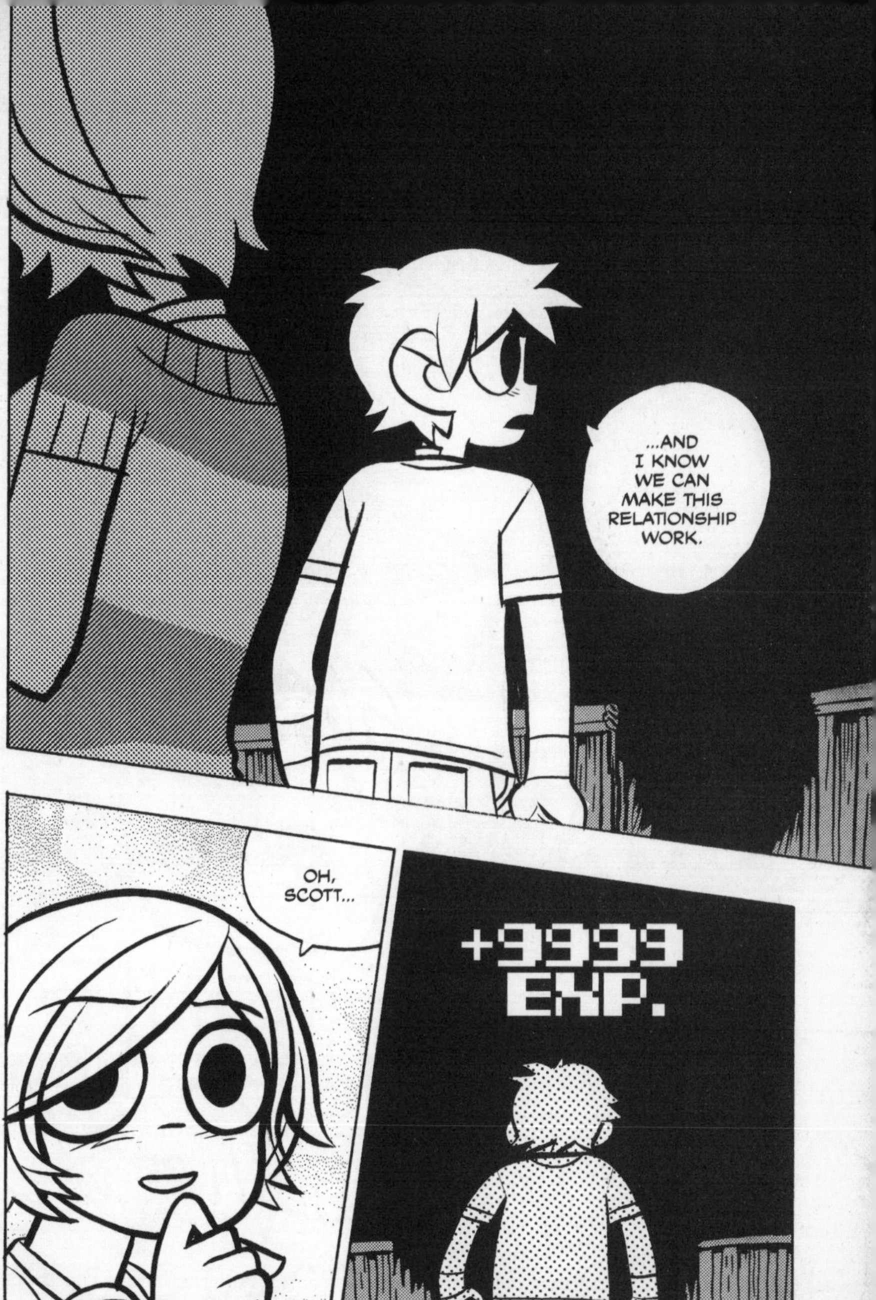
...AND I KNOW WE CAN MAKE THIS RELATIONSHIP WORK.
OH, SCOTT...
+9999 EXP.

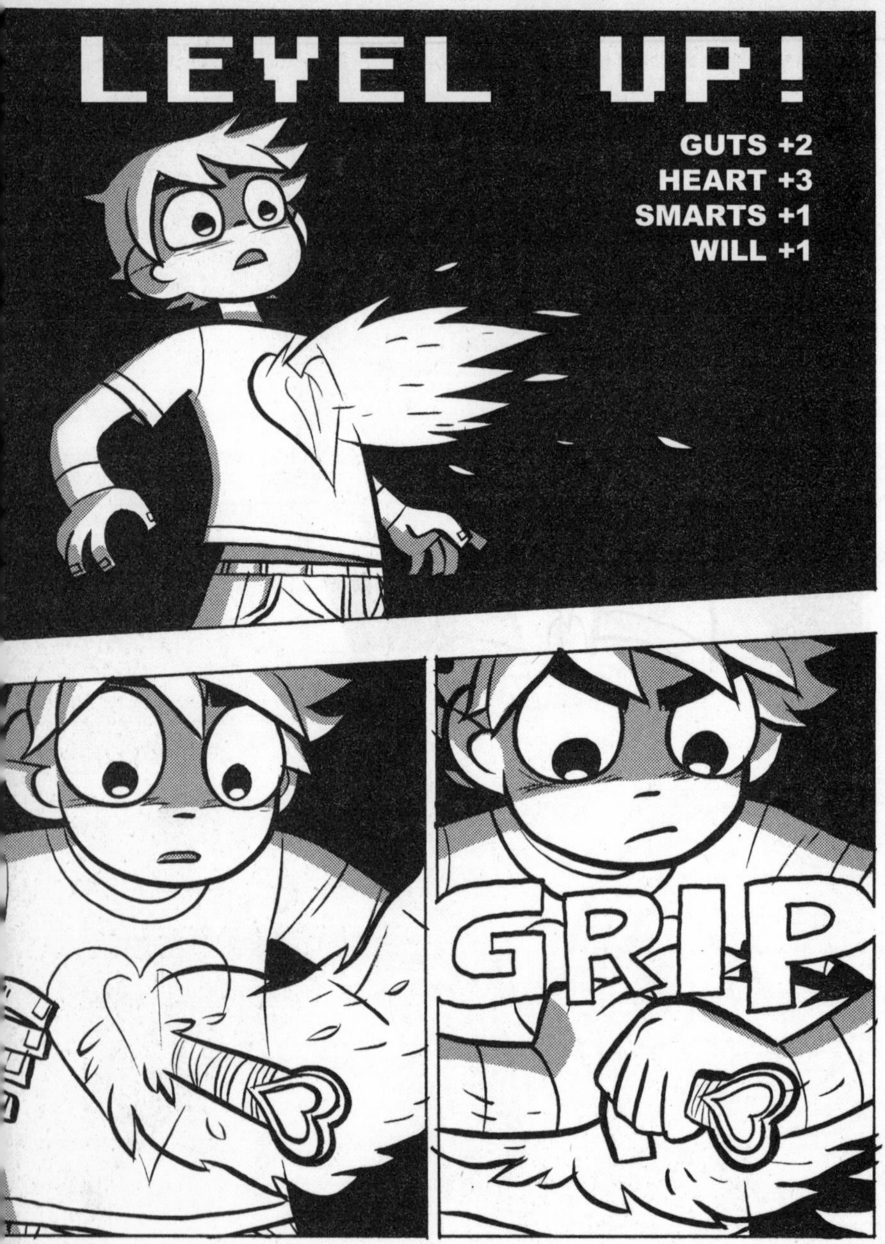
LEVEL UP!
GUTS +2
HEART +3
SMARTS +1
WILL +1
GRIP

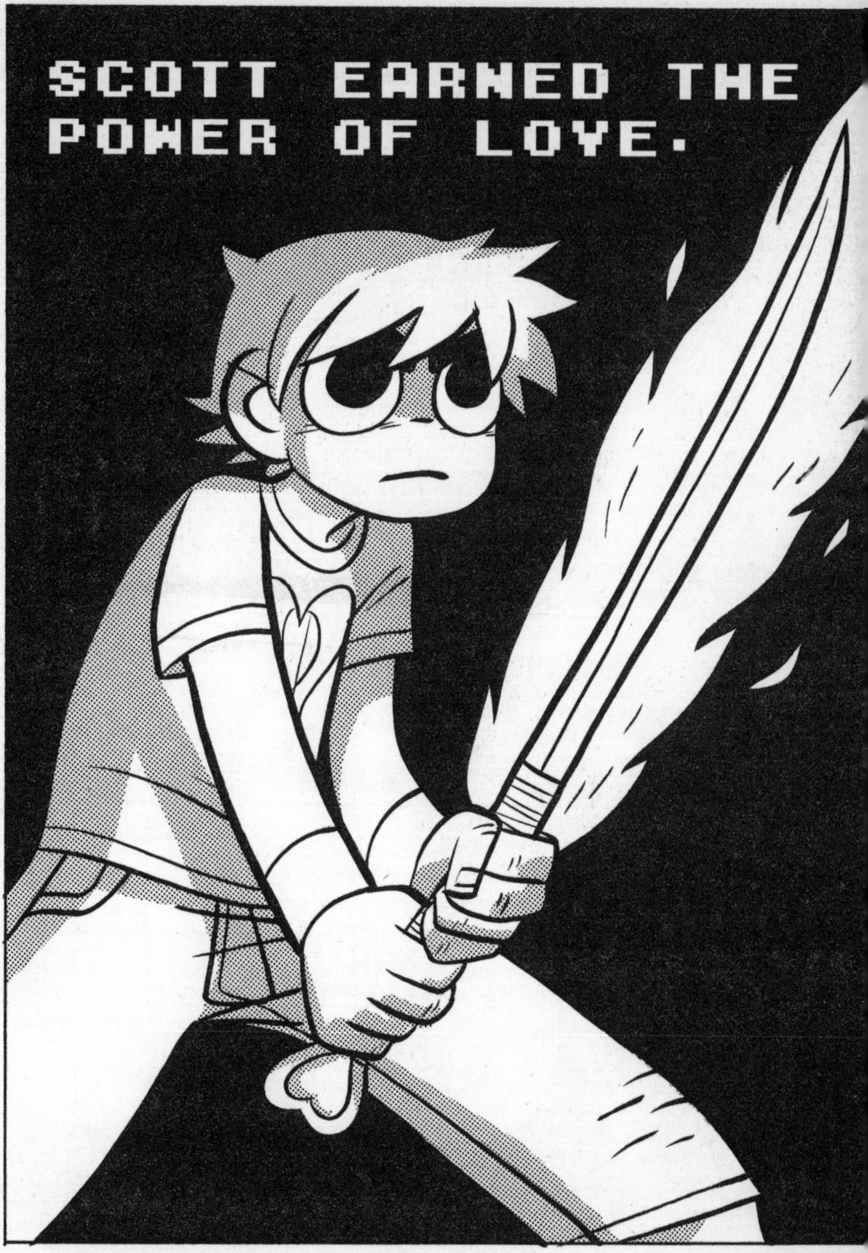
SCOTT EARNED THE POWER OF LOVE.

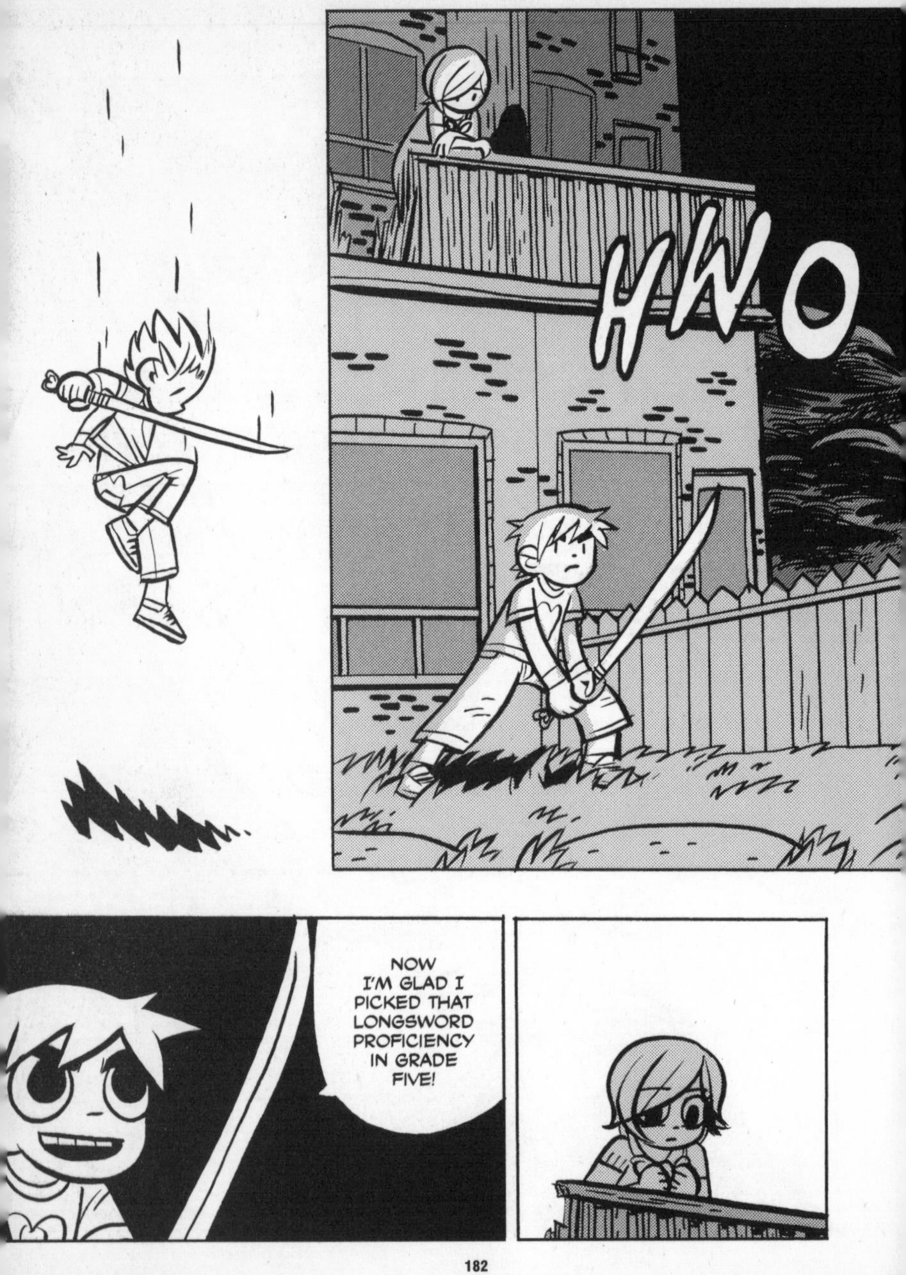
HWO
NOW I'M GLAD I PICKED THAT LONGSWORD PROFICIENCY IN GRADE FIVE!

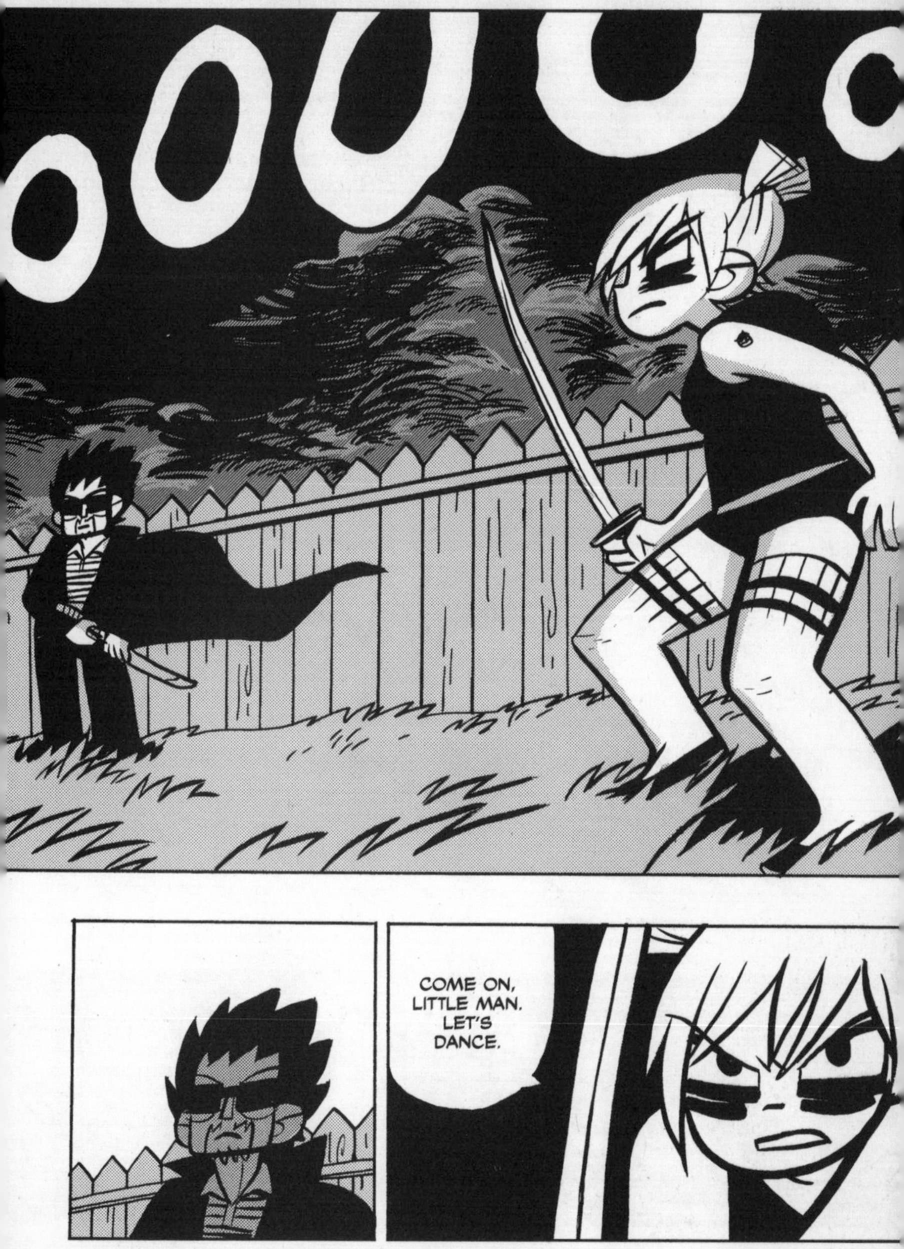
COME ON, LITTLE MAN. LET'S DANCE.

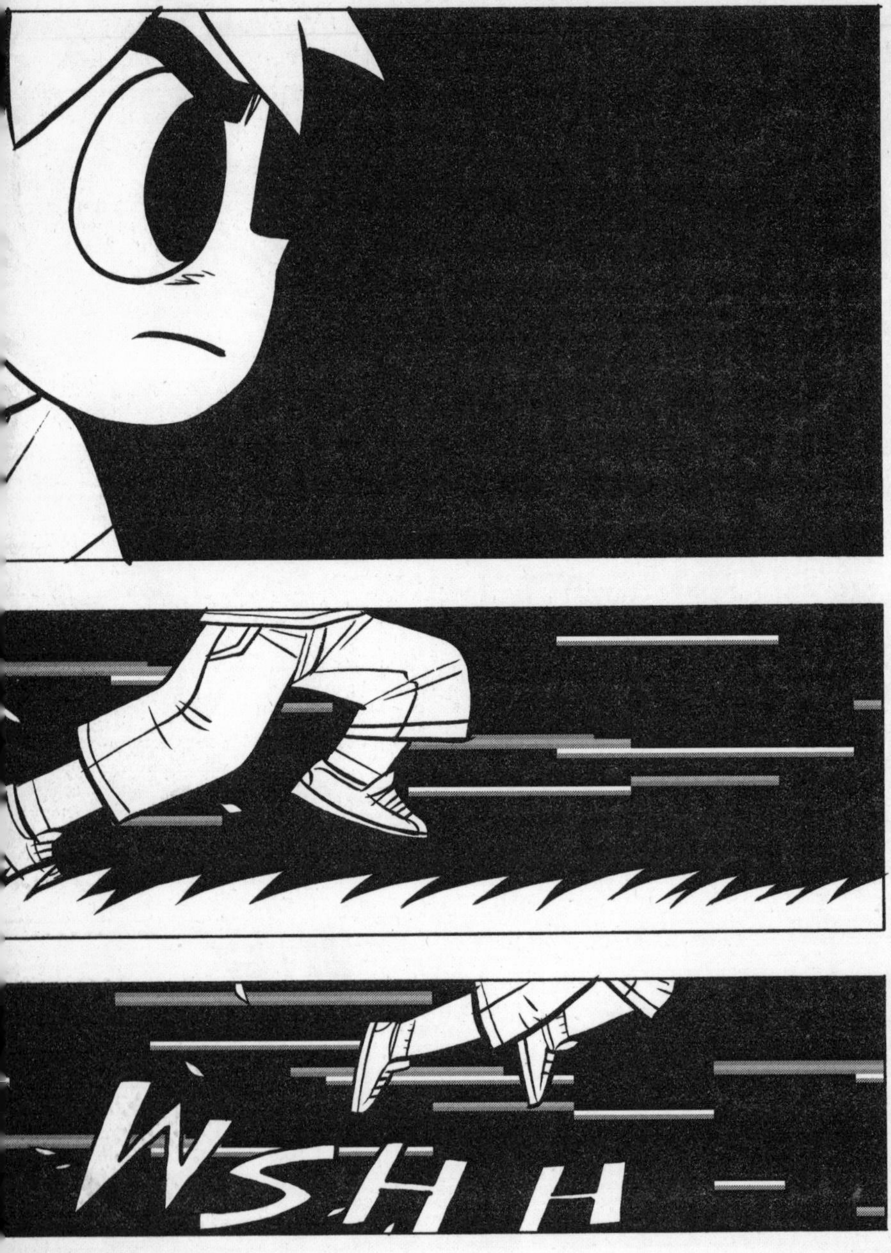
WSHH

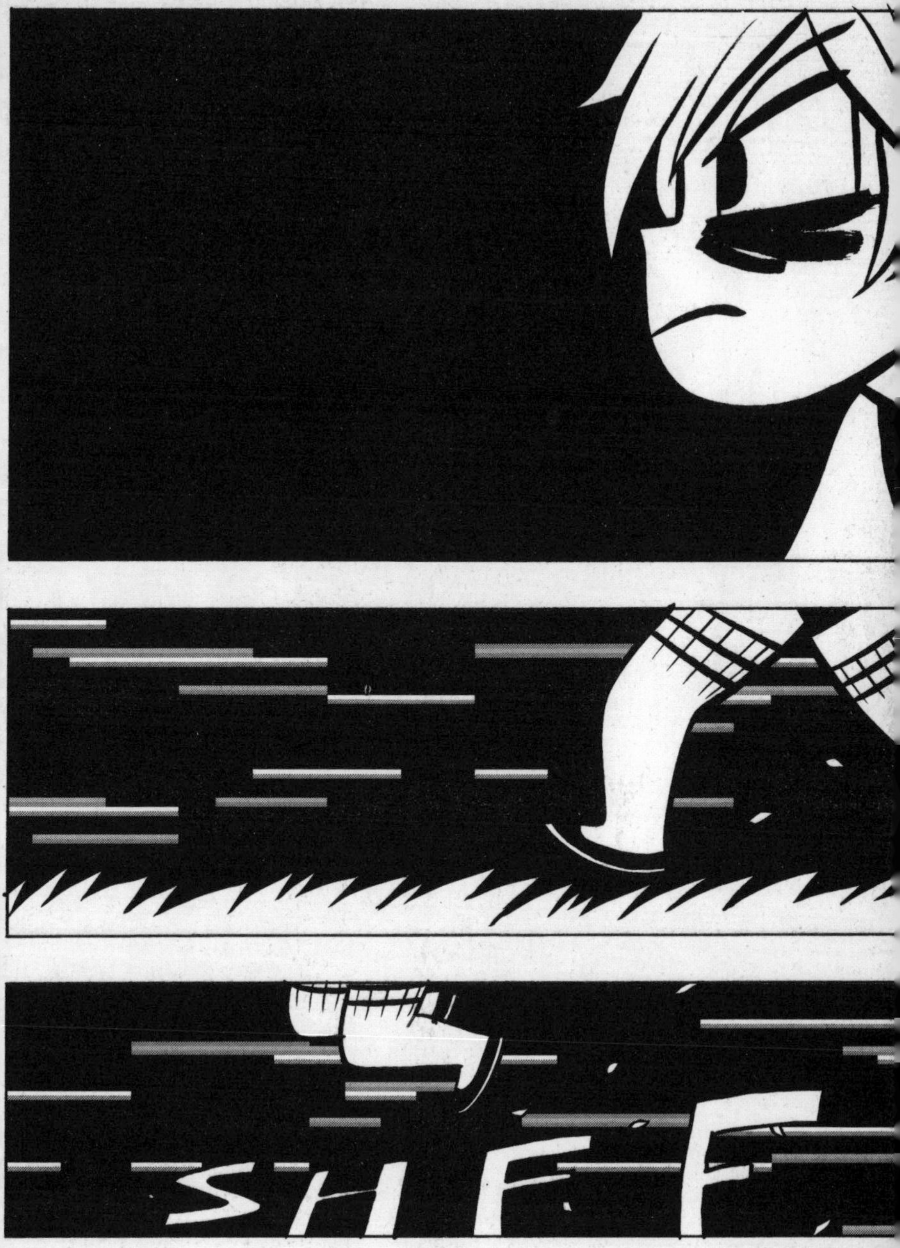
SHFF

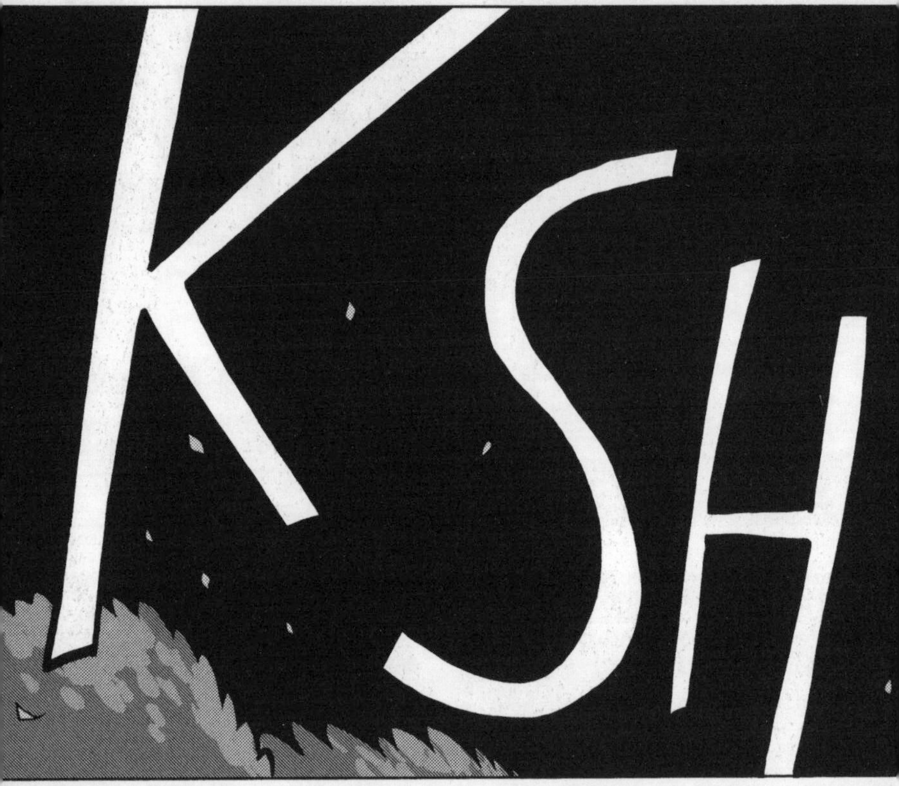
KSH

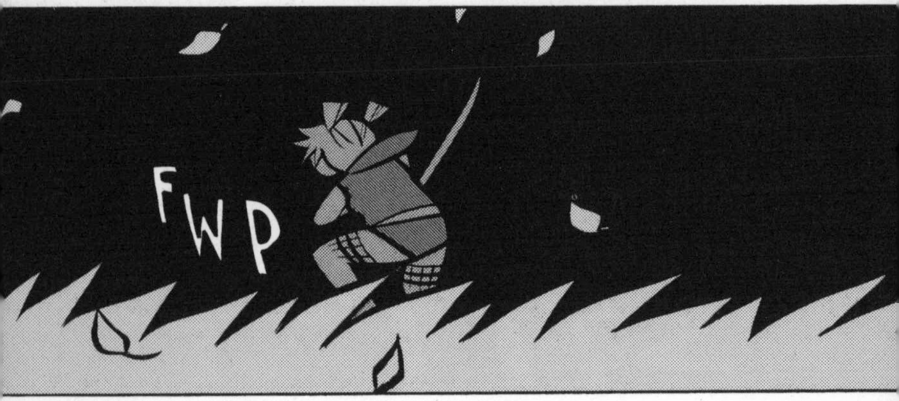
FWP

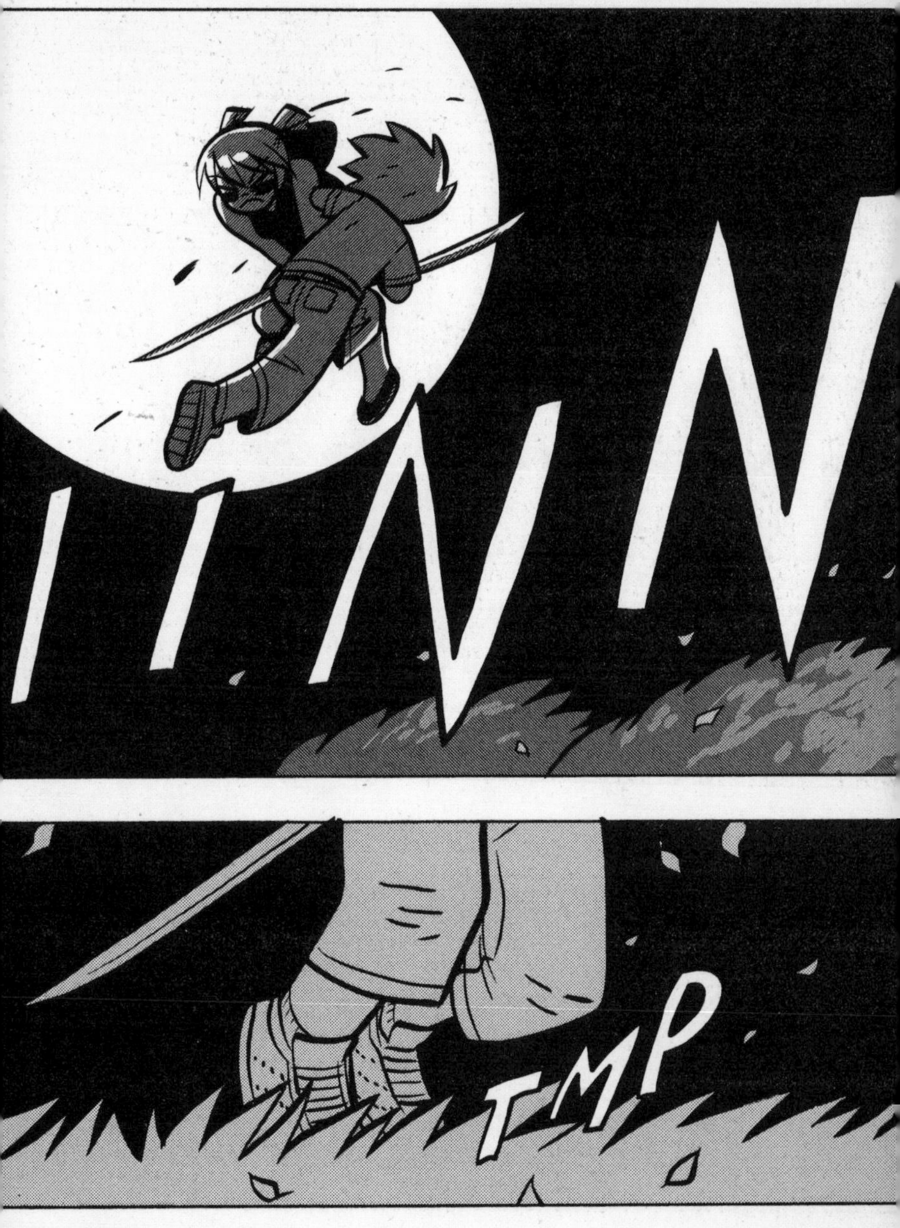
IINN
TMP

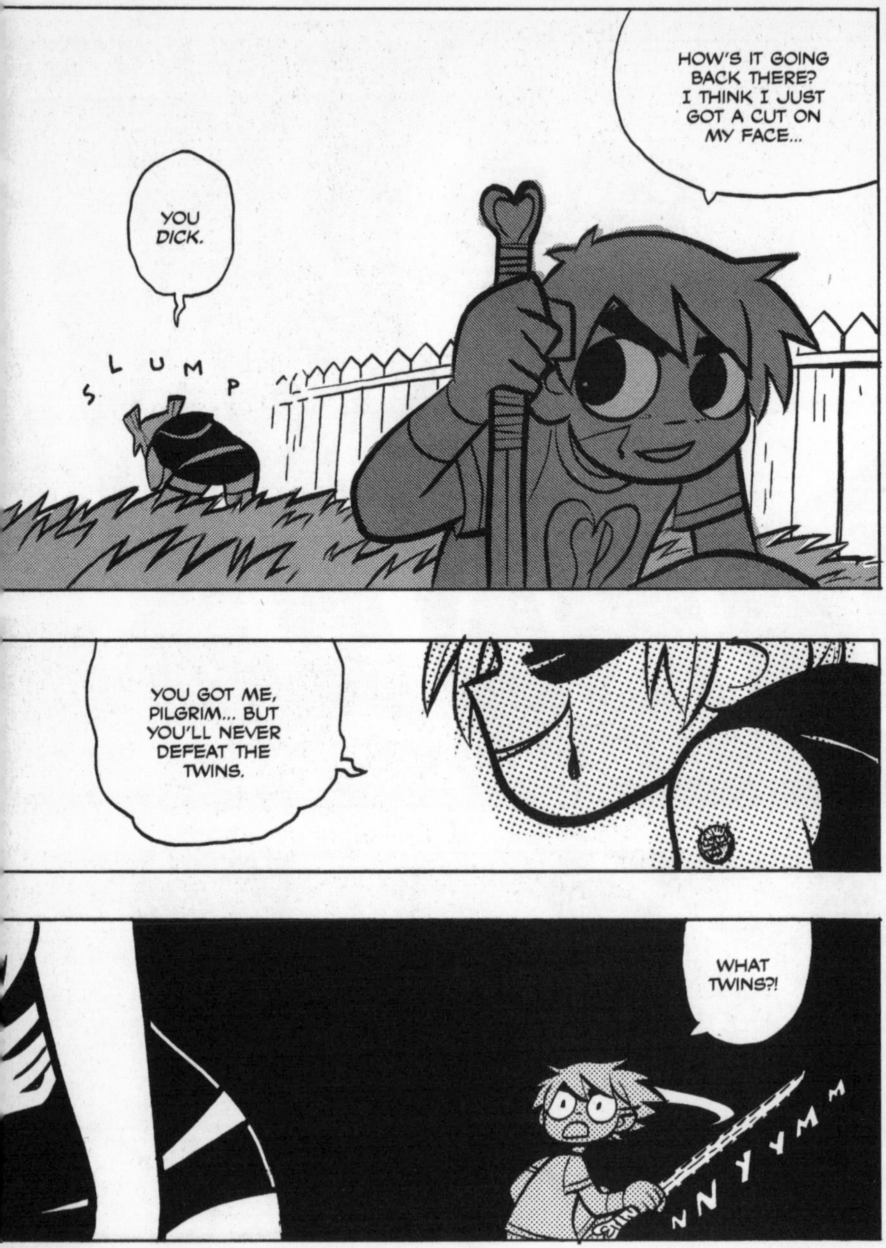
HOW'S IT GOING BACK THERE? I THINK I JUST GOT A CUT ON MY FACE...
YOU DICK.
SLUMP
YOU GOT ME, PILGRIM... BUT YOU'LL NEVER DEFEAT THE TWINS.
WHAT TWINS?!
NNYYMMM

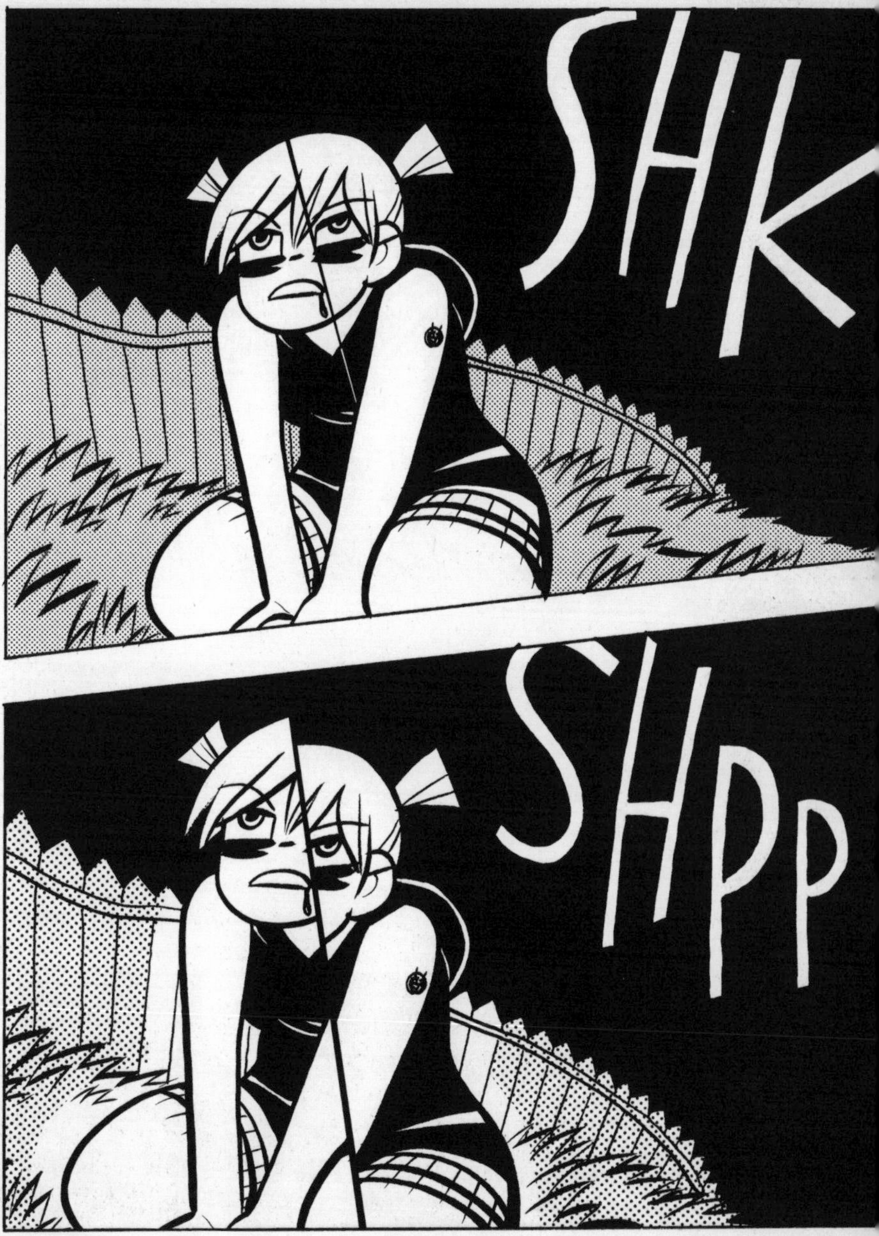
SHK
SHPP

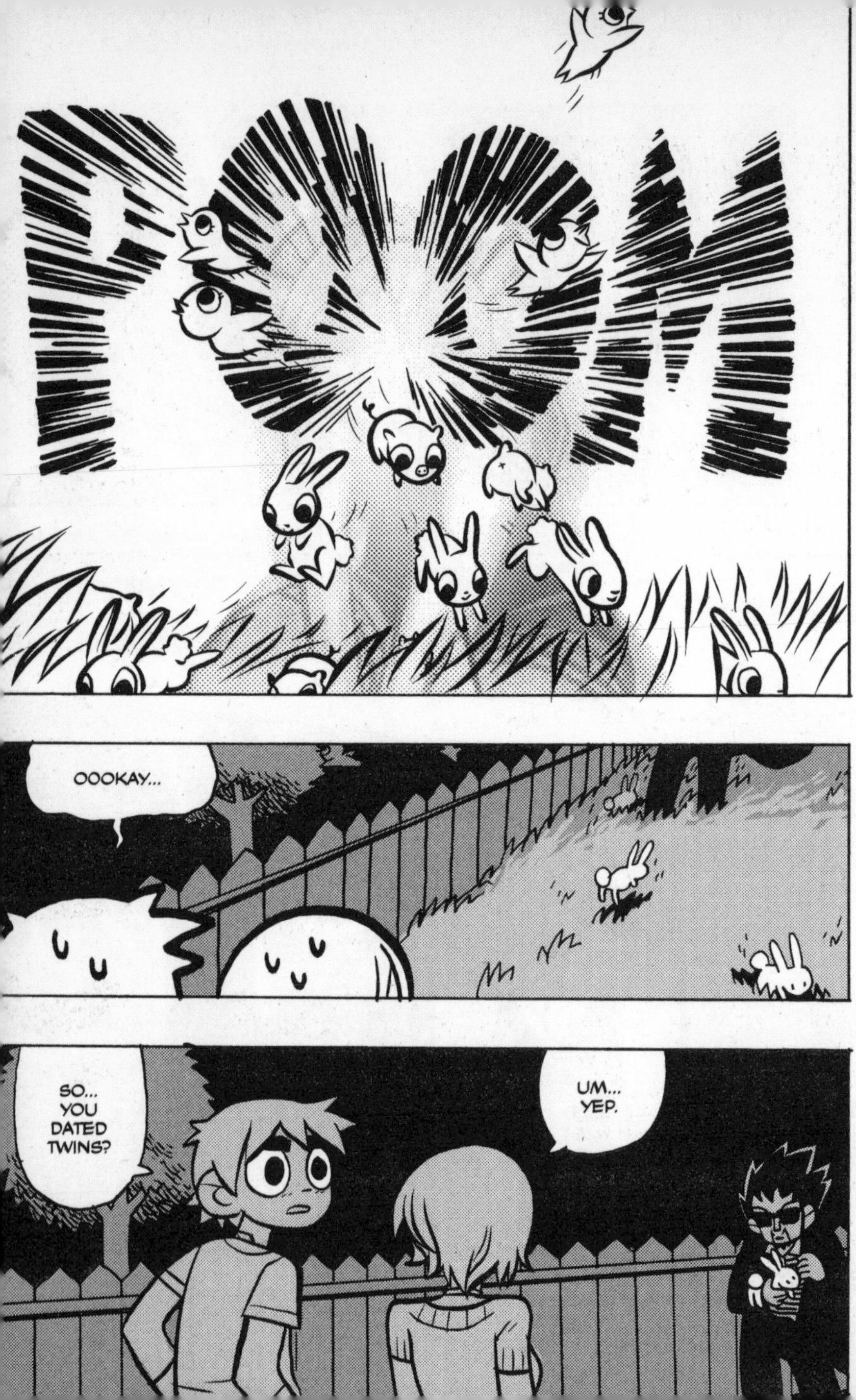
FOOM
OOOKAY...
SO... YOU DATED TWINS?
UM... YEP.

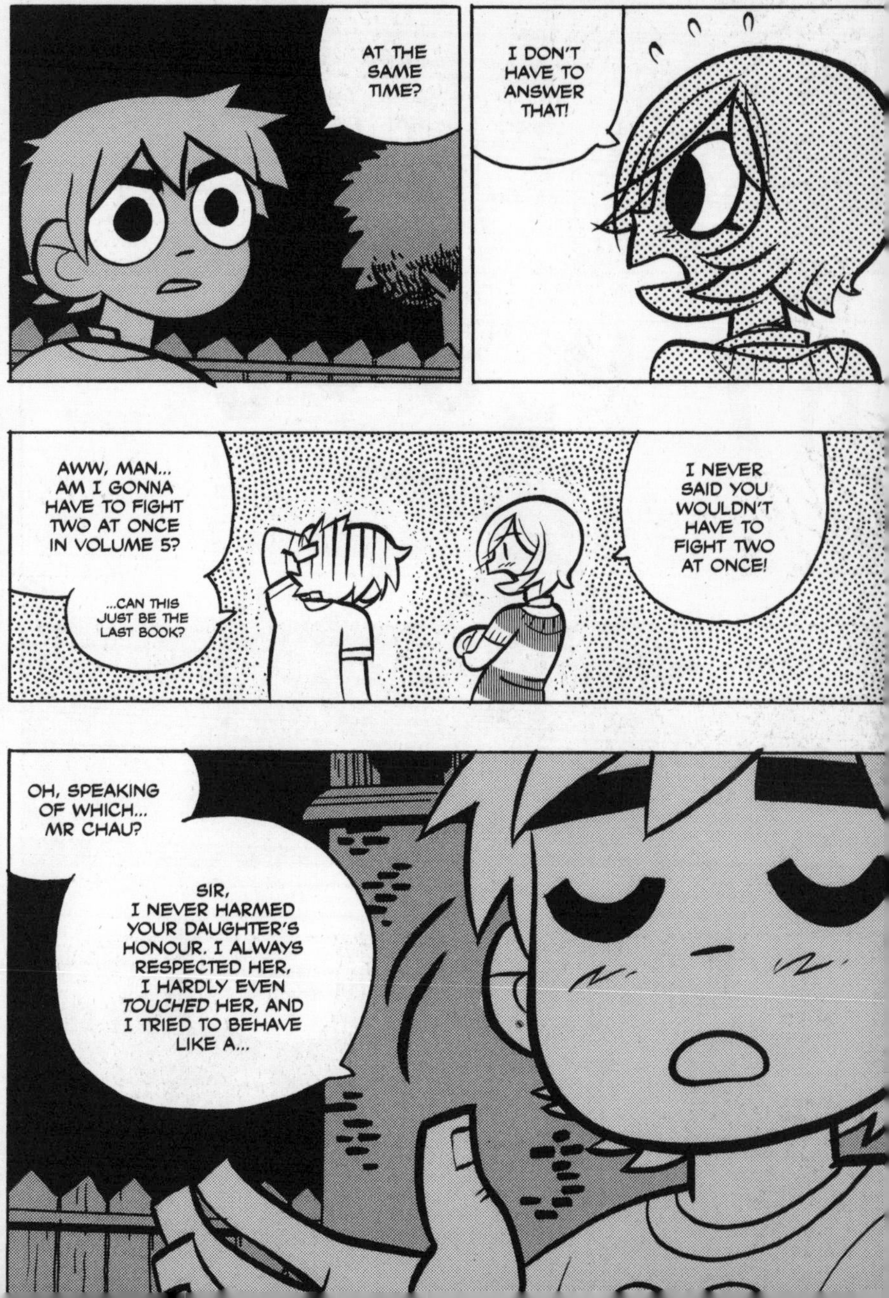
AT THE SAME TIME?
I DON'T HAVE TO ANSWER THAT!
AWW, MAN... AM I GONNA HAVE TO FIGHT TWO AT ONCE IN VOLUME 5?
...CAN THIS JUST BE THE LAST BOOK?
I NEVER SAID YOU WOULDN'T HAVE TO FIGHT TWO AT ONCE!
OH, SPEAKING OF WHICH... MR CHAU?
SIR, I NEVER HARMED YOUR DAUGHTER'S HONOUR. I ALWAYS RESPECTED HER, I HARDLY EVEN *TOUCHED* HER, AND I TRIED TO BEHAVE LIKE A...

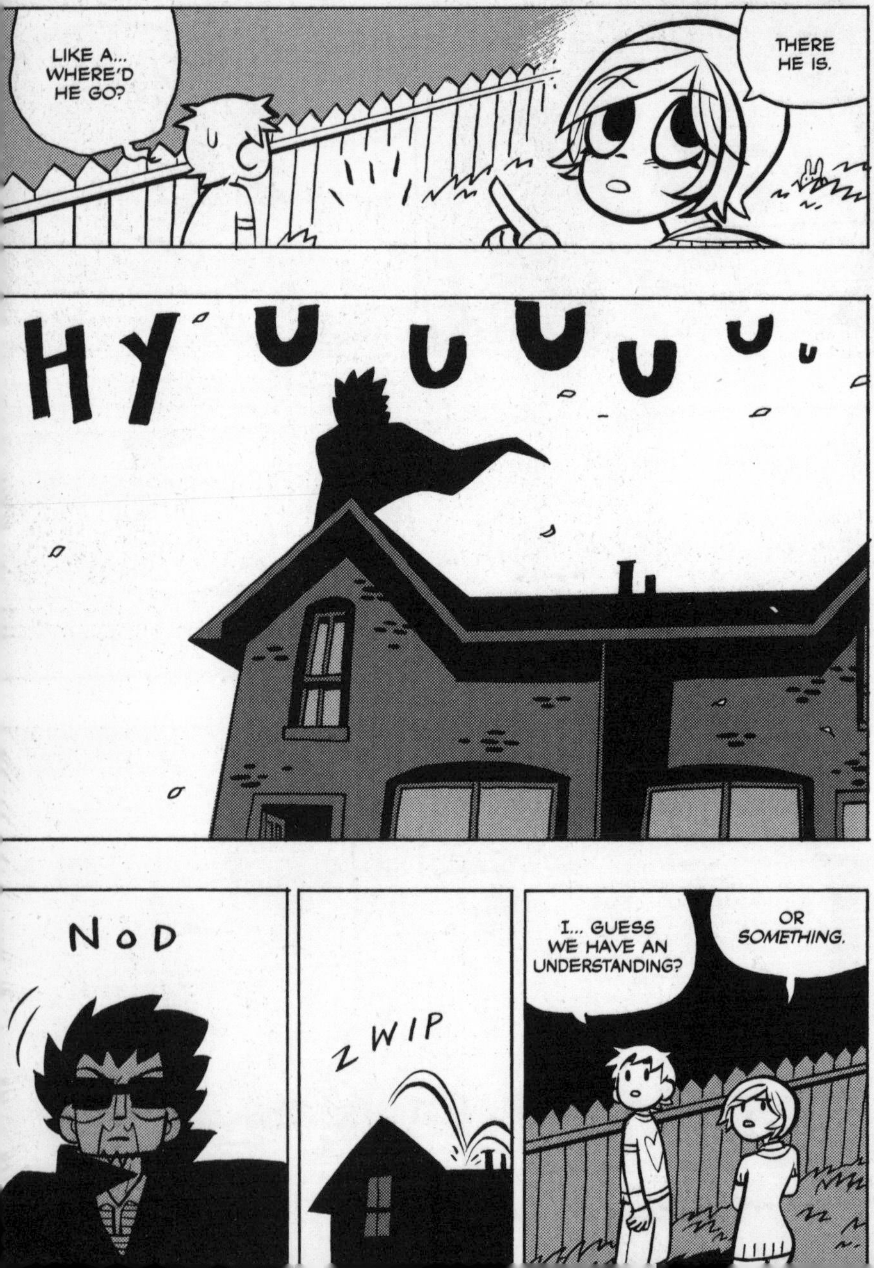
LIKE A... WHERE'D HE GO?
THERE HE IS.
HYUUUUUUU
NOD
ZWIP
I... GUESS WE HAVE AN UNDERSTANDING?
OR SOMETHING.

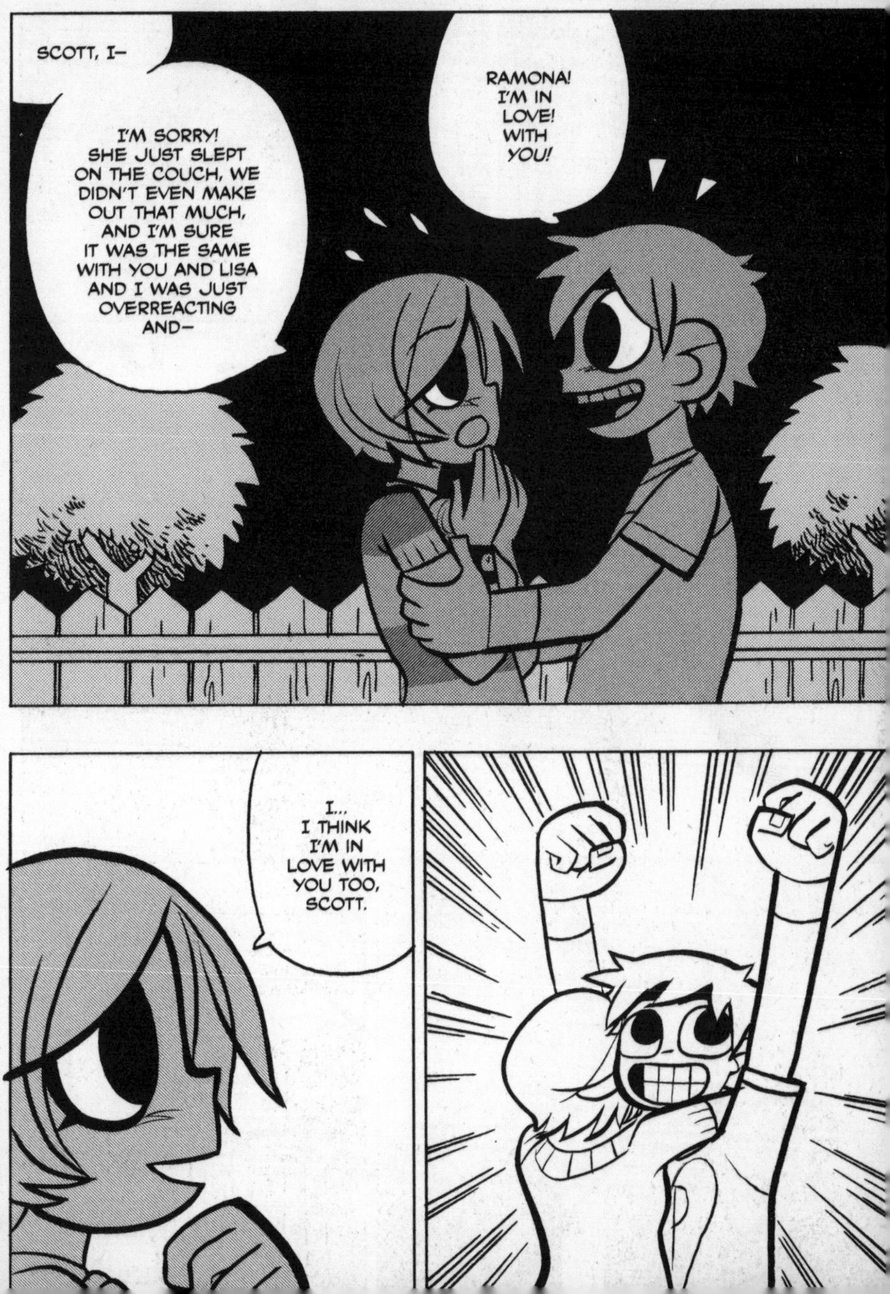
SCOTT, I-
I'M SORRY! SHE JUST SLEPT ON THE COUCH, WE DIDN'T EVEN MAKE OUT THAT MUCH, AND I'M SURE IT WAS THE SAME WITH YOU AND LISA AND I WAS JUST OVERREACTING AND-
RAMONA! I'M IN LOVE! WITH *YOU!*
I... I THINK I'M IN LOVE WITH YOU TOO, SCOTT.

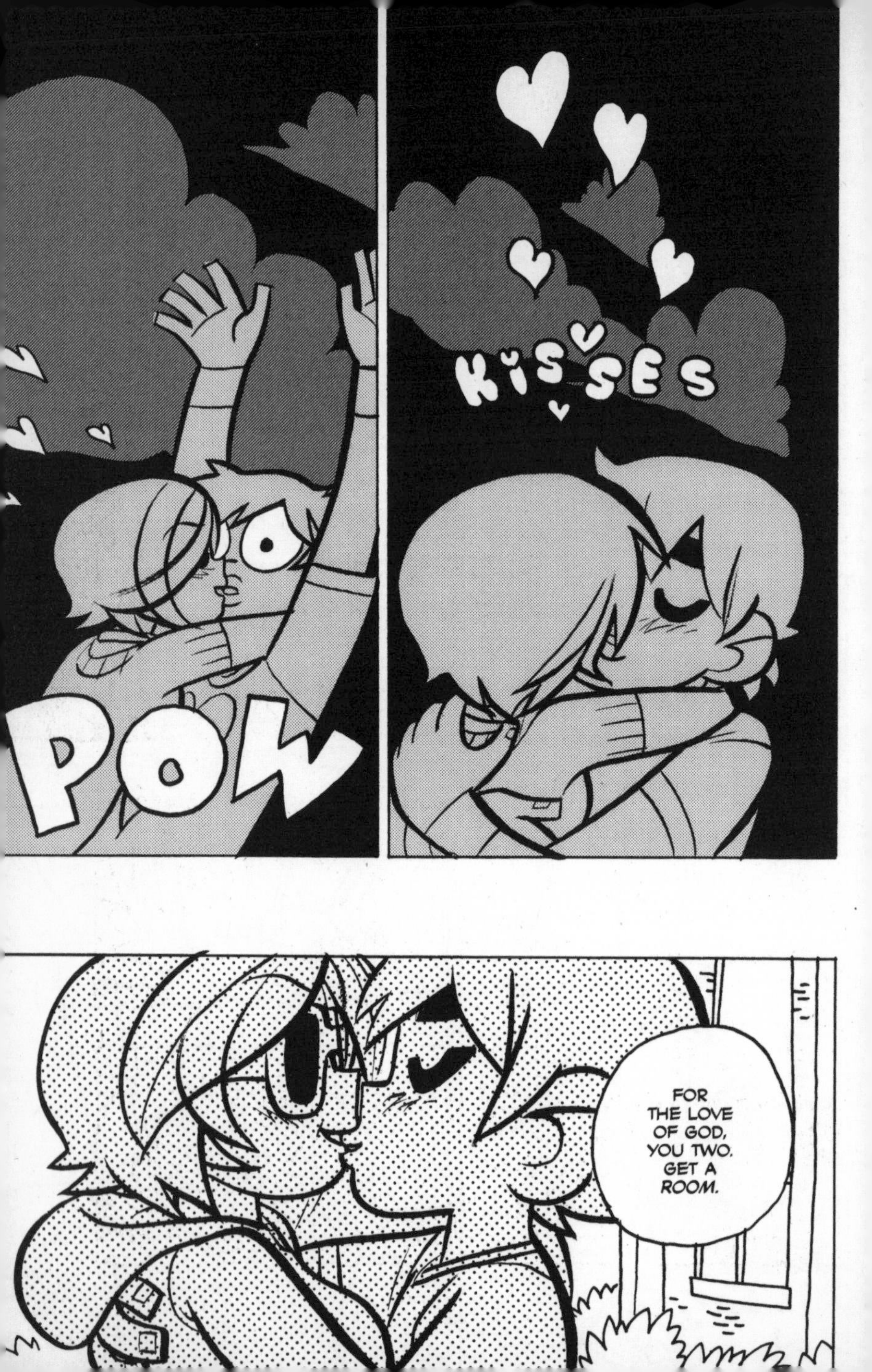
POW
KISSES
FOR THE LOVE OF GOD, YOU TWO. GET A *ROOM*.

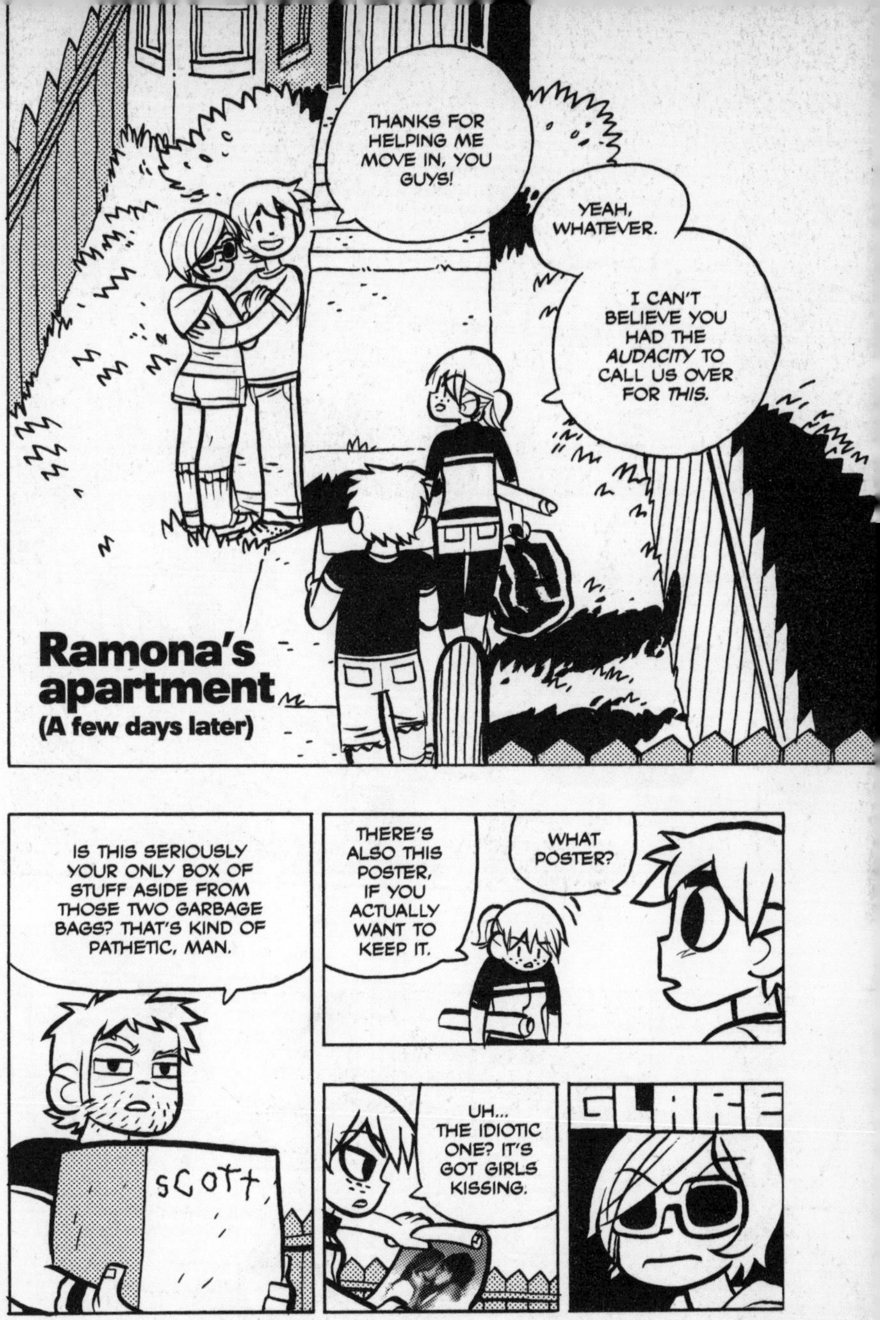
THANKS FOR HELPING ME MOVE IN, YOU GUYS!
YEAH, WHATEVER.
I CAN'T BELIEVE YOU HAD THE AUDACITY TO CALL US OVER FOR THIS.
Ramona's apartment
(A few days later)
IS THIS SERIOUSLY YOUR ONLY BOX OF STUFF ASIDE FROM THOSE TWO GARBAGE BAGS? THAT'S KIND OF PATHETIC, MAN.
SCOTT
THERE'S ALSO THIS POSTER, IF YOU ACTUALLY WANT TO KEEP IT.
WHAT POSTER?
UH... THE IDIOTIC ONE? IT'S GOT GIRLS KISSING.
GLARE

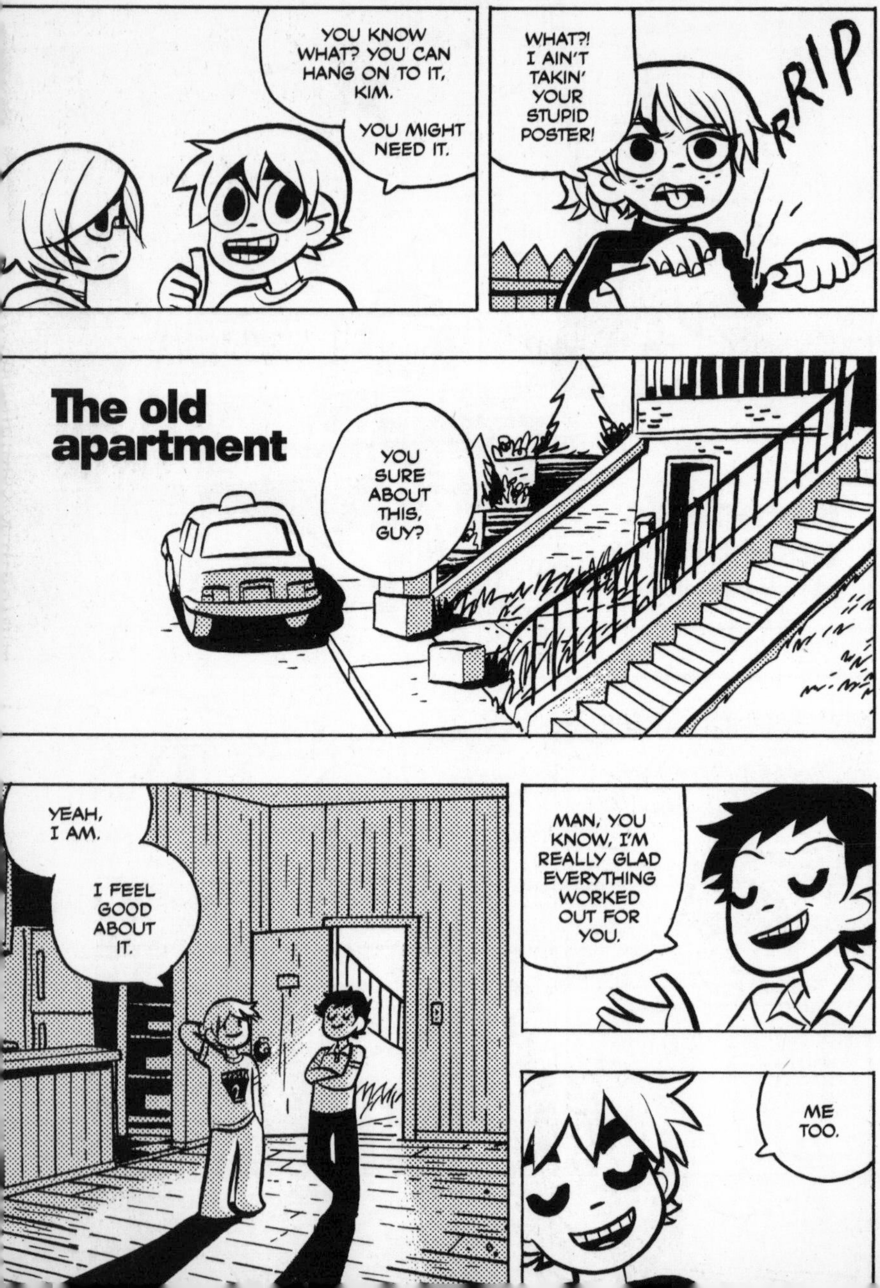
YOU KNOW WHAT? YOU CAN HANG ON TO IT, KIM.
YOU MIGHT NEED IT.
WHAT?! I AIN'T TAKIN' YOUR STUPID POSTER!
RRIP
The old apartment
YOU SURE ABOUT THIS, GUY?
YEAH, I AM.
I FEEL GOOD ABOUT IT.
MAN, YOU KNOW, I'M REALLY GLAD EVERYTHING WORKED OUT FOR YOU.
ME TOO.

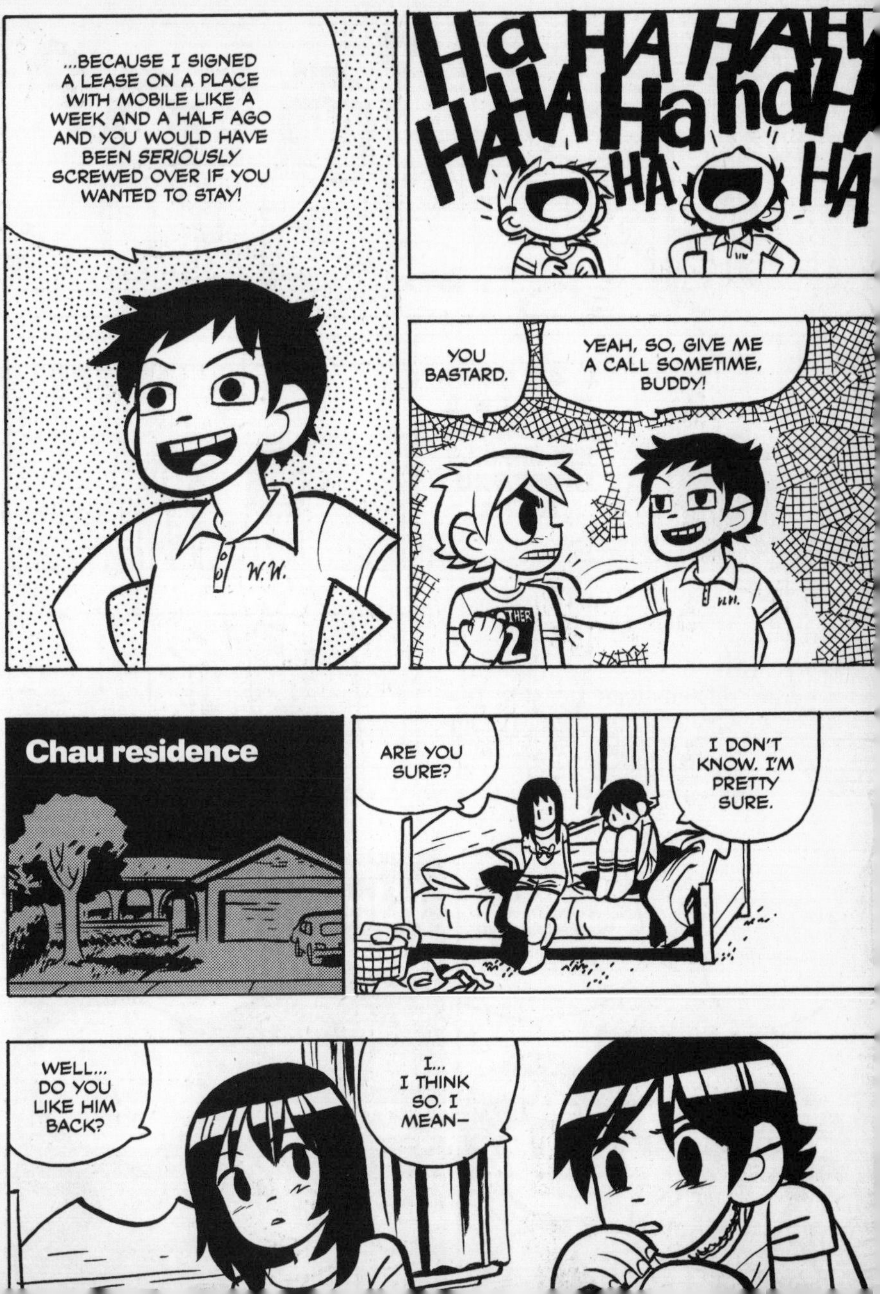
...BECAUSE I SIGNED A LEASE ON A PLACE WITH MOBILE LIKE A WEEK AND A HALF AGO AND YOU WOULD HAVE BEEN *SERIOUSLY* SCREWED OVER IF YOU WANTED TO STAY!
W.W.
HA
HA
YOU BASTARD.
YEAH, SO, GIVE ME A CALL SOMETIME, BUDDY!
Chau residence
ARE YOU SURE?
I DON'T KNOW. I'M PRETTY SURE.
WELL... DO YOU LIKE HIM BACK?
I... I THINK SO. I MEAN—

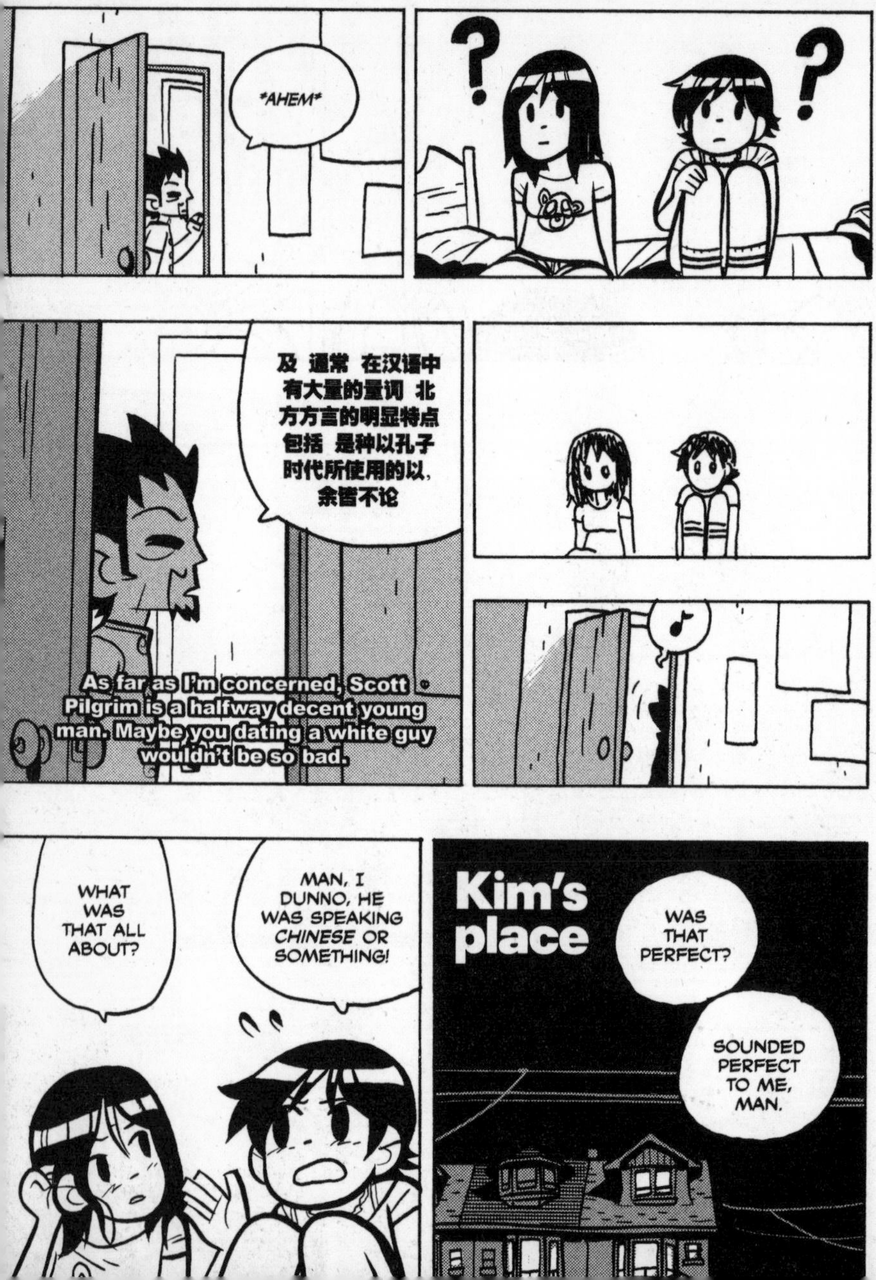
AHEM
及 通常 在汉语中 有大量的量词 北 方方言的明显特点 包括 是种以孔子 时代所使用的以, 余皆不论
As far as I'm concerned, Scott Pilgrim is a halfway decent young man. Maybe you dating a white guy wouldn't be so bad.
WHAT WAS THAT ALL ABOUT?
MAN, I DUNNO, HE WAS SPEAKING *CHINESE* OR SOMETHING!
Kim's place
WAS THAT PERFECT?
SOUNDED PERFECT TO ME, MAN.

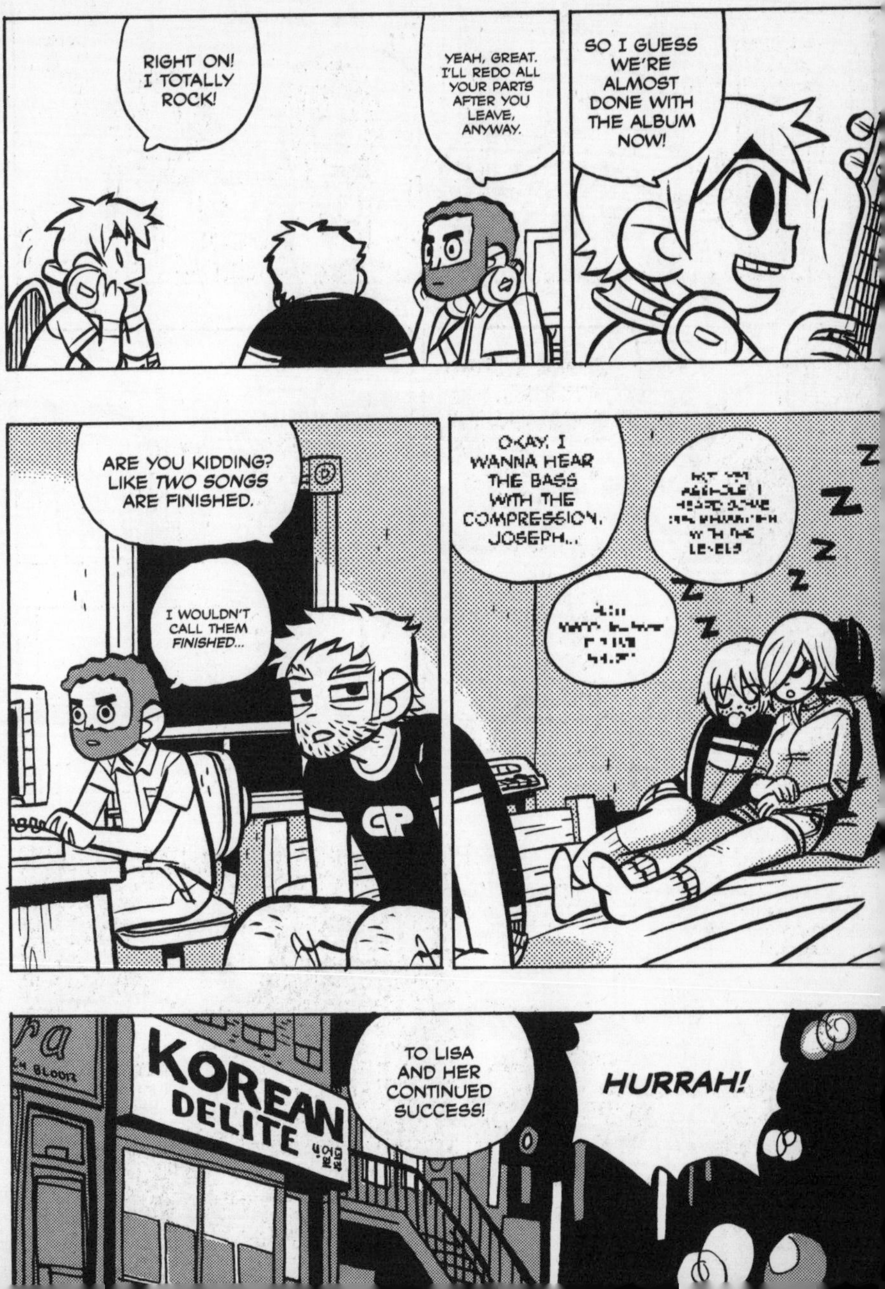
RIGHT ON! I TOTALLY ROCK!
YEAH, GREAT. I'LL REDO ALL YOUR PARTS AFTER YOU LEAVE, ANYWAY.
SO I GUESS WE'RE ALMOST DONE WITH THE ALBUM NOW!
ARE YOU KIDDING? LIKE *TWO SONGS* ARE FINISHED.
I WOULDN'T CALL THEM *FINISHED*...
OKAY, I WANNA HEAR THE BASS WITH THE COMPRESSION, JOSEPH...
Z Z Z Z Z Z Z
KOREAN DELITE
TO LISA AND HER CONTINUED SUCCESS!
HURRAH!

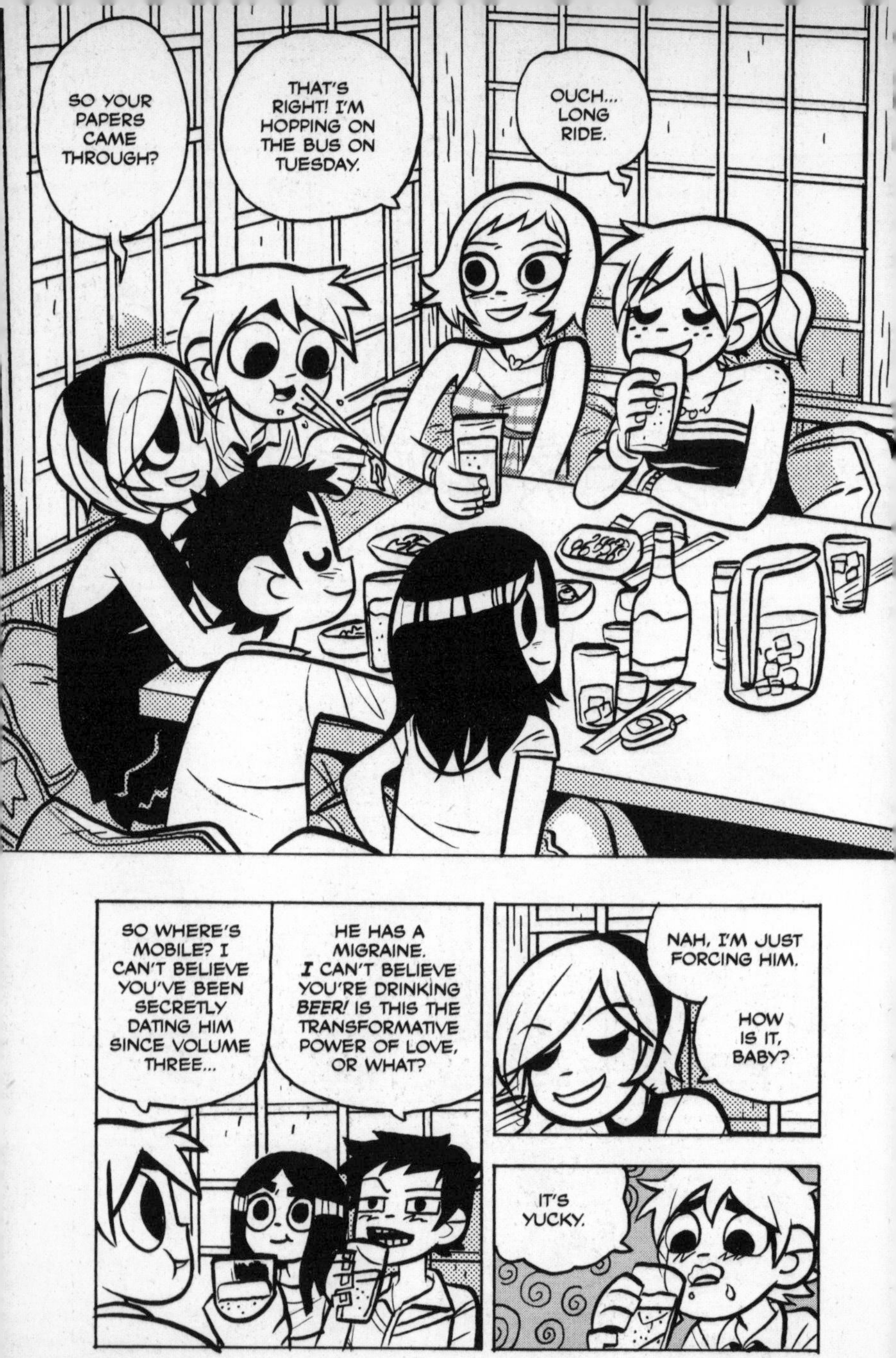
SO YOUR PAPERS CAME THROUGH?
THAT'S RIGHT! I'M HOPPING ON THE BUS ON TUESDAY.
OUCH... LONG RIDE.
SO WHERE'S MOBILE? I CAN'T BELIEVE YOU'VE BEEN SECRETLY DATING HIM SINCE VOLUME THREE...
HE HAS A MIGRAINE. *I* CAN'T BELIEVE YOU'RE DRINKING *BEER!* IS THIS THE TRANSFORMATIVE POWER OF LOVE, OR WHAT?
NAH, I'M JUST FORCING HIM.
HOW IS IT, BABY?
IT'S YUCKY.

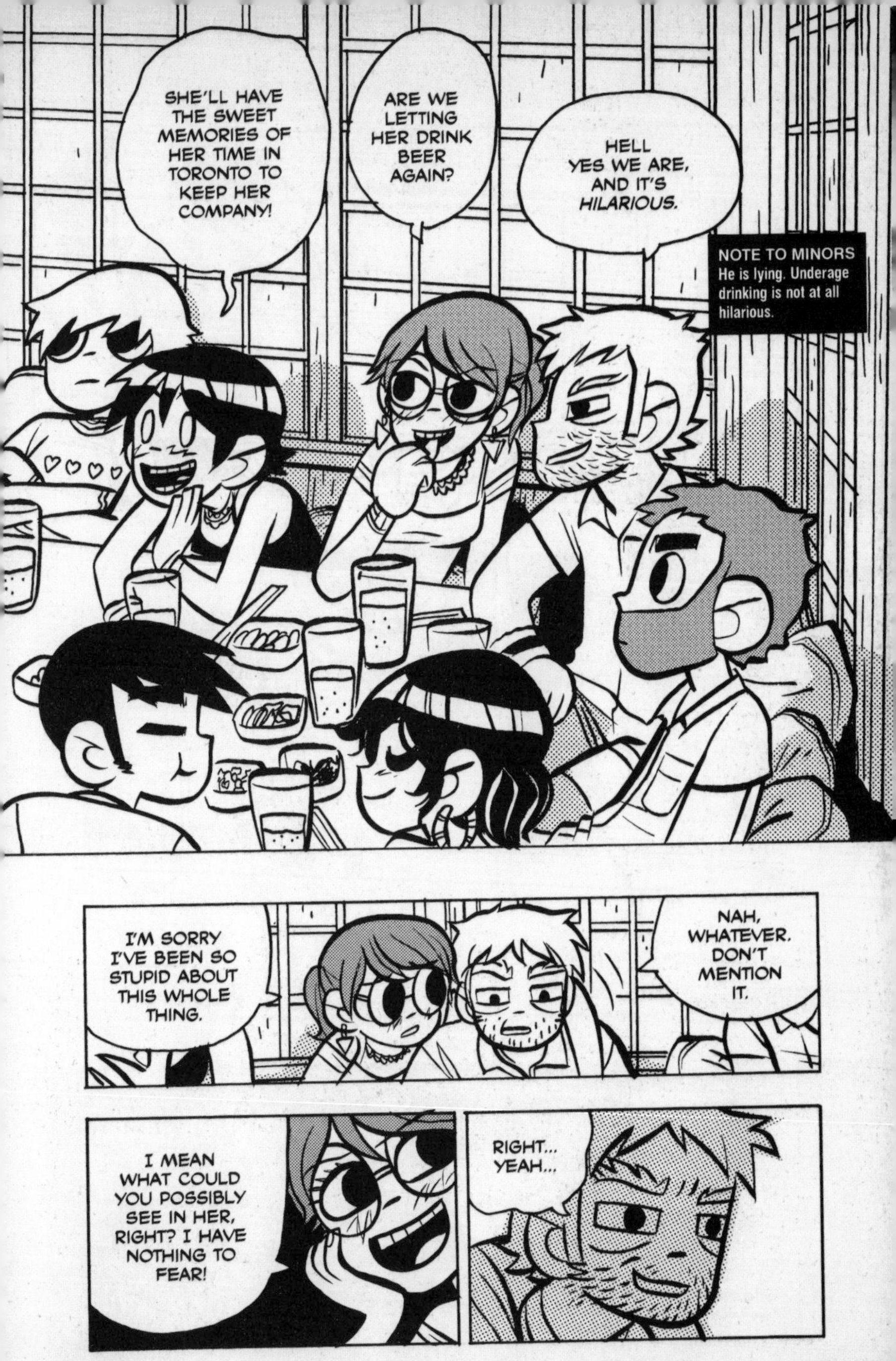
SHE'LL HAVE THE SWEET MEMORIES OF HER TIME IN TORONTO TO KEEP HER COMPANY!
ARE WE LETTING HER DRINK BEER AGAIN?
HELL YES WE ARE, AND IT'S *HILARIOUS.*
NOTE TO MINORS
He is lying. Underage drinking is not at all hilarious.
I'M SORRY I'VE BEEN SO STUPID ABOUT THIS WHOLE THING.
NAH, WHATEVER. DON'T MENTION IT.
I MEAN WHAT COULD YOU POSSIBLY SEE IN HER, RIGHT? I HAVE NOTHING TO FEAR!
RIGHT... YEAH...

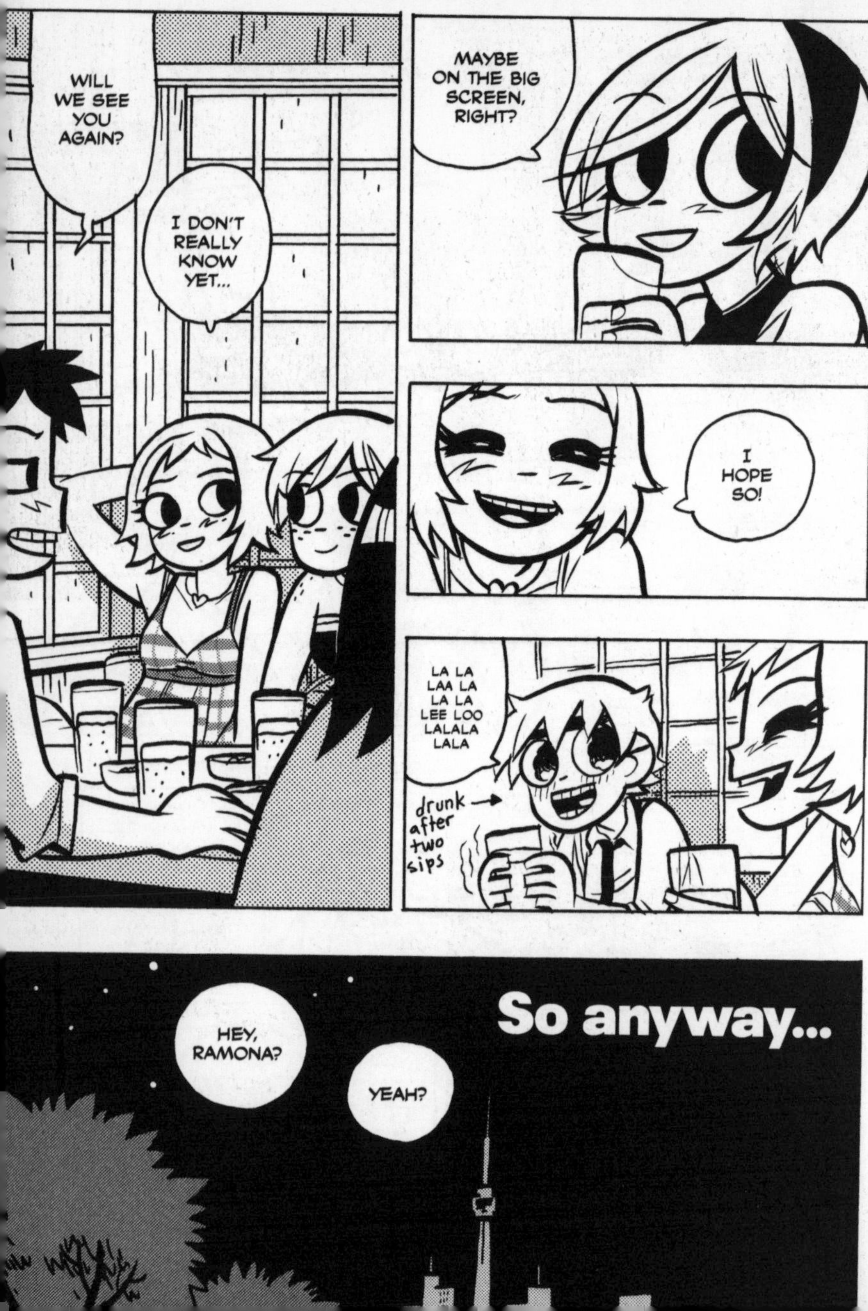
WILL WE SEE YOU AGAIN?
I DON'T REALLY KNOW YET...
MAYBE ON THE BIG SCREEN, RIGHT?
I HOPE SO!
LA LA LAA LA LA LA LEE LOO LALALA LALA
drunk after two sips
So anyway...
HEY, RAMONA?
YEAH?

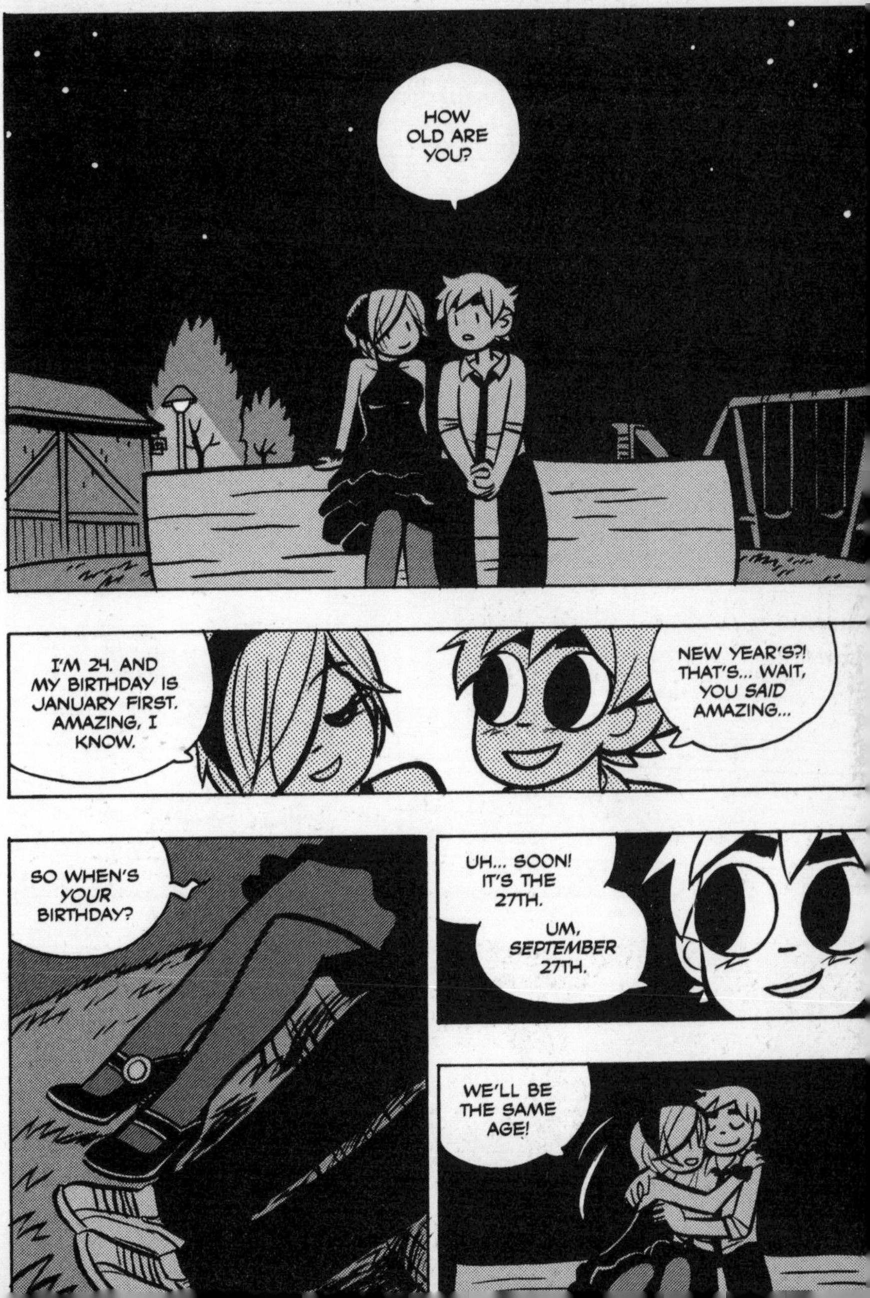
HOW OLD ARE YOU?
I'M 24. AND MY BIRTHDAY IS JANUARY FIRST. AMAZING, I KNOW.
NEW YEAR'S?! THAT'S... WAIT, YOU *SAID* AMAZING...
SO WHEN'S *YOUR* BIRTHDAY?
UH... SOON! IT'S THE 27TH.
UM, *SEPTEMBER* 27TH.
WE'LL BE THE SAME AGE!

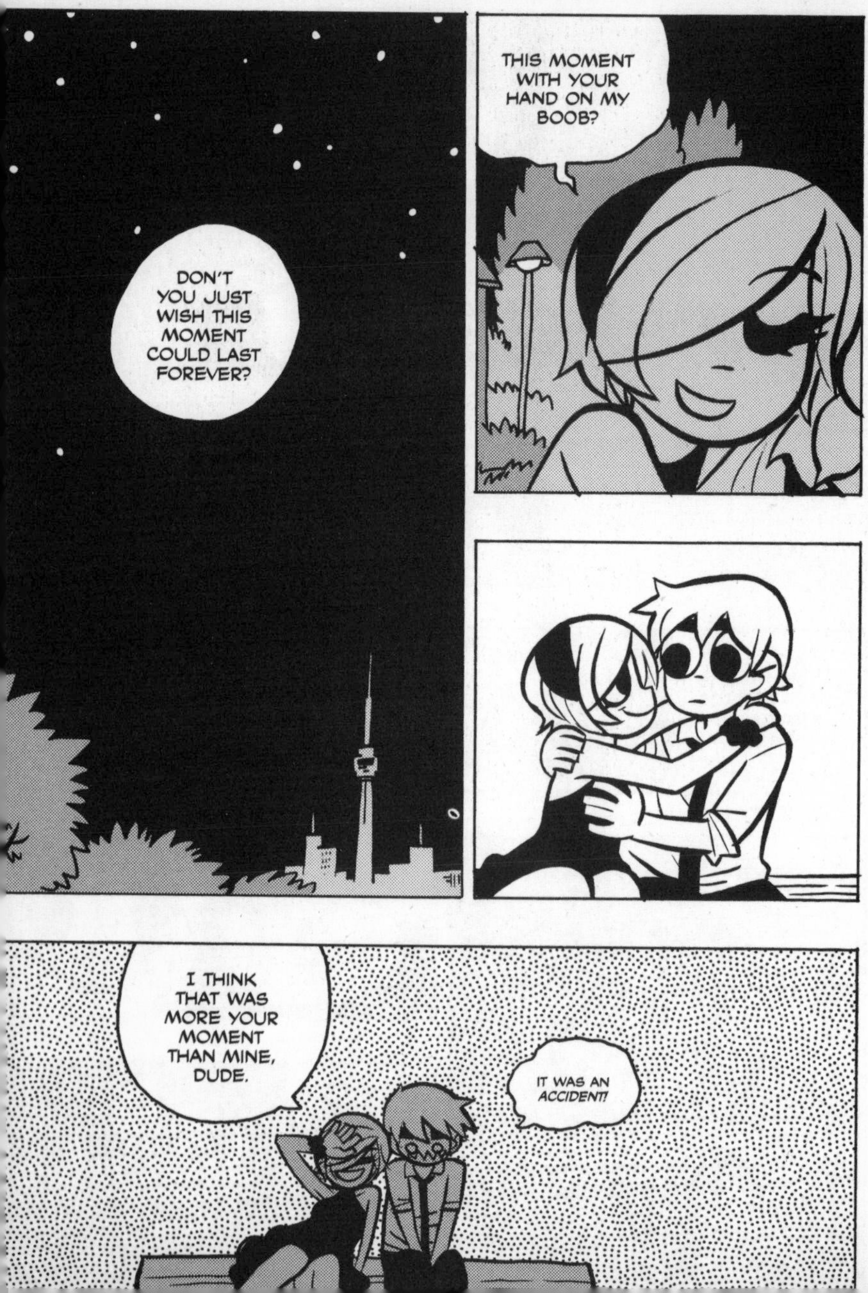
DON'T YOU JUST WISH THIS MOMENT COULD LAST FOREVER?
THIS MOMENT WITH YOUR HAND ON MY BOOB?
I THINK THAT WAS MORE YOUR MOMENT THAN MINE, DUDE.
IT WAS AN *ACCIDENT!*

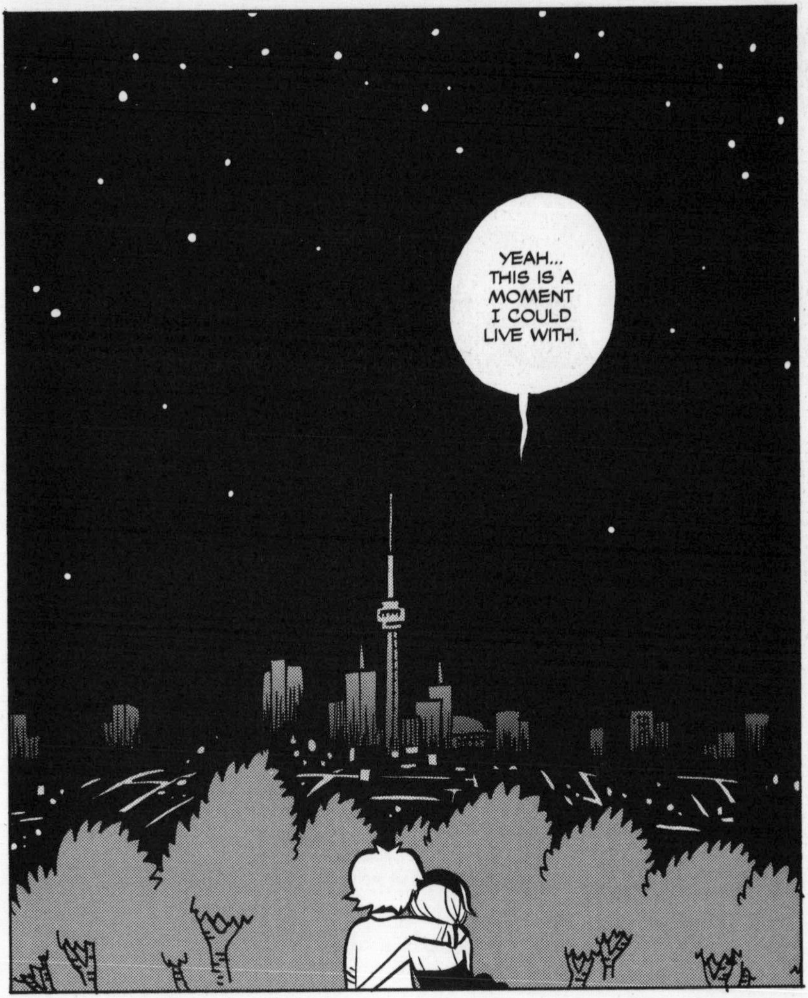
YEAH... THIS IS A MOMENT I COULD LIVE WITH.

NEXT: Twins!

Bryan Lee O'Malley has been alive since he
was born and will live until he dies, which will
probably be pretty soon. His dying wish will
be the wish that he hadn't wasted his best
years drawing this book.

His epitaph will be
whiny and narcissistic.

author portrait by **Hope Larson**

BONUS!
Guest Features

Bonus Comic **by Steve Manale**

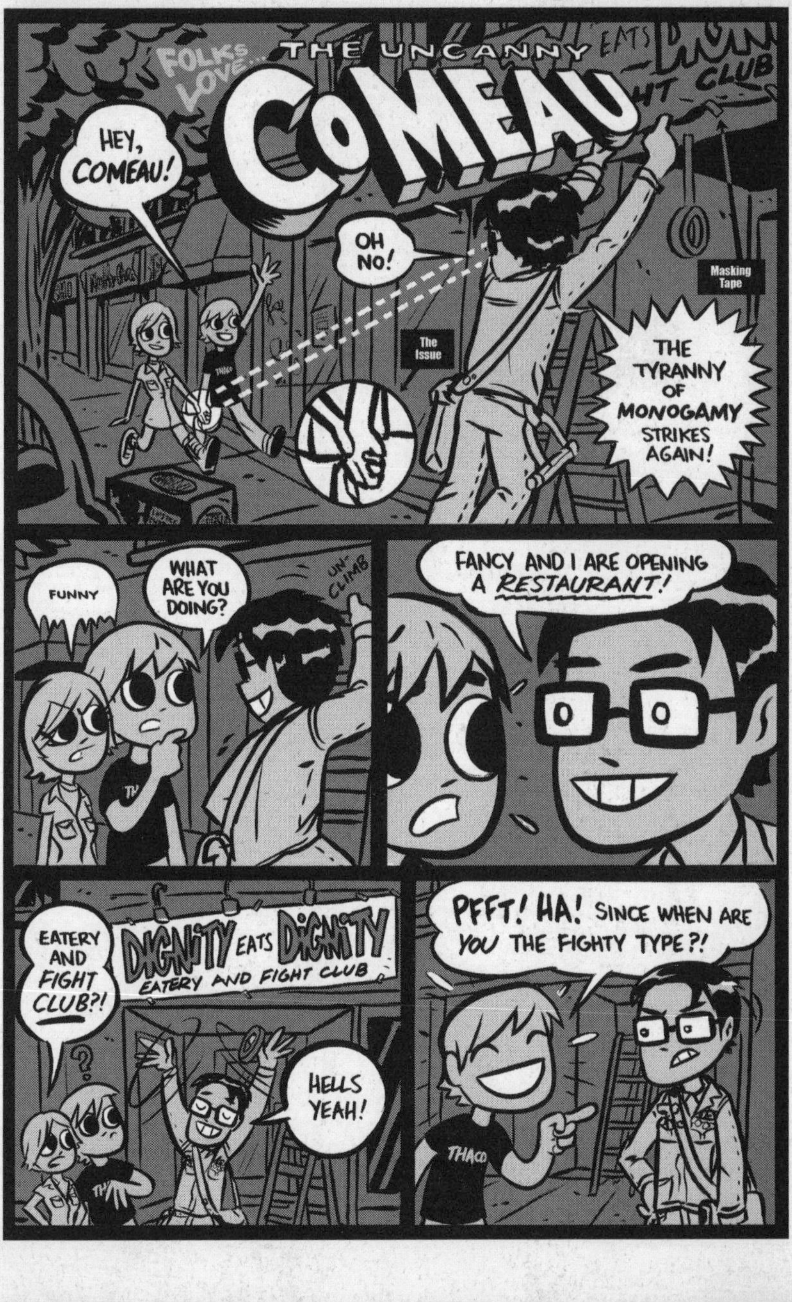
FOLKS LOVE...
THE UNCANNY
COMEAU
HEY, COMEAU!
OH NO!
Masking Tape
The Issue
THE TYRANNY OF MONOGAMY STRIKES AGAIN!
FUNNY
WHAT ARE YOU DOING?
UN-CLIMB
FANCY AND I ARE OPENING A RESTAURANT!
EATERY AND FIGHT CLUB?!
DIGNITY EATS DIGNITY
EATERY AND FIGHT CLUB
?
HELLS YEAH!
PFFT! HA! SINCE WHEN ARE YOU THE FIGHTY TYPE?!

Bonus Comic by Steve Manale

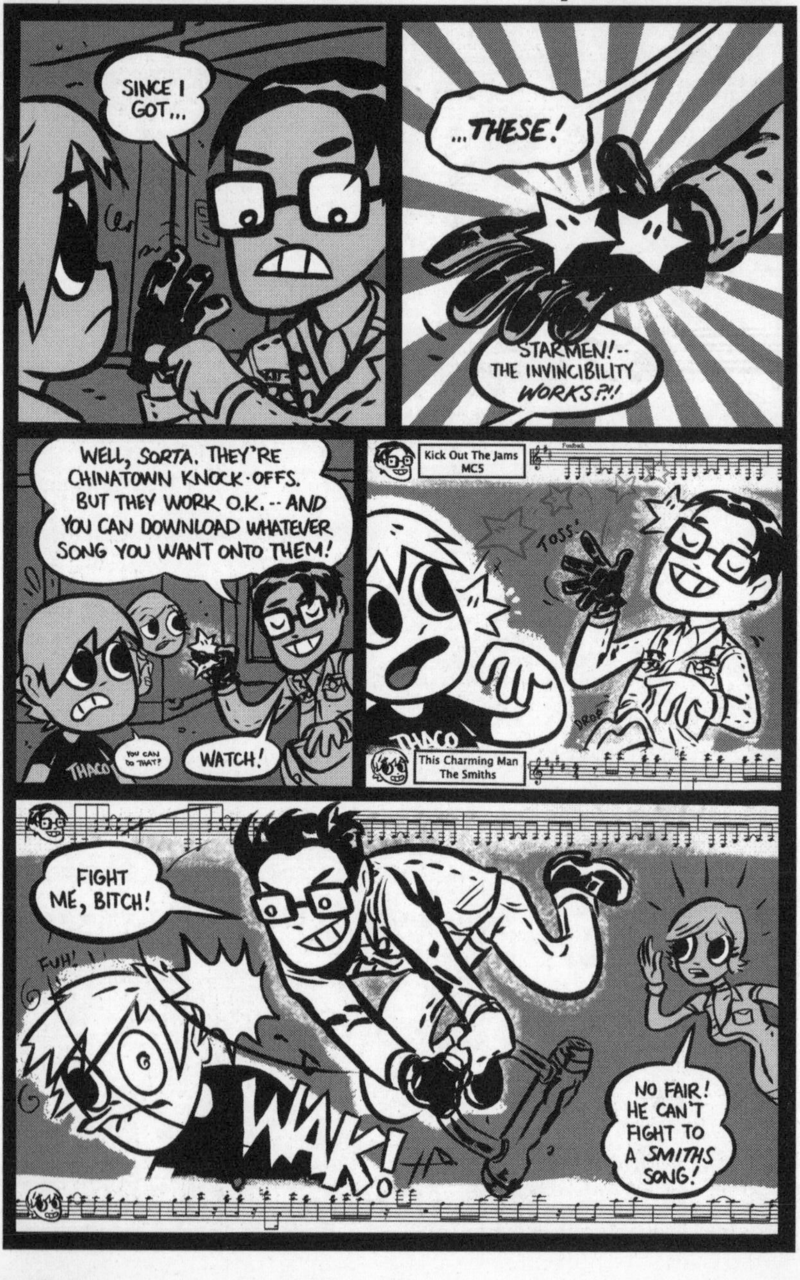
SINCE I GOT...
...THESE!
STARMEN!-- THE INVINCIBILITY WORKS?!!
WELL, SORTA. THEY'RE CHINATOWN KNOCK-OFFS. BUT THEY WORK O.K. -- AND YOU CAN DOWNLOAD WHATEVER SONG YOU WANT ONTO THEM!
THACO
YOU CAN DO THAT?
WATCH!
Kick Out The Jams
MC5
TOSS
DROP
THACO
This Charming Man
The Smiths
FIGHT ME, BITCH!
FUH!
WAK!
NO FAIR! HE CAN'T FIGHT TO A SMITHS SONG!

Bonus Comic **by Steve Manale**

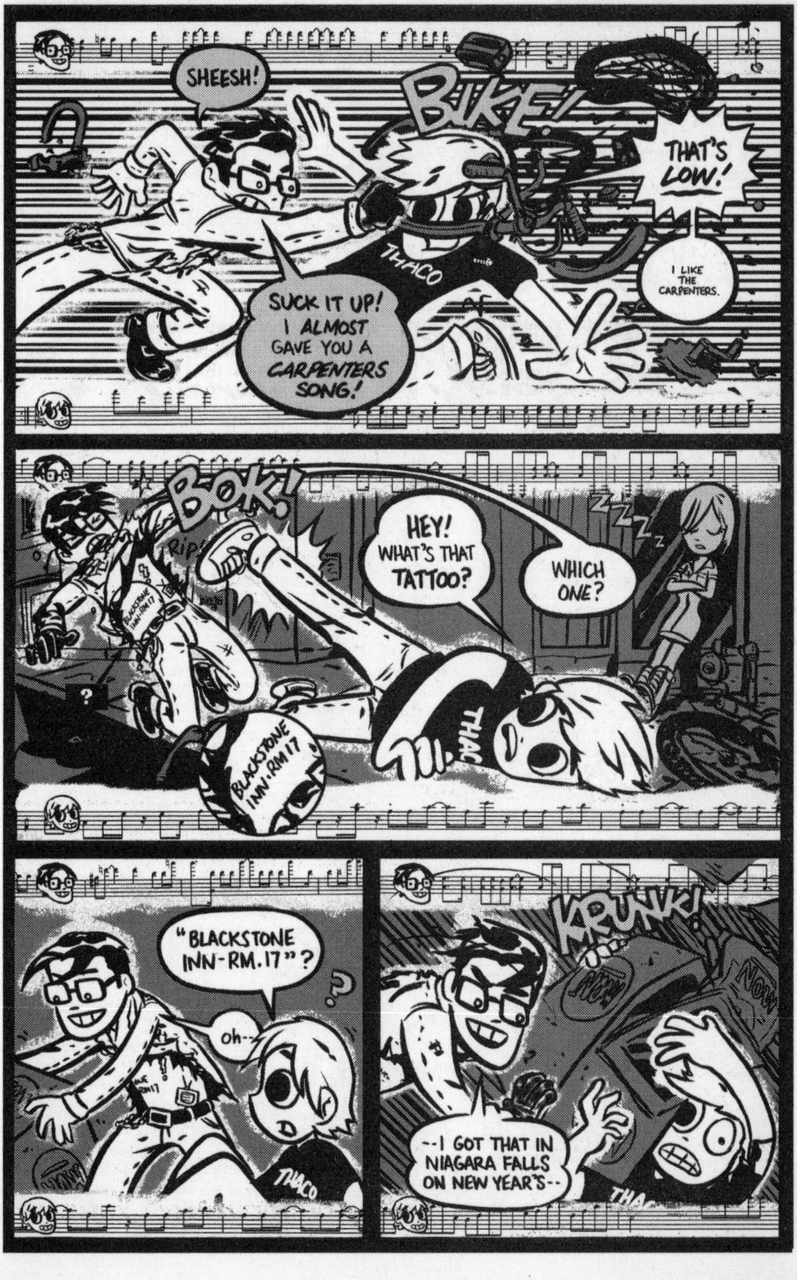
SHEESH!
BIKE!
THAT'S LOW!
I LIKE THE CARPENTERS.
SUCK IT UP! I ALMOST GAVE YOU A CARPENTERS SONG!
THACO
BOK!
RIP!
HEY! WHAT'S THAT TATTOO?
WHICH ONE?
BLACKSTONE INN·RM 17
THAC
"BLACKSTONE INN-RM.17"?
oh--
THACO
KRUNK!
--I GOT THAT IN NIAGARA FALLS ON NEW YEAR'S--
THA

Bonus Comic **by Steve Manale**

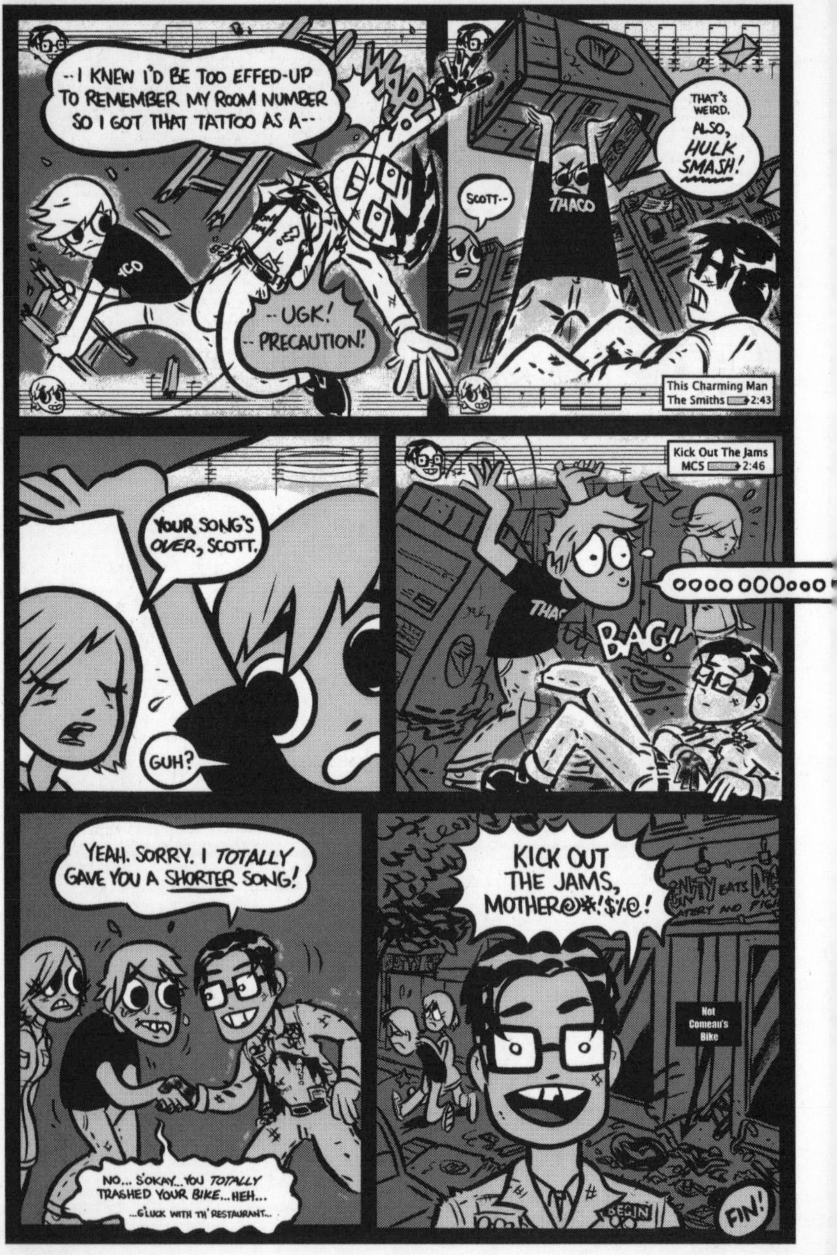
--I KNEW I'D BE TOO EFFED-UP TO REMEMBER MY ROOM NUMBER SO I GOT THAT TATTOO AS A--
WAP!
--UGK! --PRECAUTION!
THAT'S WEIRD. ALSO, HULK SMASH!
SCOTT--
THACO
This Charming Man
The Smiths 2:43
YOUR SONG'S OVER, SCOTT.
GUH?
Kick Out The Jams
MC5 2:46
oooo oOOooo
BAG!
YEAH. SORRY. I TOTALLY GAVE YOU A SHORTER SONG!
NO... S'OKAY...YOU TOTALLY TRASHED YOUR BIKE...HEH...
...G'LUCK WITH TH' RESTAURANT...
KICK OUT THE JAMS, MOTHER@*!$%@!
Not Comeau's Bike
FIN!

Bonus Comic #2 by Michael Comeau

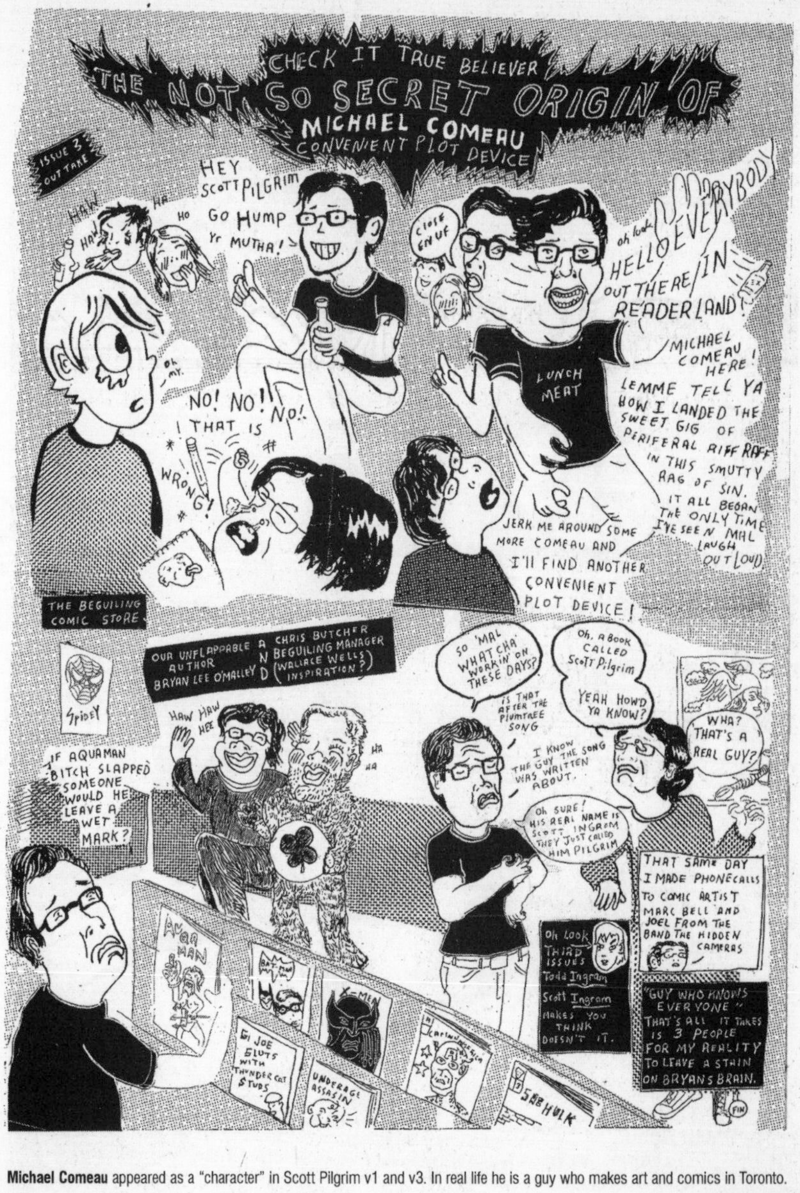
CHECK IT TRUE BELIEVER
THE NOT SO SECRET ORIGIN OF
MICHAEL COMEAU
CONVENIENT PLOT DEVICE
ISSUE 3 OUT TAKE
HEY SCOTT PILGRIM GO HUMP YR MUTHA!
HAW HAW HA HO
CLOSE ENUF
oh look HELLO EVERYBODY OUT THERE IN READERLAND!
MICHAEL COMEAU HERE!
LEMME TELL YA HOW I LANDED THE SWEET GIG OF PERIFERAL RIFF RAFF IN THIS SMUTTY RAG OF SIN.
IT ALL BEGAN THE ONLY TIME I'VE SEEN MAL LAUGH OUT LOUD
LUNCH MEAT
Oh my.
NO! NO! NO!
I THAT IS WRONG!
JERK ME AROUND SOME MORE COMEAU AND I'LL FIND ANOTHER CONVENIENT PLOT DEVICE!
THE BEGUILING COMIC STORE
OUR UNFLAPPABLE AUTHOR BRYAN LEE O'MALLEY
A N D
CHRIS BUTCHER BEGUILING MANAGER (WALLACE WELLS INSPIRATION?)
SPIDEY
HAW HAW HEE
HA HA
IF AQUAMAN BITCH SLAPPED SOMEONE WOULD HE LEAVE A WET MARK?
SO 'MAL WHATCHA WORKIN' ON THESE DAYS?
Oh, A BOOK CALLED Scott Pilgrim
IS THAT AFTER THE PLUMTREE SONG
YEAH HOW'D YA KNOW?
I KNOW THE GUY THE SONG WAS WRITTEN ABOUT.
WHA? THAT'S A REAL GUY?
Oh SURE! HIS REAL NAME IS SCOTT INGROM THEY JUST CALLED HIM PILGRIM
THAT SAME DAY I MADE PHONE CALLS TO COMIC ARTIST MARC BELL AND JOEL FROM THE BAND THE HIDDEN CAMERAS
Oh Look THIRD ISSUES Todd Ingram
Scott Ingram makes you think doesn't it.
"GUY WHO KNOWS EVERYONE" THAT'S ALL IT TAKES IS 3 PEOPLE FOR MY REALITY TO LEAVE A STAIN ON BRYANS BRAIN.
AQUAMAN
BAT-MAN
X-MEN
GI JOE SLUTS WITH THUNDERCAT STUDS
UNDERAGE ASSASIN
SHE HULK
FIN

Michael Comeau appeared as a "character" in Scott Pilgrim v1 and v3. In real life he is a guy who makes art and comics in Toronto.

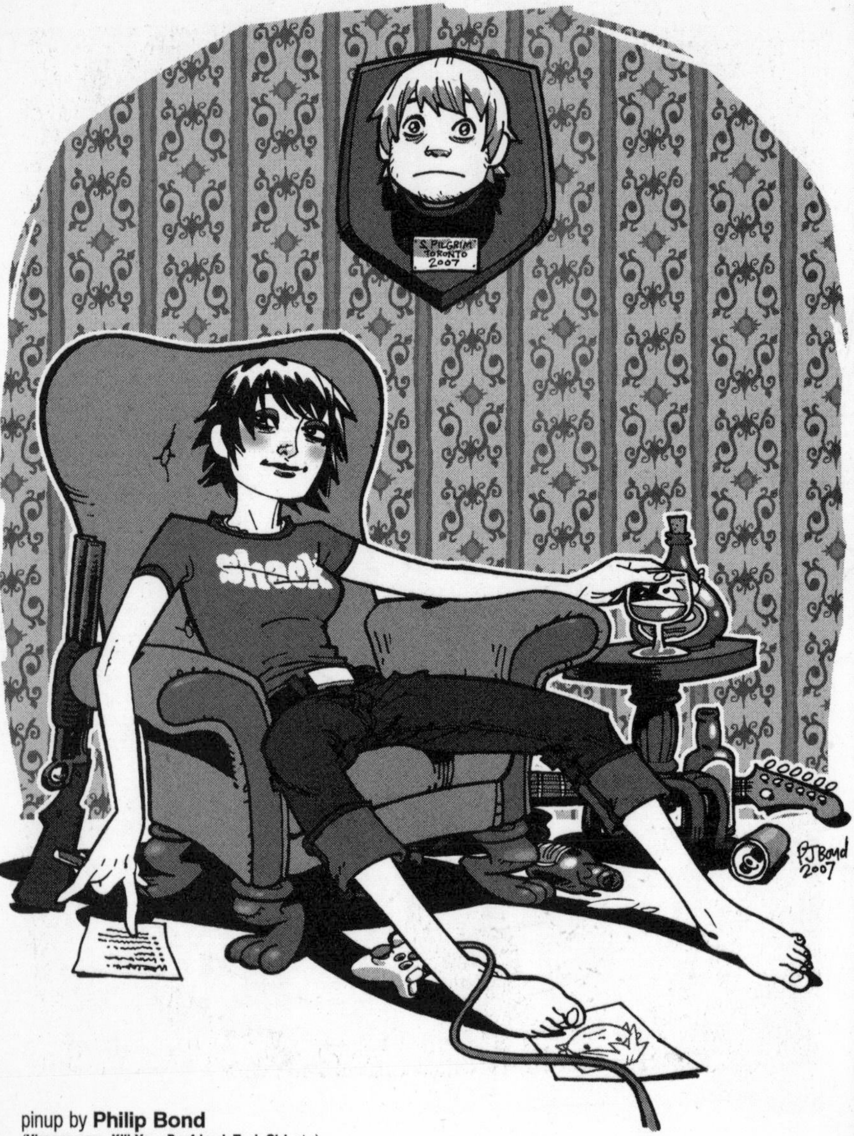
S. PILGRIM
TORONTO
2007
shock
PJBond
2007

pinup by **Philip Bond**
(**Vimanarama**, **Kill Your Boyfriend**, **Tank Girl**, etc.)